PENGUIN CLASSICS

W9-AZF-510

THE TIME REGULATION INSTITUTE

AHMET HAMDI TANPINAR (1901–62) is considered one of the most significant Turkish novelists of the twentieth century. Also a poet, short-story writer, essayist, literary historian, and professor, he created a unique cultural universe in his work, combining a European literary voice with the Ottoman sensibilities of the Near East.

MAUREEN FREELY was born in the United States, grew up in Istanbul, studied at Radcliffe, and now lives in England, where she teaches at the University of Warwick. The author of seven novels, she is the principal translator of the Nobel Prize–winning Turkish novelist, Orhan Pamuk.

ALEXANDER DAWE is an American translator of French and Turkish. He lives in Istanbul.

PANKAJ MISHRA is an award-winning novelist and essayist whose writing appears frequently in *The New York Review of Books*, *The Guardian*, and the *London Review of Books*.

AHMET HAMDI TANPINAR

The Time Regulation Institute

Translated by
MAUREEN FREELY
and
ALEXANDER DAWE

Introduction by
PANKAJ MISHRA

PENGUIN BOOKS

PENGUIN BOOKS

Published by the Penguin Group
Penguin Group (USA) LLC
375 Hudson Street
New York, New York 10014

USA | Canada | UK | Ireland | Australia | New Zealand | India | South Africa | China
penguin.com
A Penguin Random House Company

This translation first published in Penguin Books 2013

Published in Turkish as *Saatleri Ayarlama Enstitusu* by Dergah Yayinlari
Published with the support of the Turkish Ministry of Culture / Translation and
Publication Grant Program of Turkey

LIBRARY OF CONGRESS CATALOGING-IN-PUBLICATION DATA
Tanpinar, Ahmet Hamdi.
[Saatleri Ayarlama Enstitüsü. English]
The Time Regulation Institute / Ahmet Hamdi Tanpinar ; translated by Alexander Dawe
and Maureen Freely ; introduction by Pankaj Mishra.
pages cm. — (Penguin classics)
ISBN 978-0-14-310673-9 (pbk.)
PL248.T234S19513 2014
894'.3533—dc23
2013033709

Printed in the United States of America
1 3 5 7 9 10 8 6 4 2

Set in Sabon

Contents

Introduction

Orhan Pamuk has called Ahmet Hamdi Tanpınar (1901–62) the greatest Turkish novelist of the twentieth century. From the evidence of this novel—and *Huzur* (*A Mind at Peace*)—Tanpınar may have a strong claim to this distinction.

Born and educated in the old Ottoman Empire, Tanpınar was clearly a major artist and thinker—a strong influence, among other Turkish writers, on Pamuk himself. However, it is difficult for the anglophone reader to verify Pamuk's judgment. Translations from twentieth-century Turkish literature are scarce. The unique history and culture of modern Turkey is not immediately familiar to readers in English: how, for instance, in the 1920s the Muslim-majority Ottoman Empire was radically and forcibly reorganized into a secular republic by Mustafa Kemal (better known as Atatürk), and everything in its culture, from the alphabet to headwear and religion, hastily abandoned in an attempt to emulate European-style modernity.

There is another, even steeper, hurdle to understanding Atatürk's drastic cultural revolution: this is the basic assumption, shared by many Western readers, that societies must modernize and become more secular and rational, relegating their premodern past to museums or, in the case of religion, to private life. This idea—that modernization makes for enhanced national power and rapid progress and helps everyone achieve greater happiness—has its origins in the astonishing political, economic, and military successes of Western Europe in the nineteenth century. It was subsequently adopted in tradition-minded societies by powerful men ranging from autocrats such as Atatürk and Mao Tse-tung to the more democratic-minded, if paternalistic, Jawaharlal Nehru.

They felt oppressed and humiliated by the power of the industrialized West and urgently sought to match it. It did not matter that their countries lacked the human material—self-motivated and rationally self-interested individuals—apparently necessary for the pursuit of national wealth and power. A robust bureaucratic state and a suitably enlightened ruling elite could quickly forge citizens out of a scattered mass of peasants and merchants, and endow them with a sense of national identity.

But there was a tragic mismatch between the intentions of these hasty modernizers and the long historical experience of the societies they wanted to remake in the image of the modern West. No major Asian or African tradition had accommodated the notion that human beings could shape a meaningful narrative of evolution, or that the social order, too, contained the general laws discovered by modern science in the natural world, which, once identified, could be used to bring about ever-greater improvements—the potent and peculiarly European prejudice that gave conviction to such words as "progress' and "history" (as much ideological buzzwords of the nineteenth century as "democracy" and "globalization" are of the present moment). Time, in fact, was rarely conceptualized as a linear progression in Asian and African cultures. Nevertheless, scientific and technological innovations, as well as the great triumphs of Western imperialism, persuaded many Asians that they too could rationally manipulate their natural and social environment to their advantage.

As evident in Iran under Reza Pahlavi, as well as in Mao Tsetung's China, these single-minded authoritarian figures, who saw themselves as bending history to their will, ended up inflicting immense violence and suffering on their societies. The outcome was always ambiguous (as is now clear in Turkey's own turn to a moderate Islamism after decades of a secular dictatorship and the recent embrace by Chinese Communists of a worldview they previously scorned: Confucianism). For as Dostoyevsky warned, "No nation on earth, no society with a certain measure of stability, has been developed to order, on the lines of a program imported from abroad."

Dostoyevsky was speaking from the experience of nineteenth-century Russia, the first society to be coerced by its insecure rulers into imitating the West: the result was uprooted and "superfluous" men, such as those he and his compatriots wrote about, bloody revolution, and a legacy of authoritarian rule that persists to this day. Japan had then followed Russia—and preceded Turkey—in trying to do in a few decades what it took the West centuries to accomplish. Japanese writers in the last century—from Natsume Sōseki to Haruki Murakami—have attested to the profound psychic distortions and widespread intellectual confusion caused by the Japanese attempt at Westernization that peaked with the rise of Japanese militarism and, after the incineration of Hiroshima and Nagasaki in 1945, turned Japan into an American client state. Novelists as varied as Jun'ichirō Tanizaki and Yukio Mishima sought a return to an earlier "wholeness." Tanizaki tried to recreate an indigenous aesthetic by pointing to the importance of "shadows"—a whole world of subtle distinctions banished from Japanese life by the modern invention of the lightbulb. Mishima invoked, more dramatically, Japan's lost culture of the samurai. Both were fueled by rage and regret that, as Tanizaki wrote in *In Praise of Shadows*, "we have met a superior civilization and have had to surrender to it, and we have had to leave a road we have followed for thousands of years."

In recent times, Orhan Pamuk's fiction has, as he writes in his novel *The White Castle*, eloquently attested to the alienation wrought by "the transformation of people and beliefs without their knowledge" and the pathos of "witnessing the superiority of others and then trying to mimic them." But what Tanpınar identified as a peculiar "fatality of Turkish history" was not particular to his or Turkey's experience. Both China's Lu Hsün and India's Rabindranath Tagore confronted what Tanpınar described as "the awful thing we call belatedness"; that is, the experience of arriving late in the modern world, as naive pupils, to find one's future foreclosed and already defined by other people's past and present. There is much literary, historical, and sociological evidence attesting to the spiritual and psychological as well as political damage of top-down modernization. Still, most commentators in the West continue to insist that non-Western societies, especially Islamic ones, ought to quickly become modern: in other words, be more like the West. These reflexive and unexamined prejudices emerge, understandably, from the exceptional experience of Western Europe and America. But at least some of them have to be overcome before we can understand the nature and extent of Tanpınar's achievement—his sense of foreboding and loss, and his evocation, in particular, of the melancholy, or *hüzün*, of those doomed to arrive late, and spiritually destitute, in history. It requires sympathy with the trauma of writers who witnessed the devastation of their familiar landmarks, for whom the new world conjured into being by their great leaders remained agonizingly meaningless, denuded of the consolations of tradition and heaving with the tawdry illusions of modernity. It requires understanding that though Tanpınar knew his European literature—his Baudelaire, Gide, and Valéry—the anguish, as Pamuk writes, "that sustains all of his work arises from the disappearance of traditional artistry and lifestyles."

The anguish—and the resentment of being in permanent tutelage to Europe—was all the more keen for Tanpınar, who had grown up in the Ottoman Empire and knew something of the old ways before they were violently suppressed by Atatürk. He grew up, for instance, with the Ottoman music and poetry that Atatürk's cultural engineering made inaccessible to later generations. His teacher was Yahya Kemal Beyatlı, a much-loved Turkish writer, who authored nostalgic epics relying on traditional Persian *aruz* rhythm instead of the newly invented Turkish one. Tanpınar seems to have recognized that Atatürk's new republic could not be a tabula rasa, no matter how hard the state tried to eradicate the fez, Muslim calendar, and Arabic numerals and measures, and replace them with the European clock, calendar, numerals, and weights and measures.

But Tanpınar did not respond to this feckless program of Westernization with a conservative or backward-looking project like Dostoyevsky's pan-Slavism. Tanpınar hoped for a synthesis of past and present that went beyond secularist slogans and state programs for modernization. In opposition to a parochial nationalism, Tanpınar invoked the cosmopolitanism of Istanbul—something that has become a tourist-brochure cliché in our own time but wasn't so obvious in the 1930s, when the city was disdained by secular Kemalists for its centrality to the superseded Ottoman Empire. The old city brought the traditional together with the modern, the foreign with domestic, and the "beautiful with ugly"—an intermingling originally forged by "the institutions of Islam and the Ottoman Empire." And it was important to emphasize this because, Tanpınar wrote, echoing many writers in Japan and other parts of Asia, it was of no use to keep thinking of the East and West as separate; they had to be seen as "an invitation to create a vast and comprehensive synthesis [*terkip*], a life meant for us and particular to us."

Tanpınar's brooding and intricate novel *A Mind at Peace* (1939) attempts such a synthesis—one reason why it became popular in the 1980s as Turkey began to emerge from decades of soulless Kemalism. Its most cherished character is Istanbul itself—the city's poor neighborhoods, dramatic sunsets, and long Ramadan evenings—celebrated with no less lyrical intensity than Baudelaire had showered on his Paris. It is against the backdrop of the city in the 1930s that Mümtaz, a young writer, pursues a nearly mystical romance with a musically gifted woman named Nuran, while staving off the intellectual and romantic challenge of Suad, a Nietzschean dandy. His cousin, the cultivated İhsan, introduces the conventionally Westernized Mümtaz to the works of Ottoman poets and composers. As though fulfilling Proust's maxim that what we love in others is the particular world we think they represent, Nuran embodies, in the rapturous eyes of Mümtaz, the superseded Ottoman-Turkish culture.

The symbolism is rendered in a dense, opaque prose and unchronological sequences that speak of a very deliberate attempt to appropriate the techniques of modernism—the artistic movement that set itself against the great rational ideologies and epistemologies of the nineteenth century. The Kemalists had tried to enlist Turkish writers into the national task of creating new role models and educating a loyal and intelligent citizenry. But Tanpınar, with his poetics of the indolent flaneur, rejects the social-realist tradition that was dominant in Turkey (and indeed in all new national societies in the twentieth century). He seems to have taken to heart Baudelaire's dictum that the modern artist is "the painter of both the passing moment and everything in that moment that smacks of eternity." He lingers defiantly on classic Istanbul scenes: ferries with melancholy foghorns and broken marble fountains.

This literary archeology seeks to excavate different histories and memories buried within the old city. But Tanpınar's self-chosen project of synthesis in *A Mind at Peace* doesn't survive his scrupulous attention to the tormented inner lives of his characters. Failure dogs the romantic and professional life of Mümtaz, a writer entrusted with the task of developing a suitable intellectual history (biographies of sixteenth- and seventeenth-century Turkish figures) for modern Turkey. Most characters seem paralyzed by their inability to transcend their divided selves. Mümtaz's mentor, İhsan, talks—channeling Tanpınar—about the "necessity of constructing a new life unique to us and compatible to our conditions without closing ourselves to the West and by preserving our ties with the past."

But everywhere there are signs of the Turkish "intellectual indigestion." Once discarded, Tanpınar implies, tradition cannot always be retrieved and used to re-enchant the world—a warning to those who today rummage through Istanbul's cosmopolitan past for clues to their identity.

As Mümtaz looked at this shop, involuntarily, he recalled Mallarme's line: "It's ended up here through some nameless catastrophe." Here, in this dusty shop, in this place on whose walls handmade tricot stockings hung . . . In neighboring shops with wooden shutters, simple benches, and old prayer rugs rested the same luxurious and, when seen from afar, occult insights of tradition, in an order eternally alien to the various accepted ideas of classification, on shelves, over bookrests or chairs, and on the floor, piled one atop another as if preparing to be interred, or rather, as if being observed from where they lay buried. The Orient, however, couldn't be authentic anywhere, even in its grave.

Next to these books, in laid-out hawker cases, were lapfuls of testimonials to our inner transformation, our desire to adapt, and our search for ourselves in a new context and climate: pulp novels with illustrated covers, school textbooks, French yearbooks with faded green bindings, and pharmaceutical formulas. As if all the detritus of the mind of mankind had to be hastily exposed in this market . . .

The suicide of Suad, the Nietzschean radical, who hangs himself while listening to Beethoven, further hints at the impossibility of synthesis. The Orient is doomed to inauthenticity, to be forever seeking fragments it can shore against its ruins.

The Time Regulation Institute, published in 1962, confirms this despairing vision. The continuity between past and present dreamed of by Tanpınar seems no longer possible. The onward-and-upward narrative of progress, dictated by the state and embraced by a gullible people, has contaminated everything. The spiritual resources of modernism seem meager compared to the great and irreversible material changes—industrialization, mechanization, demographic shifts, middle-class consumerism, and rapid communications—introduced by Turkey's Kemalist elite.

The novel's narrator, Hayri İrdal, is one of those superfluous semimodern men familiar to us from Russian literature: more acted upon than active, simmering with inarticulate resentments and regrets, a cross between Oblomov and the protagonist of *Notes from the Underground*. Confusion marks almost everything he does:

I was fording a deep-sea cavern lined by the remains of knowledge and by all the ideas I had ever failed to grasp. As they swirled around my feet I moved forward, and with every step I felt the coil of unfounded beliefs, ungrounded frustrations, and unending despair tightening around my chest and arms.

By the early 1960s, Tanpınar had worked in a ministry and even been a member of parliament; his narrator has a keen appreciation of the absurdities of the self-perpetuating and self-justifying bureaucratic state, which, rather than self-aware individuals, embodies progress and enlightenment in Turkey. The modern age, his benefactor, Halit Ayarcı, claims, has been

> given many names, but first and foremost it is the age of bureaucracy. All the philosophers, from Spengler to Kieserling, are writing about bureaucracy. I would go as far as to say that it is an age in which bureaucracy has reached its zenith, an age of real freedom. Any man who understands is a valuable figure. I am in the process of establishing an absolute institution—a mechanism that defines its own function. What could be closer to perfection than that?

This mechanism that defines its own function turns out to be the Time Regulation Institute. Tanpınar's satirical intentions in this novel are clarified by the fact that in 1926 Atatürk had formally adopted Western time by passing the Gregorian Calendar Act. Most people in Turkey, as in nineteenth-century Asia, had not needed to know the time with the precision offered by watches. The muezzin's call to prayers or the sun's journey sufficed. But Atatürk decreed that clock towers be erected across the country. They were to be part of the new architecture and urban environment in which Turkish citizens could pretend to be modern, and anyone still adhering to Islamic time, or timekeeper's houses, was severely punished.

Atatürk was clearly influenced by Western notions of maximizing the efficiency of individual citizens. His clock towers not only cheaply propagandized the virtues of regularity, constancy, punctuality, and precision; the Western-style workday, which divided life into compartments—time carefully allocated for work, study, recreation, and the rest—promised greater economic productivity and endowed time itself with monetary value.

İrdal, however, has savored another kind of life, one in which idleness, or wasting time, is a source of happiness. As in *A Mind at Peace*, Tanpınar again evokes the modernism of the everyday—one opposed to the alienated linear time of top-down modernity. But the setting is pastoral rather than urban, and the mood is nostalgic as İrdal contrasts the easy luxuries and fulfillments of his childhood with the individual liberations promised by the modern state.

> The freedom I knew as a child was of a different kind. First, and I think most significantly, it was not something I was given. It was something I discovered on my own one day—a lump of gold concealed in my innermost depths, a bird trilling in a tree, sunlight playing on water.

İrdal dates his fall from this Eden to the time he is given a watch: "My life's rhythms were disrupted, it would seem, by the watch my uncle gave me on the occasion of my circumcision." From then on, he is a citizen of modern Turkey, expected to do his bit as an individual producer and consumer to boost its collective power. Asked by Halit Ayarcı to wear a bureaucrat's drab uniform, İrdal can sense

> a dramatic shift in my entire being. New horizons and perspectives suddenly unfurled before me. Like Halit Ayarcı, I began to perceive life as a single entity. I began to use terms like "modification," "coordination," "work structure," "mind-set shift," "metathought," and "scientific mentality"; I took to associating such terms as "ineluctability" or "impossibility" with my lack of will. I even made imprudent comparisons between East and the West, and passed judgments whose gravity left me terrified. Like him, I began to look at people with eyes that wondered, "Now, what use could he be to us?" and to see life as dough that could be kneaded by my own two hands. In a word, it seemed as if his courage and powers of invention had been transferred to me, as if it were not a suit at all but a magic cloak.

But, as Tanpınar shows, sometimes relentlessly, İrdal drifts further away, as he grows older, from any ideal of serenity and contentment. Though "born into a family fallen on hard times" he has had quite a happy childhood. "So long," İrdal writes, "as we are in harmony with those around us—assuming, of course, the right balance—poverty is never as terrifying or intolerable as we might think." In Istanbul, he knows the desperate loneliness and petty jealousies of people in relatively affluent but atomized societies. His professional career turns out to be a procession of empty and futile postures. His private life is marred by multiple broken friendships and unhappy marriages. He is hounded by a series of absurd people, among them a wealthy aunt who hilariously rises from the dead to torment him.

Tanpınar uses İrdal to take aim at many aspects of Kemalist Turkey: counterfeit tradition, for instance, as exemplified by İrdal's projected history of a seventeenth-century clock maker called Ahmet Zamanı Efendi, which tries to provide a respectable pedigree to the Kemalist state's tinkering with the old temporal order, and heals its ruptures with the past. As part of Atatürk's invention of tradition, the freshly minted Turkish Historical Association had indeed introduced a new history of Turkey, in which Turks became a primarily ethnic rather than religious community. Unlike Mümtaz in *A Mind at Peace*, who cannot get on with his account of an eighteenth-century Ottoman poet, İrdal manages to finish his book. There is, however, a problem: this account of a traditional herald of Turkish modernity, renamed Ahmet the Timely, is mostly bogus, depicting him, among other impostures, at the Ottoman siege of Vienna.

As İrdal writes, "Unfortunately a handful of armchair academics tried to spoil the fun, being so impertinent as to suggest that such a figure had never actually existed and dismissing the book as a complete fabrication." But his boss, Ayarcı, assures him that

> as important as creating a movement is maintaining its momentum. In extending our movement to the past, you have intensified its forward momentum. In addition you have shown that our forbears were both revolutionary and modern. . . . Is history material only for critical thought? Can we not stumble upon someone from the past whom we love and enjoy? Oh, you'll see how pleased everyone will be with our work!

The Ottoman past that Tanpınar once wished to retrieve for his project of synthesis appears in *The Time Regulation Institute* as a plaything of frauds and charlatans. Unlike Nuran in *A Mind at Peace*, who knows her musical tradition and can sing, İrdal's sister-in-law can only screech grotesquely and mutilate old songs. "Our life is a tale without a plot or a hero," Osip Mandelstam wrote about another spiritually marooned people, "made up out of desolation and glass, out of the feverish babble of constant digressions." Tanpınar's novel, too, has the anarchic, bleak, and almost uncontrollable energy of the "modernism of underdevelopment," which, as Marshall Berman pointed out,

> is forced to build on fantasies and dreams of modernity, to nourish itself on an intimacy and a struggle with mirages and ghosts. In order to be true to the life from which it springs, it is forced to be shrill, uncouth and inchoate. It turns in on itself and tortures itself for its inability to singlehandedly make history—or else throws itself into extravagant attempts to take on itself the whole burden of history.

That peculiar torment is very palpable in *The Time Regulation Institute*. And so is its attempted resolution. Like Tagore and Tanizaki before him, Tanpınar upheld the felt experience—the small joys and sorrows—of ordinary life against the dehumanizing abstractions and empty promises of modern ideologies. No longer seeking, as he did in *A Mind at Peace*, an immutable cultural identity in Istanbul's past, he places himself on the side of the fragmentary and the gratuitous against the imperatives of history and progress.

Tanpınar returns often to the question of human freedom—a theme that clearly preoccupied him a great deal and gave metaphysical ballast to his critique of secular modernity:

> The privilege I most treasured as a child was that of freedom. . . . Today we use the word only in its political sense, and how unfortunate for us. For I fear that those who see freedom solely as a political concept will never fully grasp its meaning. The political

pursuit of freedom can lead to its eradication on a grand scale—
or rather it opens the door to countless curtailments.

*The political pursuit of freedom can lead to its eradication
on a grand scale. The Time Regulation Institute* is to be
savored, among other things, for the brilliance of such insights.
Tanpınar presciently feared that to embrace the Western conception of progress was to be mentally enslaved by a whole new
epistemology, one that compartmentalized knowledge and concealed an instrumental view of human beings as no more than
things to be manipulated.

İrdal's career as the Kemalist state's functionary achieves its
apotheosis when he becomes an architectural designer for the
Time Regulation Institute and is praised for his "unusual staircases and the two unnecessary bridges connecting them to
the main building." But the makeover cannot but remain tragi-
cally incomplete. For İrdal, ushered late into the modern world,
feels that

> naturally all this didn't develop as smoothly as it would have for
> Halit Ayarcı. Every so often my soft, complacent, compassionate
> nature—made softer over time by poverty and despair—would
> step in to interrupt and alter my course. In effect I became
> a man whose thoughts, decisions, and speech patterns were all in
> a jumble.

How eloquently this describes the fate of many human beings,
or "things," forced into alien ways and lifestyles—the hundreds
of millions of white-shirted workers with shakily grasped European languages and irretrievably impaired mother tongues.
These are the people encountered in passing, if at all, in the
works of Western travel writers, marked off from their suave
Westernized compatriots by their broken English, seemingly
childish naïveté, and residence in a netherworld of perception
and awareness.

Max Weber, the tragic prophet of modernity, saw the bureaucratic and technological state as an "iron cage" in which we
live as "specialists without spirit, sensualists without heart."

Even worse, Weber feared, "this nullity imagines that it has attained a level of civilization never before achieved." *The Time Regulation Institute* explodes that presumption by showing us, in our postmodern cages, glimpses of another kind of civilization. It also mourns, more eloquently and sensitively than any novel I know, the obscure sufferings of people in less "developed" societies—those who, uprooted from their old ways of being, must languish eternally in the waiting room of history.

PANKAJ MISHRA

A Note on the Translation

As a young man, Ahmet Hamdi Tanpınar witnessed the transformation, almost overnight, of the ornate, opaque language we now know as Ottoman into an idiom thought to be more fitting for a modern, westernizing republic. First came the Alphabet Revolution, in 1928. Atatürk gave his new nation just three months to say good-bye to Arabic script and to master the new Latin(ate) orthography. In 1932 he launched the Language Revolution, with the aim of ridding modern Turkish of all words of Arabic or Persian origin. The Turkish Language Society, to which he entrusted this great task, did not, in the end, manage to do away with all such words, nor did it succeed in winning support for the thousands of neologisms it invented to replace them. But it did succeed in reducing the vocabulary by 60 percent. The distance between Ottoman and modern Turkish has grown with every decade, so much so that Atatürk's own orations, which still inform what Turkish schoolchildren learn about their history, have been translated twice.

Writers were intimately involved in this story from the beginning. Some allied themselves with the state; many others ended up in prison. But support for "pure Turkish" remained strong on both sides of the political divide. Tanpınar was the great exception. He revelled in Ottoman's rich blend of Persian, Arabic, and Turkish. He believed that the way forward was not to sever all links with tradition but to find graceful and harmonious ways to blend Eastern and Western influences. He refused to change his language to suit the bureaucrats. For this he was heavily criticized, dismissed in literary circles as old-fashioned and irrelevant. *The Time Regulation Institute*, first published in book form in the year of his death, was his last (and most lasting) revenge.

Its hero, Hayri İrdal, speaks a language that, however much it strains to keep pace with modern times, keeps collapsing into its old ways. As much as he tries to embrace new words and ideas, his old ones come back to claim him. This losing battle is evident in Hayri's every reminiscence. Guilelessly he climbs from clause to clause, as we count the seconds before the edifice starts to teeter.

That's how it is, at least, for those of us who have had the privilege of reading *The Time Regulation Institute* in the original. For those of us familiar with Turkey's traditions of oral storytelling, there is also the pleasure of watching Hayri walk way out on a limb, and then the limb of the limb, as we begin to ask ourselves if he and his author have perhaps lost the thread, the plot, the point, or even their minds. And then, just as our own minds begin to wander, there's a slap on the table, bringing the story, the chapter, the novel to a sudden and startling end, and all those random details fall neatly, and perfectly, into place.

How to capture these sublime feats in a language that has never suffered political interference of this order? How to convey the changes of register that are the source of so much of the comedy? For us the answer was to go beyond the usual (and in this novel, often insoluble) problems of diction and meaning, to listen instead to the music of the narration. For Tanpınar was one of the great stylists of his age. He was famed for his poetry as well as for his prose. Language was his instrument, and he brought to it all he knew of music, both Eastern and Western. Whatever games he played on the printed page, he played them first with sound.

We did things in the opposite order when shaping his sentences in English. First we put the words on the page. Then we listened for the voice, arranging, rearranging, and changing the words and clauses until we heard something of the Turkish music coming through.

Here we should point out that we are not alone in this: No one can translate Turkish into English without a great deal of arranging and rearranging. Turkish is an agglutinative language. It routinely appends strings of eight, nine, or more suffixes to its root nouns. It has a single word for he, she, and it. It offers no independently standing definite or indefinite articles. It has a much more refined understanding of time than we do. Not only can it distinguish between hearsay and that which we have seen with our own eyes, but it can also change a verb from active to passive with the addition of a two-letter, midword syllable that is all too easily missed by Anglophone eyes. It takes an easygoing approach (in our eyes, at least) to singulars and plurals. It likes cascading clauses beginning with verbal nouns that are as likely as not to be in the passive voice—as in "the doing unto of," or even "the having been done unto of." It puts the verb at the end of the sentence, and when this sentence comes from a master stylist who feels unjustly constrained by the politics of language, finding solace in a grammar too flexible for bureaucrats to contain, that verb will often turn the entire sentence on its head.

All this leaves much room, and perhaps too much room, for interpretation. So much the better, then, that there were two of us. It was easier to take a risk knowing that someone was watching to catch us if we fell—or skipped a line, perhaps to escape yet another logic-defying sentence. It was fun having company, on the bad days and the good. Our most difficult day came right at the end, when we were trying to work out the shape and dimensions of the Institute itself. The solution came to Alex in a dream. And, oh, how we laughed when we worked through it the next day, and saw how perfectly this preposterous structure reflected the author's ideas about modernization-from-above. It was a thrill to bring this metaphor, and this book, into English. We hope you enjoy it as much as we did.

MAUREEN FREELY AND ALEXANDER DAWE

Suggestions for Further Reading

Finkel, Andrew. *Turkey: What Everyone Needs to Know*. Oxford: Oxford University Press, 2012.

Finkel, Caroline. *Osman's Dream: The History of the Ottoman Empire*. New York: Basic Books, 2006.

Freely, John. *Istanbul: The Imperial City*. New York: Viking, 1997.

Freely, John and Hilary Sumner-Boyd. *Strolling through Istanbul*. London: I.B. Tauris, 2010.

Goffman, Daniel. *The Ottoman Empire and Early Modern Europe*. Cambridge: Cambridge University Press, 2002.

Goodwin, Jason. *Lords of the Horizons: A History of the Ottoman Empire*. New York: Henry Holt, 1999.

Guler, Ara. *Ara Guler's Istanbul*. London: Thames & Hudson, 2009.

Hanioğlu, M. Şükrü. *Atatürk: An Intellectual Biography*. Princeton, NJ: Princeton University Press, 2011.

Mansel, Philip. *Constantinople: City of the World's Desire, 1453–1924*. New York: St. Martin's Press, 1996.

Pamuk, Orhan. *Istanbul: Memories and the City*. New York: Alfred A. Knopf, 2005.

Pope, Hugh and Nicole Pope. *Turkey Unveiled: A History of Modern Turkey*. New York: Overlook, 1998.

Shafak, Elif. *The Flea Place*. London: Marion Boyars, 2004.

Tanpınar, Ahmet Hamdi. *A Mind at Peace*. New York: Archipelago Books, 2008.

Chronology of Turkish History

1181–1407	Five emperors with the name Andronicus rule Byzantium.
1453	Fatih Sultan Mehmed II conquers Constantinople.
1500–1700	The Golden Age of the Ottoman Empire.
1730–1754	Mahmud I reigns and the empire begins to stagnate.
1512–1867	The Ottomans control Egypt but the state is often semi-autonomous due to Ottoman governors who run rogue operations.
1808–1839	Mahmud II reigns. Military, administrative, and fiscal reforms lead to the Tanzimat (reorganization) decree and reforms that aim to emulate Western models.
1839	The Tanzimat decree, a liberal charter of political, social, and legal rights, in which all races and creeds are declared equal, is ratified but complete implementation proves untenable.
1839–1876	Abdulmecid I and Abdülaziz reign. A period of fiscal extravagance and irresponsibility inspires the Young Ottoman movement to push for democratic reform and the implementation of a constitutional monarchy.
1876–1909	Sultan Abdülhamid II reigns. Accepts the new constitution and allows for a parliament to form (1877) but dissolves it a year later, citing civil unrest as the primary cause. By the end of his reign, marked by fear, paranoia, and xenophobia, a police state manages a vast network of spies and censorship of the press.
1889	The Ottoman Union (Ittihad-I Osmanı) is founded by opponents of the Abdülhamid regime. It eventually becomes the Committee of Union and Progress (Ittihat

ve Terakki Cemiyet) the first political party in the Ottoman Empire.

1908   The Committee of Union and Progress (CUP), composed largely of members of the Young Turks movement, revolts, demanding that a parliamentary system replace the monarchy.

1909   Abdülhamid is forced to reinstate the constitution. He is deposed by the parliament and constitutional sovereignty is established.

1913   The Second Balkan War. The Balkan league dissolves over a dispute regarding the division of spoils. CUP seizes power through a military coup and rules until the end of the First World War.

1913   The assassination of Grand Vizier Mahmut Şevket is used as an excuse by the CUP to establish a military junta.

1914–1918   First World War. The Ottoman Empire enters the war on the side of Germany. CUP leaders are widely regarded as responsible for entering the war and for getting rich by controlling the trade of staple goods such as soap and sugar.

1909–1919   The reign of Mehmed V.

1918–1922   The armistice years. British mandate in Istanbul.

1919–1922   Turkish war of independence. Mustafa Kemal Atatürk repels foreign powers and establishes a Grand National Assembly in Ankara.

1923   Turkish Republic is founded and the sultanate is abolished.

1924   The Caliphate is abolished by the Turkish Grand National Assembly and the last Caliphate Abdulmecid II is exiled.

1923–1945   Period of single party rule. Rapid modernization from a top-down revolution dismisses the fledgling nation's Ottoman past, absorbs minorities under a single ethnic banner, and gives birth to a highly bureaucratized state.

1945–2000   A tumultuous transition to multiparty democracy marked by four different military coups.

2002–present   AKP (Justice and Development Party) in power.

The Time Regulation
Institute

PART I

GREAT
EXPECTATIONS

I have never cared much for reading or writing; anyone who knows me can tell you that. Unless you count Jules Verne or the Nick Carter stories I read as a child, everything I know can be traced to *A Thousand and One Nights*, *A Parrot's Tale*, the armful of history books I've had occasion to pass my eyes over (always skipping the Arabic and Persian words), and the works of the philosopher Avicenna. Before we established our institute, when I was unemployed and spent my days at home, I would often find myself leafing through my children's schoolbooks; at other times, when I was left with nothing to do but recite the Koran, I would whittle away my hours in the coffeehouses of Edirnekapı and Şehzadebaşı, reading articles in the newspaper or the odd episode of a serial.

I should also mention the psychoanalytic studies of Dr. Ramiz, who oversaw my treatment while I was under observation at the medical institute and who was so kind to me in later years. Lest I seem unworthy of the goodwill bestowed on me by this eminent scholar, I must assure you that I've read his entire oeuvre without skipping a single sentence. But while no doubt his work illuminates grave and important matters of mysterious origin, it did little to influence my taste in literature or my turn of mind. During my long conversations with Dr. Ramiz—always he would speak and I would listen—I often had occasion to profit from my many hours of reading, as they offered me, if nothing else, a way of masking my ignorance. (One never does lose the good manners one learns as a child.) My father was against our reading anything but our schoolbooks—though early on he made an exception of works

on Arabic grammar and syntax, such as *Emsile* and *Avámil*—
and it is perhaps because he censored, or rather forbade, our
reading that I lost all interest in the written word.

Nevertheless there was a time in my life when I succeeded in
writing a small book. This wasn't an act of self-promotion—
a form of posturing I abhor—for I didn't write it in the hope
that others might proclaim, "Look, our friend Hayri İrdal has
written a book!" Nor can I say I was compelled by a restless
ambition. In due course I shall explain just how this book came
into being and the purpose it served; for now let me note simply
that it numbered among the publications of the institute whose
doors have now been closed, though it might be more accurate
to say the institute has, thanks to Halit Ayarcı's fortuitous intervention, been consigned to continuous liquidation. If I have received any praise for this book illuminating the life and work of
Sheikh Zamanı, the patron saint of clock makers, all credit
must go to the founder of our institute, Halit Ayarcı, the dear
benefactor and beloved friend who plucked me from poverty
and despair and made me the person I am today, for indeed his
excellence knows no bounds. Everything in my life that is good,
beautiful, and precious belongs to this great man who was
taken from us three weeks ago in a car accident. I need only recall the moment when, having invited me to tell him everything
I had learned about clock making while working alongside the
muvakkit Nuri Efendi, he had a flash of inspiration as profound, perhaps, as that which led to the creation of the institute
itself: for not only did Halit Ayarcı discover Sheikh Ahmet
Zamanı Efendi at that precise moment; he also knew at once
that this man belonged to the reign of Mehmed IV.

These were the two discoveries that allowed for our swift
transfer to the headquarters where, in happier days, we were
able to celebrate our "time" holidays with such success. My
book was translated into several languages, and its critical
reception abroad was as solemn and profound as it had been at
home: this alone should prove that our dear friend Halit
Ayarcı—may he rest in peace—was not at all mistaken when
he divined our need for the illustrious Ahmet Zamanı to have
existed, nor was he wrong when he assigned him to the century

in question. The original idea was not my own, but when I think back on this book that bears my name, when I recall its translation into eighteen languages, and the reviews it received in foreign newspapers, and the great scholar Van Humbert, who traveled all the way from Holland to meet with me and visit the tomb of Ahmet Zamanı, I know I am remembering the most important events of my life.

This scholar, though, turned out to be rather irksome. Finding the tomb of a man who never existed in mortal form is more difficult than you might imagine, as is surviving vigorous debate with a foreign scholar, even with the aid of an interpreter. We were saved first by what the foreign papers called our "Sufi-like attitudes and detached—or, rather, indulgent—personalities," and second by the fact that our forefathers had availed themselves of pseudonyms.

After wandering the graveyards of Edirnekapı and Eyüp for several days, and visiting the Karacaahmet Cemetery, we were bound to find an Ahmet Zamanı Efendi. And so we did. I am not unduly troubled by the minor alterations I made to the identity of the actual deceased. If nothing else, the poor man had his tomb repaired and his name made known: glory and calamity are both at God's mercy. Photographs of the tomb were printed in the press, first in Holland and then in other countries around the world, but always on the condition that I would be there with one hand resting on the tombstone and the other holding my raincoat, my hat, or perhaps a newspaper.

There is only one thing that saddens me when I remember this man who wrote such lovely things about my book, who introduced me to the world and spent so many days with me searching for the tomb: never once did I allow him to pose for a photograph leaning against Zamanı's resting place. No sooner did Van Humbert ask the question than I turned him down, saying, "But you *are* a Christian—it would be a torment for Zamanı's soul!" and insisting that he stand off to my right. Thinking about it now, I can allow myself to imagine he forgave me. And considering the months of trouble the lout brought upon me, it serves him right! What business did he have swooping in like that and causing such aggravation? We are people who live in a world of our own

making! Everything is just as we like it. But as you will see in due
course, Van Humbert had his revenge.

So I never was one for reading or writing. But here I am this
morning, struggling to write my memoirs in the oversized notebook before me. In fact I woke up at five o'clock—much earlier
than usual—with this very task in mind. All the good-natured
and industrious employees at Clock Villa were still asleep: not
just our maids, but also our chef, Arif Efendi, whose only flaw is
that he isn't from the town of Bolu, though he does whip up
truly delightful dishes just the same, and our Arab *kalfa*, Zeynep
Hanım, for whom we searched far and wide, suffering a thousand hardships, just to give our home that taste of the old
world—how strange that blacks are now as rare as imported
goods while in my childhood there were so many of them in
Istanbul. So for better or worse I was left to make my own morning coffee, after which I ensconced myself in my armchair and
began trying to imagine my life, sifting through all the things I
would soon record—things that needed to be changed or embellished or omitted altogether. In short, I have tried to arrange the
events of my life into some semblance of order, bearing in mind
the many strict rules of what we might call sincere writing: these
are never as indispensable as when one is composing a memoir.

For above all else, I, Hayri İrdal, have always argued for
absolute sincerity. Why write at all if you cannot say honestly
what you mean? A sincerity of this order—disinterested and
unconditional—by its nature requires close scrutiny and constant filtering. You must agree that it would be unthinkable to
describe things as they are. If you are to avoid leaving a sentence arrested in midthought, you must plan ahead, choosing
only those points that will resonate with the reader's sentiments. For sincerity is not the work of one man alone.

But please don't assume from this that I set too high a value
on my life or that I deem it too important to be left unrecorded.
I number myself among those who believe that the Lord, our
Creator, granted us this life to be lived, for either good or evil,
and not for us to write it down. Besides, it's already there in
written form. I am alluding here to our fate as set down in the
periodicals of the Divine Presence.

No, when I say I am writing my memoirs I don't mean to say I have set out to describe my life. I simply wish to record a series of events I happened to witness. And in so doing to remember—to honor—the saintly man we laid to rest three weeks ago.

I may be the most humble and absurd man in the world and, as my wife says, the most slovenly creature you may ever meet—that is, before the founding of our institute—but I did come to know a truly great man who possessed a natural genius for invention. I spent years at his side. I watched the way he worked. I witnessed how an idea would suddenly catch fire in his mind and take shape, like a tree sprouting shoots and branches, before coming into being. It was in this spirit that I witnessed the Time Regulation Institute—perhaps the greatest and most important organization of this century—evolve from a sudden spark in his eyes to the splendor it enjoys today, or did, rather, yesterday. Without fear of ridicule or affectation, I now can say that—despite my pitiful shortcomings, I, Hayri İrdal—was able to play a vital role in the foundation of this institute, if only thanks to coincidence and a run of good luck.

It seems to me that my greatest obligation to future generations is to record all I have seen and heard. For only one person could have written the history of our institute better than myself, and that man, Halit Ayarcı, is no longer with us. Last night at the dinner table I found his chair empty once again. I will never forget the way my wife fixed her gaze upon it throughout the meal. She seemed a stranger in her own home. In the end she could bear it no longer and, wiping her eyes with a napkin, rose from the table and shut herself in her room. I'm quite sure she cried all night. And she was right to do so; for if Halıt Ayarcı was my benefactor, he was her best friend. Just considering the prospect of a memoir will have provoked in her, as in me, a grief that matches the occasion.

I lay in bed, thinking, for quite some time. "Hayri İrdal," I said to myself, "you have seen so much of the world, and you have witnessed so much as well. Although just sixty years old, you have lived the lives of several men combined. You have endured all manner of suffering and the misery of being shunned. You have bounded up the steps to your future, light-footed and never faltering. You've tackled problems that no one given only strength or time could ever solve. All this is thanks to Halit Ayarcı. He's the one who rescued you from the asylum. All the enemies in your life, all those who plagued your thoughts and peace of mind—he turned them into friends. Once you were a man who saw in the world around you only cruelty, poverty, and misery, but suddenly you found yourself amid the noblest of pleasures and a happiness that ought to be the province of all creatures on earth, and you came to understand the nobility of the human soul. You discovered the meaning of intimate love, for it was he who revealed to you the exquisite beauty in the face of your wife, Pakize. You assumed that the great Lord had sent you a rabble of pitiful creatures bent on making your life miserable, when suddenly he contrived for you the gift and joy of God's children. Must you not do everything in your power for the memory of this good, pure, and—in every sense of the word—exalted friend? Can you even contemplate the possibility of him sinking into oblivion, his memory buried in a pile of slander and scorn? Think about it for a moment: What was your life before you met Halit Ayarcı? And what are you now? Think about your house in Edirnekapı and the creditors who turned up at your door day after day, even pouncing upon you in the street. Remember how you once had to struggle to get hold of even a single piece of bread. Then behold the comfort and happiness of your life today!

II

I mentioned my life prior to meeting Halit Ayarcı. But can one really call it a life? If to live is to endure endless pain and destitution and to suffer humiliation so deep that it afflicts each and every fiber of one's being, if it means fluttering ceaselessly against the walls of a cage that will never open, then there is no doubt that I and others like me did "live," in the fullest sense of the word. But if the word encompasses a wealth of spirit and possibility, a modicum of rights, a few rare moments of inner bliss, with a dash of trust in the outside world, and a sense of fairness and balance in dealing with one's fellow man and suchlike—well, then things are quite different. You might have noticed that I make no mention whatsoever of helping others or doing anything constructive. Until I met Halit Ayarcı, I was never even aware of such pleasures. Today, however, my life has meaning. I shall leave behind a work that I believe will more or less secure me a place in the annals of history. For ten years, I acted as assistant head manager of one of the most innovative and beneficial organizations in the world. I helped not only my own immediate family but also my close and distant relatives and my friends, even those who had once betrayed me, by providing them with employment and a sense and source of well-being. In this regard I suppose it would suffice to highlight our contribution to urban development through the construction of a new district near Suadiye, as well as the services our institute provided to its workers, most of whom were in fact relatives of either myself or Halit Ayarcı. For as soon as the institute was established, Halit made the very important decision—from which we never strayed—that half the management positions and other important posts would be filled by members of our families and the other half by those who had the recommendation of a notable personage.

I am not sure if I need to mention the criticisms much aired in the papers long before it was decided to liquidate the institute or the ever more violent attacks that followed the institute's dissolution. Life can be so strange. Ten years ago the very same papers delighted in everything we did, showering us with praise and holding us aloft as a model to the world. Though they attended our every press conference and never missed an official cocktail party, these dear friends of mine now do nothing but hurl abuse.

First they condemned the organization for its unwieldy size and inefficiency. Overlooking the fact that we created jobs for so many in a country where unemployment is rampant, they railed against our excesses: three management offices, eleven management branches, forty-seven typists, and two hundred seventy control bureaus. Then they ridiculed the names of our various

branches, overlooking the fact that a watch or clock is indeed
made up of hands for minutes and hours, a spring, a pendulum,
and a pin, as if the thing we all know as time were not in fact
divided into hours, minutes, seconds, and milliseconds. Later
the papers called into question the training, expertise, and intellectual underpinnings of our licensed employees—who had garnered over ten years' experience with us—before mercilessly
denouncing my early book, *The Life and Works of Ahmet the
Timely*, which had once delighted them.

After tearing to pieces *The Life and Works of Ahmet the
Timely*, they went on to attack all our other studies. For days
on end, we would open the papers to find reproductions of our
book covers under preposterous headlines that implied the
works were somehow subversive or only worthy of derision:
*The Effect of the North Wind upon the Regulation of Cosmic
Time*, penned with such painstaking attention to detail by the
head of our Millisecond Branch (also husband to our family's
youngest sister-in-law); or *Time and Psychoanalysis* and *The
İrdal Method of Time Characterology*, both by my dear friend
Dr. Ramiz; or Halit Ayarcı's *Social Monism and Time* and *The
Second and Society*.

As if that was not enough, they went on to accuse us outright
of being frauds and charlatans, homing in on our accumulative
fining system, with its proportional reductions and the bonus
discounts that had once so amused and entertained our fellow
citizens while also allowing the institute to pursue its varied
social and scientific activities. But how warmly these same people had once applauded this system of fines, which I myself
invented, just to pass the time, while watching my wife, Pakize,
and Halit Ayarcı play endless games of backgammon for petty
cash during their gambling soirees.

One of our esteemed financiers publicly declared this system
of fines a most remarkable innovation in the history of account-
ing and took every opportunity to remind me that he would
never hesitate to put me in the same company as the illustrious
financiers Doctor Turgot, Necker, and Schacht.

And he was right. For in matters of finance—whereby money
turns people into good taxpayers—unhappiness has forever

been the rule. And in the matter of fines in particular, people inevitably feel a certain discomfort. But our system was not at all like that. When an inspector notified a citizen of his fine, the offender would initially express surprise, but upon apprehending the firm logic behind the system, a smile would spread across his face until, at last understanding this was a serious matter, he would succumb to uproarious laughter. I cannot count the number of people—especially in the early days—who would extend a business card to our inspectors, saying, "Oh please, you absolutely must come over to our house sometime. My wife really must see this. Here's my address," and offer to cover the inspector's taxi fare.

Our system of fines specified the collection of five kurus for every clock or watch not synchronized with any other clock in view, particularly those public clocks belonging to the municipality. However, the offender's fine would be doubled if his timepiece differed from that of any other in the vicinity. Thus the fine might rise proportionally when there were several timepieces nearby. Since the perfect regulation of time is impossible—because of the personal freedom afforded by watches and clocks, something I was naturally in no position at the time to explain—a single inspection, especially in one of the busier parts of town, made it possible to collect a not insignificant sum.

The last calculation required by this confusing system concerned the difference between watches or clocks that were either fast or slow. Everyone knows that a watch or clock is either fast or slow. For timepieces, there is no third state. It is an accepted axiom very much akin to the impossibility of exact regulation; that is, of course, assuming the watch or clock has not stopped altogether. But here matters become more personal. My own view is this: since man was created ruler of the universe, objects can be expected to reflect the tenor of his rule. For example, during my childhood, under the reign of Abdülhamīd II, our entire society was moribund. Our dissatisfaction stemmed from the sultan's long face, but it radiated out and infected even physical objects. Everyone my age will recall the mournful cries of the ferryboats of that era, with

their piercing foghorns. But with the favorable unfolding of
events thereafter, we find our days so full of delight that
we now hear joy in a ferryboat's horn and in the clang of a trolley's bell.

The same can be said for watches and clocks. They inevitably fall in step with an owner's natural disposition, be it ponderous or ebullient, and in the same way they reflect his
conjugal patterns and political persuasions. Certainly in a society like ours that has been swept along by one revolution after
another in its relentless march toward progress, leaving behind
diverse communities and entire generations, it is all too under-
standable that our political persuasions would find expression
in this way. Political creeds remain secret for one reason or
another. With so many sanctions hanging over us, no one is
about to stand up in a public place and proclaim, "Now, this is
what I think!" or even to say such a thing aloud, for that matter. Thus it is our watches and clocks that hold our secrets, as
well as the beliefs and habits that set us apart from others.

Just as a watch can become a man's dearest friend, ticking
with the pulse in his wrist, sharing the passions in his chest,
and growing heated with the same fervor, until they are as one,
so too may a clock sit on a table throughout the span of time
we call a day and assume the essence of its owner, thinking and
living as he does. Without going into too much detail, I can say
that we find this same tendency—to assimilate and adapt—in
all our personal belongings, even if our relationships with them
may never be as profound as the ones we have with our watches
and clocks. Do not our old hats and shoes and clothes become
more and more a part of us with the passage of time? Isn't that
why we are constantly trying to replace them? A man who dons
a new suit leaves his old self behind. How different it looks, as it
recedes in to the past! What bliss to exclaim, "I am at last a new
man!"

I can assure you that the late Halit Ayarcı—who harbored
the fear that many would come forward to discredit our
institute—strongly recommended that I avoid making these
types of declarations; but since I am no longer thus constrained,
I can claim comfortably that it is indeed possible to see in an

old hat or a pair of shoes all the whims of its owner—his foibles and particularities, even his many pains and sorrows. This may help explain the conventional wisdom that new servants coming to work in our homes should be given some of our clothes—at the very least a couple old shirts, a tie, or a pair of old shoes. Thus the servant—someone with whom we are newly acquainted—will, after putting on a shirt and tie and walking about in our shoes for a while, feel mysteriously compelled to adopt our idiosyncrasies and manners of thought, without ever knowing why. I myself experienced something like this on two occasions.

Cemal Bey, the director of the Bank of Diverse Affairs, and the man behind my dismissal from this establishment, was the architect of many of the calamities I've suffered in my life. There was a time when he offered me one of his suits. We had dramatically different personalities: he was a fussy, snobbish, grouch of a man, who judged the world by unbending rules and took great delight in belittling his staff, whereas I had a simple and compliant nature, wishing only to get by. The fact of the matter is that I never did take on his personality. That was beyond the realm of possibility. But his only weakness— his ardent love for his wife—seemed to have seeped into me through his suit. For during the week I wore that suit, I fell madly in love with Selma Hanım—I, a strict adherent to Muslim morals, father of three children, and married to Pakize, a woman far superior to me in every conceivable way. Years after I left the bank, the suit became tattered and threadbare. But my passion for Selma Hanım never waned.

The second suit was given to me by Halit Ayarcı, in the days just following the founding of our institute. He considered it best for me not to report to the institute in the clothes I was accustomed to wearing at that time. On the very first day I wore the suit, I sensed a dramatic shift in my entire being. New horizons and perspectives suddenly unfurled before me. Like Halit Ayarcı, I began to perceive life as a single entity. I began to use terms like "modification," "coordination," "work structure," "mind-set shift," "metathought," and "scientific mentality"; I took to associating such terms as "ineluctability" or "impossibility" with my lack of will. I even made imprudent comparisons between East and West, and passed judgments whose gravity left me terrified. Like him, I began to look at people with eyes that wondered, "Now, what use could he be to us?" and to see life as dough that could be kneaded by my own two hands. In a word, it seemed as if his courage and powers of invention had been transferred to me, as if it were not a suit at all but a magic cloak. In fact I no longer saw Cemal Bey's wife, Selma Hanımefendi, as a woman beyond my reach. Naturally all this didn't develop as smoothly as it would have for Halit Ayarcı. Every so often my soft, complacent, compassionate nature—made softer over time by poverty and despair—would step in to interrupt and alter my course. In effect I became a man whose thoughts, decisions, and speech patterns were all in a jumble. When the late Halit Ayarcı heard me say as much, he smiled warmly and reassured me, "That's just how it should be. It adds a certain spice. Keep it up!"

I feel I must stop here to report what was said on one of the days we discussed the matter.

"Aziz Hayri İrdal," he declared, "what you have said is entirely true. This is precisely why all great men give their clothes and personal effects to those working alongside them. Roman emperors, kings, and powerful dictators have always presented their belongings to their friends so they might think as they do. Indeed this must be the very reason Ottoman leaders would bestow their kaftans and furs on their grand viziers. You have unwittingly put your finger on one of history's great secrets, a kind of psychological mechanism!"

Without a doubt, he spoke the truth. And let us not forget that I made this discovery after putting on his suit. Yes, it was by donning his suit that I discovered this man had a genius for discovery.

But let us return to watches and clocks. Allow me to speak of *The Psychoanalysis of Clocks*, a seminal study first published by Dr. Ramiz in our institute's journal. On second thought, I fear that such digressions—even if they are of an entirely scientific nature, or of a radically different nature, for that matter—will weigh too heavily upon these memoirs, and so I shall refrain. The work is in print, and those interested may consult it if they wish.

Dr. Ramiz and I differ in one significant respect, and here I shall relate what he said to me only personally: While I approached our joint enterprise from the perspectives of general psychology and sociology, he availed himself of such concepts as sexuality, libido, and repression. I was pleased to hear this, even though I knew nothing of individual or collective psychology, and even less of sociology. As he summed up his thoughts, Dr. Ramiz, who had always been kind enough to take me seriously, took the trouble to tell me that I was a great idealist. When my wife and I later discussed the matter, she was of the opinion that—seeing as we were speaking of subjects so intimately linked to human affairs as clocks, watches, and time—my utter disregard for the role of sexuality in the social realm could not be attributed to the so-called idealism the doctor saw in me but must stem from sources far more serious: namely corporeal and hygienic.

However you look at the situation, there is undeniably a difference between fast and slow timepieces, and this difference is an extremely important one. Therefore everyone found it quite acceptable when we enforced a two-kurus increase on the cash fine we collected for slow clocks and watches. In fact people were extremely pleased. And seeing as we fined those whose timepieces were slow, we were obliged to cede a certain advantage to those whose were running fast. Humanity never did sit easily with pure equality, and people need the encouragement of a little incentive here and there. I can say with confidence that good is only ever achieved if an identifiable evil is subjected to punishment and shame. My late teacher Nuri Efendi, whom I will discuss at length in due course, spoke these very words with regard to Sufism: "A thing is possible and accepted only if its opposite also exists." In fact it was this important point that led Halit Ayarcı to agree to my proposed increase in fines.

The third particular of the system of fines I'd devised was a discount offered to repeat offenders, ranging from 10 to 30 percent. You're well aware that the punishment for a crime is greater on the second offense, as the laws and customs of the world require. This leads to a kind of standoff between the legislator and the offender, a digging in of heels.

I am not talking about a first offense. It is often the case that the first offense might, like a first marriage, leave feelings of regret. But it is common knowledge that, following a second offense—and the increased penalties it entails—a person will find himself swept away by the hopelessness he might feel at an auction when the price is spiraling beyond his means. This is why in our fining system we prevented this outcome and its natural reactive elements by implementing a reduction of fines up to 30 percent on the seventh or eighth offense. Of course this aggregative and incremental system of fines brought attention to our institute. Naturally there was a business rationale for it. We were in effect doing business with revenues neglected by the municipality. And what enterprise does not seek to extend some kind of discount to its regular customers? As it turned out, I hadn't been wrong in assuming that the people of Istanbul—who were accustomed to end-of-season sales and who could conceive of only a small fraction of the profits large businesses were making—would be pleased with our system. Suffice it to say that one is not in the habit of expecting so much from a quasi-official establishment, and so it was quite easy for the public to enjoy the system and speak highly of it to others.

And that is precisely what happened. Unable to believe such a thing was possible, or simply assuming it to be some kind of joke, people began to storm our centers with their watches in hand or to stop our inspectors on the street and ask to be fined. Throughout the city, it was suddenly all the rage to pay these fines voluntarily, and even with a smile. There was no longer any need to buy children toys; the little dears had found a more exciting way to share in the happiness of adults.

I should mention that it was not just the people of Istanbul who took a passionate interest in the fines but also those in surrounding villages and even in cities some distance away—so much so that in the initial months of enforcing the system of discounted fines, and particularly when the subscription plans were instated, the state railway management bureau was forced to add additional trains to several lines. Every day the railroad stations of Haydarpaşa and Sirkeci would be overrun with people smiling, often splitting their sides in laughter, as they cried, "My goodness, take a look at this!" or "Unbelievable, but true!"

So eager were the masses pouring in from the countryside that we were forced to take regulation teams from as far out as Pendik, on the city's Asian side, and Çatalca, in Thrace, and relocate them to stations closer to the city and the central terminals. Not only did we have to transfer some of our people to different posts, but when we needed to recruit new regulation teams in the villages, we were also obliged to hire youths, for we had insufficient manpower to carry on as it was.

It would not be incorrect to say that much of the fame our institute won abroad is due to this system of cash fines. Certainly you've read in the papers how cruise ship passengers forced captains to change course for Istanbul, where they would stay a week in the city, returning with receipts of discounted fines in hand before continuing on their journey, and how many of these passengers would not leave the city until they had been granted an interview with either myself or Halit Ayarcı, and how they scoured the city shops for our photographs.

I shall not enumerate all the indignities our institute has suffered in recent times. As I progress through these memoirs, my readers will see for themselves just what kind of cruelty was thrust upon us. Yet here again I simply cannot continue without making just one personal observation.

Like those who criticize the Time Regulation Institute, those who praise it always overlook one fundamental aspect: the strong connection it has to my person—in fact to my past. I would never deny that the institute was born of Halit Ayarcı's entrepreneurial gifts and powerful mind. In every sense and meaning of the words, he was both my benefactor and a great friend. But my role in the Time Regulation Institute was by no means what those on the outside claim or imply: I was not merely a cog, or a means to an end. It could very well be that the institute was the result of Halit's imaginative mind and that all my life I was destined to live through the contingencies born of his creation, with much pain and suffering as the price. But this is the very essence of my being.

My first responsibility in writing these memoirs is to discredit all who have slandered or scorned the institute or its late founder; my second, of no less importance, is to assert a small but very important truth.

III

I've already mentioned on several occasions my life's various misfortunes. As my memoir unfolds, my readers will see how want and privation have been my lifelong companions, together serving practically as a second skin. But it would be wrong to say that I have never been graced with happiness.

I was born into a family fallen on hard times. But I had quite a happy childhood. As long as we are in harmony with those around us—assuming, of course, the right balance—poverty is never as terrifying or intolerable as we might think. For it offers certain advantages. The privilege I most treasured as a child was that of freedom.

Today we use the word only in its political sense, and how unfortunate for us. For I fear that those who see freedom solely as a political concept will never fully grasp its meaning. The political pursuit of freedom can lead to its eradication on a grand scale—or rather it opens the door to countless curtailments. It seems that freedom is the most coveted commodity in the world: for just when one person decides to gorge upon it, those around him are deprived. Never have I known a concept so inextricable from its antithesis, and indeed entirely crushed under its weight. I have been made to understand that in my lifetime freedom has been kind enough to visit our country seven or eight times. Yes, seven or eight times, and no one ever bothered to say when it left; but whenever it came back again, we would leap out of our seats in joy and pour into the streets to blow our horns and beat our drums.

Where does it come from? And how does it vanish with such

stealth? Are those who bring us freedom the very ones who snatch it away? Or do we simply lose interest from one moment to the next, passing it on to others as a gift, saying, "Here you are, sir. I have already had my share of pleasure from this. Now it's yours. Perhaps it will be of some use to you!"? Or is it like those treasure troves that sit gleaming at the back of fairy-tale caverns, only to turn into coal or a pile of dust at first touch? I must confess I've always found freedom an elusive concept.

At the end of the day, I must conclude that no one really needs such a thing in the first place. This love of liberty—and here I'll borrow a phrase much loved by Halit Ayarcı, as he can no longer reprimand or tease me for dipping into his personal lexicon—this love of liberty is nothing more than a kind of snobbism. If we really needed such a thing, or if we truly felt passionately about it, then wouldn't we have grasped onto one of its many avatars and never let it out of our sight? But to what end? The next day it already would have vanished. How strange that we accustom ourselves to its absence so quickly. We are content to invoke its name in the odd poem or schoolbook or public speech.

The freedom I knew as a child was of a different kind. First, and I think most significantly, it was not something I was given. It was something I discovered on my own one day—a lump of gold concealed in my innermost depths, a bird trilling in a tree, sunlight playing on water. There was no going back; from the moment I discovered it, everything changed: my humble existence, our humble home, the very world in which we lived. In time I would lose them all. Nevertheless I owe all the most precious things in my life to freedom. It has filled my days with miracles that neither the miseries of my early years nor the comforts of today could ever take from me. It has taught me how to live without possessions, without a care in the world.

I never chased after things I didn't need. I never wore myself out trying to fulfill doomed passions or ambitions. I never longed to be first in my class, or second or twentieth, for that matter.

The crowded classrooms of Fatih College offered me the chance to observe the ritual of competition from the back rows or, if you like, from the royal opera box. From there, I learned to observe human affairs with detachment.

I wasn't accompanied to school by a servant or page, as most of my friends were. And I didn't wear new or flamboyantly stylish clothes, waterproof boots, or a warm cloak. I wandered the streets with patches on my knees and my elbows almost popping out from my sleeves. No one kissed me and sent me off to school with a thousand warnings, nor did anyone wait impatiently for my arrival home. In fact the later I returned home, the better it suited my family. But I was happy. Though I lacked love and affection, I had my life and the street. The seasons were mine, in all their varied and playful guises, as was all humanity, the animal kingdom, and the inanimate world.

Twice a day I would walk from Edirnekapı to Fatih, plunging into a new fantasy with every dawdling step. But as I approached the age of ten, a passion came to sully this happiness. My life's rhythms were disrupted, it would seem, by the watch my uncle gave me on the occasion of my circumcision. For no matter how innocent a passion might be, it is still a dangerous thing. But I was saved by my spirited nature. It even gave my life direction. One might almost say it gave my life shape. For it may well have been this passion that led me to freedom's door.

IV

When my father recorded my birthday in the back of an old book as the sixteenth day of the holy month of Receb in the year 1310 of the Islamic calendar, he did so with the same conviction as I do now, in proclaiming that Hayri İrdal's true date of birth was the very day he received this watch. From the moment they placed it on my pillow—its blue ribbon a testament to the lengths my aunt was willing to go to avoid paying for a chain—my life changed, its deeper meanings suddenly emerging. First the little timepiece nullified my little world, and then it claimed its rightful place, forcing me to abandon my earlier loves: I forgot about those two glorious minarets carved out of chipboard that my uncle had given me (perhaps because my father was the caretaker of a mosque, and also because we lived just beside the Mihrimah Mosque, my uncle always gave me such gifts, despite the fact that he gave his own children toys that were—to use words still relevant today—modern and secular); and so it was for the enormous kite I so lovingly assembled with the neighborhood children in the courtyard of our house, and the karagöz puppet set I bought after pilfering scraps of lead from various parts of the mosque and selling them to the chickpea peddler, and Ibrahim Efendi's fickle goat I sometimes took out to graze in the cemetery in Edirnekapı and along the old city walls, suffering its mischief when I knew all too well that the stubborn beast wasn't even mine. For me, the importance of each and every one simply disappeared.

I fear that readers of these memoirs may glance over what I have written thus far and think that up until that day I'd never seen a watch or that we had no way of keeping time in our home. But in fact our house was host to several clocks.

Everyone knows that in former times our lives revolved around the clock. According to what I learned from Nuri Efendi, the best customers of Europe's clockmakers were always Muslims, and some of the most pious Muslims were to be found in our country. The clock dictated all manner of worship: the five daily prayers, as well as meals during the holy month of Ramadan, the evening *iftar* and morning *sahur*. A clock offered the most reliable path to God, and our forefathers regulated their lives with this in mind.

Time-setting workshops could be found almost everywhere in the city. Even a man with the most pressing business would come to a sudden halt before the office window to pull out a pocket watch befitting his wealth and age—of gold, silver, or enamel, with or without chains, as plump as a pin cushion or a baby turtle, or flat and thin—and, praying that this moment would be auspicious for him and his children, would utter a *bismillah* in the name of God and reset the timepiece before bringing it to his ear, as if to hear the triumphant tidings that had been promised him in both the near and distant future. To listen to a watch was to listen to the waters that ran from the ablutionary fountains in the mosque courtyards; it was the

sound of an infinite and eternal faith, a sound like no other
that reverberated in this world or the one beyond. Its ticking
set the pace of the day, defined its myriad tasks, and led the listener down immaculate pathways, bringing him ever closer to
the dream of eternal bliss.

A large grandfather clock stood in the living room on the top
floor of our house, and whenever my father was hard-pressed
for cash, he would try to sell it, but for various reasons, which
I shall soon explain, he never could. The calligraphic panels of
various sizes hanging on the walls, the cool damp smell of the
straw mattresses on the floor, the thick curtains draped over
the doorways and the entrances to stairways, and this clock my
father had inherited from his grandfather—all gave the impression of being inside a little mosque.

Some of our neighbors—in particular Ibrahim Bey the owner
of that fickle goat—took pleasure in slander, accusing my father
of having lifted the clock from the small wooden mosque where
he had once served as caretaker. According to these extravagant
lies, my father came home one night with a whole slew of things
he said he had rescued from a fire, including the various panels of
calligraphy and the clock. In our neighbors' minds, everything
had come from the mosque—even the heavy drapes, the ostrich
egg on the console, and the brooms from Mecca that dangled
from the ceiling.

Undone by these false accusations, my poor father would
sink into silence for days on end. Why do people lie and peddle
such slander? In my humble opinion, such calumny is not only
repugnant but also pathetic and absurd. Those compelled by
the flaws of their own nature to disparage others find ready
fodder in the lives of their enemies. For in the life of one individual, there are more imperfections than any imagination
could ever concoct; and over an individual's lifetime these flaws
congeal to define his character." This must be the source of the
saying "nobody's perfect." He who strays from its wisdom,
denigrating his neighbor instead of trying to understand him,
is no more himself than if he were wearing clothes chosen at
random from a rack in some bazaar. Personally, I have always
adhered to the wisdom that so many choose to ignore. And for

this very reason, readers of this memoir will not find in it a single lie or disparaging remark but rather will uncover truths that until now have been kept under lock and key. Perhaps as I relate them I shall make the odd amendment, as befits an author who has assigned himself the task of writing his memoirs.

My father had several weaknesses, which the poor man was unable to conceal. His sudden marriage, wholly approved by Islamic law, to a miserable woman who had begun renting a room in our house just a few days earlier, and who had divorced her former husband that very week, is perhaps the prime example; at the time my father could hardly support his first wife and her children.

The worst of it was that he was entirely devoted to my mother—he married the wretched lodger only because he thought she was rich. But the poor creature was penniless. Her wealth amounted to no more than the silver pieces stashed in the oversized coin purse she kept buried in her bosom, of which we caught a glimpse only when she had to pay rent or a long-overdue court fee. All the same, my father never managed to divorce the woman and remained a bigamist for the rest of his life.

My aim here is not to speak ill of the dead. From the beginning of time, our family has been afflicted by a fixation with marriage, and I too have suffered my share of this misfortune.

So, yes, like anyone else, my father had his shortcomings, and our neighbors were right to take advantage of them. But to accuse him of stealing—and from a mosque!—the property of a pious institution that had been ravaged by fire! No, sir, this is not the sort of thing my father would ever do.

In any case, the story of this grandfather clock is really quite unique. My father's grandfather, Ahmet Efendi the Signer, was a civil servant at the Sublime Porte; having suffered the shame and frustration of slander during the Egyptian Affair—indeed there was even a period when his life was in danger—vowed that if he ever disentangled himself from the debacle, he would fund the construction of a mosque. The affair was finally settled, and after taking a moment to catch his breath, he took to the task; but fearing he might not have sufficient funds to complete the project, he did not proceed with construction beyond buying the plot. In any event, it was only after this mosque of his dreams was granted the status of a charitable foundation that he purchased, in addition to several other buildings, the large villa in Edirnekapı whose stable and servant quarters housed our entire family for many years.

He went on to use any remaining funds to procure furnishings that were eventually to be destined for the mosque: large wool carpets and kilims, a grandfather clock to stand by the door, and lamps and calligraphic panels to be hung on the walls. However, after taking care of these finer details, and before he could begin construction, he lost his job once again, and as such troubles were to plague him for the rest of his life, he was forced to pass on the fulfillment of his good deed to the next generation, although it shouldn't be forgotten that the foundations for the mosque already had been prepared.

If anyone asked when he thought his charitable endeavor would be complete, he would always reply, "God willing, it will come to pass sometime in the next year!" And so toward the end of his life, he, his wife, and close friends knew him as Ahmet Efendi the Some Timer, not the Signer.

After Ahmet Efendi's death it came out that his son Numan Bey, my grandfather, had been mentioned in his will in connection with the mosque: "My responsibility remains, as I was unable to realize my goal. God never granted me the chance. So it now rests in your hands. Finish the job as quickly as you can!" The imperative was Numan Bey's ruination, for he inherited hardly a kurus apart from the house, which he was all but forced to sell, along with just about everything else, in order to meet his father's obligation; but still he was never able to begin construction, and so it was that our family lived in that little house, surrounded by furnishings destined for a mosque.

As it was with my grandfather, so it was with my father: the inheritance virtually destroyed his life. Though he'd once enjoyed a respectable position as a civil servant at a pious foundation, he was, after a series of bungled affairs, demoted to the modest post of caretaker of a small mosque.

My father saw the clock as a kind of creditor and held it responsible for his misfortune; it irked him terribly to have to walk past it every day. And he suffered the neighborhood gossip in silence, not wishing to dredge up the story of the abandoned project, a story he himself would never tell. In time that clock would become his single most secret obsession—and his downfall.

It might have been the gossip that turned me against the clock, or it might have been the gloom it cast over the room. But still it was a beautiful piece. With a rhythm all its own, it was like a packhorse that had strayed from its caravan. Following whose calendar? In which year? What was it waiting for when it stopped running for days before suddenly heralding some mysterious event with a resounding clang that filled the space around it? We hadn't the slightest idea. The free-spirited clock never submitted to adjustments or repairs. It followed a time all its own, far removed from human affairs. On occasion it would release an unexpected sequence of deep chimes, after which its pendulum would swing silently for months on end. My mother looked kindly on the clock's elderly disposition. To her mind it was either a prophet or a being blessed with mystical powers. A fearful reverence for the clock was ingrained in us all on the death of Ibrahim Bey, for it sounded its deepest chimes that evening, perhaps at the precise time he passed away. The clock had been in disrepair for weeks. From that day on, my mother referred to it as the Blessed One. Despite all his religious fervor, my father maintained a more humanist outlook on life and called the clock the Calamity. Saint or calamity, the clock still embodies the spirit of my childhood.

In addition to the grandfather clock, a small clock sat on a table in my parents' bedroom. Unlike the aforementioned timepiece, this one was neither religious nor destined for the world beyond. On the contrary, it was a secular clock with a unique spring mechanism that when properly set played a popular Turkish song at the start of every hour. When radios became popular, song-playing alarm clocks disappeared. Truth be told, I much prefer the singing alarm clock to the radio—though it might not seem entirely fair to harbor such an opinion, considering how my oldest sister-in-law, buoyed by our esteemed institute, has become a renowned chanteuse of popular songs, in a voice reminiscent of a door's ungodly squeak, utterly failing to

identify more than three basic Turkish *makamsher*. Her rise to
stardom was essentially made possible by the support of Halit
Ayarcı. But, then, what can I say? The radio was a needless
invention. If nothing else, an alarm clock doesn't warble without respite throughout the day, or bounce about to dance numbers as if possessed by an evil djinn, nor does it vex its listeners
with warnings of a dangerous storm, and of course just when
your radio goes quiet your neighbor's cranks into action. In my
opinion, as much as I am capable of judging the matter, of
course—for, dear reader, as you listen to these ideas you mustn't
forget that they come from an old man who had a patchy education at best and has spent the better part of his life on wooden
benches in coffeehouses!—the radio does little more than feed
people useless ideas. Sometimes I consider just what strange
creatures we are: we bemoan the brevity of our lives but do
everything in our power to squander this thing we call "the
day" as quickly and mindlessly as we can. Even at this age, I sit
beside a radio for hours when I should be working, listening
endlessly to commentaries on boxing and football matches I've
only ever seen in the newsreels they show before films.

The third timepiece in our household was my father's pocket
watch, a strange contraption equipped with a compass, a hand
that showed the direction of Mecca, and a calendar of universal time that told both existent and nonexistent *alaturca* and
alafranga time. It had but one flaw: that even a master watchmaker found it impossible to familiarize himself with its many
functions. Even Nuri Efendi wasn't convinced he could bring all
its features to optimum working order. Once the thing broke, it
was no small task to repair it. Half of the watch remained out of
order, like a house whose middle floor was lived in but whose
ground and upper floors were vacant and silent. But the watch
did strengthen my father's friendship with Nuri Efendi.

My master Nuri Efendi, a true practitioner of the art, became
so exasperated with having to repair the watch over and over
again that he finally went so far as to forbid my father to wind
it himself.

So as you can see, my uncle's gift to me of a watch was not
wholly surprising. The place it would fill in my life had long

since been primed. Could a boy that age receive a watch and not wonder what made it tick—especially a boy who spent his entire childhood in a house with a grandfather clock that to all intents and purposes had cast a spell over its surroundings? Up until that point, I had seen only the exteriors of timepieces, fearing I would be scolded if I looked inside. I would only observe them, taking pleasure in their presence. But my uncle's gift sparked my desire to know timepieces more intimately, to plumb their depths. The first day I held it in my hand, my intellectual plane was elevated tenfold. And from that moment, I was plagued by questions: Whither? Whence? And how?

Need I say that only a few weeks after I received my uncle's gift, it had become nothing but a mass of twisted and jagged bits of shiny and rusty metal, and no longer served any purpose at all? The experience revealed two things to me: my overwhelming desire to take apart and understand every watch and clock I came across, and my total indifference to the rest of the world.

I had to repeat a year at school because of that watch, and the same happened the following year, when I found another very old watch on the way to school. By the end of my third year, I was able to begin my second year of college, both because the administration took pity on my father and because the entire school and neighborhood supported my cause. But I had lost all desire to study. And so I began to spend most of my time at Nuri Efendi's time-setting workshop. Strange how my truancy had a positive effect on my school life: As my teachers saw less of me, they saw fewer of my flaws. So I never again had to repeat a year at college. I became one of those dim students left to God. For the rest of my life, I was greeted with short, dismissive nods and pitying smiles or the sniggers and grins of the less polite.

V

In Nuri Efendi's workshop, where I passed my days, there was no room for nods, insinuating smiles, or laughter. There were only watches and clocks: elaborate table clocks ticked on every windowsill; grandfather clocks lined up against the walls like the very guardians of time; a suspended clock dangled over the master's divan, just to its right; and in every corner of the room—scattered along the windowsills, strewn over the divans, and on every little shelf—piles upon piles of watches and clocks waited to be repaired, some half-finished, some still in pieces, others entirely bare, and some with only their cases removed. Nuri Efendi busied himself with these throughout the day, and when his eyes grew tired, he would lean back on his divan and cry, "A coffee!" Resting for a spell in the little stone room, listening to the din of ticking clocks, he would dream of all the clocks in the world he had not yet seen and might never see—the clocks whose hands he would never touch and whose voices he would never hear.

When I first became acquainted with Nuri Efendi, he was already in his late fifties, of average height, thin, shriveled, but robust. He told me he'd never once fallen ill, never once suffered so much as a toothache, and that he attributed this to his Thracian roots. "My father was a wrestler, and I too did my share of wrestling when I was young," he explained as he flexed his powerful biceps, a true sight to behold in a man so frail. When he was angry, or simply in a sour mood, he would throw his arms around one of the gigantic stones in the courtyard of the mosque—left over from an old restoration project—and heave it around the grounds.

With large chestnut-colored eyes, an elongated square face, and a straggly white beard, he had an unearthly look. His was the gentle gaze of a man who could do nothing but good. There was something to him of the old man in a fairy tale who appears out of nowhere to give you three hairs from his beard, so that later, when you find yourself in a tight spot, you can burn them and he will swoop in to rescue you. Though he'd been in the same workshop for thirty-five years, no one had ever seen him lose his temper or so much as raise his voice.

Nuri Efendi had a charming way of speaking: he would choose his words carefully, intoning each and every syllable. And the topic he especially enjoyed was horology. Some friends and acquaintances took him for a great scholar, while others thought him a kind of quasi saint. In reality he had had little education, managing only a few years of religious study at a mosque, but he never tried to hide this from anyone and would often proclaim, "Watches and clocks made me the man I am!"

I suppose he was the best clock repairman in the neighborhood. But he was no mere artisan: he had the joy of a man who was passionate about his work. He never haggled with those who brought him a watch or clock to repair, accepting whatever he was offered.

Upon receiving a timepiece from a customer, he'd say, "Now, don't come back to pick this up until I send word that it's ready!" Or sometimes he'd cry out to a customer already halfway out of the workshop, "Now, don't you rush me! For I won't be rushed!" After opening up the watch or clock entrusted to him, he would place it in a glass jar and simply observe it, sometimes for weeks, without laying a hand on it, and if it began to tick, he would lean over the jar and listen. These deliberations gave me the impression that Nuri Efendi was more clock doctor than repairman.

Nuri Efendi equated people with clocks. He'd often say, "The Great Almighty made man in his image, and men made watches in theirs." Sometimes he'd expound on this idea, adding, "Man must never forsake his clocks, for consider his ruination if forsaken by God!" And there were those times when his musings on watches and clocks became far more profound: "The clock itself creates space, and man regulates the clock's tempo and time, which means time coexists with space within man."

He came up with countless other adages that proposed similar comparisons: "Metals are not forged on their own. The same follows for man. Righteousness and goodness come to us through the grace of God. Such values are manifest in a watch or clock." For Nuri Efendi, love of timepieces was rooted in morals: "Accustom yourself to observing a broken watch as if tending to the sick or needy." And he practiced what he preached. Here I should mention that the watches and clocks that most fascinated him were the trammeled and broken ones destined for the dump; indeed they were the very ones that were already there! And whenever he came upon a watch in such a sorry state, his face would soften and, trembling with compassion, he would say, "His heart no longer beats—his cranium has been crushed," or ask, "How will you ever turn again, my poor soul, when you are deprived of both your hands?"

He'd buy broken watches and clocks from street peddlers whose paths he crossed, and after replacing most of the parts, he'd bequeath the watch or clock to a friend in need. "Here, have this," he'd say. "At least now you'll be the master of your time. The rest our God of Grace will oversee!" Such was his answer for those friends who bemoaned their misfortune, assuming they were poor. And so thanks to Nuri Efendi, a person would once again become master of his time and would be thrilled, as if he was about to make peace with his disgruntled wife or see his children regain good health or find relief that very day from all his debts. There is no doubt that in presenting these gifts he believed he was doing two good deeds at once: not only had he resuscitated a dying watch, but he had also given a fellow human both time and an awareness of his own existence.

Nuri Efendi called these watches the "amended"—a slightly ironic reference to the recycling of weapons in that era. The springs, mechanisms, and cogs of these watches all came from different manufacturers and craftsmen, and after having been treated with certain fundamental repairs, the watches were realigned with the racing chariots of time. Turning one such watch over in his hand, he would say, "How much they resemble us—the spitting image of our lives!" This was, to employ the term Halit Ayarcı later used for him, Nuri Efendi's "sociological" aspect.

Years later, when I conveyed these very words to Halit Ayarcı, my esteemed benefactor, he fairly swooned with excitement, nearly throwing his arms around me as he cried, "But, my good friend, you have worked alongside a great philosopher!" Later I will describe in full detail the day, or rather the evening, I first met Halit Ayarcı. But I will note here only that our institute's slogans, which surprised, amused, and even challenged the minds of the people of Istanbul, were born of these sayings first uttered by Nuri Efendi.

How strange that for years as I listened to these and all the other sayings born of my late master, I suffered under the illusion that I was squandering my youth. In reality it was these very words that would lead me to enjoy the success and well-being that only heartfelt public service can provide.

But what other road was open to me? In those years I was struggling to finish college (a goal I was likely to achieve only if I stayed as far away as possible from my teachers and the school itself), so what could I really have understood of the affinities Nuri Efendi saw between watches and human beings, and watches and society? And with no explanation forthcoming, how was I to see these affinities reflected in his life and his philosophy of human fellowship? Because indeed it was an authentic philosophy, according to what both Halit Ayarcı and Dr. Ramiz later told me. But let me make this clear at once: Dr. Ramiz came to understand the value of Nuri Efendi's words only after Halit Ayarcı declared his own admiration for them, though he had heard those words many a time, and long before he ever introduced me to my benefactor. Dr. Ramiz was so absorbed in his own world that he found everything beyond it difficult to comprehend. Certainly he was not inclined to stray far from public opinion. And the same applies to his dealings with me: He was always unfailingly pleasant and kind. He enjoyed his chats with me and never tired of listening to my troubles. If our paths didn't cross, he would seek me out to ask after my children's health and even offer to help with minor matters. It was through him that I came to know Halit Ayarcı. But he didn't see my true worth; he saw me only as others saw me, which is to say that he took me for a reprobate redeemed by a paltry array of virtues, a half-deranged eccentric who viewed the world in a singular way. But upon discovering Halit Ayarcı's admiration for me, he changed his opinion, and from then on he never ceased to sing my praises. So much so that in the indexes of his four most recent works, the name that appears most often after those of Freud and Jung is none other than my own. I appear almost as frequently as my late mentor Nuri Efendi and Şeyh Ahmet Zamanı. Though in my view he went a bit too far. I'm not the kind of man worthy of being discussed

in such scientific studies. Of course, considering my love for
humanity, I wasn't about to overlook these flatteries: I had
Ramiz duly remunerated. I've always supported the man with
modest increases in what I paid him. But let me not be entirely
unfair: Dr. Ramiz treated me for quite some time, and he had
much to do with making me aware of the part of my life that
was bound to that of another, Seyit Lutfullah, as my readers
will discover in due course. This only goes to show that Halit
Ayarcı was the first person to appreciate me and Nuri—or,
more correctly, Nuri through me, and, naturally, me through
him—and the first person to discern the preternatural role that
time pieces play in our lives, with time itself ruling them by
imperial decree.

And let us not forget one of Halit Ayarcı's more outstanding
qualities: his knack for uncovering hidden talents and treasures.

Nuri Efendi and Halit Ayarcı—my life circled these two
great poles. One I met when I was still quite young, at a time
when my eyes had only just opened to the world and the people
in it. The other stepped into my life when I had lost all hope,
when I believed the story of my life was at an end. These two
men, so distinct in virtue and mentality, were likewise distinct
in their understandings of time, but in me their opposites
merged in such a way as to never again diverge. I was the product of their combined efforts. I was like the secondhand watches
Nuri Efendi repaired by carefully assembling parts made by
different craftsmen; I was a mechanism made of two personalities combined and harnessed to the caravan of time, an
"amended" alloy, a composite work of art.

Nuri Efendi was perhaps more meticulous in regulating
watches and clocks than in repairing them. An unregulated
timepiece would drive this otherwise mild-mannered man to
despair. As more and more clocks appeared around the city
following the reestablishment of the constitution in 1908, he
would no longer set foot outside his workshop for fear of
"exposure to an unregulated clock." To him a broken or dam-
aged clock was like a sick human being, and while it was natural for man to fall ill, an unregulated clock had no such excuse.
To his mind it was a social affront, a mortal sin. And it was

inevitable that these unregulated timepieces would provide the devil with yet another way to delude humanity, driving men from the road to God and robbing them of their time.

As Nuri Efendi so often said, "Regulation is chasing down the seconds!" This was yet another of his deft turns of phrase that so astonished Halit Ayarcı:

"Think about the implications of these words, my dear friend Hayri İrdal. This means that a properly regulated clock never loses a single second! And what are we doing about it? What about the people in this city, in the country at large? We're losing half our time with unregulated clocks. If every person loses one second per hour, we lose a total of eighteen million seconds in that hour. Assuming the essentially useful part of the day consists of ten hours, we are left with one hundred eighty million seconds. So in just one day a hundred eighty million seconds—in other words three million minutes; this means a loss of fifty thousand hours per day. Now perform the calculations and see how many lifetimes suddenly slip away every year. And half of these eighteen million people don't even own watches; and if they do, they don't work. Among them you'll find some that are half an hour, even a whole hour, behind standard time. It's a maddening loss of time . . . a loss in terms of our work, our lives, and our everyday economy. Can you now see the immensity of Nuri Efendi's mind, his genius? Thanks to his inspiration, we shall make up the loss. Therein lies the truly beneficial aspect of our institute. Let the critics say what they will. Our society will undertake this vital task. I want you to get right to work on an accurate and comprehensive statistical field report, so we can print brochures this weekend . . . But, then again, I'll prepare them myself—I mustn't delegate such a delicate job. You shall write the life of Nuri Efendi, a book in the European style. Only you can meet such a challenge—it is your duty to introduce this man to the world."

I never wrote the book; instead I wrote *The Life and Works of Ahmet the Timely*, using all the same ideas and materials, as it was deemed more beneficial and more contributive to the politics of our institute. Was this a betrayal of my master?

Nuri Efendi never gave me much work, and what he did pass

on to me he never expected me to finish right away. There was
never any need to rush. He was the proprietor of time. He'd
spend it as he wished, and, to a certain extent, he gave the same
privilege to the people around him. More than anything, he
had accepted me as an avid listener. From time to time he'd say,
"Hayri, my son. I cannot say if you'll ever become a fine watchmaker. Of course I'd be the first to wish you such good fortune,
for you'll be sure to face grave problems in the future if you
don't fully commit yourself to a profession early on. But as the
humble image of the Great Creator, you lack the fortitude to
endure this life and everything it will thrust upon you. Only
work can save you, and it's a shame that you lack the necessary
focus for this kind of work." Then to flatter me, he'd say, "Nevertheless you love watches and clocks, and you take pity on
them. That is important. What's more, you're a good listener.
Of that I am sure. You know how to listen, and that is a rare
talent. If nothing else, it masks one's shortcomings and elevates
one to the level of an interlocutor!"

Every year Nuri Efendi published an almanac. Toward the
end of November, he would begin compiling the material,
transferring a large part of the almanac from the previous year,
so by the middle of February it would be ready for me to take
to the printer in Nuruosmaniye. I would watch in awe as the
work unfolded before my very eyes: the months from both Arabic and Gregorian calendars; other divisions of time and years,
from elsewhere, that were older than the seasons to which they
were respectively aligned; the solar and lunar eclipses; the
meticulously calculated times for morning, noon, afternoon,
sunset, and evening prayers; the great storms and the seasonal
winds, the latter, according to his calculations, no less relevant
than the former; the solstices; the days scheduled to be bitterly
cold or unbearably hot. Dream after dream came to life from
his brass inkpot as he sat on his low divan in the small room
beside the mosque, a skullcap on his head and a reed in his
hand; he would line up his calculations like little grains of rice
on the scrolls propped up on his right knee, and they all swirled
together in a corner of the room where the light was most dim

and the sound of all the watches and clocks was most concentrated, as if waiting for their time to rule the world.

On days when he was working on his almanac, I would lose myself in a mysterious haze as I watched the miracle unfold. Knowing that the previous year's almanac had been similarly elaborated, and that the accumulated work would embrace all the various stages of our lives, I felt myself bathed in a light born of its creator's will, in a world rearranged by his very hand, as the passionate connection I felt to my late master was infused with a little fear.

VI

Among those who came to visit Nuri Efendi were Seyit Lutfullah the Mad, who lived like an owl in a dilapidated *medrese* on the hill between Vefa and Küçükpazar; Abdüsselam Bey, a Tunisian aristocrat who indulged in an extravagant lifestyle in an enormous villa with a broad ocher facade, near the Burmalı Mescit and just below the Şehzade Mosque; the hunter Naşit Bey, who lived behind the Halveti dervish lodge in Hırkaişerif; and the pharmacist Aristidi Efendi, a Christian of modest repute who managed his apothecary in the largely Muslim neighborhood of Vezneciler.

Abdüsselam Bey was a wealthy, exuberant man whose entire tribe lived with him in his villa of some twenty or thirty rooms. The house had an uncanny way of trapping anyone who had the misfortune of being born there and many, it seems, who merely set foot inside. This old Istanbul aristocrat, so distinguished and refined in his starched white shirts, had stuffed his vast mansion with relatives and servants from every corner of the Ottoman Empire: the in-laws, young brides and grooms, countless children, ancient maternal and paternal aunts, youthful nephews and nieces, pages, and at least a dozen female slaves. At my father's insistence, my mother visited the lady of the house on several occasions and each time returned home exhausted and exasperated, her head still reeling from the ordeal. Once, when I was very young, I tagged along.

I shall never forget that day, which I spent dazed and bewildered in a throng of nearly twenty women, young and old (and just as many children), dressed in extravagant headdresses, petticoats, gowns of white silk, and low-cut lace blouses whose sleeves billowed down to their wrists, finishing with ornaments and gently undulating lace fringes. Although the house looked infinite from the outside, the people inside it lived virtually on top of one another. And for all the domestic confusion, there was no denying that we were in distinguished company. Abdüsselam's first wife was a close relative of the bey of Tunis and a direct descendent of the Şerif line. His second wife was an elegant Circassian who had served in the Ottoman palace and was said to have once been intimate with Sultan Abdülhamīd. The wife of one of Abdüsselam's many brothers was from the eminent Hidiv family, and the wife of another was the daughter of the warlord of a far-flung Caucasian tribe. If the brides were not daughters of famous field marshals or grand viziers, they were granddaughters of Albanian beys. Fearing that under the reign of Sultan Abdülhamīd a family so disordered might give rise to gossip and endless paranoia, Abdüsselam succeeded in marrying one of his brother's daughters to an agent who was highly praised by the sultan himself. This honored individual was a secretary to the Council of State, of which Abdüsselam was also a member; thus the agent was able to keep a close eye on Abdüsselam Bey, both at home and at work. People who knew them took great delight in watching Abdüsselam and Ferhat Bey, his brother's son-in-law, travel together to and from the Council of State in their rubber-wheeled phaeton. The strange thing about it was that while the above-mentioned relation felt oppressed by his obligation to spy on a man he truly loved and considered something of a benefactor, Abdüsselam Bey was more than pleased with this friendship of forced circumstances, for Abdüsselam Bey was the sort of man who would scream "fire!" if left alone for more than an hour—the sort of man who always sat next to the only other passenger on a trolley or, if it was empty, hovered over the conductor.

I became much more intimate with Abdüsselam during the Armistice years, from 1919 to 1922. Although he had grown rather old by then, his memory was more or less intact. When he reminisced about the old days, he would remember Ferhat Bey's timid demeanor and burst out laughing. After I returned from military service, Abdüsselam took pity on me for being alone—both my mother and my father had passed away. Having welcomed me into the small home in Beyazıt where he then lived with his youngest daughter, he arranged for me to marry a young girl they had raised there. And so, yes, my first wife, the mother of Zehra and Ahmet, had grown up in his villa.

Abdüsselam Bey's villa carried on in the same way until the declaration of the reinstated constitution. To give you an idea of the colorful crew that populated the villa and the expenses it accrued, suffice to say that the neighborhood's sweetshop, butcher, and two grocery stores survived pretty much on the villa alone. The lion's share of the pharmacist Aristidi Efendi's revenue came from the residence as well. Following the Declaration of Independence, the villa began slowly to dissolve, a decline that in some aspects echoed that of the Ottoman Empire. First there was the fall of Bosnia-Herzegovina, Bulgaria, eastern Thrace, and northern Africa, whereupon Abdüsselam's brothers and their wives departed; this was followed by the Balkan Wars, when the younger men and their wives also abandoned the estate. Toward the end, only the spying Ferhat Bey and a few of his children remained. Ferhat Bey and Abdüsselam lived together until the end, harnessed to each other like the swarthy steeds of Hungarian and British blood that pulled their rubber-wheeled phaeton to the Council of State every morning and back home in the evening. In the end conversation between the two men went no further than recitals of the weekly reports on life in the villa that Ferhat Bey submitted to Sultan Abdülhamīd.

Though these bulletins flushed Abdüsselam Bey's face a deep crimson, with each week they revealed to him a new aspect of the ancient villa's inner world, transporting him back to the time when fortune still smiled on him, when he was still young, rich, and virile—the master of a household arranged just to his liking, where no one language held sway for long, strong

personalities jostled for space, and life was infused with the
warmth of humankind.

Yet there was something a little odd about the way Abdüsselam Bey would conjure up his lost world during these recitals
losing himself in its immensity before my very eyes. As he listened to Ferhat Bey, his nostalgia would take on a sinister
aspect: his eyes sparkling with a strange malice and with a smile
that seemed to mock the frailty of humankind, he would launch
into stories that only deepened Ferhat Bey's embarrassment.

One day Abdüsselam Bey, former member of the Council of
State, revealed his secret to me:

"My poor son-in-law, the truth is his work made him all too
anxious and ashamed. He had absolutely no idea that I submitted my own weekly report on *him*."

Around the time I began frequenting Nuri Efendi's workshop, there were just thirty-seven people still living in Abdüsselam Bey's villa. Not counting the children, the house was only
inhabited by semiretired servants (one of life's odd reversals),
distant relatives of Abdüsselam's siblings, and aged aunts whose
affiliation with the family was debated daily. Abdüsselam was
deeply saddened by all this and could not understand how
independence—which we had apparently all been longing for in
secret—had deprived his home of the cheerful cries of children.
He could not understand why his domestic expenses kept rising.
As he struggled to make ends meet, Abdüsselam was further
confounded by all these distant relatives, whom he found as
unreadable as texts whose principle sentences had been effaced
or rendered indecipherable; all the same, he still welcomed this
absurd crowd with open arms, for fear of ending up alone.

VII

Though Abdüsselam Bey squandered much of his fortune on
passing fancies, he was also indulgent of those around him,
particularly his nephews. He called to mind those kindly uncles
one meets in operettas, those comical creatures who are either

quietly brooding or flying off the handle, and who fritter their lives away on little pleasures before suddenly, and outrageously, coming to the rescue of a young relation. Whatever his quirks and idiosyncrasies, they combined to suggest a man of consequence.

Seyit Lutfullah was something else altogether: a ghostly shadow in the void, a mask on loan, a living lie: Imagine the lead actor in a fantastical play who—still wearing his costume and cloaked in his assumed personality—springs off the stage to continue his performance in the crowded city streets. Seyit Lutfullah was such a man. He inspired his little coterie to all kinds of pastimes and passions, taking people who would otherwise have led rather mundane existences and turning their worlds upside down. But with him it was never clear where his strange beneficence ended and his lies began.

He was not from Medina, as most people claimed, nor was he a descendant of the prophet Mohammed. In fact he probably adopted his name somewhere along the way. According to Nuri Efendi, he took the name Seyit, given to descendants of the prophet Muhammad, when he was engaged to a woman during his time in Iraq. But he actually hailed from the province of Baluchistan in Afghanistan. He left his native land when he was still quite young and, after traversing the Orient, arrived at last in Istanbul, where his beautiful and moving recitations of the Koran at the Arab Mosque attracted much attention, which made it possible for him to marry the daughter of a gardener who tended the grounds for a rich family in Emirgân, and even afforded him the opportunity to proselytize at a local mosque. Those who had known him from his first appearance described him as a morally upstanding and rather fanatical exponent of sharia law who, in his sermons and deliberations, would vociferously berate his flock. According to what my father reported, the man prohibited most everything in life save prayer, going so far as to place restrictions on eating, drinking, and sometimes even speaking.

His first stint in Istanbul lasted only three years. Then his wife died, and he resumed his travels, leaving everything behind. He returned to Istanbul ten years later, and two years before the reinstatement of the constitution he settled into the ruined *medrese*. But Seyit Lutfullah was no longer the same. One of his eyes had turned entirely white, his lips were slightly parted, and his body was at the mercy of a tic that left his primary motor functions intact but sent a continuous series of short, awkward, involuntary spasms through his entire body. His left arm swung back and forth, as if he were soothing a sleeping child in a perambulator, and his neck twitched violently, as if he were working out a painful cramp. With his dark and leathery half-paralyzed face, his humpback, his enormous height, and one foot forever dragging behind him, Seyit Lutfullah seemed more evil djinn than human being. He might have been a creature standing guard over treasure at the end of an epic journey. Yet in his youth he'd been considered rather handsome.

Seyit Lutfullah attributed his transformation to his battles in the world beyond. By his own account, while preparing most fervently to become a medium to the spirit world, he had stumbled upon a disgruntled group of guardian spirits, and it was they who had left him in this horrific state. When Nuri Efendi spoke of him, he said, "This is just what the holy Koran tells us. Such is the fate of those who meddle with spirits." But in truth he was hoping to hear the whole lurid story—curiosity being Nuri Efendi's only real shortcoming—and so he could never quite bring himself to forsake the man who rubbed shoulders with blasphemy.

Almost everyone had an opinion of Seyit Lutfullah. Dismissing him as a charlatan, Aristidi Efendi attributed his physical transformation to either a congenital condition or rampant syphilis. For Abdüsselam Bey's sake, the pharmacist tried to cure Seyit Lutfullah with various concoctions prepared according to old manuscripts in which he had little faith. While Abdüsselam Bey remained wary of Seyit Lutfullah's dealings with the spiritual world, he still considered the man a vast repository of ancient lore and hoped the experiments carried out in Aristidi Efendi's laboratory might help him regain his squandered fortune—a case in point being that he sincerely believed one day they would discover, for indeed it had been promised them, the treasure of the emperor Andronikos. Seyit

Lutfullah had long since become a native of Istanbul and had even forgotten his Arabic, but as with Abdüsselam Bey, the old Maghrebi of Tunisia, his ancient superstitions endured.

In those days it was hard not to see Abdüsselam Bey as a gambler with a few cards perennially up his sleeve, poised for the most improbable of exploits.

Convinced that one day they would succeed in making gold, Abdüsselam covered all the costs of Aristidi Efendi's researches in his secret laboratory, located just behind his pharmacy. But Aristidi Efendi's approach was different from that of his friends: he believed the project was achievable through the application of modern chemistry alone. Abdüsselam Bey, on the other hand, was eager to try both magic and the questionable chemical formulae Seyit Lutfullah brought to the laboratory.

The truth of the matter is that each of these men was mired in a tireless search for a tunnel that would take him to the other side of the wall he called reality. Did Abdüsselam Bey really believe in Seyit Lutfullah? I cannot say. To my mind, these men acted in response to something more important than mere belief. All three held most fervently that there should be no limit to the concept of the "possible." Everything existed within a universe in which anything could happen: objects, matter, human beings—all stood on a threshold of infinite potential, waiting for a magic word, prayer, or experiment to transform them in an instant. The flaw these men shared was to mistrust anything they could see with their own eyes or touch with their own hands.

Though he was the most realistic member of this entourage, my ruined father was nevertheless susceptible to its mad schemes, and in Seyit Lutfullah he saw his final hope of bringing his grandfather's pious mission to fruition. But his partners never really accepted him, for they saw themselves in him; that is to say, they recognized his desperation to sacrifice everything he owned, and this led my father to feel a certain animosity toward them. Even so, Nuri Efendi still repaired my father's watch for free, and Abdüsselam Bey was always willing to extend a helping hand, while the hunter Naşit Bey's support for my father was boundless. Deep down, if only intermittently, my father did enjoy the company of these men, and so he never showed his anger; it was with the fury of a man brutally scorned and cast aside that he leveled his ire against Seyit Lutfullah. To my father, Lutfullah was "a miserable dope fiend and a liar." He wasn't a medium in contact with guardian spirits, nor did he have anything to do with treasure or the world beyond. The stroke that had turned his face into a heap of ghastly junk was brought about by opium, wild philandering, and a blatant disregard for his health. But in denouncing him as a sloth, a swindler, an adulterer, and a trickster, my father was in fact echoing views Aristidi expressed in more measured terms.

Lutfullah made no secret of his dabbling in opium. For him the drug was not a dangerous pleasure so much as a means to beauty, truth, and exultation or, to use his own vague terminology, "a mystic path." There was, he said, no way of achieving truth without casting aside reason, and indeed there were many occasions when he would wander about semiconscious. Deep in these fogs, he would ramble on about "the other side of the curtain," enumerating the delights that awaited us in the world beyond our sight.

Listening to him, it was difficult not to believe that the man walked in a world we could not see: among turquoise palaces filled with gold, jewels, and silver-laced tapestries, a world that promised a thousand and one delights. While wandering about that pleasure-filled world, he enjoyed a lover named Aselban, a beautiful creature with whom he frolicked among ever-blooming roses, at the edge of a crystal pool, listening to the rippling of cool waters and the songs of nightingales, taking delight in the fragrances of jasmine and rose as she strummed her *bağlama* beside the harem's fairest ladies or sat alone at a window, her hands busy with embroidery, ever dreaming of him. Aselban's hair was darker than night, her skin fairer than jasmine flowers, and even the pheasants swooned with envy at her heavenly sway.

This magnificent creature was madly in love with our friend but, sadly, a union between them was a "philosophical impossibility." For first Lutfullah had to discover the treasure of the emperor Andronikos, a condition put forward by those who lived in the world beyond—namely Aselban's mother, father, and violent sister, whose beauty was not inferior to Aselban's. The treasure itself was merely an illusion created by a magic spell. And of course Lutfullah had no need for such riches, so sure was he that all his desires would be met in the world beyond—provided he met the conditions set by its inhabitants. Once Seyit Lutfullah found the treasure, Aselban would become human, and he would regain his true sunlike countenance. They would live together happily ever after, as just rulers and paragons of grace.

When in low spirits, Seyit Lutfullah could not but despair over the difficulty, even impossibility, of his task, but when his mood lifted—which is to say, when he was thoroughly out of his gourd—he would assure us that he was not the person we saw: the blinding effect of the dazzling beauty of his face rendered it invisible. According to our dear friend, who often slept at Aselban's feet during his visits to his mysterious retreat, he bore a close resemblance to the oriental princes and Indian rajas that were popular in American films of the time.

"I was out hunting with Aselban the other day, when suddenly a hundred greyhounds were bounding alongside us! Oh, the gazelles we bagged, and the tigers . . . There was one that . . ."

And if the hunter Naşit Bey was in attendance, with his greyhound so decrepit it could barely rouse itself for a hunt, the tales grew longer still.

But when Lutfullah spoke with Abdüsselam Bey, he skipped over the hunts and concentrated on the lively hordes that peopled his world of bliss. In the palace of Aselban's father there were nearly a thousand children, and up to three times as many close relatives of all ages, forever overflowing with love and worry for one another, never apart for more than a moment. And when Lutfullah described the orgies that Aselban's father enjoyed with the forty young concubines who lived at his beck and call, Abdüsselam Bey nearly lost his mind.

Just one thing darkened Lutfullah's happiness: he could travel to the world beyond only at Aselban's invitation. When

none was forthcoming, he would wander, sometimes for
months on end, through our worthless world, as worn as the
rags that clothed him, as ruined as the ruin in which he dwelt.
Ill-tempered and belligerent, he avoided human society, for he
was given to violent bouts of rage that seemed very much like
epileptic seizures; these horrifying episodes clearly took a toll
on his constitution.

His chest pumping with pride and his mouth spewing foam,
he'd sputter a string of strange and indecipherable profanities,
inviting damnation upon his enemies, threatening to murder
and destroy them with his own grisly hands. "I . . . Ah, yes,
I . . . I . . . Does the individual not know who I am? The individual knows not who I am? I shall rain misfortune upon the
head of this individual." Lutfullah's opponent was always an
"individual" or at least addressed in the third person: "Is he
aware that I shall burn him to a crisp?"

His rage was like the opium, a kind of divine madness, and
in those rages Seyit Lutfullah was himself the master of life and
death, his hubris justified by a mad philosophy that claimed to
explain both the animate and inanimate worlds. But when his
rage subsided, he was overcome by sadness. "The other day my
enemies—the ones from the world beyond, of course—they
provoked me. I disclosed many secrets. Now the journey will
be more difficult. Until further notice they will not allow me to
exercise my powers to their full extent!"

My father actually believed in some of these powers.

"There's something about that brute," he'd say. "The baker
Ahmet Efendi would never have ended up as he did. In just
three days his house and business were burned to the ground,
his family destroyed. Now the fellow's ruined and living in the
poor house."

Shuddering at the thought of Lutfullah's gruesome powers,
he'd adjust his collar and hock a ball of phlegm to the ground.

"He's not a man. He's a devil! God protect us from the stones
this monster might send down upon us. Why doesn't the government put the evil wizard behind bars? Just last night I saw
him hobbling toward the graveyard in Edirnekapı. Has he done
someone in?"

It was rumored that whenever Seyit Lutfullah convened with his auspicious spirits by turning his head toward the wall, his prophecies always came true, and that his breath, and even his hand, had a healing effect on people afflicted with certain nervous disorders.

In 1906, the year Lutfullah's fame began to spread, Abdüsselam Bey became convinced he'd lost a valuable gold watch. Through Nuri Efendi he consulted Seyit Lutfullah, who, after holding long talks with the world beyond, told Abdüsselam in his mangled Turkish:

"The watch a lady's trunk, the trunk the hull of a ship, the ship the middle of the sea . . . Send telegraph at once . . . For if not . . ."

Such was his answer.

Three days later we discovered that the truth was really quite different. The watch was found in the pocket of a waistcoat in the bedroom wardrobe of a chambermaid who had been brought from Egypt by Abdüsselam's second wife. But consider the coincidence: at around the same time, the following telegraph was received concerning a servant from Ünye who had left the household to return to her native village.

"Woman found. A cheap knock-off table clock in her trunk. Both clock and woman in custody. Waiting further instructions."

One might say that Seyit Lutfullah owed his renown in Istanbul to this misinterpretation, which was somewhat correct in its details but muddled in its context.

Indeed this slight error in context was what made the man's astounding powers apparent. Seen through this distorting prism, his divine inspiration was as clear as a lone ship on rough seas in the dead of night. After all, when asked to account for the discrepancies, Seyit Lutfullah never once claimed that his mediation with the spirits was entirely conclusive.

So the discrepancy came to seem like no more than a missing link—very much like that mosque (I can never remember which one) with no fewer than nine hundred ninety-nine windows. For if Lutfullah's prophesy had come true, the whole thing would have been written off as mere coincidence, its assorted details forgotten. Yet not one of the details revealed by this

minor error was lost; in light of the mistake, all the particulars—
the watch, the servant who left Abdüsselam Bey's villa, the hull
of the ferryboat, the chest—were illuminated like roadside inns
along an arduous journey. I am left to wonder whether there
can be an example that better illustrates the crucial—and sup-
portive—role error plays in human affairs.

From then on Seyit Lutfullah was one of the most esteemed
guests at the Tunisian's villa. His every word was believed. His
attire, his lifestyle, and his ruin of a *medrese* all helped to con-
solidate his position. He dismissed with a vague gesture any
advice about moderate alterations to his dress; alluding to an
ominous dark power, he'd say, "They'd never allow it." He
once accepted a robe and turban at Abdüsselam Bey's insistence, only to return them three days later, saying, "They were
not authorized. May the patron forgive me." Seyit Lutfullah
knew how to forge a legend that would last.

He liked to say that it was his auspicious guardian spirits
who had directed him to the *medrese* that was his home.

I've seen very few places like this ruin of a *medrese*: its
every fragment spoke of the effort and precision of its creator.
You might almost think that this building and its miniature
neighboring mosque—attributed to the reign of Mahmud I—
began their slow descent into ruin the moment they left the
hands of the architects, in strict accordance with a plan that
foresaw its current state.

The paving stones in the courtyard had been either broken or
dislodged by an enormous plane tree surging out in all directions. Most of the rooms on the three wings—save for Seyit
Lutfullah's—were partly or completely in ruins. As for the little
mosque on the left side of the courtyard, all that remained were
four front steps leading up to the minaret. In a charming little
graveyard off to one side lay four or five esteemed personages
from the era, along with the *kahvecıbaşı* who built both *medrese*
and mosque; it was separated from the street by a flimsy fence
that was barely standing.

Trees and dry vegetation dominated the *medrese*'s entire
courtyard, as well as the graveyard and the plot where the
mosque had once stood; a few trees had thrust their roots out

from beneath toppled columns. The oddest sight was the slender and elegant cypress sapling that grew on the roof of the room where Seyit Lutfullah slept, rustling in the wind like the flowers of a silk *oya*. On cloudier days it seemed no more than a smudge against the ashen void of the sky, an arrow pointing toward an infinite and unassailable nature.

Marked with this strange herald, the *medrese* teetered like a giant scale at the top of a hill from which it would one day fall. Seyit Lutfullah slept on a mattress tossed on the floor of the ruin's only intact room, which was mildewed and perpetually dark. Beside his mattress were a handful of large bottles that seemed to hold his provisions and, strange as it may seem, a tortoise—a gift from Aselban, coyly named Çeşminigâr, "the fountain of beauty"—which trundled about under the feet of Lutfullah's visitors, entirely at ease with humans.

Rumor had it that auspicious spirits had directed Lutfullah to the *medrese* because it was close to the treasure of Andronikos. This tallied with Seyit Lutfullah's endless tales of his quest in the world beyond for this treasure dating back to the days of that emperor.

But, then again, judging by what my dear friend told me in strict confidence, the *medrese* was neither devastated nor in the ruined state that we saw before us. It was, on the contrary, a sumptuous and resplendent *saray*; We were as incapable of seeing the true splendor of this palace as we were of seeing Seyit Lutfullah's true beauty. Only when the treasure was uncovered would its pillars of pure gold and its diamond-encrusted turquoise domes shine forth. Then everything would fall into place. Aselban would agree to appear in human form, her lover would be reunited with his true face, and at last they would be joined in eternal bliss.

"Thereafter I will reign over the entire world," he would say, "and everything I desire will come true." He'd banish misery and injustice from the world and govern with absolute justice. For this strange man had peculiar ideas about the struggle between justice and injustice, leading one to wonder whether his activities might not be directed by larger forces after all, and, in the end, casting some light on his true nature.

By this logic, Seyit Lutfullah was the type of man to scorn and repudiate the riches offered by chance, so he might attain the otherworldly pleasures and power of eternal life. He was an idealist with a lofty soul. To have "everything" in life, he chose to live in the barren desert of "nothing."

When I explained these various eccentricities to Dr. Ramiz, he homed in on this one aspect of Lutfullah's personality, and on countless subsequent occasions he told me this problem of justice and injustice could very well be the key, or at least one of the keys, to unlocking the Seyit Lutfullah affair. My dear friend, so zealously devoted to avant-garde scientific methods, once went so far as to ask me if Seyit Lutfullah had read Marx. Quite often he'd flare up and say, "I am most certain the man has read either Engels or Marx. What a pity you have never inquired."

"How could such a lowly creature have read the work of such lofty intellects? The miserable soul doesn't even speak proper Turkish!" I'd reply.

And he'd challenge me.

"Your kind is always the same. You lose sight of mankind's superior virtues, just as you are lost to the feelings of inferiority that constrict your soul. My dear friend, relinquish these airs. I am now thoroughly convinced the man knows German and has read the full body of socialist literature. Otherwise he never would have bent himself so forcefully to this question of justice and injustice—the question of our age—nor would he have made such sacrifices in its name." And he'd silence me, vowing that the man must be one of the founders of socialism.

Conversations with Dr. Ramiz were always like this. He would pounce on a single minor point and within seconds be on the verge of an avalanche. Due to my modest understanding of matters intellectual, I never found the nerve to criticize the great scholar to his face. But why lie, considering all I knew about my friend's life? I had never encountered in his ideas anything that might have inspired people to such a cause.

The passions of Aristidi Efendi, Naşit Bey, and Abdüsselam Bey were more finite. After Aristidi Efendi learned from an elderly brother-in-law, a priest on the island of Heybeliada, that the emperor Andronikos was in all probability the emperor Hadrian, he came to perceive the quest as a purely scientific enterprise. He had no faith in Seyit Lutfullah's deliberations or in the orders he received from the world beyond, instructing him to wait. Work should begin at once, with shovels and a pickax. But in the world of spirits, the rules were precise and the time preordained.

The great event of 1909 was Aristidi Efendi's decision to begin, alone, in the dead of night, his search for the treasure of the emperor Andronikos. But after several hours of digging, he found it necessary to reassign the treasure's true location, and so the secret search continued. What he found at the bottom of a shallow pit were not amphorae brimming with gold and jewels, or precious cloth and palatial treasures, or gilded manuscripts and miniature statues of saints made of ivory and gold; he found only a few bones and a jar that held a single coin dating back to the reign of Sultan Mahmud I, and it was at this point that Aristidi Efendi began to ask questions about the treasure's actual location. When Seyit Lutfullah told the chemist the following day that it had never been a question of *actually* finding the treasure, and that it would now take months just to reassign it to its *original* location, Aristidi Efendi nearly died of sadness and remorse. As with the story of Abdüsselam Bey's watch, this bungled operation drained Aristidi Efendi of any energy he might have mustered to oppose Seyit Lutfullah.

From then on, one could see the flicker of superstitious fear in the indulgent European smile Aristidi Efendi had once flashed in the face of Lutfullah's ignorance; in the company of our friend he became as restive and indecisive as an army with no option of retreat.

What Seyit Lutfullah really wanted was the power to unlock the mystery of the universe and thus gain spiritual control over matter. "Gold is not to be made in an alembic but forged of the soul. How much of it is already in the earth? The problem is to produce it without using our hands," he would say.

But when leading experiments in the secret laboratory behind Aristidi Efendi's pharmacy, surrounded by alembics and vials and various bottles and stills, he was ready to try anything, as

were all the others; he'd present Aristidi Efendi with questionable formulae fished from old manuscripts, and heated arguments would ensue, often lasting days.

Through these battles, Aristidi Efendi's well-mannered European patience and indulgence were challenged by Seyit Lutfullah's humility, as well as his proud and powerful hold on the
spiritual world, and the two opposing powers swirled around
each other as if melding in a great cauldron set over an open
fire. All I remember of the great debates I myself witnessed are
Lutfullah's favorite terms: "purification," "putrefaction" "thick-
ening," "marriage," "birth," "dissolution," and "connections";
they shimmered like doors to a greater world, answering only to
powerful displays of will.

And yet we have all witnessed, in the most unexpected of circumstances, such doors bursting open before us. Aristidi Efendi
(who liked to claim all the glory for these experiments, despite
the fact that they were funded mainly by Abdüsselam Bey) was
working alone one night when an alembic cracked and his laboratory went up in flames. Only an hour later did the fire department and neighborhood volunteers make it to the scene and find
the body of Aristidi Efendi half-consumed by the fire. It was
February 1912, and with Aristidi Efendi's death all effort to
make gold in an alembic came to an end. And so the only hope
that remained for the small group was the treasure.

VIII

But why have I burdened my chronicle of the Time Regulation
Institute with these distant reveries? And why have I allowed
myself to be seized by these shadows of the past? People today
fail to grasp the importance of such questions. They overlook
the truths and absurdities that lie beneath. I myself am now far
too old to take pleasure in visits to the past or even, for that
matter, from simple reminiscing. But even so, there is no dis-
puting the fact that from the moment Halit Ayarcı came into
my life I became a new man. I became more at ease with

reality, more accustomed to confronting it. Indeed the man created a whole new life for me. I now feel distant from all these characters and long-ago events; a part of me has turned away from the past, though I still claim it as my own. But however I might regret it, I cannot explain myself without looking back. I lived among these men for years and with them chased after their dreams. There were times when I even dressed like them, adopting aspects of their personalities. Without my quite knowing, I would on occasion even *become* Nuri Efendi or Abdüsselam Bey or, yes, even Seyit Lutfullah. They were my models, the masks I hardly knew to be masks. I would don one personality or another before heading out to mingle with the crowds. And still today when I look in the mirror I can see these men reflected in my face. First I see Nuri Efendi's indulgent smile, and then Lutfullah's deceitful gaze, and I shudder at the thought of the horrible things I might have done. Or I am devastated to detect the desperate jealousy and impatience of my father. I can see these men's traits in my attire too. The moment I put on a suit sewn for me by one of those celebrated tailors, I can be no other than Abdüsselam. And just the other day I noticed I needed new spectacles: off I went to look for a new pair with gold rims exactly like the ones Aristidi Efendi used to wear, though I knew the style was well out of fashion. Perhaps this is what we mean by "personality": the rich array of masks we store in the warehouses of our minds and the eccentricities of those who manifest themselves in our person.

But there may be a deeper and more powerful force that intervenes on occasion to obstruct these inherited traits. This is something I've always had in me. I cannot say that the same goes for everyone. Naturally there are those who live differently, those who consider themselves stronger and closer to reality, and unique.

Such matters are distant from the memoir I am writing. I am busy with my own chronicle. But to return to my earlier point, I was never quite able to escape the hold these friends had on me. As my son once told me, I had no experience of what he called "proper, organized employment." Like my friends, I wandered from whim to whim. Ahmet was never like me;

indeed he made a concerted effort not to be. And for this he deprived himself of numerous opportunities. Nevertheless, as soon as he finished high school he won himself a state scholarship. And although I suggested he continue his studies in America after completing medical school, a choice befitting our wealth and position at the time, he rejected the idea out of hand and instead went to Anatolia. Thereafter he lived without ever consulting me on such matters, forever refusing all I offered.

It would be wrong to say he never loved me. Yet he was vehemently opposed to my mode of thinking, which was not in harmony with his way of seeing the world. Nevertheless I maintain that a part of me lives on in him. I even saw this for myself one day, as I watched him examining a patient at his clinic. I would have examined a watch in exactly the same way. Or rather it was how Nuri Efendi would have examined a watch; I always wished my son would one day resemble this man, for he was always more master of the trade than I.

For whatever reason, it is my past, and not my current position in life, that holds the key to my problems; I can neither escape from it nor entirely accept its mandate.

IX

Some four years ago, I discovered a piece of an old balustrade. Having bought it on the spot, I had it mounted over the French door in my office, which looks out onto the Clock Villa's veranda and garden, with its seasonal flowers. I am in no doubt that this balustrade is what has led me to labor over certain points in my memoirs. When I look up at its star-and-tulip motif I have the impression of looking deep into my despairing and poverty-stricken past, but at the same time I can see through to my childhood and its days of fantasy and hope. Whenever, in those days, I went to see Seyit Lutfullah, to give him various items people had abandoned at Nuri Efendi's workshop, and would pass through that ruined *medrese*, I would stop before this same balustrade and daydream about the share I would receive of the treasure Lutfullah was sure to unearth one day, or the mercury that Aristidi Efendi would one day transmute into gold—though no one had ever actually promised me a share, I was convinced that someday, somewhere, something would come to me—and I would dream, too, of repairing the cemetery and its toppled walls and maybe even the mosque itself.

But fortune and chance ushered in quite the opposite. Although I had vowed to bequeath our grandfather clock to a mosque when I was older and in secure financial circumstances, I eventually, some twelve years ago, sold it; and something similar happened with this balustrade. One day I'd found it dangling from the wall, like the wings of one of the hunter Naşit Bey's birds, and I made off with it in broad daylight and sold it to an antique dealer for just thirty liras.

At the time those liras filled me with the thrill I might once have felt on discovering Andronikos's glorious treasure or turning all the mercury in the world into gold in Aristidi's alembics.

With this money, I bought a few modest little gifts for my wife, Pakize, and once again sent my older sister-in-law's oud for repair (she was a music lover, and at the very least I knew this time the instrument would be returned to us promptly). I was also able, at last, to purchase a particular belt for my younger sister-in-law, who had mustered the courage to enter, for the fourth time, the beauty contest that put such a strain on our budget; Pakize wholeheartedly believed (99.9 percent of the time) that the belt, captivating as it was, would lead her sister to be crowned queen, although it barely managed to cinch the woman's amply flowing gown. As for my remaining two liras, I gave them to my dear old friend Ali Efendi, an itinerant street peddler, who returned to me the watch of our neighbor and local shopkeeper Hulki Efendi, which I had pawned a few nights earlier so I could take the whole family to an open-air cinema.

This balustrade brought me, if only for a time, the comfort and powers of perception that had eluded me for so long. Yet the sadness in me endured. I had betrayed my past and, in particular, a childhood vow. I had always believed in the saintliness of the man who lay beneath the enormous turbaned tombstone that leaned just behind the balustrade, perhaps because of the mulberry tree right beside it, which had grown to such extraordinary size. When my mother was ill, I would go there every evening to pray and light candles in front of the balustrade.

But who could have imagined that four years ago, while wandering in and out of old antique shops—I'd do this from time to time, not with the aim of selling anything, but in search of objects and artifacts for the Clock Villa—I would stumble upon that piece of balustrade? If I had known its future price would be even more than the handsome figure I've already quoted, I would have seized it instantly and embraced it like a long-lost friend. But who would have known? The sneak caught on right away, despite all my efforts to show reserve. Perhaps he saw the way my hands were trembling despite my attempt to keep them hidden from view. Thus, after pouring most of my energy into haggling over an Indian lectern, I asked in a most offhand way for the price of the balustrade. "Nine hundred liras," he replied. "A very important piece . . . from Konya . . . worthy of a museum, that one." From thirty liras to nine hundred! Exactly thirty times more expensive. The square root of the sum, as my son would have said. Dazzled by the elegance of these figures, I nearly cried, "Done! Have it sent to my home," but I rallied to counter with one hundred fifty. He groaned. I raised it to a hundred sixty. Then he claimed I was merely clowning. It was as if we had found ourselves in the same minaret but on different flights of stairs that passed through the same balconies as they twisted through the tower, and within the tower's thick walls we could catch glimpses of each other trying to calculate just how we could meet exactly in middle, but he was slowly plodding down as I was storming up. I must have miscalculated, for Mandalin Efendi was fixed on a step much higher than my own, at four hundred seventy-five. Perhaps only to avenge myself of my defeat, I gave the man his money and bent over the balustrade to kiss its bottom, which still bore the marks where it had been scorched by candles in my childhood. There was no longer any reason to conceal the joy I felt in recapturing this fragment of my past. But I went one step further:

"Mandalin Efendi," I said, "you haven't proved yourself a very good salesman today. Indeed this piece is worthy of a museum, but I know better than anyone that it does not originate from Konya, and I also know you could have sold it to me for much more."

Mandalin Efendi looked at me for a moment and then threw his arms up into the air as if about to fly away:

"Well, my good sir, what's done is done, a sealed deal," the Jewish merchant cried. "The better for you and the better for all of us . . . There are always other customers."

Some might find it shameful that I took home, as private property, a piece of the Kahvecıbaşı Cemetery. This saddens me a little, I admit. There is something rather disquieting about the whole thing. But this is not to say that I can find no consolation in the affair. First, both the *medrese* and the mosque are no longer there. Thus there is no incontestable owner of the balustrade to whom I might be compelled to return it. It is true that by pinching the balustrade I might have had something to do with the demolition of the building itself. But as I've already explained, the structure was derelict beyond repair. And of course you already know of the circumstances that compelled me to remove the piece in the first place. My fellow citizens should find some consolation when they see the new apartment buildings that now stand on those grounds. The neighborhood has sprung to life. The way things are developing we can expect an entirely modern neighborhood within a few years. I applaud the modern man, and I too enjoy modern comforts and modern architecture.

It doesn't weigh too heavily upon me to see cemeteries disappear or to see priceless, exquisitely carved and inscribed tombstones used as basins, ornaments over public fountains, or makeshift shelves on radiators. As for this coffeehouse proprietor Salih Ağa, after whom the cemetery was named, I've known for some time that the man was not a saint. Despite my vows and all the candles I lit in that mosque, my mother still passed away; and so, saint or no saint, I'd never been able to forgive him. At this point in my life, I am not about to bemoan the fact that one can no longer find a single cemetery in the city center!

Modern life commands us to stay far from the notion of death.

And why not, good sir? Are we to live or are we to await death sitting down?

Returning to the balustrade, I was the first to discover this sublime work of art and to grant it the admiration it deserved. I was the one who marveled at its beauty. I was the one who later spotted it, there in the antique shop, and prevented it from falling into the wrong hands and being taken away by people with no understanding of its value. You might say I was even its savior. What could be more just than rescuing this objet d'art and taking it to the safety of my home, never again to be drawn into a wild adventure? And who would receive more pleasure from such a thing than I? Who else could descry his own past in its arabesque motifs or recognize the strange souls who once gave it life?

As I write these lines, I lift my head from time to time to let my eyes linger on the piece. Just a few steps beyond, under the cedar tree and the poplar beside it—this too I uprooted, from an old garden on the Bosphorus, and planted here—I can see my grandchildren playing with my youngest daughter, Halide, granted to me by the Almighty in my sixtieth year. They're holding colorful little pails and shovels; no sooner have they filled the pails with sand from the garden than they empty them out. Though their nannies are watching over them—that moronic Swedish governess my daughter should never have hired to look after her children, and that sweet, ever-smiling, plump, wheat-skinned Asiye Hanım, whom I hired to take care of my dear Halide—I am well aware that they are nurtured and protected by altogether loftier beings. Yes, why would I lie, for I sincerely believe that Nuri Efendi and Abdüsselam and even Seyit Lutfullah in his disheveled robes—a gift to him from Aselban—are keeping the children company at this very moment. Who knows? The spirit who beckoned to Halide, who led her to the sundial at the center of one of the flower beds, her blue bloomers hanging so daintily from her short dress, who allowed her to fall where the rock gave way under her hands, must be none other than Nuri Efendi. I was not at all mistaken in naming her after the late Halit Ayarcı, at the behest of Pakize. As the days go by, she resembles him more and more. His lines appear on her little rose-petal face, in fact her temperament becomes more and more like his. Like him, she can bend anyone to her will; she can have anything she wants without asking.

This must mean that Seyit Lutfullah was not exaggerating when he spoke of the effect names can have on our destiny. I am quite sure that if I had given Halide another name, she would not seem so very much like my late benefactor.

X

Nineteen twelve was one of the most painful years of my life, as Nuri Efendi passed away at the very start. His death set in motion a series of events that caused me no end of trouble. Returning from the funeral, I had to face the fact that I was already unemployed at seventeen. Up until the age of fourteen, I had managed to continue my studies at college, but after my friendship with Seyit Lutfullah intensified, I had stopped attending school altogether. I was adrift. School is of course extremely important for children. Above all else, it allows us to put off answering childhood's most troubling question: what will I be when I grow up? School reminds me of a train that carries you to a destination—providing you arrive on time, make all the right connections and wait patiently for the journey's end. But I had jumped off the train in the middle of a desert, far from my destination.

Gradually I became the subject of magnanimous and high-pitched concern. My mother never stopped asking, "What will become of this child?" And when entering into conversation with my father, the neighbors said, "Whatever will you do with your son?" Some thought I should concentrate on my studies, while others believed I should be schooled in a trade. But all were united in the opinion that my father had no choice but to take a forceful stand.

There were even those who said, "There's no way that boy will ever find a job. You might as well marry him off."

I too was asking questions, which is not to say that I was

considering a career or a job or even remotely thinking about a
way to earn money. But still there was this thing we call time,
this thing we deem the day. And I had to find some way to
make short shrift of it. Up until that point in my life, I hadn't
been interested in anything but watches and clocks; matters
more profound than these were beyond my comprehension. I
had acquired from the late Nuri Efendi a vast store of knowledge about timepieces and their vicissitudes, but I had never
seriously considered the profession of horology. I was all
thumbs. My hand-eye coordination was unremarkable; the
two seemed to exist in entirely separate worlds. And I was a
born amateur. I quickly lost interest in anything undertaken as
work. A path would unfurl in my mind, and I'd meander
toward it, leaving behind the work at hand. I had always been
like this: at school, at Nuri Efendi's workshop, and at the dervish lodge I visited with my father on Thursdays and Fridays
from the age of seven. Yet I had to do something. So I began to
work as an apprentice for a clockmaker just a little way down
the road from Nuri Efendi's workshop. The poor man was penniless and had almost no customers; he hardly made his daily
bread. But he took me in all the same. He was even willing to
give me a few pennies from the clock and watch repairs I undertook myself. But—just my luck—not one customer came into
the shop on the days I worked. So, as master and apprentice,
we sat opposite each other in silence.

Asım Efendi was not at all like Nuri Efendi. He possessed
neither ideas nor any particular philosophy pertaining to
watches and clocks. One day I felt I should share with him
some of what I had learned from Nuri Efendi, but the man
could not comprehend a word I said. When I said that watches
and clocks were just like human beings, he cried, "Look here, I
don't humor that kind of claptrap!"

Meanwhile Seyit Lutfullah never left me alone. He had
become accustomed to my assistance in his finagling with the
world beyond. He would drop by the shop almost every other
day and cry, "On your feet, look alive. An order has arrived.
Onward to Etyemez!" Then he'd entreat my master to give me
leave, and if he protested, Lutfullah would threaten the old man

with his demons. Etyemez, Eyüpsultan, Vaniköy—in short, all
Istanbul was ours. With a dirty turban wrapped around his
head and his robes billowing out in the slightest breeze, Lutfullah took the lead, dragging his half-crippled leg in his wake,
while I trailed behind in my bedraggled and patched attire, and
we wandered the streets of Istanbul.

All the same, and for better or worse, I managed to work with
Asım Efendi for a few months. True, the old man lacked a philosophy of timepieces, but he did know how to repair them, and
he was able to teach me a thing or two. Sadly, I was forced,
through an unfortunate turn of events, to leave his shop. One
day Seyit Lutfullah absconded with a watch that was waiting to
be repaired. When the crime was discovered, I was blamed. They
detained me at the police station for hours. Finally they remembered that Lutfullah had come into the shop the day before, and
he was promptly called in. In his defense the wretched creature
explained that he had stolen the watch to buy incense to burn at
the foot of the treasure of the emperor Andronikos. And he
showed them where he had pawned the watch for next to nothing. He claimed he had done everything at the insistence of a
spirit medium who had told him his quest would not move forward without the theft of such an object. Once it became clear
that he was the true culprit, I was released. But I couldn't just
abandon the miserable fellow—I didn't have it in my heart. In
the end I thought of Abdüsselam Bey, and it was with his assistance that Lutfullah was spared prosecution for both drug use
and theft. Abdüsselam bought the watch back from where it had
been sold for a few silver coins, but Asım Efendi refused to take
me back. And he was right: it was dangerous to keep an apprentice with such irresponsible and good-for-nothing friends.

XI

This episode with the watch would no doubt have had far more
significant (and disquieting, even dangerous) repercussions at
home than at the police station. But as luck would have it, a

momentous event on the very next day shook our family to its
core, igniting my father's fury and raising my mother's complaints to an unprecedented pitch.

This is how it always happens. Such crises never simply vanish of their own accord; other ones arrive to push the previous
one aside, lightening the impact of the former and dissolving
any possibility of blame. Thus only one day after my father had
been summoned so abruptly to the police station to account for
his son, my paternal aunt passed away. And just as she was
being lowered into the earth—following the late-afternoon call
to prayer—she sprang briskly back to life. This second catastrophe turned our lives inside out, and my father never recovered from the shock.

My aunt was the only family my father had in the world.
And perhaps it was this enforced intimacy that led them to
become so dramatically different in temperament, disposition,
and even appearance.

My father was a vigorous man, the kind who could devour a
stone. He had a colossal and consuming appetite for life. For
him the universe was like a heap of grain to be threshed and
sold, or at least that's what those who knew him liked to say.
But my aunt, she had been sickly since childhood. She was feeble, malicious, and self-absorbed. Though reasonably devout,
my father had a cheerful disposition and a taste for music and
conversation. My aunt, however, was dark and moody, fervently pious, proud, yet fragile—she was a miserable little
woman who loved nothing more than to descry the work of the
devil in the sensual. These two had but one thing in common:
each lived under the weight of a terrible depression. My father
was depressed because he was penniless; the man was forever
chasing after chimeras, kept afloat by hopes of the impossible;
my aunt was burdened by a meanness that propelled her into
an existence so frugal she could barely make ends meet, despite
a good-sized fortune accruing interest in the hands of money
lenders, an assortment of stocks and bonds, her grand villa in
Etyemez (left to her by her late husband, the warden of the
street sweeper's trade guild) and several Ottoman *hans* and
hamams. In fact she never risked remarriage for fear she might

lose her fortune, preferring to live like a lonely owl in her monstrous sixteen-room villa with no one save the half-crazed chambermaid she'd adopted as a child and an old servant who was just as fervent and mean as she was, not to mention a terrible busybody. It was no more than a week after her husband's death that she put an end to my father's visits, he being inclined to probe into her affairs. This is why we saw her only on religious holidays such as Ramadan and Kandil, when we would visit to pay our respects and kiss her hand. She also made it her custom to come and stay with us on the second week of Ramadan, as we lived closer to various mosques. Whenever we went to visit her, we were offered the cheapest refreshments, cakes, and cookies Istanbul could provide, and, along with mountains of advice and admonishments, we would be given tawdry little presents of nominal value. Yet when she came to visit, she expected us to observe full decorum in what we offered her, and when displeased she would fly into a gruesome rage. The prospect of having to host this bilious guest and her two servants would strike fear into our household a full two months before their arrival. Our aunt would never have been able to change her eating habits so dramatically from the moment of her arrival—suddenly she became ravenous—had she not followed a diet beginning on Şaban, the eighth holy month of the Muslim calendar, which became ever stricter with the approach of the holy month of Ramadan. But nothing was more difficult than enduring the barrage of advice and criticism she dispensed over the course of the holy week.

Truth be told, she liked neither my father nor me. And it was a joy for her to make this perfectly clear. There was no doubt she considered us more legal inheritors than close family. For her, our household was nothing more than the lever of a great machine that groaned behind that terrible eventuality, death, when in fact, considering the finality of the affair, we were really the entire contraption itself. Weighed down as she was with this vast inheritance, my aunt couldn't think of dying without recalling that she would be dying for our sake. She interpreted almost everything we did in this light, lambasting us even when we had spoken with the best intentions. Naturally all the advice she meted out on this matter revolved around her paranoia. Her favorite motto was, "The greatest mortal sin is wishing death upon someone other than oneself!" This despite the fact that no one harbored such a morbid desire, to begin with. My father took pity on his sister and even wished for her to be happy. After she was widowed, he strongly encouraged her to marry Naşit Bey. But my aunt refused even to entertain the idea, so convinced was she of the hunter's moral repugnance. "I'm not looking for a man to gobble up my fortune," she'd mutter. She even suspected my father of some deviant ploy in his wish to marry her off, especially since he had just arranged for my engagement to Naşit Bey's daughter—though we were both far too young.

Once, when my aunt fell ill, my father sent a doctor to her villa, paying for the visit out of his pocket. No one there could ever forget how she screamed at my father as she drove him and the doctor away: "Why the rush? Sooner or later it'll all be yours!" I won't deny the fact that as my father's financial situation worsened he came to see my aunt's estate as his only hope for salvation. Moreover, my aunt's health had sharply declined—a result of her peculiarly sparse diet, her ceaseless agitation, and her paranoia about her wealth. Her spirits were at an all-time low. She refused to leave my father alone, demanding unimaginable sacrifices in return for the inheritance he was soon to receive and taking every opportunity to shame and abuse him. Gradually my aunt ceased to be my father's sister: she became his burden.

Toward the end my aunt lost control of half her body. My father just could not understand how she could carry on living semiparalyzed, especially since she continued to harangue him as vigorously as ever, and he put it down to rancorous sentiments she must have harbored for him since childhood. According to my father, she continued living only to spite him. After suffering a day of malicious torment at the invalid's bedside, he would return from the villa in Etyemez and whimper: "Is it really possible? Who would continue to live like that? The miserable creature is tormenting me, just out of spite. But God is great . . ."

All this goes to show that my father saw himself as the oppressed party.

But at last the fateful day arrived. With tears pouring from her eyes, the half-crazed chambermaid came to inform us that my aunt had passed away. My father rushed off to her villa to take the required preliminary measures. Funeral prayers were performed in Lâleli. My father delegated the burial to our neighbor Ibrahim Bey, so he could return directly to the villa in Etyemez after prayers, to watch over its contents so that nothing might go missing. To my mind, this was his gravest mistake in the whole affair. For if he hadn't been swept away by the fear of losing her estate and its property, my aunt would have been buried in a timely fashion, thereby reducing the likeliness of her resurrection. And—even if she had been destined to rise again from the dead—my father would have been standing at the head of her grave, desperate and aggrieved, beating his head with his hands and tearing at his clothes, with tears flowing from his eyes—all of which would have ensured a happy outcome. Instead we were met with a very unhappy outcome indeed. Ibrahim Bey had arranged a pauper's funeral, entirely unbefitting the bride of the warden of the street sweeper's trade guild, just so he could skim from the money my father had given him for the burial proceedings. And because it proved difficult to locate her late husband's tomb—not a soul from the family was there to watch her burial beside it— the grave diggers began late: from start to finish, the entire operation was marred by infelicitous delays. When at last the coffin lid was cut open to tip the corpse into the freshly dug grave, my aunt awoke from a deep coma, and because she was the type of creature who was never caught unawares, even in the most extraordinary of circumstances, she heaved the coffin lid aside and assessed the scene, and with what she later viewed as her eternal powers of perspicacity, she grasped the situation immediately, shouting out to the only person she recognized there, the imam from Etyemez: "Quick, hurry up and take me home!"

As Ibrahim Bey told me later, most of the mourners were terrified, and at once took to their heels, thus making the task of returning the casket from the cemetery in Merkezefendi to my aunt's villa all the more difficult. Had she not given a ferocious scolding to those who had not been so quick off the mark, it's unlikely she would have made it home at all.

First she ordered the imam to give her a coatlike cape that had been abandoned by one of the diggers at the graveside, and after wrapping it tightly around her, she proceeded to direct the procession from the stretcher that held the coffin. With half her body jutting out of the casket, and shouting out instructions to the luckless souls charged with carrying her back to her villa in Etyemez (she had the gall to order them to take her all the way back home in the very manner they had brought her to the graveyard—no less would have been expected of her), she even managed to stop off at the first pastry shop they came across after entering the city, purchasing a savory bun to relieve her hunger.

This bizarre return from the world beyond, and the fantastical death of my aunt, now alive in her coffin and nibbling on her savory bun, attracted much attention in the backstreets of various neighborhoods as they lumbered along, so that by the time they reached the home my aunt had once entered as a bride, they had almost half the population of the district behind them; the procession had taken on the aura of a victory march.

Meanwhile my father, knowing nothing of the resurrection, was still at the villa. He had seized the premises and terrorized its servants before extracting everything that seemed of any value, including items buried in the coal cellar, light in weight but heavy in worth, and he had strewn it all in the middle of the floor; his pockets were stuffed with jewels, bonds, and gold that he had rustled out from the drawers of my aunt's bedside table, and his eyes were still searching as if to say, "Where's the rest?" In the meantime I had dismantled the dining room clock, which had captured my imagination as a child—and always been kept well out of my reach—and was busy fiddling with its pieces in a vain and furious attempt to repair it.

I was the one who opened the door. My aunt brusquely ordered her removal from the casket they had by then lowered. There cannot have been a commander in recorded history who, after seizing victory in the battlefield, showed as much composure as my aunt when her coffin was lowered to the ground. She was in complete command, calling to mind the pictures of Caesar I'd seen in history books. Sadly, she didn't afford me the chance to express my admiration. In fact she hardly even gave me the chance to applaud. Thrusting me aside, she stepped into the foyer, whereupon, without even looking me in the face, she cried:

"Where is that brute of a man, your father?"

Awestruck, I could only indicate with a trembling nod that he was upstairs.

"Well then take me upstairs. At once!" she cried.

But without waiting a moment for assistance, she flew up the stairs. The crowd stood stunned. My crippled aunt, who had been at death's door, who had in fact just returned from the dead, was now walking unassisted—indeed she was bounding up the stairs!

I had never loved my father in the same way after his second marriage. Unable to distinguish the genuine man among his many masks, I was rarely convinced by his shows of suffering. But I shall never forget his face that day. The moment he saw his sister in her funeral shroud—his stingy and cantankerous sister, whom he thought he had sent off to heaven just a few hours ago—the poor man was rendered speechless by shock, or rather fear. His face trembled, white as waxed cloth, and his whole body shook. Not a word passed between them until my aunt calmly intoned: "Put everything down."

Trying his very best to mumble something along the lines of "Welcome home, sister," my father pulled out the various items he had stuffed into his pockets and down his shirt, his hands still trembling with fear. Five minutes later he resembled a leech dipped in ash. He had given back all he had taken, in fact even more. He'd given back more because he had, at just that precise moment, given up all hope for the future. My aunt waited patiently, clocking my father's every movement until she was sure there was nothing left on his person save his soul, and then said:

"Now leave. And take all these people and that dimwit son of yours too. But at the very least you can make my bed before you go, and brew me some linden tea. Hurry up now, I seem to have caught a chill. It is rather cold outside."

Father and son, we stumbled out of the house in a daze.

Now, I must confess that this ghastly business did not have the same effect on me as it had on my father. Undoubtedly my aunt was being entirely unfair with us. But I had never believed I had any right to her fortune in the first place. Like so many others born aggrieved, I tended to weigh any misfortune that befell me against those tragedies I had been able to avoid. It was never a matter of right or wrong. It was more complicated than that. Looking back on my life—and I am of course of an age to be doing such a thing—I see I have always had a spectator's frame of mind. My concern with the welfare and demeanor of others has always distracted me from my own woes.

This was certainly the case that day. For despite all we lost on the day my aunt came back to life, I still found enchantment in the miracle that had unfolded before my eyes.

But there was more. Even if my father had not been so devastated as to hire a car to take us home, I would still have found delight in witnessing an event never before seen or heard in the history of our family.

There was nothing comical about my aunt's imperial posturing, or my father's frozen shock, or Ibrahim Bey's dramatic retelling of the affair—even when he pounded his fists against his chest to illustrate the losses suffered. In the end what mattered most was not the great fortune, even though it had been my family's last hope, nor was it the announcement of my aunt's death in the papers, conveyed in the biggest and most brightly lit letters the world has ever seen; it was the one thing passed on to us from the fortune of the warden of the street sweeper's trade guild: the enormous pendulum of the villa's clock, which was buried deep in one of my pockets, taken from the villa that we, as father and son, had conquered, if only for a fleeting spell.

Let my father say whatever he may, but I for one got my share of the inheritance. At one point Ibrahim flashed my father a fearful look and wailed, "It's all my fault. I could have finished the job sooner."

My father lifted his head and mumbled, "There's no need for you to worry, Ibrahim Bey. It was the will of God." And after a moment's pause he added: "Then things would have been far worse. God willing, this will be a lesson to her that will encourage her to fulfill her grandfather's will. If only he were still alive . . ."

My father never recovered from this affair, one that few in this world ever suffer through. He was never able to shake off the tremor it gave to his hands or the heaviness that remained in his tongue.

There comes a point in any man's life when he becomes conscious of his destiny. My father discovered his in the cruelest way imaginable. Once aware of his fate, he saw no point in curbing his carelessness or impatience, though it had been these very shortcomings that had led to our ruination. He sank into a strange silence. He became a quiet and gentle man who kept to his own corner. Yet occasionally he would glance at the pendulum (which for whatever reason he had hung on the entrance wall, never to be removed), and as he jumped to his feet, a strange and tortured smile would flash across his face.

I still marvel at how this tempestuous and eternally dissatisfied man could sink so abruptly into silent defiance.

All of us—even those not endowed with a hopeful disposition—have thought, even dreamed, of life after death. It is the reward we project onto the unknown and distant future, promising consolation for this string of catastrophes we know as life. It is a game of cards played with the very best hand, one we're always destined to win, a wild desire that no man is ready to relinquish: the dream of living another life, provided of course there remains a narrow recollection of the past to make him conscious of the change and pleased to have left the other world behind. My aunt was the one person out of a million to taste such happiness. Sadly, her life after death—her resurrection—proved not to be the hoped-for empyrean.

Despite the unexpected manner of her return from the cliffs of eternity, on the surface she was still the same old aunt we had always known. But deep down she had undergone a profound change. This might be better understood as a revolution, seeing as my aunt's return from the grave overturned what we, along with all her acquaintances, saw as the regulated order of her life—and in my view it rests on the following three fundamental points:

First, my aunt no longer despised the body that had carried her back in such a miserable state from the world beyond, following a death that had proved temporary. Confronted by the faults she was incapable of changing—her age, her malformations, her overall unseemliness—she no longer condemned herself. Having accepted her body as her sole source of support in this game of blindman's bluff that we call life, she came to appreciate its value.

The second change could be seen in her regard for her wealth. Her fortune (to which formerly she had been so attached, thinking herself its sole custodian) had, if only for a few hours, found its way into her brother's hands and pockets, and although her brother was in some way dear to her, he was still another human being; having seen how easily a fortune could change hands, she set about changing her relationship to it. Until then my aunt would have said, "I'll hide it whatever the cost—it can only increase in value." She had transformed her coal cellar into a kind of bank vault. But that day it was as if suddenly she had decided, "No, I shan't keep a penny of it, and I shall no longer worry about the return. I shall sit right here and eat my way through it!"

Having turned against all those she assumed had their sights set on her money, my aunt now turned against her own fortune.

But whatever the peacemakers among us might have insisted, this did not lead to a dramatic change in the way she treated it. My aunt and her fortune had long lived in opposition to one another, like two radically different spheres, coexisting as polar opposites, and it was the conflict itself that brought about a certain equilibrium. At the time of her provisional death, my aunt had relinquished everything, but following her miraculous resurrection she took possession of her fortune most forcefully.

In making that outlandish journey from the graveyard back to her home, in drawing upon the strength of her will to subdue all those around her—for the crowd surely would have preferred the serenity of a burial to the fated resurrection—in embarking on this adventure, my aunt had at last discovered this thing called life. Swayed by a soft March sun shimmering behind a thin curtain of gently falling snow, and by the biting wind blowing over the old city walls, not to mention the ever-multiplying, weeping crowds and the faces looming over her, she was beset by emotions that until then had lain dormant. Life did exist after all! Both the rich and the poor were alive. They laughed, shouted, cried, worried, loved, and grieved, but above all they lived. Why would she not do the same? Especially now, when she had so much of what these people most desired. She had discovered life on her journey home; crossing over her hearth to watch my father remove precious stones from under his shirt and out of his pockets, she discovered the true value of her fortune.

The third and final change was physical. The fearful joy she'd felt at eluding death and the surge of panic she'd endured while recapturing her fortune combined to jolt my aunt out of illness and paralysis.

The result, you might well ask? It was this: my aunt, who was taken home in a victory chariot like Caesar, accompanied perhaps by a third of the city, woke up the next day from a long and peaceful sleep in perfect condition, and she bounded right out of bed.

The first thing she did was send for the imam, to whom she gave her late husband's entire wardrobe, along with personal effects she had kept as memento mori. Then she hopped in a carriage and set off to visit a financier who took her to the finest seamstresses in all of Beyoğlu. For days, she busied herself with the latest fashions. Meanwhile she had the villa of the warden of the street sweeper's trade guild cleaned, restored, whitewashed, and renovated. And she even bought herself a small carriage with black rubber wheels.

The day the new carriage arrived, a butler, a male cook, and a new team of chambermaids began working at the villa. Once this team was in place, my aunt relieved her ward, Safinaz Hanım, of the title *ahretlik,* thus emancipating her from indentured service. In severing this immortal bond, she relinquished all concern with the world to come. The poor woman left the house in a hired carriage with two trunks and a few pennies in her pocket. In the space of a week (seeing as human beings always need companionship), Naşit Bey had taken her place, moving into the villa with his son and daughter to become my aunt's second husband and our new relative. Six months later they went together to Vienna to take the cure, and not long after their return, Naşit Bey became a deputy member of the Committee for Union and Progress. Thereafter he embarked on a significant business venture, availing himself of my aunt's fortune.

In all this our only acquisition, apart from the pendulum, was Safinaz Hanım. After living for a short while with a relative in Beşiktaş, she ran out of money, only to remember that her former guardian had a brother who lived in a small, comfortable, modest, and cozy little four-roomed home in Edirnekapı, and with the last penny in her pocket she hired a carriage and directed it to take her and her empty trunk to our home.

XII

Aristidi Efendi's death brought an end to our quest for gold. And my aunt's rebirth wiped out all hope of an inheritance. All we had left was Seyit Lutfullah and the treasure he was still so passionately seeking. Needless to say, another ill-fated and untimely event ruined this, our last, chance.

Seyit Lutfullah had begun delivering sermons on certain days at a small mosque somewhere near the Yemiş Pier. During one of these sermons, the poor soul suddenly felt called upon to reveal a startling truth that he had kept secret from everyone until that moment.

After enumerating various material and spiritual threats to the Islamic world and bemoaning the mounting chaos around us, he told the faithful gathered before him that things simply could not carry on as they were and that the time was ripe for a new *mehdi*, a messiah who was soon to arrive to put an end to the confusion; and at the end of his speech, he trumpeted the good tidings at the top of his lungs: "Lo, I am that new messiah! I have only to make myself known. But I will do so soon enough . . . and then you shall all flock to my side."

Though Lutfullah conveyed his triumphant message with astounding lucidity, he pinned his coming to an indefinite date, leaving us with a fair idea as to how much opium he had consumed that day. This did little to help his case, as the government in power took a dim view of the affair; Mahmud Şevket Pasha had not yet been assassinated and Istanbul was seething with political unrest.

Thank God Lutfullah was able to speak more clearly on the matter once the effects of the drugs had faded, particularly during his first interrogation. He spoke at length about Aselban, the treasure of Andronikos, the battles waged by his guardian spirits at the sight of the treasure, and the disgruntled treachery of those evil spirits who pestered him, dressed up to resemble some sort of fifth column. Perhaps the messiah idea had been instilled in him by those same evil and capricious spirits. Having shunted the blame to Abdazah, a spirit so evil as to be well beyond the grasp of any government or police force, he came around to the idea that his case should be viewed as exceptional.

Following Lutfullah's detention, I was called into the police station, along with my father, Abdüsselam Bey, and Sadi Efendi from Isparta, who had taken Nuri Efendi's place at the Time Workshop. While waiting in the corridor to give our statements, Naşit Bey (whom we hadn't seen since his marriage to my aunt) entered the building. And what an entrance it was.

This was not the Naşit Bey we had known—that avuncular man whose face, if not reflecting the simple joy of being alive, conveyed sadness and anxiety about his finances. Now his entire being exuded grandeur and gravitas. His moustache, which had previously drooped over his jowls, pointed upward in defiance of gravity, while his eyes, narrowed by sadness, were as hard as stones, with a piercing gaze that seemed to cut through the seen world to confront the one beyond. With a honey-colored overcoat in place of his old hunting jacket and a golden cane in his hand, he ambled toward us with ponderous steps that bespoke the seriousness of the occasion, which is to say that he left us in no doubt about the significance of his coming all the way down to the station to rescue us. Striding past us with a pride that reflected a fortune worth a couple of hundred thousand liras, and with all the power and prestige of the Committee for Union and Progress behind him, he stepped into the room where Abdüsselam Bey was undergoing his police interview.

About ten minutes later, they burst from the room. My father took this opportunity to congratulate his old friend and new relation and wish him every happiness. I took Naşit Bey's hand and kissed it before pressing it to my forehead. Ah, the good old days. This man who used to stop me on the street in Büyükçekmece to urge me to take his daughter's hand in marriage, this man who'd had nothing to say beyond a single bland assurance—"In just a couple years now you'll be the new young man in our family"—now reluctantly offered me his hand, and after I had kissed it, he abruptly pulled it back to wipe it clean with a handkerchief before putting on his gloves. But having him there—Abdüsselam played a small part in the matter as well—did seem to expedite matters. After the men of importance had given their statements, it seemed unnecessary for us to do the same—in fact it took on the colors of a tiresome chore: "We'll call you when we need you," the police officer grumbled, and sent us home.

Two days later Seyit Lutfullah (having been declared "a drug user and, while not in full possession of his mental faculties, nevertheless a madman and a risk to society at this point in time") was exiled to Sinop on the coast of the Black Sea.

On the evening of the day Lutfullah left town, a police officer brought us a basket with Çeşminigâr inside; using rather strong language, he urged us to do everything we could to look after the tortoise. "The hoca efendi took all his books with him," he told us. Thus we inherited what you might call our share of Andronikos's treasure.

But Çeşminigâr did not prove to be as loyal as Safinaz. The creature never warmed to our home. While Safinaz Hanım never left the little bay window nook, the only spot in the house where you could actually breathe and observe the outside world, the tortoise escaped from the house, whenever it could, to trundle about the neighborhood. Almost every day one of us, or one of our neighbors, would find the little beast in the Mihrimah Mosque, in one of the neighbors' gardens, or beneath the hooves of a carriage horse.

I have noticed that fairy tales always start with a name. Assign a name to your jacket or bow tie, and though they may be lacking in function or beauty, their identity suddenly shifts—voilà! they have acquired a personality. The people in our neighborhood gave Çeşminigâr the name Emanet, or Bond, probably because they found the name Çeşminigâr a little antiquated. And of course no one in the neighborhood wanted to lose their Bond. We all patrolled the streets with our eyes glued to the ground. The extraordinary attention we attach to benevolent deeds meant that someone was sure to find Bond in some secluded corner and hasten him back to our house, scolding us for having ever let him escape. To many on the outside, these hunts for Bond seemed futile, but with every escape, the tortoise internalized the topography of the neighborhood, until one day it went missing for good. It was with fear that I conveyed the terrible news to Lutfullah. The response we received from the castle in Sinop was truly remarkable. In his letter, scribbled in nearly illegible safranine ink, the political exile told us the tortoise had found him in Sinop and that we had nothing to worry about, that he—Lutfullah, not the tortoise—was in good health and busy in the region of Seyit Bilal with the hunt for the treasure of Gülsüm the Illiterate, which he would soon be unearthing, and upon doing so he would realize all his dreams, and, given these circumstances, he no longer needed the treasure of Andronikos and was bequeathing it to me. "I have been meeting with Aselban day and night, and during our travels together we converse. She has made you a brother of this world. And as a present she has given you the treasure of the emperor Andronikos. But you must come to know its true worth. As it now lies under the Maiden's Tower, it might seem unattainable, but with our arrangements and our prayers, you need not harbor the slightest doubt that we shall have it transported to a neighborhood from which it will prove far easier to unearth. If not . . ."

So after losing almost everything, we found it all again—both the power and the fortune.

XIII

Following the banishment of Seyit Lutfullah, the question of my future was raised yet again. Like it or not, I had no choice but to return to the old watch repairman's shop. The chief obstacle having been removed, the old master greeted me with open arms. But I was no longer the Hayri he once knew. The days when I would study watches and clocks and their secrets with love and admiration in Nuri Efendi's Time Workshop were long over. I had been exposed to other ideas since then, and passed through many new forms during my schooling with Lutfullah. There was no longer any connection in my mind between the words "life" and "work." For me, life was a fairy tale you invented while keeping your hands stuffed deep in your pockets. I found no joy sitting at the feet of an old man afflicted with rheumatism, listening to his endless complaints about whatever happened to cross his mind. So one day I placed before him the pin, the magnifying glass, and the key to the shop and dashed out to the street with the ten pennies or so I had left in my pocket from my earnings the day before. In one breath I was on the city walls. I was elated, as if all my problems had vanished in a flash. I spent that evening at one of the theaters in Şehzadebaşı. The whistles, the applause, the laughter, the cries of ticket salesmen on the streets, the lights on the stage, and above all the languorous look of that Armenian singer at the peak of her career, and her piquant voice—all seemed to promise new horizons. But what I loved most was watching how these men I met every day in the street or coffeehouse were made anew on the illuminated stage, as the brass band blared on. It was a dream come true! That night I made my decision. And three days later, I was a member of one of these improvisatory theater groups.

Naturally they never gave me an important role. And I was never under the illusion that we performed anything noteworthy. Nevertheless 1913 was perhaps my finest year. My days were my own, from start to finish. Toward evening we would congregate in the theater, as if plotting surreptitiously against someone's life. Then it would all begin in a great fury. The drums, horns, and clarinet on the streets would announce that the night was now ours, and we'd prepare the stage as if it were a parallel world. The audience would gather on the other side of the curtain, and the sound of their footsteps, the commotion, the screams, the jostling of the crowd, the impatient catcalls shook the foundations of the makeshift theater before the curtain finally opened. We would watch the first cantos from behind the audience. The old woman would shake her great belly before the crowd, and all would roar with applause, wise to the buffoonery but perhaps enjoying it all the more for that very reason, their whistles cutting through the air like it was cloth.

Everything was shabby, old, miserable, and cheap. But because I had passed through the school of Lutfullah, these cheap and miserable things seemed all the more beautiful to me for the illusions they helped create. The first garment I wore—a pair of aristocratic pantaloons from the era of Napoléon III—was torn in three places. As for the lady, or rather the countess, with whom I was to fall in love, she easily could have given birth to my mother. But what did any of this matter? The important thing was that my name was no longer Hayri, and that I was able, for a time, to break free of reality's grip. In a word, it was an escape. I was living in an enchanted world of lies and illusion, and that was all I wanted.

What didn't we perform? Our repertoire included all the great works. No Don Quixote ever stormed the windmills with such courage or panache. Sadly, in my third month there were retrenchments. And I was among those who had to go. So I decided to join a troupe in Kadıköy that performed kuşdili in a rundown hall. My earnings from such endeavors were meager. I made hardly enough to cover my transportation. But this time the women in the group were young—as the troupe was new and undiscovered—and I fell in love with each and every one of them.

I would return to the European side of Istanbul, in the solitude of the final ferryboat, my mind dazzled by images of their loveliness and my body infested with lice left behind by previous passengers. But I should say that for once fortune actually smiled on me. I had even managed to take second and third supporting roles in our plays.

The third stage of my career again took place in Kadıköy; this time it was an operetta. I was able to try out my voice in these musicals, which vacillated between *alaturca* and *alafranga* styles. I managed to infuse the performances with the Hüzzam and Hüseyin *makams* I sang with my father every Thursday evening and Friday at the dervish lodge we frequented. Our director had only one obsession: the cleaning of his monocle! And the light reflected from that monocle seemed to ennoble everything it touched.

After the operetta we dabbled in traditional Ottoman mime theater, and then, at the insistence of Abdüsselam Bey, I joined the Municipal Theater Group, but I understood nothing of Antoine's lessons. It was the Great War that rescued me from the chaos of this strange and tiring world that largely eluded my understanding. With the war, it seemed I finally set my feet on firm ground. But as always it felt too late.

PART II

LITTLE TRUTHS

I

Following my discharge from the army, I returned to Istanbul, where I found the city and its people much changed. Signs of poverty were everywhere; chaos and desperation reigned. My father had died in the war. My stepmother was living alone. The moment I set foot in the house, I knew those four years had been spent in vain. At home nothing had changed: The same calligraphic panels hung on the walls, and the same curtains, now more tattered and worn, hung from the doorways leading to rooms and the entrance hall; the house was as closed to the outside world as ever. In the front room, the lone straw mat on the floor, a footstep away from disintegration, filled the place with the stench of mold and mildew; and the Blessed One (our dustier-than-ever grandfather clock) huddled in the same old corner, calling to mind a decrepit camel fallen ill somewhere in the Caucasian deserts, dreaming deliriously of a time beyond all order.

As soon as I stepped inside I knew I had returned to my paternal home, to my childhood, to my youth—or whatever you would like to call it. What could I expect after those four years? I was as indolent as ever, indifferent to everything around me.

But those first days were not unduly depressing. My stepmother was born to show compassion. She was pitifully lonely, accustomed to living with only the idea of me; the day I arrived in person I thought she might die of joy. During those four desperate years, she had tended fastidiously to the great array of fruits in our large garden, making and then stockpiling preserves. I was shocked to see all the jars lined up on the breakfast table. "Have some of this plum jam. I made it when your father was still alive . . . And this sour cherry jam . . . I made last year. I kept it for you. No, dear, this sort of jam doesn't go bad . . . And this apricot one here, oh, come now, just a little spoonful . . ." And so in one sitting I was force-fed jams for all seasons. The poor woman wouldn't stop crying or throwing her arms around me. She thought me handsome, heroic, and resourceful; she wanted to hear of my noble adventures. If I tried to express my fears about the future, she would interrupt me and say, "Oh, come now. A man like you? How could a man like you not find a job?" And slowly I began to believe her.

I looked for work constantly, but at the time there were tens of thousands of other newly discharged young men like me looking for work in Istanbul. Every day the boats would bring in hundreds of new prisoners of war. I simply couldn't find employment. My back wages provided a degree of comfort, but my life became a precarious balancing act on a wire spanning an abyss.

Not wishing to get tangled in the web of the past, I refrained from seeing my old acquaintances. Besides, there was no one left save for Abdüsselam Bey. To guarantee I would not cross paths with the poor man I'd once loved so dearly, I changed my walking route, avoiding the direct road to the War Office, which I visited quite frequently in those days, and taking the streets behind the Şehzade Mosque and Direklerarası instead.

But in the end the old man came and found me. This was three months after my return. Early one morning a carriage pulled up in front of our house and with some reluctance I peered out of the window and saw Abdüsselam stepping down. "Where's that unfortunate son of yours?" he bellowed at the doorstep.

He didn't come up to find me but waited for me in the courtyard as I dressed. Then he took me to his new villa in Soğanağa, a smaller and more modest abode.

The splendor of his former villa, with its carriages and horses, its servants and abundant comforts, was not yet a distant memory. But its denizens had dispersed. Now the poor man lived with only his youngest daughter and his son-in-law, their children, Ferhat Bey (whose wife had died), two old servants, and Emine the chambermaid, who had been raised in his household, and whom I was to marry in two weeks' time, as if there were nothing more important for me to do.

We went up to his room on the second floor. He sat me down on the divan, on which was perched a small chest of drawers from India. On top of the chest was a pile of envelopes, and from these he pulled out photographs one by one, describing where each had been taken.

I told him about my difficulties finding work, and he promised to help with my search. But nothing came of it. Abdüsselam Bey's former friends had either vanished or changed so much that they no longer considered the man of any real import. After a few days pursuing leads, we decided it would be best for me to complete my studies. With his encouragement, and Ferhat Bey's even more enthusiastic support, I enrolled in the Post and Telegraphy Academy. I don't know why they chose this particular school, which seemed rather modest, at least from the outside; it was, after all, a time when most schools were so hard up for students that they had no choice but to rely on recruiting agents, even offer financial incentives to recruit students. Though the two men were very fond of me, their feelings about me hadn't really changed. And Abdüsselam Bey had more important considerations in mind. My education wouldn't last long; moreover, students were given a little pocket money. We came to the conclusion that working with telegraphs was not so different from working with watches and clocks—perhaps because they too ticked and had inside them this thing known as a mechanism.

"You already have this penchant for fiddling with such things—now at least you'll be able to fiddle with them for a living," they said.

After I had enrolled in the academy, or rather after I had negotiated the first step into a moderately secure future of my very own, Abdüsselam Bey announced that I was to marry Emine as soon as possible. The fact was that by that point I hardly ever left his home. Day and night he badgered me to propose. Marriage, I thought, might lessen my intimacy with him.

As he was almost a father to me already, an exchange of vows with Emine could serve only to formalize our relationship. It is unlikely she would have found anyone better than me; but, on second thought, she might have. As indeed she should have. Poor Emine! It's hard to imagine myself ever finding anyone more perfect! There was never any strangeness between us; we had no problems getting along. And as we were all going to live together in the house in Soğanağa, there was no need to worry about the things that impoverished newlyweds might find daunting, such as decorating a new home or making ends meet, and certainly not the "loneliness" of suddenly being left to ourselves—Abdüsselam made a point of stressing the loneliness. And so for all parties God's will was done, bringing me comfort and peace of mind. Moreover—of course Abdüsselam never openly admitted this—in such a troubled time, when his business affairs, to use market terminology, were approaching collapse, new members could always join the household and, if pushed, my stepmother too. By drawing her into his home, he would have his revenge on the misfortune that had dogged him for so long.

My stepmother didn't come to live with us. She was reluctant to leave the home where she believed she had been happy with my father. A human being's conception of happiness can be very strange indeed. Consulting books or listening to what people have to say on the matter, you might well conclude that we are creatures of reason—that mental faculty meant to distinguish us from animals. To use a tired phrase, man is king of the jungle. But if we examine how we manage our affairs, we are hard-pressed to find any trace of reason at all. And neither does reason influence our apprehensions or affections. When my stepmother turned down the invitation to come live with us in the house in Soğanağa, it would have made more sense for her to justify her decision by saying, "What business do I have in someone else's home? Perhaps if I were your biological mother, but even then . . . Anyone can tell with a glance that we aren't family." But after keeping her distance for so many years, the old parasite had burrowed her way into our home. Saddled with an invalid husband, and perpetually ill-tempered, before the war she'd never fully accepted the place as her own—so it drove me to distraction to hear her say it was her happy memories of the place that prevented her from leaving. It was beyond all logic or reason—as absurd as Abdüsselam Bey's insistence on my marrying Emine or Emine's exuberant acceptance of my proposal. The two reactions were no different. My stepmother was under the delusion that she had been happy in our home. She had so inflated the joy of being a part of the family (for years, before marrying my father, she had lived in a separate world, even imagining our family beyond her reach) that she was now unable to leave, but the fact remained that her arrival at our home was entirely inauspicious and not at all a source of happiness. Founded on supposition and hinged on the loosest of recollections, her happy memories proved so powerful that Abdüsselam Bey was obliged to respect her choice.

Emine was a charming and innocent young woman; above all she had a good heart. In the face of adversity she showed remarkable courage. Her life in Abdüsselam Bey's villa had been that of a caged bird. Her world was made up of only the people she knew there. At the time of our marriage she was a stranger to the outside world; taking her first tentative step into it, she nearly turned around and scampered back inside. But she seemed to have been wise since birth: almost never was she caught off guard. Not even the strangest situations fazed her. Always possessed of sound judgment, she was brave and affable to the end.

Our first years together were happy. Once I finished school I took a position at the Post and Telegraph Office. Later on, with the help of one of Abdüsselam Bey's friends, I found a job at the Tünel management office. At the time I was earning a respectable sum of money. I had no complaints, apart from the loss of our first child at birth. But the fact remained that we had no life to ourselves. Yes, everything at home was comfortable, plentiful, and secure, but we were never truly free and were certainly never left alone.

There was no escaping Abdüsselam Bey's ministrations; no one in the house could elude him. If he heard so much as a footstep or a light cough, be it in the entrance hall or in one of the bedrooms, and at any time of night, Abdüsselam Bey would race to the rescue, never allowing anyone to remain alone for more than a minute. Except for my time at work, I lived under his thumb. We would have breakfast together. And before I left, he would give me the name of the coffeehouse where I could find him that evening, and he would be sure to arrive there an hour early. Ferhat Bey, who had recently retired, would usually be there with him. Later in the evening we would go home together and sit and talk until bedtime, which he never failed to find a way to postpone. Meanwhile his real son-in-law—his youngest daughter's husband—would be out carousing, on behalf, he claimed, of all the men in the household; sometimes he even took his wife along with him.

Emine and I made the decision to move out at the first opportunity. In fact Emine had already visited my old home several times to see how she might put the place in order, while always taking care to show due respect to my stepmother's fond memories of the past; after throwing away the moldy wicker mats in the front hall, she took the clock pendulum off the wall and hid it somewhere in the attic—my aunt having told her long before we were married the story of how it came into our possession.

"I don't understand why you don't like it! It's a charming little home. You'll see. I'll make it a paradise. We must free ourselves of the smothering love in our present home."

Emine couldn't have known anything of the language of the melodramatic Turkish cinema in those days, but describing our predicament in Abdüsselam Bey's home, she'd naively say we were "slaves to love."

It wasn't just Abdüsselam Bey's attentions that convinced us to leave. The old man's ever-worsening financial woes made us more and more uncomfortable. Everything he owned had been sold, and whatever was left had been pawned. Deep in debt, Abdüsselam Bey hid the severity of his financial problems from us all. Despite our concentrated efforts, Ferhat Bey and his stepson and I were unable to persuade him to let us share the household expenses. And so his good cheer slowly faded. He became distracted and pensive. The man who had never before set foot outside unaccompanied now crept out alone at night in secret search of loans. In the end, Emine and I decided it would be wrong to continue to burden him.

But we were unable to carry through with our plan. The very day we'd hoped to tell Abdüsselam Bey of our decision, his son-in-law managed to get himself posted somewhere in Anatolia. After protracted deliberations, protests, and complaints, Abdüsselam Bey at last gave up and let his son-in-law and daughter go. As she left the house, Ayşe Hanımefendi cried out to us, "Our father's now in your hands. In a way, he's your father too." Her husband, standing at her side, said more or less the same thing. But after she moved out of earshot, he whispered, "God give you patience." We were stuck. We simply couldn't abandon the old man. And the fact was that he needed to be cared for by someone truly committed. His body, like his memory, was failing. And it was more than just forgetfulness: he was becoming increasingly confused.

So I contacted his eldest son, who lived in Çamlıca, as well as the middle son in Anatolia, asking them to come and take him. It was the least I could do for this poor man who had done so much for me over the years.

The middle son simply sent a telegraph, during Şeker Bayram, with his salutations to his father and a few photographs of his family. The son living in Çamlıca came to pay his respects over the holiday, along with his younger brother, as he always did, taking this opportunity to explain just how difficult it would be for him to welcome his father into his home. "My wife made me swear on the matter. I just couldn't," he said.

"At least you could help him a little," I said. "He has no money, and he's up to his eyes in debt. I give him everything I earn, but secretly. I'm always afraid he'll find out. He'd never accept money from me. If things continue like this, you'll wind up in debt yourself."

But he didn't believe me.

"You don't know my father," he asserted. "There's money somewhere—that's for sure. Who knows where he's hiding it."

"Fine," I replied. "But if something happens to him, we'll be ruined. And Emine and I will be incriminated. That would be uncalled for, wouldn't you say? Why don't you come and live with the man. Come and claim what is rightfully yours!"

He shrugged off my proposal. By then his father was already in the room with us. As he left, the son looked long and hard at me. "I have faith in you," he said. But it was not a look I could trust. A strange fear came over me.

That year, after Kurban Bayram, Ferhat Bey married a widow in Kadıköy and left the house. Echoing the old man's other son-in-law, he said, "May God give you patience and lighten your burden!" Then he added before he left, "And if there's a shred of reason left in your head, you should by all means follow my lead."

Now we were alone with Abdüsselam Bey in his home. Here was the man who had once lived in that enormous villa behind the Burmalı Mescit, amid a vast tribe of sons, grandchildren, and relatives close and distant. Now he would die in the hands of two virtual strangers. Such was his fate.

Throughout my life I have seen how it is often the case that a man ends up with the very thing he fears most. Not long after the night Aristidi Efendi burned to death following an explosion in one of his alembics, I found myself back in Nuri Efendi's Time Workshop. Everyone had something to say about the accident. Someone—I cannot, just now, recall whom—spoke of it as a curious coincidence, seeing as Aristidi Efendi had always feared this eventuality. Nuri Efendi had been listening to us in silence when suddenly he dropped the watch he was holding and said:

"As far as I am concerned there's nothing strange about it at all. Indeed we might even consider it natural. For there's no such thing as the present: there is only a past, and a future at its beck and call. In our subconscious minds we are forever constructing our futures. From the moment Aristidi Efendi began conducting his experiments, his fate shifted. He became, in effect, the architect of his own death. Why are you gentlemen so surprised to hear that he had sensed this all along?"

Abdüsselam Bey may have set the stage for this ultimate solitude through his overabundance of affection—one might even see it as a kind of addiction—for humankind and his overwhelming love for his family, near or far. Had he not been burdened with an overabundance of love and a dread of solitude, then surely those near and dear to him would not have abandoned him so hastily, and he wouldn't have suffered the desolate loneliness that marked his decline.

The following year not one relative came to see Abdüsselam Bey over Şeker Bayram. Yet for each holy night of Kandil, and on all the other religious holidays, he would purchase gifts for every son-in-law, daughter-in-law, and grandchild, as well as all his other living relatives, and perhaps even some no longer alive, according to their age and standing in the family hierarchy. Who could say how he found the money for all this.

Silk handkerchiefs and ties and shirts by the dozen, cheap jewelry for the girls, watches for the boys, and flowing robes for retired servants—it was all piled up in a room. And dressed in his old redingote and a freshly starched shirt, his gleaming spectacles perched on his nose, his hand stroking his neatly trimmed beard, his eyes glued to the clock on the opposite wall, and his ears alert to the slightest movement on the street, he sat and waited three long days, convinced the doorbell would ring at any moment, and when he heard footsteps at the door he would leap up to see who was there.

Great holiday feasts were prepared—enough to feed all who had once lived in the old villa, enough to give them all a taste of the dishes they liked best. We knew only too well that we'd have no visitors, and yet the table was ready to be set at a moment's notice. On the evening of the fourth day of Kandil, Abdüsselam Bey would turn to Emine with a look of despair that he could no longer mask and say:

"Emine, my good child, take these packages away and put them in the children's room. They can pick them up when they stop by."

The children's room had become a sort of emotional depot for Abdüsselam. A mountain of meaningless castaway objects accumulated dust: eleven cradles, two or three mattresses (all victims to Abdüsselam Bey's conjugal nights), wardrobes, mirrors, old toys, and chests—in short, a whole collection of odds and ends his daughter and son-in-law couldn't bring themselves to pass on to junk dealers when they moved out of that monstrous villa. Abdüsselam Bey called it the children's room, though not a single child was born there or ever lived there, and the strange thing was that the name somehow stuck. Perhaps it was the name alone that made the room feel haunted—for eventually we all came to believe that the spirit of the old villa resided in that room. It was a room of remembrance and loss, piled high with farewells, with the dead stacked one on top of the other, where each of us could see the death of our own childhood and youth; the furniture heaped together in its center like a ship run aground was a steadfast reminder. The room was Abdüsselam Bey's heart, in every sense of the word. Only those who ventured inside could begin to grasp how disturbing it might be to share a life with this good-natured man, because here, in this realm beyond time, he had drained all these objects of their indifference. The key hung on the door, but no one dared venture inside.

Despite her sunny disposition and her rational frame of mind, Emine had so absorbed her master's misery that she wouldn't so much as walk past the door. She carried inside her all the psychological traumas of the house that had been her home since childhood.

Faced with Emine's refusal to carry the packages into the room, I was the one left to do it, albeit with reluctance. Tripping over the old, abandoned furniture, when I crept into the room I'd be startled by a faded, ghostlike, and altogether unfamiliar reflection of myself in a mirror that was suddenly illuminated by a beam of light from the outside; and a peculiar fear of unknown origin would pass through me.

Where did it come from? And how very strange that it could take dominion over my entire person. These were, after all, the days when I was meant to be dizzy with love. My wife and I were expecting a baby. Every now and then Emine would turn to me, smiling, and say, "Kicking up a storm down there . . . must be a girl!" She complained constantly of these little kicks and affected serious concern when she said, "But how will I ever manage?" Even the low-spirited Abdüsselam Bey was overjoyed, and he never tired of saying, "How many days left? Go and ask." And he would always insist that I do so. Then he would do the calculations on his fingers, measuring each new answer against its predecessor. It had been some time since a child had been born in the house. The man couldn't stop exclaiming, "Oh, I shall be a grandfather once again!"

When it came time to put away the packages, he would give us a meaningful look and say, "Let's hold on to these—their rightful owners will be here soon enough." Emine would blush deeply as she left the room. And Abdüsselam Bey's face would light up with one of his rare smiles.

"Haven't you spoken with Ferhat Bey? Why did he go off to live with his wife in Kadıköy rather than bring her here? We could have all lived together. How could someone up and leave the house that was his home for so many years?"

"The woman refused to leave her father's house. She simply wouldn't leave!"

Abdüsselam Bey looked me directly in the eye. "Then why did he marry her? Couldn't he have found himself a poor and wretched wife?"

I was shocked. That old fear of mine now took on a sharper form, gripping me more violently. Where a pure love for humanity had once resided, there now was only the terror of solitude. But that wasn't all: something more significant was happening. We had surrendered ourselves to this miserable man because I lacked the will to stand up to him.

Zehra's birth eased Abdüsselam's anguish at being forgotten by all his relatives. He called for the most splendid cradle in the house to be rescued from the children's room. The latest grandchild in the family of Ahmet the Signer took her first sleep in this heavy cradle, made of walnut, inlaid with silver and mother-of-pearl, and as large as a train compartment. It goes without saying that Abdüsselam never left it untended from the day the baby was born. In line with an old custom of the villa, it was he who named the baby, not me. And though he had

intended to give the child the name of my mother, Zahide, in
the confusion of the moment he chose his own mother's name,
Zehra.

I I

This tiny mistake set off a series of catastrophes. At first the
old man was able to laugh with us about it, but soon he became
distressed and accused himself of having committed a terrible
offense. In the end it became a full-blown crisis of conscience:
He came to believe he had robbed us of our child. And he was
convinced he would be held accountable in the afterlife for
doing so. However, this served only to strengthen his bond
with Zehra, and he even took to addressing her as "Mother"
on account of her name. He began to plan for her future. Soon
the house was awash in legal documents willing to the child
what remained of his fortune. God knows how many he drew
up on a daily basis. During the last three years of his life, such
documents could be found almost anywhere in the house:
hidden under carpets, kilims, and pillows or stashed away in
desk and dresser drawers. Though Emine and I would tear up
at least a few of these every day, great piles of them emerged
after his death; almost all stated that he was bequeathing his
remaining wealth to his "mother Zehra Hanım" and strongly
urged us to give the utmost attention to her education and upbringing.

"That her mother and my daughter, Emine Hanım, and her
father and my son, Hayri Efendi, look after Zehra and pay due
attention to her education and upbringing until she is married . . . ," and so on—thus a gentle old man's will entrusted us
with the care of our own daughter.

As the war in Anatolia had long since finished and a good
number of soldiers had already returned to Istanbul, many of
Abdüsselam's relatives and friends were in the city when he
passed away. They flocked to the house the following day, each
with a different version of his will. But of course by then their

wills were out-of-date and legally void. Some time ago we had, however, agreed that we would take only our child and our personal effects when we left the house. And that's just what we did. But a few days after our departure, the atmosphere changed. In a number of his wills, Abdüsselam Bey had bequeathed to my daughter a great many things he had already pawned, and for quite considerable sums, and for some reason he had left wills with two different notaries. And so to settle the affair we were obliged to go to court.

Despite the fact that there was nothing even remotely resembling an inheritance, most of the potential heirs believed— among other far-fetched scenarios—that we had taken advantage of the old man's dementia to trick him into thinking our daughter was his mother.

And when we claimed, in self-defense, that the man had not been in full possession of his mental faculties during the last few years of his life, we were accused of disrespecting our dear benefactor and making a mockery of his memory. "Slander!" they cried. "Slander, defamation, ingratitude . . ." No sooner had we turned our backs than they interpreted everything in their favor: "Did you hear that? How they confessed to it all?"

Good God! so much was jointly owned, and the legal formalities were endless. If ever a sixth, seventh, or even a tenth of a plot of land or property had gone up for sale, my late father-in-law had bought in. Who knows, perhaps he thought he might extract a profit when the prices rose. His drawers were crammed full of property deeds, but every year he accrued an equivalent bill of debt. His real estate was not a source of revenue but, rather, a kind of stamp collection. At first the judges we spoke with found humor in the thought of this grown man taking his adopted maid's daughter for his mother, but with time the deceitful statements made by Abdüsselam Bey's many heirs led them to suspect us of foul play. I did my best to explain the situation:

"Sir, the late efendi was a playful man at heart. This is just the kind of little joke he liked to play on my daughter, whom he treated as his own child . . ."

"Are you trying to say he played jokes on a three-year-old

child?" the judge asked reproachfully. "First you say he treated her like his child, and now you're saying he acted clownishly, taking her to be his own mother. Make up your mind!"

"I am in no position to choose. The deceased availed himself of both techniques."

"Some of the wills date back to when she was only six months old. What is this? What part of this joke would a six-month-old baby understand?"

"Nothing at all, absolutely nothing, but everyone does this sort of thing. Who doesn't change his voice when speaking to a child? And we don't limit this role-playing to children. Consider when we play with cats and dogs—we either stoop to their level or demand they rise to our own. In this regard the deceased had struck just the right balance. The parties were engaged in mutual dependency but were in fact independently at variance."

I had picked up some legal terminology.

"Well fine, then. But how do you account for the child—or the mother, if you will—referring to the deceased as her son? The witnesses' statements are quite clear: Since he passed away, the child weeps and cries out, 'Oh, where's my son?'"

Indeed this was the case. Abdüsselam Bey had even managed to teach our daughter Zehra to address him as her son. Now the little girl drowned herself in tears as she cried out for her missing son. Again I did my best to interpret this conundrum for the court.

"That's right, sir. This is what he taught her. The two would spend the entire day together. Besides, isn't that how all this started in the first place? In his last years, the poor man just wasn't thinking very clearly . . ."

Feelings were running so high by now that it was extremely difficult to speak without offending someone. Oh how happy and relieved I would have been if I could have just shouted at the top of my lungs that this man I had loved so dearly had gone senile. Had he not been demented, he would never have bombarded us with stories of incest as bizarre as any story ever told about the Egyptian pharaohs. In the end the will (which in any case had never been legally binding) was annulled, and I was merely reprimanded, first for showing disrespect to the memory of my guardian, and then for speaking nonsense in a court of law.

By the time it looked as if the matter had been resolved, I had genuinely begun to fear that the words "guardian," "father," and "inheritance" would be my undoing. But it didn't end there: next the public entered into the fray.

III

The annulment of the will left our small circle reeling. Everyone we knew, or at least a significant majority, claimed that we, and in particular my daughter, had been deprived of what was legally our due. By now I had left the Tünel for a private institution, and everyone in my office, as well as in my neighborhood, was up in arms about the injustice that had been visited upon us, with each of our supporters reacting in his own particular way. Some took pity on me and my daughter. Others forgot us altogether, so angry were they with the heirs for disrespecting their father's last wishes at a time when he had only scant worldly possessions to his name. Others avowed that it was through my own foolish incompetence that the fortune had slipped from my grasp. In heated debates, the matter might be swept away with a quick gesture or built up into an avalanche or deemed to be of no significance whatsoever, depending on the speaker's mood and inclination. Those who viewed the matter in moral terms had little concern for the fortune itself, preferring to leave it in the hands of God. And those who believed man to be inherently avaricious and conniving took pleasure in calculating our losses and my ineptitude.

But they all had one thing in common: they never listened to what I had to say. It would have made no difference had I said, "But the man had no money. He was up to his ears in debt. I actually haven't lost a thing. For there was nothing I ever wanted to begin with!"

Even my employer was swept up in the tide of public opinion.

So convinced was he that I'd been robbed that he offered me a sudden five-lira raise in consolation.

My boss's gesture of pity served only to deepen the compassion that surrounded me. Some even thought I had suffered a blow from which I would never recover. One night, as I left the office, a friend took me by the arm and said:

"Come now, good Hayri. Let's go round the corner and knock back a few glasses of rakı together. It's the cure to all misery."

"Let's drink, yes, let's have a drink, but not out of misery, for I'm not at all troubled. We'll drink for the pleasure of the drink itself. But if you like, why not come to our house? We can drink there. It wouldn't be right for me to leave my wife alone at a time like this."

My wife was then pregnant with our second child, Ahmet. But Sabri Bey was set on misinterpreting everything I said:

"Of course . . . You've both suffered a terrible blow. The poor woman has every right to feel . . ."

And so he used all his powers to persuade me. He wouldn't come home with me as he didn't want to put us out any further; he was determined to console me in a *meyhane*, and I agreed, hoping this might give me a chance to explain how the inheritance had been misunderstood. At least in a public tavern he'd have to relinquish his grip on my arm when he sat across from me at the table. Sabri was a rather ugly man, but his great bulk was somehow reassuring.

When at last we were settled in the *meyhane*, I did my best to explain how I'd landed in this predicament:

"I loved the man like my own father. And I was a witness to his many kind deeds. But I never expected more from him— I had no right. Anyway he's been penniless for the past six years. He survived on loans. As for the will and all that, well that's just what happens when a man loses his mind. If there had been anything like a real inheritance, I doubt I'd ever have been able to sleep at night, but the man was so deep in debt . . ."

And so on and so forth. But Sabri Bey pursued the issue:

"But, then, how could he keep taking out new loans?"

"By pawning odds and ends. And I'm sure he contracted other debts too."

I offered one explanation after another, still hoping I could convince him. He nodded as I spoke but always returned to the same question:

"Yes, but why would they keep giving the man more if they knew he was already in debt? What I mean is, just how did he deceive them?"

By then my patience had run out:

"How should I know? Perhaps he had a method of some kind . . . a system . . ."

Sabri Bey's ear pricked up at the idea. Clearly he was after such a system for himself, because the moment the magic word fell from my lips he called out for the second bottle of rakı:

"My dear friend, there's nothing strange in all this. There was hardly anyone Abdüsselam Bey didn't know. Perhaps he was relying on an inheritance of his own . . . or there was land somewhere, in Tunisia, Algeria . . ."

"No, no, too far away. There must have been something else."

"Then perhaps there was something he could never sell, something everyone knew about, at least all the creditors. Something extremely valuable . . . A diamond, for example . . ."

His curiosity had unlocked my imagination. A vision of Seyit Lutfullah flashed before my eyes. Once while speaking of the treasure of the emperor Andronikos, he had told me its many jewels would include the rare and priceless Şerbetçibaşı, or Head Sherbet Maker's, Diamond.

Could I not enjoy a little joke on this fool who had dragged me into this tavern out of errant pity and was now trying to uncover some new way to deceive people?

"Imagine if he had the Şerbetçibaşı. Then surely he could've said to his creditors something to the effect of, 'I'll never sell it. It's an heirloom. But it will repay all my debts when my children eventually do sell it!'"

"That's right!" Sabri Bey cried. "That's exactly what must have happened."

And he called for a third bottle. He leaned over the table, his face dripping with sweat from the summer heat, and asked, "The Şerbetçibaşı . . ." His eyes flashed with curiosity. "Have you ever seen it?"

"My good fellow, I just made the thing up. Didn't we just do so together? I mean, weren't we just speculating?"

"But you know the name!"

"Think about it: I may have heard of such a jewel in a fairy tale from my childhood. Or perhaps someone mentioned something like it to me once. It could've just popped into my mind when you mentioned diamonds. Whereas in reality . . ."

"But that's simply not possible. No doubt it's something like the Kaşıkçı, the Spoon Maker's, Diamond. The same size and value . . . Don't you think?"

He filled up our glasses again, and we drank.

"Naturally he showed it to you?"

"What?"

"The Şerbetçibaşı."

Suddenly it dawned on me what sort of trouble I had brought upon myself with this practical joke. I called the waiter and handed him the last twenty-five lira note I had in my pocket. Sabri Bey watched me in silence. His eyes narrowed. Clearly there was more he wanted to know, but I flew out the door without so much as a good-bye.

A terrible pain swept through me, as if I'd accidentally cut off my own arm or leg, as if I had committed a grave error that would cause me or, even worse, my children, immense suffering—it was one of those wild fears that turn your life upside down.

"Why in the world did you ever agree to drink rakı with that fool?" Emine scolded me, before adding in consolation, "But there's really nothing to worry about. Just forget it. What could come of such a thing anyway? Can't a person joke now and again? A man might say anything when he's drunk."

The next day was a holiday. I spent all day at home, tinkering with the old watches that Abdüsselam Bey's children had given us as compensation for our share of the inheritance. I hadn't touched a watch or clock since returning from the war.

By evening I felt a little more at peace. I had convinced myself that Sabri Bey must have forgotten about the whole thing.

But the next day he jumped up from his seat the moment I stepped foot in the office, scurrying over to me to hiss these ominous words into my ear:

"The diamond."

There was that same flickering light in his squinting eyes. Who knows what he was trying to tell me.

The next evening the boss called me into his office. He wanted to hear the story of the Şerbetçibaşı Diamond from the source. I told him what had happened. He seemed somewhat convinced. But soon the story spread, and eventually everyone I knew had heard it. Everyone I bumped into would latch onto me and say:

"Good man, you never told me about this diamond of yours! You can't just keep such an enticing story all to yourself . . ."

It got to the point where I couldn't even pass by the neighborhood coffeehouses because all sorts of people would leap up with backgammon pieces, dice, cards, dominoes still in their hands to stop me in the middle of the street, and say, "Wouldn't you like a tea?" before pulling me inside. They wanted to hear about the Şerbetçibaşı. Some admired my honor and humility in denying the diamond's existence, but others found me wanting in resolve and would carp behind my back the moment I left the room.

Before long they were all claiming to have heard the diamond's story; drawing upon every scrap of ancient lore they could summon, they proceeded to solder together the legend behind a diamond that had never existed. My wife I and were distraught.

It was around this time that a number of creditors holding bonds for various items pawned by Abdüsselam Bey began legal proceedings against the heirs. Almost all of them had heard the story of the diamond. And most wanted compensation from this undeclared inheritance. I had no choice but to become embroiled in their lawsuits.

IV

First I was presented to the court as just another witness whose personal opinion might help to clarify matters. Then suddenly I was the centerpiece of the entire case. Because we had lived with the old man until his death, it was assumed we'd had

perfect knowledge of all his possessions and so must know
where the diamond was hidden. At this stage they were only a
few steps away from concluding that the Şerbetçibaşı Diamond
was indeed in our possession. Just a few more statements about
probabilities and likely consequences and the gap would close.
As indeed it did. Several hearings later the court was unani-
mous in believing we had the diamond. To make matters worse,
Abdüsselam Bey had used rather vague and suggestive language in his will: "the remainder of my fortune following the
completion of my debts," or "what remains of my estate." Similar wording appeared in the letters he wrote to his creditors.
And of course I myself had openly alluded to the diamond (if
only in jest).

Sabri Bey became the hero of the proceedings, just as he had
been in the investigations about me prior to the trial. His statements stuck like olive oil stains and did not cease. At almost
every hearing he came up with another detail I was meant to
have divulged to him that night. Despite his cordiality throughout the trial, he pursued his version of the truth with extraordinary vigor. After extended interrogations running over several
hearings, we all (myself included) came to learn that the wily
princess Saliha Sultan had finagled the Şerbetçibaşı away from
the Head Sherbet Maker himself, that after her death it had
been housed in the imperial treasury, and that later still
Abdülhamīd I had offered it to one of his most prized courte-
sans.

But of course no one had the slightest interest in the relationship between the Şerbetçibaşı and Saliha Sultan. All they cared
to know was that the diamond, after centuries of being lost
and rediscovered, had at last come into the possession of
Abdüsselam's family. When asked to confirm this story, I said:

"No, the diamond was part of the treasure of the emperor
Andronikos!"

My answer didn't please them one bit: they put it down as an
attempt to appear mentally unfit.

My aunt's husband, Naşit Bey, was one of the creditors. He
kept an attentive eye on me, assuming the air of a close relative.
He was extremely conscientious in answering questions. But he

didn't know me; he didn't know me at all. No, Abdüsselam Bey had never spoken to him of such a diamond. He had once promised him that he would repay him "when things got better." And the old man had once told him, "I am richer than you might imagine." They had known each other for a long time. And indeed Abdüsselam Bey was a rich man. As for the diamond, Naşit Bey went on to say that such an heirloom might exist in an old family of this repute: "A dynasty stretching back a hundred fifty years . . ." And they seemed satisfied that my own intentions in the matter were good. At least that is what they said. My aunt herself had said as much during the trial. My father, she said, had paid little attention to my upbringing. He'd always had his eye on making money; he'd thought of little else. He had even tried to stop my aunt from marrying Naşit Bey, asking Seyit Lutfullah to work his magic on them. So my aunt had said to Naşit Bey, "Yes, let's get married. I absolutely must save Hayri from the grip of his money-grubbing father!" But my aunt had thoroughly despised me from the moment my father, taking advantage of her temporary loss of consciousness, had tried to bury her, using me as an accomplice.

"The truth is the whole family is a little greedy. My wife is the only generous one—she at least is endowed with a humane touch," Naşit Bey said at one point during the trial.

Of course we also heard about the mosque whose construction had been handed down to us by Ahmet Efendi the Some Timer, but the story was horribly mangled in the telling: According to this version, my father had squandered all the money his grandfather had put aside for the mosque.

Naşit Bey paused repeatedly to pull his handkerchief from his pocket and clean the lenses of his spectacles or mop the sweat from his brow. He kept calm, speaking at a slow and steady pace and offering prompt answers, but only when addressed. Even so, he spoke in such a way as to leave a certain ambiguity in the air, as if to invite further interrogation about other family concerns that had yet to be addressed, even as he swore it had never been his intention to bring any of these matters into question in the first place. It was by following this strategy that he was at last able to bring up the temporary death of my aunt. It was like watching a man dispatch a polished object across a smooth table with only the slightest flick of his finger.

Why was Naşit Bey treating me with such hostility? What did he want from me? Why was he so bent on ruining me, and why and where had he mustered such ambition? It was beyond comprehension. His speech sent me spinning. But even before he so much as opened his mouth, I could feel my blood coursing through my body, robbing me of all peace. I had, I suppose, been undone by his cold and clever calculations, his ironclad determination.

Then something snapped. I felt instantly lighter, as if relieved of an immense burden, as if layer upon layer of worry had suddenly evaporated. From the very beginning of this bizarre and absurd trial, I had been expecting—and dreading—a change of heart along just these lines. This lightness in my soul—this impertinent indifference—signaled the opening of a door that had remained tightly shut since my marriage to Emine.

It was as if Naşit Bey had deliberately set out to pull Emine away from the door she had been guarding with such angelic vigilance. So the moment he finished speaking, I called out in the loudest voice I could possibly muster:

"No, no! My aunt actually died. And she was about to be buried when she came back to life—and now she lives among us as a ghost! She came back from the dead because she couldn't part with her money. If you don't believe me, then ask for a picture and see for yourselves. It's the latest fashion these days, getting your picture taken. Take a good look at these pictures, or summon her here and see her in the flesh. Have a word with her! Then you'll see that what I say is true!"

Everyone was shocked. But what did I care? I couldn't have felt more comfortable. I was calm, and there was a lightness in my soul. The others were all clinging to their own particular version of the truth, bending time to suit their purposes; I saw no reason not to follow suit.

I continued:

"As for my aunt's humane disposition—well, she said she never again wanted to see my face, never mind allow me to pay her a visit. She never lets anyone visit her. And she's never loved anyone. She's a mean and ill-tempered woman, a slave to her whims and desires. So afraid that someone might rob her, she slept in the coal cellar, with the money she hid there. There was just one man she could bear: this swindler, this profiteer who got fat on the war . . . She even tolerated his beanpole of a daughter."

And then I added:

"His original plan was to foist her on me. But I refused: I couldn't bear the sight of her. Back then, Naşit Bey was poorer than I was. But now that he's rich, he's suddenly become my enemy. Probably because he knows that when my aunt dies, her entire fortune will go to me."

I still blush when I think back on all this. Naşit Bey had turned me into a man I didn't recognize. At that moment I gladly would have been turned into a snake, just so I could lash out and bite him. Though such metamorphosis was denied me, I could at least stab my finger at him as I cried:

"War profiteer! Soap and sugar smuggler! What do you want from me?"

Another rumble of dissent from the crowd. The hearing went to a recess. Naşit Bey flashed me a saccharine smile before leaving the hall. I had given him everything he wanted, in fact even more.

Fifteen minutes later they announced that I was to be sent to the Department of Justice Medical Facility.

This is where I came to meet Dr. Ramiz. When they took me into the office, he was waiting for me with the director of the facility. He gave my story the utmost attention, declaring an interest in my case and accepting me as a patient. After leaving the director, we went straight to the doctor's office. At the time the medical institute was in one of the annexes of the Dolmabahçe Palace. Dr. Ramiz's office was in the basement. It was a narrow and depressing little room whose only window looked at the garden wall. Against one wall of the office was a sink with a leaking faucet. Upon entering the room, Dr. Ramiz went straight to the sink and washed his hands, while I stood in the corner, contemplating my fate.

On my way over to Dolmabahçe I'd caught a glimpse of the sea, and for just a moment I was pulled away from the fate to which I had become accustomed, losing myself in those deep-blue waters, awash in the glow of the autumn sun.

My thoughts were in disarray. My wife, my children, and my home seemed a million miles away, lost to me forever.

Once again I was seized by the fear that had haunted me throughout the proceedings. What if they involved my wife? It was strange that the judge had kept her out of the trial. This gave me hope. I took it to mean that he didn't take the accusations against me seriously. But if that was the case, then why had he sent me here? No, he was just buying time. Soon enough they would entangle Emine in this infernal web. Though ten days had passed since my detention, I was able to visit with my wife in the courtyard before I was taken away—her arms tightly wrapped around my neck, her eyes drawn, her cheeks hollow, her voice hoarse, her hands burning with fever. I thought of her as I stood before the window, studying the last flowers of the season, dusty and forlorn, at the base of the garden wall, struggling to stay alive but surrounded by misery. A bee buzzed lazily over my head and landed on the window screen, a few inches from my nose. Cries of pain and anguish echoed through the building: Never before had I heard such sounds. Ramiz Bey had finished washing his hands and was now busy dousing them with the lemon cologne he had taken out of his bag.

There was a knock at the door; a warden opened it and suddenly the screams from down the hall were much louder.

"Salim Bey says we're to open the body. Aren't you coming?"

My entire body shuddered in fear. Vigorously shaking his cologne-soaked hand, Ramiz Bey replied:

"No, I'm busy here. Have them boil the intestines. I'll come have a look later."

Then he turned to me.

"There's been a case of poisoning, or rather we suspect as much."

Once again he picked up his briefcase. It was made of yellow leather, with a handsome and intricate interior, and there was a lock on the outside. It soon became apparent that my future friend never carried any of his personal effects on him, keeping them instead in this briefcase; and each time he replaced an item he had just used, he would close and lock the case with considerable haste. He took out a packet of cigarettes and offered me one. Then he took one for himself. I searched for my matchbox but couldn't find it, so he lit both our cigarettes before ordering coffee from the warden, who was still standing at the door.

Dr. Ramiz was a young man, somewhere in his thirties, slightly taller than average, with a light-olive complexion and a physique bordering on plump. His large, vacant eyes were pitch black. But on first looking at him you didn't notice his eyes or his rather ordinary face. You were nevertheless left feeling that there was something about it that wasn't right. Then, as you came to know him, you began to see how badly put together it all was, with his overgrown forehead, his overly symmetrical bone structure, and, last but not least, his chin, which ended abruptly, like a fugitive struggling to break free of its unnatural contours. And it was the same with his voice: he would start off in a bizarre and articulated accent that trailed off into a kind of muttering, until finally it vanished into nothingness. For some reason it conjured up spirals made of uneven curves, and so, too, did his face.

Dr. Ramiz had just returned from his studies in Vienna. Later I heard from just about everyone that he was a respected doctor whose reputation rested on diplomas of distinction. His specialty was psychoanalysis, which he'd practiced at various institutions for several years.

Even that first day I could see that Dr. Ramiz was interested in psychoanalysis less as a means of treatment for individual patients than as a science that might remake the world in its image, a road to salvation that rivaled the established religions. To him, this new science was everything: crime, murder, disease, greed, poverty, misery, misfortune, congenital disabilities, and archrivals—these things didn't exist. No living hell lay beyond the reason of man's will. There was only psychoanalysis. Sooner or later everything came back to it. With this one humble key, he proposed to explain all life's mysteries.

Returning to his homeland, he had been refused both the position and the funding he would need to cure the entire nation with his miraculous practice and, by the time we met, resentment had seeped into almost every aspect of his person.

Dr. Ramiz's great passion for social issues served only to feed his anger. After speaking with him for several hours, or rather suffering his complaints, his analyses of social ills, and his assorted musings on the future, I could neither imagine nor indeed genuinely wish for a world in which all might attain happiness through work befitting their person or capacity.

And so it was on that first day that I realized Dr. Ramiz was the incarnation of discontent. Although possessed of a fine arsenal of bons mots—words and phrases like "adolescence," "domestic issues," "public education," "production," and, in particular, "activity," were forever trickling out of his mouth— he was the kind of man who never could apply himself to a task for very long and who was only content when complaining or occupying himself with mandatory tasks, which is why, despite a fine position and a fixed place in society, he saw himself as a miserable and mistreated man with a dim future. Perhaps he took a liking to me and offered his protection because he saw in me another sorrowful outcast. Since his return from Vienna, he had, in his bitterness, swept his life empty of friends.

Still standing, we began to discuss the current state of the nation. More than ready to see the world through rose-colored glasses—provided, of course, I could first extract myself from the trouble that had befallen me—I nevertheless understood little of what the doctor said. But slowly I learned how to follow his line of thinking. He liked nothing at all about our country. The mind-set of its people was démodé. Young men like him (and me!) were denied the opportunity to advance ourselves. We had only to consider my own situation to see how bad things really were in this country of ours. Was this the kind of treatment a man of my caliber deserved? Since his return from Vienna two years ago, Dr. Ramiz had indeed been unable to practice psychoanalysis. Now, for the first time, he had a patient. As a "case" I was extremely important, and thank God for that. I was at least a goodly source of consolation.

In Europe, however—in particular in Vienna and in Germany—
the situation was quite different. There they had a respect for
specialization; for them, psychoanalysis was as fundamental as
their daily bread.

When our coffees arrived, Dr. Ramiz moved to the head of the
table and had me sit directly opposite him. He then opened his
briefcase once again and took out his cigarettes. After we each lit
one, he placed the pack back in his briefcase and locked it.

"No, they don't like me very much here," he said. "They use
such antiquated methods that . . . But anyway, it's not really my
place. I'm doing my mandatory service. But now they've
assigned me to you. The director promised: 'If a suitable case
comes along . . .'"

How clear it was from that moment. Our fates were entwined
for all eternity!

Following his explanation of the situation at hand, we briefly
returned to the topic of Vienna and the Teutonic nations.
Together we pined for their order and beneficence.

When we had finished our coffees, he stood up and pushed
our cups aside.

"Now tell me what's happened," he said.

He allowed me to lead the discussion. I briefly explained the
case to him. Then he asked me to explain my entire life story.
He took notes on a piece of paper in front of him as I spoke. He
paid special attention to my childhood and asked me to repeat
almost everything I told him. He was particularly taken by the
Blessed One, and asked endless questions about the old clock,
always using the name my mother had given it.

"What was it like?" he asked.

"An enormous grandfather clock . . . of very high quality, old
English workmanship, purchased during the reign of Sultan
Abdülmecid. But broken. My wife has it up in the attic. But it's
still possible for you to see it, if you'd like. It produces the most
wonderful sounds."

And I gazed into his eyes, hopeful that he might wish to buy
our clock. It wouldn't have been the end of the world had he
done so. When I was in the detention center, one of the guards
told me about a well-heeled Jew in the adjacent cell who had

sold to an Iranian from Benderbouchir a sunken ship salvaged
in Lisbon; and the guard had even received his commission in
advance. I might do the same myself. Finally, no longer able to
resist, I cried out: "I'll give it to you for a fine price. And if you
like, we can go have a look at it right now!"

This was of course for my benefit. I was speaking directly
from the heart and only could think, "Oh, if he shows enough
interest, we'll go back to my home where I'll fill my eyes with
the sight of Emine pumping water from the well in the courtyard, and I'll wash my face with its waters and sing children's
songs with Zehra . . ."

"Didn't you say it was broken?"

"Broken? Just in need of a little repair!"

He thought for a moment:

"Yes, of course, that must be it . . ."

But what was it that must be? I couldn't quite understand
what he meant. Nuri Efendi said a watch or clock should
always be in working order, in fact it should never stop at all. I
shrugged my shoulders. When would our conversation return
to my present situation? Perhaps never. After many hours had
passed, Dr. Ramiz moved the subject to my father. And after
my father, it was my mother, and after my mother, Nuri Efendi.
He was curious to know about all my acquaintances. And then
he zeroed in on the story of the mosque that Ahmet the Signer
had never found the wherewithal to build.

"Was this mosque discussed often at home?"

"No," I said. "Or at least not very often. Whenever my father
had the slightest hope of a little money coming his way, he
might bring it up. Otherwise he'd never let anyone even mention it. Actually the clock reminded him of the mosque, so he
harbored rather hostile feelings toward it."

"Which clock?"

"The big one."

"You mean the Blessed One? But why don't you use its
proper name?" he scolded me. "When something has a name,
it should be addressed with that name."

Saddened that I had overlooked this simple truth, and delighted that he had discovered a new aphorism, I let the discus-

sion return to the Blessed One. The doctor presented me with a steady stream of questions, and I explained everything as best I could remember, innocent of what lay ahead:

"One night we were all sitting together at home when suddenly the clock began to chime. My father flew into a rage. 'Enough!' he shrieked. 'You know just like everyone else that I'm broke. It's simply impossible right now. We can barely get by as it is. Things are not like they used to be. Why do you keep harassing me?'"

"He said all this to the Blessed One?"

"Yes, I mean, I suppose so . . . I don't know!"

"Yes, it must be . . . A very interesting case indeed . . . Extremely typical, but, then again, just as rare. Thank you very much. Thank you very much indeed . . ."

The man was thanking me for having gotten myself into this sorry state.

"And those were the man's very words, right?"

His attentions and intentions were evident from head to toe as he peered into my face. "I will most certainly write a report about this for the congress . . . Now, tell me again what you just said a moment ago?"

I went over the episode again.

"This is a rare case of tremendous significance—one might almost call it a taboo encircled by a web of complexes. But similar cases have been documented."

And he told me how infertile women on a Javanese island, or some such place, were in the custom of visiting an ancient cannon that their people venerated as a prophet, tying strips of cloth to it in the hope of curing their condition. Hoping to change the subject, I said:

"We have similar stories too. The old war ship *Mahmudiye* was like that. You know, the one that supposedly had three hulls? At night the ship sailed by stealth across the Black Sea to attack Sebastopol, unloading its cannons on the bastions and returning before morning. My father remembers it well. The inside was as large as the Selimiye Barracks—"

"It was inside your house?" he asked me.

Was he daydreaming, or did he just assume I was completely out of my mind? Or even more terrifying . . .

"No, no!" I cried. "In our country. I mean, it was in Istanbul."

And so I tried my best to articulate my thoughts clearly so as to prove I was sane.

"How could such a battleship ever fit inside a house? You would need something the size of Hagia Sophia to hold such an enormous vessel."

"Hagia Sophia?"

I saw now where I had gone wrong.

"I mean, these are merely figures of speech," I said. And without allowing him a chance to speak, I returned to my story.

He listened with grave attention, all the while taking notes. Then, thanking me once again, he offered his opinion:

"This, too, is extremely interesting, but rather different. Which is to say, it's something else entirely . . ."

At various points in our discussion he stopped to clean his fingernails with the pocketknife he'd taken from his briefcase. When he finished the job, I was sure he'd pass the knife to me, which really wouldn't have been all that bad, seeing as the best thing to do would be to fiddle with something, anything to keep my mind off the absurdity of my situation. But he didn't offer me the knife, instead placing it back in his briefcase before we doused ourselves in more lemon cologne. Then out came the cigarette pack all over again, and I could bear it no longer.

"Doctor," I cried. "Why not just keep all these things out on the table?"

For a moment terror overtook me, but then he smiled softly and said, "It's easier this way."

The doctor's conception of ease was no different from my stepmother's conception of happiness. Ah, humankind . . .

"You are quite a wonderful fellow, Hayri Bey. If only we had met in Vienna."

And of course we went right back to talking about Vienna—Dr. Ramiz's beloved city always took precedence over my case. Then we turned to a more inauspicious topic of discussion.

"The Blessed One was quite important for your mother, wasn't he?"

"I suppose."

"Try to remember."

He was looking me straight in the eye again.

"Perhaps what I mean to say is, it was a quirky old clock with its own strange moods. It had a whimsical—or, rather, idiosyncratic—way of working, though perhaps that was only because it was broken. And the things it would do in its different moods—well, we found them rather strange."

As I spoke, his face radiated joy, and he nodded eagerly as he listened. Then he read over his notes.

"Strange, quirky, odd, strange moods, idiosyncratic, whimsical, the things it could do . . . That's right, isn't it? Very interesting . . . And then?"

"That's it."

By then I had had enough. What about my examination? He had made absolutely no mention of it.

"Yes, I'm listening. And your mother?"

"In the end she was terribly frightened of the clock. You know the type, from the older generation—she was a superstitious woman."

"There's no such thing as old or new in our field. The most primitive person is no different from ourselves. Conscious and unconscious lives are the same anywhere. Psychoanalysis . . ."

And that was how the word I would hear so often for the rest of my life popped out of his mouth and plopped down before me like a soft-boiled egg.

He got up.

"We'll continue tomorrow. Now let's make sure you get some rest! Has your bed arrived?"

"My wife's sending it over."

"Well, that's good, then. You'll sleep here in this room. You'd only be bored in the reformatory, and uncomfortable. I'll have a word with the director about it."

He seemed distraught.

"They don't like me here. They never listen to what I have to say. But seeing that you are now my patient . . ."

"But, Doctor, I'm not ill. Now you know everything. And still you believe I am ill?"

Without listening to me in the slightest, he left the room.

I stood there, thinking for a while as I watched him leave.

I dashed to the sink to splash water on my face. The discussion had worn me out. The doctor had left the door open, and a cold draft blew into the room, carrying with it painful cries, sharper now and all the more horrifying. What was going on? Were these the voices of the truly insane? Or were they just patients? That man who had come in earlier had said something about opening a cadaver. I wondered if they'd started dissecting. Perhaps they were just now closing it up! The doctor hadn't shut the door behind him. Perhaps they hadn't closed the body. But why were they opening it in the first place? Suddenly I was overwhelmed with a desperate desire to flee. I fearfully stepped out of the office, heading in the direction from which I assumed we had come. As I tiptoed down the corridor, the screams grew only louder. This can't be the way, I said to myself. But it was as if the screams were drawing me to them. There were voices behind a half-opened door. I poked my head in and then instantly leapt back, my entire body trembling in fear. No, they hadn't finished closing it up. I turned on my heels, scrambled back to the office, slammed the door shut, and hunkered down in my chair.

Dr. Ramiz returned a little later, his face lit with joy.

"It's done. At first there were difficulties, but I explained that you were a patient with problems that pertain to my field in particular, and they finally agreed."

"But, Doctor, I'm not ill. Good God! I've told you everything."

Again he fixed his eyes on mine and stopped me, his voice full of resolve.

"You are ill. It is the fate we all share since the birth of psychoanalysis."

"Well, then what difference is there between me and the people who are free?"

"That's another matter. I shall be looking after you from now on."

"Well, then what's going to happen?"

"We'll treat you. Besides, yours is not a very difficult case. In such cases the diagnosis is almost tantamount to treatment. Which is to say that if we follow a tight schedule we should be able to finish in a few years."

I was beside myself.

"A few years? I need your report, Doctor. My wife is ill. You can see clearly by just looking at her face that she's ill. You must get me out of here as soon as possible."

"That's another matter, which we've already covered."

Then he changed direction.

"You'll spend the evenings here, where you'll be comfortable. Don't wander about the building. Try not to think too much. And no cigarettes—they're forbidden. I promised the director there would be no smoking in the evenings."

Not long after Dr. Ramiz had left, one of my neighbors arrived with my bedroll and some food. Emine had not been able to come herself, but she hadn't forgotten a thing.

From the following day on, Dr. Ramiz occupied himself exclusively with my case. Now he was interested in my dreams. Who knows, perhaps it was just my nature not to have many dreams? But like anyone else, I did occasionally have strange dreams that you might call nightmares. I described everything and anything I could remember.

On the fourth day Dr. Ramiz changed his method of treatment. The curtains were drawn, and I was asked to lie down on a sofa facing the wall. He no longer asked me questions but rather invited me to say anything and everything that came to mind. And so I kept speaking. I kept speaking under the impression that in so doing I was deceiving him. But the hold he had on me slowly began to tighten. It was as if my thoughts had been drawn into a dark cellar, a cellar from which it was impossible to escape. Then suddenly a word, a memory, would light up like a window thrown open in the darkness. I was walking directly toward it. When he pulled back the curtains I'd be utterly exhausted. And we continued like this, day in and day out, until the end.

My despair and frustration were driving me mad, but Emine never forgot me; she would either come to see me herself or find someone to come in her place. All in all, I became quite comfortable. I found a way to fill those previously vacant hours: I began repairing watches for the institute's staff, starting with the director's. And so the man gradually took a liking to me.

From time to time, he'd call me to his office, and we would sit and chat. He was particularly interested in the story of the Şerbetçibaşı Diamond.

"You know, if something like that were in my hands . . . I mean, if the name's anything to go by, the thing must be the size of a walnut. And why not, Hayri Bey . . . ? Just hold on for a few more days until Ramiz Bey finishes his report."

Just as I was stepping out the door, he called me back and fished a watch out from one of his vest pockets. Handing it to me, he said, "I almost forgot. This is my wife's. It hasn't been working properly for some time. If you could just have a look at it . . ."

The following day the warden brought me a "friend's watch." Some of these I repaired, but on many occasions I could only diagnose the problem and prescribe a fix, as I didn't have adequate equipment at hand. In the meantime, my psychoanalytic treatment continued unabated.

I was suspicious of the light that flashed in the director's eyes whenever Dr. Ramiz's name came up in our conversations, but I never could muster the courage to ask about my situation. How could I possibly risk saying anything that might compromise a man so good-hearted? But the clock was ticking, and I truly began to despair. Emine became weaker and more desperate every day. Since my detainment, she had been bearing our terrible burden alone. I had to stop work when the trial began, and we were now on the verge of utter poverty. Ten days after I was committed for treatment, Dr. Ramiz cut me off abruptly during one of our discussions.

"So we have finished with stage one," he announced.

He paced about the room a few times, then stopped in front of me and placed his hand on my shoulder.

"Yes. I have determined your illness. What you have is a typical case of a father complex. Apparently you never liked the man. But this isn't too grave. This may in fact provide the quickest path to maturity. But you have succeeded in something far more fascinating."

I was wringing my hands, and my temples were covered in sweat.

"Doctor, please!"

"Now, there's no need for that. Your condition has been diagnosed. I had in fact already stumbled upon the possibility of such an illness while listening to your life story. It became more evident to me in your dreams. And today I saw it all with great clarity. It is impossible that I have erred in my diagnosis."

My very soul was atremble as I listened.

"Then what do I have, Doctor?"

"A grave illness . . . , which could have been worse. And there's certainly no need for you to be alarmed, for this is something we can address easily. A typical case, but harmless . . ."

He stepped away from me and pulled out a chair from the other end of the room as if he might crouch down behind it. Leaning against the back of it, he continued:

"As I said, your father, you don't like the man, apparently you never did."

"For goodness sake, Doctor!"

"Listen to me. Please try to listen. You never liked your father, and instead of eventually taking his place, you have never stopped looking for new father figures. In other words, you never fully matured. You're simply still a child! Wouldn't you agree?"

I leapt out of my chair. This was surely going too far. It was clearly slanderous, perfidious, not to mention cruel; in one fell swoop he had rendered me an outcast from society.

"Such a thought would never cross my mind. And never did. That's ridiculous, sheer nonsense! Why would I look for another father? I'm the man's son whether I like it or not. How could I deny my own father?"

"Sadly, this is just the case. It's been like this all your life. This is the source of the continuing confusion in your life, at work, and in your sense of self."

I looked around the room in utter bewilderment. No one was there to rescue me from this terrible situation. If I was going to get out of it, I'd have to do it myself. So I rallied all my strength.

"Look, Doctor," I began, "there's nothing wrong with me. I just have bad luck. I always end up embroiled in the most unseemly scenarios. And I don't know where this bad luck will take me next. Now I find myself stuck in this absurd situation. And why? I spoke out when there was no need. One little word dropped from my mouth, and around it they concocted an entire fairy tale. And they went as far as to make it my ruination. Sadly, I'm the victim of a lie that I myself devised. How could I have done such a thing? Why did I do such a thing? I really don't know. But that's just how it happened. I just rambled on and on . . . Nothing more than that. Perhaps I'm no different from all the rest of humankind combined. We are enslaved by our own stories. But mine was on a different scale—for I ended up paying dearly for it, and my children and my wife are paying for it too. Try to understand me. These people simply thrust it all upon me. There's really nothing else to it . . ."

If I had thought it possible, I would have thrown myself on the floor and groveled at his feet. This was how I saw myself throughout my tirade. I wanted to embrace something, to beg and plead, until everyone, even fate itself, believed me.

"Calm yourself, Hayri Bey," he kept saying. But I continued.

"It's a lie. Please understand. An insignificant, simple lie. A joke!"

I tried to pull myself together and explain.

"Simply take out the lie and nothing's there—I'd be saved. I'm not sick at all. If you're looking for someone who is, well, there's my wife! I'm terribly worried about her—she's very ill. She looked dreadful the other day. She wasn't that bad when I left home, but as for myself, I'm absolutely fine! A man in perfect health."

Oh, the sound of my voice then. How well I know that voice and the way it makes my entire body heave. How many times in my life have I woken up from dreams with this same fear inside me, with this voice wet with tears still ringing in my ears? Fear. Fear and man, fear and man's destiny, the struggle of man against man, and needless hostility. But who was I fooling? To whom could I explain myself? For what can a man ever really convey? What grief can one man truly share with another? The stars might speak to one another, but man can never communicate with man.

The worst of it was that Ramiz Bey had no intention of trying to understand what I was saying, let alone even listen. He was interested only in my illness, or, rather, his diagnosis. And really, why would I ever disavow my own father?

"Please stay calm," he said. "Unfortunately you don't like the man but not liking someone doesn't mean rejecting him out of hand. You're rather mixed up about the whole thing. The confusion began with the Blessed One. Its past exerted an exalted and sacred stranglehold on your home. Domestic values were turned upside down, and your father was relegated to second fiddle."

"The clock!? That wretched thing? A crotchety old clock . . . a family heirloom?"

"Don't you see? Miserable, old, crotchety . . . You continually speak of it as if it's a human being. Pay attention to your words: first 'wretched' and then 'old.' What I mean is that first you spoke of it as if it were a human being, and then you caught yourself and said it was 'old,' as if to characterize it as just a piece of furniture. But you weren't entirely satisfied with that word, and so you added the word 'crotchety' . . ." He riffled through his notes. "On the first day you used the following words and phrases: 'strange,' 'bizarre disposition,' 'flights of fancy,' 'idiosyncratic,' and 'those things it would always do.'"

"And?"

"In other words, you spent your childhood in a home dominated by this clock. Even your father was jealous of it. Although your mother named it the Blessed One, your father called it the Calamity. I'm surprised the man never smashed it to pieces, because your father realized the danger it presented well before you did."

"But he never wanted to smash the thing. He wanted to sell it."

Delighted, the doctor bounced out of his seat. I'd supplied him with yet another piece of evidence for his case.

"So he wanted it out of the house."

I bowed my head. It was true. My father behaved as if the clock was a bitter rival, and he would often moan, "The thing never leaves me alone. Oh, the Calamity has practically taken over my home."

Again I rallied my strength and began to explain. What else was there for me to do?

"Doctor, please! All this is quite unreasonable. Just because the poor man let a few words slip . . . No one could really be jealous of a clock. Have you ever seen someone jealous of an object? I could understand if it were a person . . . but why would someone be jealous of their own property? Perhaps they might find it distasteful or become tired of it or throw it away— sell it, burn it, smash it to bits, but . . ."

"And then there's Nuri Efendi, Seyit Lutfullah, and Abdüs-selam Bey."

"Nuri was my master, and the best man I've ever known. Lutfullah was a hopeless madman, but I was always amused by his words and actions. I liked him as I might like a fairy tale. As for Abdüsselam, the man was very kind to me."

"Yes, but they all fit into different periods of your life. You followed a different man at each stage in your life."

Panic slowly welled up inside me. Was that really the case? There's no doubt I was in some way attached to all these men. Dr. Ramiz suddenly and quite mercilessly interrupted my thoughts:

"How do you explain Abdüsselam naming your first child?"

I held up my hands and once again implored him to return to reason and logic, the only sound approach to all this.

"Have mercy, Doctor, a little mercy . . . It was a matter of courtesy, for I was living in his home. He had been so kind to me on so many other occasions. He was my benefactor. So call it whatever you like: a blessing, an act of piety to the man, or as the elders call it 'an auspicious consecration.'"

"So, in a word, he was a father to you. And you wholeheart-edly accepted him as such. You accepted him to such an extent that you even allowed the poor man to give your daughter his mother's name."

"And that is my fault? He gave her the name—and by mistake."

"Naturally you were the one who thrust the role upon him. A matter of influence . . . You're a powerful man, Hayri Bey, or, rather, a powerful patient."

By this point all my resistance was broken. There was nothing I could do but stare at him, transfixed by his interpretation. It was the same way I had, for days, stared at everyone in the courtroom in utter surprise. In the same state of mind I had cried, "How can these people actually believe all this?" I suppose it is this state of shock in the face of our fellow human beings that prevents us from going mad several times a day.

Snuffing out my cigarette, I stood up.

"Don't you think this has all gone too far, Doctor?" I asked. "True, I was never a great admirer of my father. He had such strange moods. He was cantankerous, and he spoke too much, and he had no self control. All in all, he wasn't the kind of man anyone really loved, respected, or, for that matter, held in much esteem. He'd had bad luck—that was certain. But he was still my father. I pitied him even if I didn't love him. He had such a soft and battered soul . . . To look for someone to replace him, and so many years after he passed away? Now, maybe if I *were* my mother, I might be able to choose another man for myself . . ." He gestured for me to sit down.

"This is true, quite true . . . But what can be done? Such is your condition. Your own words indicate as much. Didn't you say the deceased was not the kind of man to be loved, respected, or esteemed? Yet a father should always be loved—should be someone who is always respected. This is the case whether you like it or not. You see, you aren't at all envious of your father, but normally a father is envied. Things would be quite different if there were envy. But you were never envious of your father."

"What aspect of the man could I envy?"

Every time I spoke, the doctor's smile took on new shades of meaning.

"You were never envious of him because you never found anything of merit in the man! Now, now—there's no need to panic. These kinds of conditions are found in almost everyone. You're just a little late in this regard. You still haven't become a father. But when you do, all this will pass."

"I never became a father?! But I have two children. I even named the second child myself. Goodness me, I was the one who decided on the name Ahmet."

"Because Abdüsselam Bey is now dead. But with the death of your father you should have achieved a certain freedom or maturity. The question now is how to free yourself of the consequences of this complex. Yet as the complex exists in the subconscious mind it's insignificant, as long as it remains the same—insignificant and in fact entirely natural, especially in today's society. For in today's world almost all of us suffer from this condition. Just look around: we all complain about the past; everyone is preoccupied with it. This is why we seek to change it. What does this mean? A father complex, no? Don't we all, both young and old, wrestle with this very condition? Observe our obsession with the Hittites and Phrygians and God knows what other ancient tribes. Is this anything but a deep father complex?"

I stood up again. I wanted to flee, but our coffees had just arrived and so I sat down.

"Isn't this enough for today?" I begged.

"No, sit down and listen. You know well enough that psychoanalysis . . ."

I lowered my head and opened my arms.

"But Doctor, whatever could I possibly know about it? I'm an uneducated man. You've heard my life story ten times over. I never really went to school. My father never demanded anything of me. He never forced me to go to school."

I suddenly stopped. I was giving myself away again. I was yet again speaking unfavorably of my father. I tried to change the topic.

"All I know is a bit of this and that about watches and clocks, nothing more!"

Of course once I mentioned clocks, the Blessed One and my supposed second father, the late Nuri Efendi, came to mind, and I went quiet. This father complex was a terrible thing. It could stop you from speaking at all.

Thank God, Dr. Ramiz wasn't listening. He never really did.

"Yes, I know all this . . . I'm aware. But you mustn't worry. Do you think anything would be different if you had completed your studies? If you do not understand psychoanalysis, then everything is . . ."

He thought for a moment, opened his briefcase, and took out his cigarettes. He offered me one and then lit his own before locking the pack back in his briefcase.

Why doesn't he keep them in his pocket? I thought angrily. Then I felt angry with myself. I had contracted the most ridiculous disease in the world, and here I was worrying about other people.

Dr. Ramiz looked at me with something akin to compassion.

"Best would be to start from the beginning. I will teach you the basics. Psychoanalysis—"

"Have mercy, gracious no! Fire! Anything but psychoanalysis . . ."

My first lesson continued until nightfall. Before he left he gave me one of his conference papers published in German. That night, as I lay on my bedroll, I began mulling over everything that had befallen me. It was nearing the end of the second week, and still there was no sign of a report. And even worse, I'd seemingly just enrolled in a course on psychoanalysis. I picked up the publication; it was written in that horrible language, German. But had it been composed in my dear native tongue, what would I have understood? I tucked it under my pillow, thinking the subject matter might be revealed to me in a dream.

The following day I was informed I had a visitor. It was Emine. Her face was even paler than before, and her cheeks were drawn. She looked at me hopefully, but she could hardly hold back her tears. I tried to seem cheerful so as to offer some consolation.

"Haven't you been released yet?" she asked.

"No," I said. "We've just begun. I had my first lesson yesterday."

"Lesson? Have you lost your mind?"

"Just a lesson really. I'm studying psychoanalysis!"

I gave her a brief account of what had happened. It was heartbreaking to see the shadow of a smile pass over her face beneath her teary eyes. She understood the absurdity of the situation but didn't have the heart to laugh.

"Are these people mad?" she asked. "This is all we need at a time like this."

Then in consolation she said, "There's no such condition. Don't pay any attention to them! Just say, 'yes, of course, sir,' and get them to write the report! Beg them, pretend you're sane, or you're insane, whatever you have to do. Just get yourself out of here!"

That day Ramiz Bey said nothing about my report. He did however continue his lecture on psychoanalysis. Only, this time he began to explain the science using everyday analogies. And so everything went a little haywire: on the one hand, I knew I really didn't understanding anything, yet I supposed there were a few things I did comprehend. At one point he brought up the conference paper he'd left with me the night before.

"Did you have a look at it?" he asked.

"But how could I? I don't know a word of German. And even if I did, this is advanced science."

"Ah, of course," he mumbled. "I forgot about that. Not to worry. I'll just explain it all to you."

Thank God this time the memory of a German girl he had met at the conference waylaid his lecture, and from the girl we moved on to her friend who was a nurse. Throughout his musings he never stopped opening and closing his briefcase. He would take out his cigarettes and then promptly lock them up. A little later he would do the same with his English pocketknife: he would open the briefcase all over again, rummage through it, pull out the knife, and begin cleaning under his fingernails. Later it was the cologne, which of course needed to be extracted from the briefcase before he could douse his hands with its lemony vapors. Meanwhile all the young girls he'd ever known were paraded before our eyes: one connected to the next like the cars on a funicular moving up and down a mountainside. At close to two in the afternoon he told me he had important business to attend to and left.

The next day we occupied ourselves entirely with my dreams. This time the doctor behaved as if he'd never known a single woman in Germany. Quite unlike the day before, he was irritable and tired. There were bulging purple bags under his eyes; maybe he hadn't slept much the night before. And perhaps, aggravated and tired, he wasn't pleased with any of the dreams

I recounted. He accused me of not having the kinds of dreams that someone like me—who didn't like his father and who replaced him with anyone suitable who came along—should have.

"How can this be? It's inconceivable that an individual like you hasn't had a single dream that befits your condition. You might at least try a little harder."

And with this last pronouncement, he began a new stage in my treatment. That day he was silent until evening, angrily pacing the room, virtually ignoring me before coming to a sudden stop in front of me and intoning, in the most imperious voice he could muster:

"I want you to have dreams that are more in line with your illness. Do you understand me? Use everything in your power to try and have the right kind of dreams. First you must free yourself of symbols. Once you see your father's true face in your dreams, everything will change, and from there everything will fall into place."

"I always see the true face of my father in my dreams. Besides, if it's not his face, then naturally it's not my father but someone else."

"It's not that simple. Such things occur without you commanding them. This is why you need to rally your willpower and do your best to free your father of the symbolic associations he has taken on. When these symbols are removed, it will be that much easier for you to free yourself from him—which is to say, from this inferiority complex you have inherited from him. I shall write you a list of the dreams you shall have this week."

And a few minutes later he handed me a piece of paper.

"But, Doctor, can dreams be ordered up in such way? A prescription for dreams . . . ? This is impossible."

"This is a forward-thinking science, my good friend. No objections allowed!"

All this contributed to my moving that much closer to bona fide insanity, and without recourse to any of the spurious fire and light shows that my lawyer had recommended if I ever needed to prove I was insane. But really I had no choice. It was thanks to my illness that I was not sharing an overcrowded cell with madmen, murderers, and opium addicts and instead spending my days in the company of this intelligent, well-mannered, knowledgeable, warmhearted, and most humane man, having as many cigarettes and cups of coffee as I desired, or, rather, as many as he desired.

Naturally I wanted to give at least something in return for all the kindness the doctor had shown me. So before going to bed I did everything in my power to conjure up thoughts of my father, recalling him in all the various stages of my life. But as if to spite me, he never appeared in my dreams, or if so, only as one of Dr. Ramiz's symbols. I would see in my dreams either a dangerously narrow bridge nearing collapse or a smashed sidewalk covered with mud puddles, or occasionally I was in a little canoe being tossed by rough seas, a pitch-black ferry bearing down on me. I would wake up fearful that I hadn't followed the doctor's orders, and, squeezing my eyes shut, I'd concentrate on my father's face. Having exhausted this method, I would drift back to sleep where—as the doctor put it—I exhibited an absence of self-control and had dreams of a different nature.

The truth was that I couldn't stop worrying about my family's future or Emine's worsening health. Asleep or awake I thought only of Emine. Plagued by visions of misery and chaos that belied my actual state of mind, I would wake up to her pale face and reproachful eyes. Dr. Ramiz was angry with me for this and elaborated on his techniques:

"I am using the very latest methods with you, a personal method I discovered myself. I call it the 'directed dream' method. After diagnosing a patient according to his or her prior dreams, the treatment begins with the examination of subsequent dreams that are strictly guided and controlled. Though you were the patient that inspired the method, you are now showing no effort to help the treatment succeed. What a strange person you are! Have you no willpower whatsoever? Are you concerned only with the present day? Try thinking about your life as a unified whole."

Sadly, I lacked sufficient willpower for the treatment. In fact the problem was universal. But willpower was everything (if nothing else). According to Dr. Ramiz, willpower was the one thing that could be placed alongside psychoanalysis, fit to share a life with it, as a king might share his reign with his queen. All the great philosophers spoke of it, which of course meant all the names came flooding in, names that might be seen as willpower embodied: Nietzsche, Schopenhauer . . . And because Dr. Ramiz assumed I had read them all, he would make vague references to their work and apply models drawn from their books to daily life, to his own life, to my life, and to the matters facing our country; and from there we moved on to German music. According to him—later I learned that most people who had studied in Germany were the same—it was mandatory to be as familiar with Beethoven as with the man who lived around the corner. As for Wagner, well, there was no doubt in his mind that we were both related to the man. We would often finish our discussions by listening to either the "Ode to Joy" from Beethoven's Ninth or the "Grand March" from *Tannhäuser*, followed by the doctor's personal reflections on his past. His reminiscing complete, he would jump to his feet and stand above me like a god poised to create the world out of the abyss, intoning once again that powerful and mysterious word that could save humanity from the void:

"Will!" he boomed. "Do you understand? Will . . . Everything lies in this very word."

And with his raincoat and briefcase tucked under his arm, he would bound out of the room, whistling either the "Grand March" or "Ode to Joy," and leaving me alone with the mysterious word he had entrusted to me.

Alone in the room with my head between my hands, I repeated the words over and over in numb confusion: "Beethoven, Nietzsche, willpower, Schopenhauer, psychoanalysis . . . Oh, words and names and the happiness that comes to us through our belief in them . . ."

That night I was attacked by a lion in my dream. Thank God, I escaped unscathed. In my childhood, well before I became the thief of the Şerbetçibaşı Diamond, a swindler of inheritances, or a patient of Dr. Ramiz, when I was happy and in good health, we would all share at the breakfast table the dreams we had had the night before. That's how I learned that—at least according to the prevailing interpretation of the time—a lion represented justice. The lion I had seen in my dream never touched me, which certainly meant I would be saved. In the morning I greeted Dr. Ramiz with the wonderful news and recounted my dream to him. At first he seemed pleased.

"Yes . . ."

Then he stepped past me without a word, whereupon his expression abruptly changed.

"Is that all?"

"Yes, that's all. I woke up immediately, in a terrible fright, but not without some joy, as a lion symbolizes justice or political power."

But he wasn't listening:

"How unfortunate! You've missed a golden opportunity. What a terrible shame!"

Thinking a little more on the matter, he added: "You should have fed yourself to the lion."

Shivers went down my spine:

"Dear Lord, Doctor!"

"Yes, it's true . . . Or you should have slain the beast and donned its fur. Either way, somehow you should have lost yourself inside the creature so you could be reincarnated later on. Only then would everything be resolved. Haven't you noticed how this works in fairy tales? People get lost . . . they get lost—that is to say, they die before being born anew. There's no more certain way to break free from a complex than this. But you were unable to do so. Indeed you failed to do so. You missed your chance!"

Wringing his hands, he paced the room, sadness and despair written all over his face.

"You were unable to do it. You have ruined all my efforts. You were to be reborn, but you have remained exactly the same."

I did the best I possibly could to console him.

"Please don't be discouraged by this, Doctor. I shall try hard tonight. Besides, the beast never really went away. Perhaps he will return tonight."

"There's no use. With such incompetence . . . don't even bother!"

Then he set his eyes on mine again and with obvious despair said: "My dear friend, let us not deceive each other any longer. You simply do not want to get better! How could the creature ever return? Does the departed ever return?"

He had a point; he must have understood that the lion, just like my father, would never again appear in my dreams.

Nevertheless, the lion had somehow brought me a little peace of mind. A day later Dr. Ramiz asked me, "You said the lion in your dream symbolized justice. What did you mean by that?" And I told him about our old dream-interpretation manuals.

"Our forebears considered the interpretation of dreams to be of the utmost importance. But not as in psychoanalysis, nothing at all like that . . ."

"You mean we have our own manual for dream interpretation?"

"No, no, not just a manual . . . A whole book! With descriptions and analysis for everything you might dream about."

Dr. Ramiz was always charmed by things that were particular to our country, but they troubled him too—not because he had lived abroad for several years, but because they lit up the void he inhabited, suspended between two lives. "That's right, yes. That's right," he muttered, and as he recalled the aforementioned dream-interpretation books, he began nodding his head.

"My dear friend," he said, "it is truly vast, even endless, this treasure trove we've inherited from the people of the past."

Why must we always nod our heads when remembering our ancestors? Was this some kind of custom, a tradition, or a new malady we'd contracted?

That day we talked about the dream-interpretation manuals until evening. Dr. Ramiz planned to write a report on them for a congress to be held in Vienna. Assuring me that I was well versed in the topic, he asked for my help. His opinion of me suddenly had changed: he was no longer my doctor; he no longer saw me as a patient committed to the Department of Justice Medical Facility; we were now just two good friends. Every other moment he slapped me on the back and told me how important it was that we succeed.

Leaving him that evening, I asked which dreams I should have that night. He looked at me with confusion in his eyes. "The paper," he said, "just write the paper! The congress is right around the corner!"

Naturally the paper was never written. But my new friend had inadvertently introduced me to an entirely new field of research. All at once he had recognized the importance of our old practices: onomancy, numerology, alchemy, sensology—the full gamut of Seyit Lutfullah's repertoire (to use the parlance of the theater) and every other bit of hopeless, shoddily conceived science I might find hidden in a vast expanse of old manuscripts. The strangest thing was that he planned to acquire all this learning through me.

"My dear doctor, there are already books covering these topics. A brief wander through the bookstalls in Beyazıt will make that all too clear. You can purchase a stack of such tomes for less than ten liras!"

"But first you must explain it to me. Then of course we shall consult the books. But science, you see, is an oral tradition. Marvel at how I taught you psychoanalysis in only a few days."

Thank God just around that time the judge responsible for my case finally read through my file with a little more care and found that my statements agreed with those of Abdüsselam's daughter and son-in-law, and determined, at least in terms of the articles of the case that applied to me, that enough evidence had been compiled. On one of those days when Dr. Ramiz made no reference to the report he was to write on the condition of my health (so consumed was he by his work in his new field of dream interpretation), the judge came to the miraculous conclusion that I had been cured and was to be acquitted of all charges or, better put, that I was to remain outside the realm of the case.

Good and evil are interchangeable. And they travel in pairs.

The night before my acquittal was announced, I succeeded in conjuring up a dream that would very much have pleased Dr. Ramiz, a dream that will forever cause me to question my personality and that will poison my thoughts each time I remember it.

V

I dreamt I was in the laboratory behind Aristidi Efendi's pharmacy. Almost everyone I knew was there—Nuri Efendi, Seyit Lutfullah, Abdüsselam Bey and his eldest son, and Dr. Ramiz—and they were all eagerly observing one of Aristidi Efendi's experiments. But was it the laboratory or the children's room in our home? I couldn't see the enormous heap of furniture, the mirrors, dressers, or cradles. Yet somehow it was the children's room and the laboratory at the same time. And all those people weren't really there, but I knew they were—I knew we were all there together, for suddenly we were all peering into that strange mirror that startled me whenever I crept into the children's room at night, the light from the corridor revealing my reflection in the glass. The alembic and the mirror had become one, or was it that the tube was bubbling inside the frame? A terra-cotta-colored mixture was boiling furiously in the alembic, and a blackish cloud of smoke with veins the color of sulfur swelled up and down inside the tube.

I heard a shout beside me:

"They're about to separate. Watch out!"

And with ever-increasing agitation, we stared at the mud- and earth-colored cloud of smoke hovering above the alembic as it coiled like some strange creature.

Suddenly I heard Seyit Lutfullah's voice.

"Aha! That's it . . . It's done!"

And just then a bright-green light flashed above the alembic, and the black cloud collapsed inside the tube like a clod of mud. A feathery vapor rose slowly from the center of the sulfurous light. My heart pounding in fear, I leaned over as far as I could, as if I were stepping into the mirror.

"That's it . . . Oh yes! Now, now . . . ," Lutfullah cried, and then continued with his strange incantations.

My heart was still racing and it seemed as if somehow I knew what was about to happen. I begged him: "Don't do it. Abort the plan. Don't do it!"

Suddenly the white cloud changed shape, and I saw Emine's face, her hair aflame in the sulfurous cloud, her lips pale, and her eyes open wide. "Save me!" she cried. I tried to leap toward the alembic or the mirror, but I couldn't move; it seemed like hundreds of hands were holding me down, and I just couldn't move. Horrified, torn by love and despair and pity, half-crazed, I struggled to reach her, and I begged them to let me go.

"Save me, save me," Emine gasped.

And Seyit Lutfullah turned to me and said, "Oh no, and after all that effort . . ." Then he threw himself at me, shouting, "Stop! Stop!"

They all had a hold on me. Inside the alembic, with her eyes wide with fear and her hair in flames, Emine was still begging me to help her. I was desperately struggling to reach her, but Seyit Lutfullah's hands had latched onto me like hooks. How many did he have? What a terrible hold he had on me! It was as if every piece of my body were clamped in a vice. I couldn't breathe; I felt like I was suffocating. "Let me go! Let me go!" I begged as I wrestled to get free. But I knew they'd never let go, that I'd never be able to free myself from them. Still I struggled and flailed about desperately. "She's gone. Oh, I'm finished. Let me go!" I cried.

The image of Emine in the mirror had begun to change.

A moment later nothing but her two eyes remained—two eyes staring straight at me, wide with fear. Two enormous terrified and accusing eyes bore into me through a continuous swirl of harsh, pale-green light, mouthing the words, "This is all your fault." They were Emine's eyes.

Then I saw something more horrifying still. A great gust of wind sent everything flying up into the air, and in less than an instant the roof was blown off the house and the walls collapsed and we were all swept away by the wind.

A little later I found myself walking down a hill in the darkness of night. Dr. Ramiz was beside me. He was mumbling something as he led me, his arm in mine, down the cliff. At the bottom there was a brightly illuminated house. But I knew that the road ahead of us was long and that even if I did reach the end, it wouldn't matter. Still I stumbled frantically forward, telling the doctor, "Just hold on a little longer, Doctor, just a little more . . ." Suddenly a shadow loomed over us, and as it grew before our eyes we realized it was Seyit Lutfullah's tortoise, Çeşminigâr. Truly a gruesome sight to behold, it was slowly expanding, like dough, like water, like wind, swelling up to smother everything around it. Nothing could stop it. Growing larger and larger every second, it buzzed like a swarm of locusts. My teeth chattered as I whimpered, "It will grow and grow and fill up all the earth and sky!" Terrified, I woke up.

I was drenched in sweat. My teeth still tightly clenched, I looked around the room, listening to my pounding heart. It was still night, and there was a strange silence in the air. Like a cap-sized ship undulating in dead waters, the enormous building seemed almost to be swimming in a silence that blacked out all around it. But at least my feet were on firm ground. The horror I had just suffered was nothing but a dream. I lit a cigarette. I took a few deep drags and got out of bed and sat down at the desk, repeating to myself that it was nothing but a dream. Still I couldn't get the image of Emine's screaming face out of my mind, and so I closed my eyes, hoping to rid myself of those eyes. Suddenly I was woken by a sharp jolt. I had fallen asleep with my cigarette still in my mouth, and the butt had burned my lips. I tossed it to the floor, put on my slippers, and shut my eyes.

I felt a hand on my shoulder. Confused, I looked up at a face I couldn't at first recognize. Soon I realized it was Dr. Ramiz's warden. It was ten o'clock, and the director wanted to see me. I got dressed, still badly shaken by the dream. Convinced I would be given the same bad news, I didn't even bother to ask the warden why I had been summoned. I couldn't even look him in the eye. It was all over.

Upstairs in his office, the director beamed as he read to me the court decision. He announced that I was now entirely free to go. My eyes were fixed on him as if to say, "But what will I

do once I get home? I've already lost Emine . . ." I feared
reopening an old wound even though it had been dressed and
bandaged long ago; I feared seeing the gaping and untreatable
wound that would never fully heal.

Finally the director asked, "But what's wrong?"

"Nothing," I said. "I'm just afraid. Afraid of everything."

He was a fatherly man and knew the workings of the
human soul.

"All that will pass," he said. "You're now free! No need to
worry about a thing!"

And he rose to his feet and told me his side of the story.

"Well, we've sent your report to the committee."

Down in his office, Dr. Ramiz threw his arms around me
and cried, "We'll continue our work elsewhere! Besides, your
treatment is over, more or less. We'll just do a few more ses-
sions and that's that. And then we'll prepare that report."

I suddenly lost my temper. "What report?" I cried.

"My dear, the report for the congress . . . the formal submission, as they call it, about the interpretation manuals."

Oh dear!

He helped me pack my things. And he insisted on driving me
all the way home. What a kind man! There was now no doubt
in my mind that he was genuinely fond of me. Yet for six whole
weeks he never made the least effort to submit the other report
he'd promised me since the beginning.

Now all this was forgotten: happy as a child, he nattered on
about new projects to be conducted in the name of our friendship. Sadly, I was unable to share in his joy, so I couldn't really
answer any of his questions. The whole time he spoke I could
think only of that terrible dream.

Finally I was seized by a desperate impatience. "Yes, right
away, as soon as we can," I muttered.

Everything and everyone I passed on the streets wore the
ghostly pallor of the nightmare that by now had invaded my
entire being. I made my way through the streets of my neighborhood, living among the living, until we arrived at my home
and I knocked on the door with dread.

The dread persisted right up until I saw with my own eyes

Emine's face lighting up in joy. You might say I didn't really wake up until I saw her. She'd become a little thin, but the same warmth was there in her neck and in her hands. And there she was, really and truly standing before me, smiling with her usual warmth and good cheer. Her smile brought back all I thought I had lost.

I went upstairs with Dr. Ramiz, who suddenly cried, "The Blessed One!" He ran over to the family heirloom: immaculate and shining, it was standing triumphantly in its rightful place once again.

I looked at my wife in surprise.

Laughing, she confessed: "What can I say? So much has happened to us that even I began believing in these things. I took it out last week. Doesn't look too bad, eh? That spot seemed so empty without him."

Dr. Ramiz had forgotten all about us; unaware that little Zehra had wobbled up to him, her hand extended for a kiss, he was down on his knees, engrossed in the old clock. Written on his face was the joy of being reunited with a long-lost love. Emine smiled, looking first at me and then at him, as if to ask, "Where did you find this one?" I shrugged my shoulders and took advantage of our new uncle's reverie to embrace my daughter once again. All was right in the world.

VI

With the passage of time, Emine's courage and good cheer soothed my rattled nerves, and I began to forget about our strange misadventure. And perhaps more importantly, the shock and terror of that frightful dream faded away. Even the rage I felt toward Dr. Ramiz eventually dwindled; how many days had he wasted and to what absurd lengths had he gone only to pester me into having a particular kind of dream? But when he examined Emine and told me there was nothing wrong with her, I felt nothing but gratitude toward him.

Of course I spent my first few days of freedom seeking

employment. I believe I already mentioned that the moment my trial began, my position was filled and I was made redundant. But one day I ran into an old teacher of mine, who suggested I visit the director of the post office in Fener. "A position has just become available," he said. And he was right. I started work that very day, before the opening was even posted. The salary was much reduced from that of my previous job. But it wouldn't matter at all. As long as we tightened our belts, we'd manage fine. I'd regained my freedom, my home, my children, and a world filled with people who led good and decent lives. Even the oddities and idiosyncrasies of Dr. Ramiz didn't trouble me as they had before. And, besides, from my first week of freedom he had pulled me into a new world so bizarre that I lost the capacity to see anything strange in his behavior or disposition.

Dr. Ramiz liked to spend his time in one of the larger coffeehouses in Şehzadebaşı. During my stay in the Department of Justice Medical Facility, my dear friend had spoken warmly of me to all his friends at the coffeehouse—praising my various talents, my knowledge of our old ways, and my proficiency in repairing watches and clocks—and he had given them a poignant account of my life's adventures, highlighting in particular the details pertaining to my illness, so that when I stepped foot in the establishment, a cry of joy exploded from the patrons.

I was welcomed as an old friend and hero of the day. Dr. Ramiz stopped everyone who passed by our table, introducing me by saying, "This man here has conquered a true father complex. You see before you the most important patient of my career," whereupon he would tell the whole story again in full detail.

"Now the man understands both his disease and its treatment. Truly an extraordinary individual, and one who has an impressive store of cultural knowledge, not to mention his tremendous willpower—oh dear me—thanks to which he conjured such a dream!" He would say all this while vigorously rubbing my back, and then he'd launch into his absurd rendition of my life.

One might expect he'd finish his exposé with "Come now and take a few steps for your uncle," or "Haven't you memorized a new poem? Why don't you recite it for these nice gentlemen?"

At first I was really quite flustered by all the attention and rather fearful of the consequences. But indeed this was a very strange place, one where no one ever seemed surprised by anything and no subject was ever explored for very long. Here a man was accepted for who he was, with all his idiosyncrasies, shortcomings, and defects. And the more flaws the better, although this didn't mean you were absolved of anything. On the contrary, nothing was ever forgotten: events and details were lodged forever in the collective memory of the group. Indeed this communal information became as immutable as the traits of an uncompromising personality, as defiant as a name or date of birth inscribed in a passport. Years later we saw one of these coffeehouse acquaintances win a seat in the National Assembly. His success as a politician was most alarming, but in this peculiar coffeehouse he remained a fixture in the collective memory of the place; when his name came up in conversation everyone still remembered the same old things and passed the same judgments.

The character of the place derived from its proprietor, who would eventually go bankrupt. Not once in his life had the man bothered to take life seriously, though he did seem to know half of Istanbul. He needed to meet a man only once to become his lifelong friend. And thanks to him the coffeehouse became a kind of clubhouse.

He was handsome, well built, and devilishly charming. He might well have become a high-flying businessman had he not considered the domain of the eccentric the only place worth living. He had concocted a language all his own, as affected and artificial as his attire, both of which vacillated between old and new, and he wore a little pointed goatee in the French fashion. With his ridiculous attire and his pretentious little beard, he gossiped from morning till night, spinning tales of unimaginable slander with his bogus turns of phrase, while always taking care not to implicate himself. And if he was really at a loss for something to talk about, he would draw from his personal arsenal, telling tales that would have been best left untold. He was forever falling in love, and since he chose women who seemed incapable of ever loving anyone but him, he was obliged to marry each in due course, and was thus eternally entangled in burdensome divorce suits. The fact of the matter was that he lived in a glass jar, which is to say very much exposed to the public eye.

The coffeehouse was frequented by all sorts: the sons of old money, tradesmen both bankrupt and successful, unsung poets, journalists, painters, high officials, masters of chess and backgammon and other games, former wrestlers, actors and musicians, and the usual gang of university professors and students; all told, there was someone from nearly every walk of life. And though each belonged to a clique, they also gave the impression of living as one. You were on intimate terms with any of them the day after meeting him for the first time. There were no secrets. The laundry—dirty or clean—was hung out for everyone to see. Each garment was openly fingered, examined, and even sniffed, and any elements deemed interesting were promptly paraded about. Here every good deed, every moment of despair, every shocking piece of scandalous news was judged with the same severity, or if need be, compassion, before gaining official acceptance. Pederasty, unwarranted philandering, hoodwinks large and small—all was laid bare to be bandied about by the crowd.

Every coffeehouse regular, even the proprietor, was assigned a nickname, and the moment any given character stepped foot in the establishment, someone in the crowd would tell a story or two about him, polishing each detail as he went.

I'd been around most of these people almost all my life. Some I knew from work, and others I'd met in their homes. Later a good number of them worked with me, and by that I mean they worked at the Time Regulation Institute. All were more or less honorable, or at least they were willing to risk anything to appear that way. And some had already attained important posts. Not one was unhappy with his lot in life; in fact the great majority seemed rather content. But of course there were a few who encouraged their friends to make jokes at their expense, so afraid were they of being forgotten.

What wasn't discussed in the coffeehouse? History, the philosophy of Bergson, Aristotelian logic, Greek poetry, psychoanalysis, spiritualism, everyday gossip, lewd adventures, tales of terror and intrigue, the political events of the day—all gathered up into one swollen conversation that burst like a spring deluge, carrying away everything in its path, as surprising as it was senseless, one topic seething forward before the other was finished. But, then, of course, nothing was ever discussed in detail. In the coffeehouse a story would rise up as if from a long slumber, or like a faint memory of the ancient echo of a death. As conversation turned deliriously from one subject to the next, Alexander the Great would join forces with Hannibal or the Kantian imperative, all to serve as antidotes to daily life. With even the most benign adventure, the pleasure was in the retelling. The patrons had listened to one another for so long that they could guess more or less what would happen in any story. Conversation was merely a platform for the speaker to display his eloquence; it was more like a play, or the recitation of a dearly loved work, for the exchanges were executed according to predetermined conditions—not at all unlike the traditional Turkish mime theater, *ortaoyunu*. The story would be interrupted by the same interjections, and laughter would follow; if certain members of the crowd were directly involved in the tale, they would make their defining pronouncements at just the right moment. If the narrator introduced new details, he would be cut off at once with, "You made that up!" But it was these new twists that people came to enjoy most in later recitations. And no one ever found the endless—and mandatory—repetitions tedious. In fact it was only the out of the ordinary that met with some resistance. New ideas were at first humored out of courtesy and a slight curiosity, but they would remain unaddressed until the crowd's ever-vigilant imagination had recast them as pleasantries, thus assimilating them to their own idiom. This is what happened to any attempt at serious conversation. A new story was accepted into the repertory only once it had been reduced to a base sexual escapade, a tale of pederasty, a piece of slapstick shadow-puppet humor, or the replica of an *ortaoyunu*. There was a specific name given to those who discussed serious matters: they were known as the "world regulators," the aristocrats who busied themselves with the regulation of the world. Below them was a larger group called the "Eastern Plebeians." Armed with only just enough culture to be active members of the coffeehouse commune, they had little to say about life's simple pleasures or even the hardships of making ends meet, preferring instead to indulge in an innocuous flair for the comical by drawing attention to the imperfections of others around them. Finally there were the "irregulars"; devoid of social refinement and utterly ill at ease in the urban environment, they were men still in thrall to their primal urges. An irregular could pick a fight with anyone, but a plebian or a regulator would fight in earnest only if confronted by an irregular. To some degree the irregulars represented the primitive element, and perhaps because they were largest in number, they were the only ones with a subgroup: the "pseudo-irregulars."

At first this bizarre crowd and the life that came with it rather bored me; the people seemed like traditional *meddah*, or fugitives from improvisatory performances of *ortaoyunu* or shadow-puppet theater. It filled me with terror just to enter such a world, seeing as I suffered from a diagnosed medical condition and from the assorted inscrutable personality quirks that came with it. But by the third day people were asking earnestly after the Blessed One, going almost so far as to ask whether the clock was a bachelor or enjoyed conjugal life. My memories of Abdüsselam Bey, Seyit Lutfullah, and Nuri Efendi were refreshed the moment I walked in—they had all lived in this neighborhood, and almost all the coffeehouse regulars had known the latter two personally.

That Lutfullah had entrusted me with the treasure of the emperor Andronikos—that it was now entirely in my possession—had not escaped their attention. In fact my reputation in the coffeehouse preceded me, although I had never wished for or sought such recognition. Certainly no other community would have welcomed me with the same warmth. The week following my arrival with Dr. Ramiz, everyone heatedly discussed—in my presence—just which group I should be assigned to. My reserved demeanor, my preoccupation with my personal affairs, and the seriousness with which I approached these deliberations seemed to place me with the world regulators. But following Emine's death, any balance in my life became seriously disrupted, and my standing in this esteemed company suffered. So slowly but surely I was relegated to the Eastern Plebeians. And they were right to place me there!

After assigning me to the appropriate class, they began thinking about a suitable nickname. This wasn't so easy; it was a matter that required not a few discussions. Eventually they decided on the Fatherless Waif, because of my illness—that is to say, my father complex. But there were many other stories swirling around. Naşit Bey's sudden demise revived the story of my aunt who had come back from the dead. And then there was her commitment to a dervish lodge to purge the pain of losing her husband; her subsequent attachment to the sheikh, renowned among the ladies of the day; and her wealth, which made her the prized disciple of the entire lodge—all of which served to enhance the notoriety of her later misadventures. As if refusing to believe she might be overlooked by coffeehouse society, she took to writing rapturous odes to God. And the truth was that every chance encounter in my life only enhanced her notoriety. In the second week after I began frequenting the coffeehouse, a certain honest and warmhearted man who worked in the *bedesten*, an inspector of the covered market's scales, took a keen interest in Aristidi Efendi's quest to make gold. The man never left my side, and, forever clutching a manuscript he'd purchased from the secondhand book market, he pestered me tirelessly with questions about the secrets of the art. Inevitably the Şehzadebaşı Diamond became the principal topic of discussion on almost any given day. No sooner had the coffeehouse proprietor taken his first sip of strong, unsweetened coffee than he began to recount a dream he'd never actually had, embellishing the tale with elaborate descriptions of the diamond: "Last night in the dream world, may the Great Almighty deem it good fortune, the diamond was yet again presented to me on a golden platter." On the second telling the dream was slightly altered, with the diamond being brought to him by a *banu*, which is to say, a lady, and then the third time, the *banu* became a *cadu*, a witch or a ghost—in other words, my aunt.

Slowly I grew accustomed to my new life. How carefree and comfortable! The relaxed atmosphere allowed you to leave everything behind, beginning with your own person. No sooner had I left work than I'd dash off to the coffeehouse, and once inside I would become someone else, far from the worries of the day amid the banter and jesting. I would think back on my life of just half an hour earlier, or ponder my future, as if it belonged to someone else. I even had a different name: I was the Fatherless Waif.

The doctor whiled away his hours at one of the tables, amusing himself by opening and closing his briefcase, or trimming his nails, or complaining that the country was falling prey to indolence, or expounding on psychoanalysis, or simply listening to the chatter around him. He was intensely attentive to everything going on in the coffeehouse and was only too delighted if one side of an idea allowed him to generate useful social commentary while the other gave him an opportunity to invoke Jung or Freud. When I asked him if these strange conversations ever frustrated him, he said:

"Are you crazy? Could there be any more interesting case studies than these? In fact it was this very coffeehouse that led me to cherish my profession so dearly. Where else could I find people like these? Even as an organic whole this community is terribly important! There could be no better place for the practice of social psychoanalysis. Look how the past carries on in the present and how the serious and the absurd are held fast. They each live in entirely separate, imaginary worlds. Yet they dream as a collective society."

On another occasion he said:

"Where else could I find such an enlightened crowd? Each individual has his own specialty. They're all immersed in national affairs and follow new developments closely. There's no newspaper that could cover as many stories as this one coffeehouse.

You'll see when I publish my memoirs—you'll read just what I learned from these people, listening from one day to the next."

What the doctor meant by "national affairs" and "enlightened" conversation was in reality nothing more than ordinary gossip. But of course the scholar's perspicacious eye transformed its very nature.

Later I brought Dr. Ramiz's ideas to bear on Lazybones Asaf Bey, whom I strongly encouraged to work at the institute with Halit Ayarcı—later you will see how Lazybones was appointed head of our Termination Department—and my good benefactor said:

"To my mind, it must have something to do with an inability to adapt to professional life. This is what happens to a life if it doesn't create a trajectory of its own. When I listen to you talk about this coffeehouse, I imagine all its patrons—most of whom are already known to me—living in some kind of limbo. You might see them as the ones who have been locked out. They lead indolent lives, half the time taking the world seriously, half the time dismissing it as a joke, simply because their failure to adjust to the modern age has so confused them! Surely this has something to do with their ties to some distant past or another!"

"But they all have jobs," I'd object, to which he'd say:

"Well, there's work and there's work. First of all, work requires a certain mentality and a certain conception of time. I'm astonished that you believe a genuine business life was even possible in our country before the establishment of our institute. Work exists only within a defined order. And you, with all your experience, and who lent such moral support to the institute at its inception, how could you consider this work?"

Was there or was there not a valid work ethic in our country before the establishment of our institute? I couldn't give you a definitive answer. I have changed so much since embarking on these memoirs that I am no longer in a position to claim that I view the institute—currently being dismantled—with the same eyes as I once did. It seems to me now that it was more effective in providing jobs for a number of people in our country who happened to be unemployed than it was in constructing a valid work ethic. In so saying, I am not denying the substantial benefits it offered society; I am merely noting that the passage of time has slowly allowed us to see our work from a different perspective. Perhaps this is because I am no longer dependent on the institute for money or well-being. Naturally when our personal interests aren't at stake, we begin to see things in a new and more realistic light; indeed we come to see them in a truer light, to judge them in the round. Perhaps this is why I had such a heated argument with my son Ahmet the other day. His scathing criticism of the institute may have put these ideas in my head; when he heard I was composing my memoirs, he changed his family name posthaste, fearing that one day the book might actually be published.

Although I cannot say I ever fully accepted Halit Ayarcı's many ideas about work, I can concede that his diagnosis of the people at the coffeehouse was quite astute. For indeed here life was suspended. And the people inside never considered unlocking the door and stepping out; they stood forever with one foot on the threshold. The tiniest disturbance could serve as an excuse to escape, or to maintain a sense of freedom. But what were they running away from, and why? Did they not have the power to resist? Or were they truly estranged from the world around them, detached from life itself? No, the coffeehouse offered something more along the lines of a sedative, something akin to opium.

But without a doubt, personal interests were always the first priority in the coffeehouse, and when personal interests came to the fore, all the rules changed. There were daily scuffles over money, endless calculations and clandestine conversations that could last for weeks. We didn't need to witness such things to understand what was going on. We could get a clear idea of the situation just by talking for half an hour to the owner, or to a party who was directly involved, or to someone who knew the truth behind the affair. These schemes, conspiracies, and misunderstandings most often finished in ferocious quarrels that cast even our most mild-mannered friends in a different light. Thus illuminated, they reminded us that they were people obsessed with the petty calculations of their personal accounts, who could follow the journey of a ten-lira bill with peevishly rapt attention—supremely avaricious and terminally conniving.

Among the patrons were two friends as inseparable as newborn twins, who always ate and drank together; but one day they would come to blows over a money matter, and suddenly all pretense of brotherhood and equality would vanish as one became the master and the other his slave: this unfortunate shift in the balance of power would last for days, even months. Sometimes it would happen without so much as a dispute. One of the two would have a windfall, and the new dynamic would drop into place without fanfare. Or some other grueling episode would effect a new balance. But then something unexpected would again disrupt the new order.

Once we watched as the two regulars tucked themselves away in a corner of the coffeehouse where they remained for days. The second time we saw them, they were with a shabbily dressed man. And on the third day a rather smartly dressed, well-heeled gentleman joined the party, and from that day on these four were inseparable. They convened in the coffeehouse several times a day for private discussions, or one would drop in to leave a message for another. Then each began carrying a briefcase. This all started toward the end of winter. With the arrival of spring, the shabbily dressed man appeared in flashy new attire. He was now a suave and sophisticated Efendi, his gaze perspicacious and his smile firm and steady. This man who just a few months before had slipped almost like a ghost through the crowd now paraded about the coffeehouse, greeting everyone left and right as if he were selling radios or refrigerators. It was around then that he took to coming and going in a private car. He spoke of his "chauffeur," or rather "our chauffeur," sometimes softly and with deference, and sometimes with impatient rage, depending on the occasion, but never without reminding us of his social class and its attendant privileges or drawing our attention to the status that only vast expense and a great many cylinders and miles per hour could confer.

Every age, every way of life, has its own disposition, its turn of mind and hard, undeniable truths. An example, without a doubt, is the word "chauffeur," a word that speaks of refinement, superiority, society, civilization. Have you ever noticed how the first syllable is like a kiss while the second seems to retract what those pursed lips have left hovering in the air? It is one of the most prized acquisitions in the Turkish language. Say it with whatever accent you like: its meaning remains unmistakable.

By the beginning of summer these three had finally disappeared. And then the rumors began to circulate: it seems that with the aid of a crafty lawyer well versed in financial affairs, these friends of ours had managed to attach themselves to a highly complicated inheritance case initiated by a poor fellow who considered himself the rightful heir. Now they were falling over themselves trying to entertain this man, who had, thanks to their efforts, come into a splendid fortune.

After we learned all this, there was no end to the daily updates, sometimes brief and sometimes elaborate and detailed; from the gravity of our tone, one might have thought we were sending out bulletins on the movements of a star and its orbiting satellites. It was as if all the beaches and secret pleasure spots of Istanbul had been shifted to our very neighborhood, or even our very midst, unveiling secrets through glass doors or windows with their toile curtains drawn. And we would hear of innocent young girls, beautiful girls, the kind known by sobriquets taken from the poetic and imaginary lexicon of the previous generation, to aid their ascent into the middle class; these fair creatures emerged from our lukewarm cordials and lemonades before removing their clothes before our very eyes. Every new day brought cruder and lewder tales of summer revelry; they continued until the autumn rains.

With our flannel vests stuck to our sweat-drenched backs, we rubbed this way and that against our chairs to soothe our summer rashes, but once inside these stories we bathed in cool, moonlit waters, made love in dimly lit beach cabins, and locked horns like billy goats among the trees on windswept hilltops. Then there were the stories of the bars in Beyoğlu: now we were treated to half-naked women driven out of all parts of Europe by a succession of financial crises, peeling off their bathing suits and underclothes to the heartrending wail of a saxophone solo and dolling themselves up in jewels and fur coats—which is to say that they put them on after stripping themselves of all other attire for our benefit.

There was one night when Emine relinquished all concern for frugality, agreeing to step out for an evening of entertainment without first considering the state of Ahmet's shoes or Zehra's blouse, and it was then that we heard of the fair-skinned blondes and brunettes about whom, Emine exclaimed, in her eternal naïveté, "Good gracious! They're angels, not humans." Like pureblood Arab mares they pranced into the little domain of our coffeehouse, dancing the fox-trot or writhing their way through a tango, their loosened hair thrashing against their hips, and cried out in breathless triumph as we uncorked imaginary bottles of champagne in our minds, thus drowning out the slap of backgammon pieces in the background.

By midwinter these extravagant parties came to an abrupt end. And the camera swiveled back to our coffeehouse. One night the four men met in the coffeehouse. They looked exhausted and rather agitated. First they had a hushed discussion in a corner; title deeds and receipts were pulled out from dossiers and promptly returned. Then, without warning, their voices rose and words like "disgrace," "cretin," and "trickster" cracked in the air like a coachman's whip. Fists were shaken menacingly and threats delivered: "I'm going to show you, yes I will!" Then all at once they were on top of one another. Eventually the heir and his two friends drove the lawyer right out of the coffeehouse. Pompous and supercilious, the lawyer had shown little interest in making our acquaintance when he first came onto the scene; now he could drag himself out of the mud without our help. As he wiped the blood off his cheek, he cursed like the unsavory brute he was. His spectacles had been smashed in the scuffle, so I had to pick up his hat myself and stuff it back onto his head.

Two weeks later the very same dispute sprung up between

the heir and the two friends. This time it was the benefactor's turn to be relegated, in similar fashion, to the curb. Yet the result of that evening's fracas was not what we had expected. The following morning the two remaining friends decided to air their troubles to the entire coffeehouse, and within a few days their complaints had traveled so far as to reach the highest star in heaven. No doubt they had had quite a jolly year together, but now there was nothing left to show for it. Somewhere along the line the heir had managed to divest the two friends of all their legal rights via a rather complex business arrangement; he had even succeeded in appropriating one friend's family home as well as the profitable business that the other friend owned somewhere—who knows where. Both were now penniless. And to top it all off, the friend ousted from his profitable business had fallen madly in love with one of the girls who'd been coaxed into their pleasure dens, thus ensuring her fall from grace.

None of this stopped the heir from sitting down with us one day, wearing the world's most serene and cloying smile. He spoke in private with the coffeehouse proprietor for nearly two hours. As he listened to the heir, the proprietor grew increasingly angry, the blood racing to his head. The very next evening there was an extended backgammon game with the former owner of the profitable business. The heir shook the dice ferociously in the palm of his hand before hurling them onto the board, and then, his face as innocent as a child's, he leaned over the board as if he might actually dive in after the bouncing dice and clapped his hands in delight every time he rolled double sixes. Two weeks later we heard that the bankrupt former owner of the profitable business had married his paramour. Then three months later—miracle of miracles—a baby was born. The joyous news sparked raucous discussions in the coffeehouse, and with a majority vote the child was given the name Potpourri.

With all its unexpected developments and digressions, this episode kept us entertained for months. But then something else happened, and it was quickly consigned to the shadows. Two Bulgarians had come to Istanbul in search of a treasure that had been buried in some village in Thrace during the Balkan Wars. Who had given these men the address of our coffeehouse? What had led them to us? Needless to say, a committee was formed that spring, after which camping supplies fit for a North Pole expedition were procured and a little steamboat rented for the journey. Within two weeks, the area in question had been subjected to an exhaustive search. Those who stayed behind followed each new development in eager anticipation. The size of the fortune changed from day to day. It began at ten thousand pieces of gold, descended to five, then shot up to twenty before finally peaking at a hundred thousand. Quite possibly the entire summer would have carried on like this had it not been for the local council, which finally intervened, thank God, putting an end to the search. When the expedition returned, an argument broke out over the costs incurred. But calm was soon restored when one of our acclaimed historians began a riveting recitation of the battle of Holy Ali, a performance that lasted nearly three hours. That was one of the most emotional evenings the coffeehouse has ever known. Though Emine was unwell at the time, I accepted, instead of going home, Dr. Ramiz's rather uninspiring offer of rakı and a few simple mezes.

That night we lost the two Bulgarians, but a Swiss-German orientalist arrived to fill their shoes. How happy the miserable man was to have stumbled upon a community as high-minded and intellectual as ours. His face was as yellow as a potato, and a broad smile split it into two halves that seemed incapable of ever reuniting. His poor Turkish prevented him from following discussions and becoming a close friend, but he certainly found us at just the right time: a week after his arrival his money ran out, and the community took him on as its ward. Then he decided he could earn a living as an architect. So he set up his office at a table on the right side of the coffeehouse, where he negotiated with customers and constructed scale models with matchboxes, making the necessary alterations before offering the final plans, all under the attentive eye of the regulars. There couldn't have been an easier or more practical way of running a business.

He carried on his work like this for four whole years. No architect could have been more patient, thoughtful, or attentive to the needs of his clients. If a client asked, "Now, what if we place these two boxes here?" Dr. Mussak would close his eye and think for a moment before knocking down his model building and starting again from scratch. It was then that I understood the vast difference between designs drawn up on paper and those realized in solid materials of three dimensions. As his work was conducted out in the open, for all to see, it was not just the coffeehouse proprietor but also his customers and even the waiters who were involved in the process; we all offered suggestions, and Dr. Mussak would hear us out with unflagging interest, on many occasions even agreeing with us. I don't really know who invented cooperative housing, but clearly this friend of ours had discovered cooperative architecture. Sadly, a freak accident put a sudden end to his work: Our dear friend forgot to install stairs in a three-story house he had constructed near the İbrahim Pasha Fountain in Süleymaniye. Once the scaffolding was taken down, it became clear that the three floors were not separate so much as completely cut off from one another. Even the enormous villa that Dr. Ramiz used to illustrate the configuration of the conscious and subconscious minds in his lectures on psychoanalysis at the Department of Justice Medical Facility seemed somehow more logical and correct—and while its cellar and attic were complete, the first floor was either empty or unfinished.

But allow me to say this: these two buildings—which at the time utterly confounded me, being beyond my comprehension—these two buildings, along with the models Dr. Mussak built out of matchboxes, later proved extremely valuable to me, for when they decided to commission a new institute building, I rejected all proposals and took on the job myself. Drawing on what I had learned from these two men, I created the acclaimed institute building so admired by the public. In due course I shall discuss the building in more detail; after all, for three years it was a topic of intense debate all over the world. But for now suffice it to say that this building, whose second floor was left unfinished like some kind of covered terrace—it contained nothing but structural pillars, an elevator, and a cavity where the staircase should have been—was directly inspired by the house in Süleymaniye and the aforementioned villa as described to me by Dr. Ramiz.

So the house in Süleymaniye was the next source of vigorous debate in the coffeehouse, and for whatever reason, it seemed to have fallen to us to assign a function to the two floors unconnected by stairs.

It was always the same: any enterprise, however serious at its outset, would soon be undone by an inscrutable logic. Once handed over to the crowd inside, what had seemed crystal clear just two steps away from the coffeehouse would be twisted into a muddy mockery of fate.

This was the marshland we knew as "the absurd." And though I couldn't see it, I was up to my neck in it.

I was as in thrall to this world, as if I had fallen into the grips of a densely feathered beast, engulfed by its many soft arms and ticklish wings while its husky voice lulled me into a languid stupor. I was living in a world without connection, or without any connection that wasn't meaningless or absurd: I felt myself to be in a fairground torn asunder by a violent tornado that had come out of nowhere. Where had the storm started? What uncanny worlds of opposites had it plundered, which disparate armadas had it so rattled to the core that it was now quite impossible to identify the true faces of those who are blown our way? Objects would appear one after the other, as if pulled out of a magician's hat, and then it would emerge that they were somehow linked to one another. At the time I found the experience quite pleasant, but when I consider it in retrospect, I see the traces of a nightmare.

I was fording a deep-sea cavern lined by the remains of knowledge and by all the ideas I had ever failed to grasp. As they swirled around my feet I moved forward, and with every step I felt the coil of unfounded beliefs, ungrounded frustrations, and unending despair tightening around my chest and arms; whereupon, like rotten seaweed, they pulled me deeper into the depths of the sea; and every time I opened my eyes, gruesome leviathans larger than the eye could see would lunge toward me through the murky void. Then suddenly they would vanish, like giant squid eclipsed by their own clouds of ink, and I found myself face to face with Dr. Ramiz or Lazybones Asaf, my head turned toward the wild laughter that was cutting through the thunderous chaos in my head—a clanging in my ears rising from the depths I had just been wandering—and I would look around me as if I'd just woken from a dream, recognizing nothing.

"Yes, my dear friend," Ramiz Bey was saying. "There's no end to all this! The youth must take action and cast off the shackles of this *fatalisme `a l'Orient!*"

The doctor's face darkened. As if in response to a command, Asaf Bey dragged his feet and arms away from the four chairs he usually commandeered, and then, as if to reward himself for this arduous task, nested his head on the table, in his crossed arms, and fell into a deep sleep.

Lazybones Asaf was forever lethargic, and his sleep was the most sublime, the most innocent in all the world. When he closed his eyes, a gentle hum would fill the room, inviting reveries of a hundred angels with effervescent wings flittering about in the air above him, singing or softly whispering lullabies into his ear as they filled the honeycomb of his sleep with the ambrosia of innocent dreams.

Then all at once I felt a painful knot in my stomach. "Emine!" I cried, and I leapt from my chair and hurried home. She was ill. What the doctors had diagnosed as a minor case of fatigue had become a dangerous condition of fatal consequence. I had seen this coming long before the doctors did. I had known about it since I had dreamed that dream at the Department of Justice Medical Facility. The fatal alembic had boiled away before my eyes, and inside had been Emine's face; she was always on the other end of my pillow, on my lips, and in the palms of my hands, but slowly slipping away from me, and staring at me with wide-open eyes. Let her speak to her heart's content, I tried to say, let her laugh and dream about the future, and see Zehra marry one day, and Ahmet's graduation from medical school, but still her face was fading into the distance, and still her eyes were looking at me, even from so far away, looking at me as if to say, "Try what you like, but there's no cure!" It was hideous and cruel. Emine was falling into death as the tears fell from my eyes. And I could do nothing about it, nor could anyone else.

VII

Emine's death sent me headlong into a void, as if the branch I'd been clutching had suddenly snapped. So overwhelmed was I by the loss that at first it made absolutely no sense to me. Nor could I grasp how deeply I'd been affected. All I felt was a dark and terrible heaviness deep inside me. But there was also something else—a sense of liberation. The ordeal had come to an end. Emine would never die again; she'd never have to suffer another illness. In my mind she'd remain as she was. No doubt other terrors awaited me; other catastrophes were in store. But my worst fear—that of losing Emine—was gone. No longer would I view the world through the prism of her pain and ill health; never again would fear well up inside me to smother my entire being.

Our home had been destroyed; left alone with our two children, I lost the will to work, and, even worse, I lost all faith. But I was no longer afraid. The worst that could happen had happened. Now I was free.

With no Emine to keep my feet on the ground, I was ready to be swept away by any passing current. And the closest current was the coffeehouse and my friends there. Just a week after Emine's death, I found myself among the regulars once again. I sat there, in the second hall behind the shops on the main boulevard, with playing cards in one hand, a glass of rakı in the other, a cigarette in my mouth, and the din of stories in my ears; I was, in short, at ease with my surroundings, joking and smoking and for all appearances having a jolly good time. Had I forgotten everything? Was I really having fun? Absolutely not.

I felt anguish like never before. It wasn't fear or pain but the grief suffered by only those who have betrayed themselves—an odd sensation I greeted with revulsion. It was on a day like this that it happened. All at once my reflection in the mirror melted into my impression of myself. The face I saw between the coats hanging on either side of the mirror was smug but hopeless, despicable and weak willed, irresolute and resigned to his fate, so much so that for a moment I thought the glass might vomit back my image and toss my head onto my feet. But no, nothing of the sort happened. On second and third glance I grew more comfortable with the apparition. A balance had been regained.

I hired an old woman to look after the children at home. When I managed to get myself up in the morning, I'd go to work, and after that it was straight to the coffeehouse before rolling out to a local *meyhane*, with Dr. Ramiz or some other companion, to drink the night away, returning home late. I'd be pleased to find the children already fast asleep, and on some nights I'd go straight to bed myself—another day done, and I had made it through unscathed. But all too often I found the children waiting up for me, huddled in a corner. Thus the most wrenching part of the day would begin.

I had to take them up in my arms and lift their spirits without once giving them the faintest idea of what was running through my head: I had to tousle their hair and dry their tears—make them laugh. Why were they so sad? Why did they cry so much? Why were they so needy? Didn't their very existence make it difficult enough? Hadn't they tied me to one place with their very presence, condemning me forever to circle like a workhorse around the same little spot?

The moment I saw them I'd crumble in compassion; cursing myself for my spinelessness and ill fortune, I'd fight the urge to pound my head against the wall for hours on end. At times like these Emine would appear from the shadows of the house and waft toward me, placing her hand on my shoulder, as she always did, and saying, "Pull yourself together!"

And I would do just that. Decisions, promises, and resolutions came one after the other: tears were shed in darkness. But to what end? I detested the life I was living but lacked the strength to start another. I had severed all ties. I had no bonds with the world save the compassion I felt for my children. I had no choice but to endure it all—or at least tolerate the world around me. The moment I set foot outside I was a prisoner of my wandering and endlessly colluding mind, which led me off to exotic worlds whose enticements beckoned, only to stay beyond my reach.

I was driven wild by letters and postcards from distant lands. They came from all over the world: Peru, Argentina, Canada, Egypt, and the Cape of Good Hope . . . The old Jewish woman who lived amid fleas in her single room just two streets down from us had a brother in Mexico, and her neighbor—the sister of a rabbi—traded in Argentinean furs. The son of the Greek grocer across the way lived in Egypt. And his nephew was a teacher in Chicago. When I saw their letters, my eyes would shut of their own volition—I became someone else, somewhere else. Oh, to leave everything behind and just go!

But no, I would have to be a different sort of man to do such a thing. I would have to push myself beyond the shackles of my habits and routines, not just run, move, jump, and desire but also persevere. Such things were not for me. I was a hopeless shadow: a miserable, slovenly shadow who followed any man who happened to brush by, who, the moment after breaking company with this man, found himself bound to his children, huddling in each other's arms like kittens, laughing, crying, but most of all crying—a man who laughed when told to laugh, cried when told to cry, spoke when told to speak, wept when told to weep. I was a miserable creature who became interesting only when considered so by others, who existed on those rare days when people looked him in the eye.

This of course reminded me to hurry to the coffeehouse, where I could be among people whose lives were more or less different from my own and who, unlike me, did not suffer the gaze of others. When I was with them, I felt I had a life of my own; I could live and I could think.

But perhaps it wasn't quite like that. There were other factors at play. I didn't actually like the people there. I took refuge among them. I was like a man who flees a snowy night on the peak of a lonely mountain battered by heavy winds, to take refuge in one of those caravanserais that double as stables, where the

warm aroma of manure mingles with the fragrance of freshly
made tea and coffee amid the hum of human voices and the
shuffling of horses' hooves. It was this happy, saturated chaos
that kept me warm.

No doubt a day would come when I would forget the dissatisfaction I felt for the place and its people and leave myself
entirely at their mercy. Already from time to time I'd say, "Ah,
now this is life! Such peace and happiness . . . What a delightful
cast of characters!" And I lived like this until my son Ahmet's
grave illness brought me back to my senses. My fear of losing
him compelled me to accept my fate.

It was at around this time that Dr. Ramiz finally realized the
project he'd been mulling over for the last six years: the Psychoanalytic Society. I was one of the twenty members of the
society—none of whom, apart from Dr. Ramiz, were medical
doctors; I was even made its director. So, yes, I must concede
that when I was made deputy director at the Time Regulation
Institute, I was not completely without experience. Before
becoming director of the Society for Psychoanalysis, I'd been
the accountant for the Spiritualist Society, which was more or
less the same sort of organization. As director I was the holder
of the key to the society's meeting room, whose rent was paid
over the years by my dear friend the founder of the organization. Only twice did the society open its doors to the public for
conferences. At his first conference, Dr. Ramiz introduced me
as the first patient he'd treated in Turkey, providing details that
made my hair stand on end. It was thanks to these mentions
that my second wife, Pakize, first took a shine to me. At his
second conference, the doctor read a lithographed reproduc-
tion of an entire seventy-page-long dream manual, annotated
with his own comparisons and explanations along the way.

It was summer; waves of hot air blew in through the society's
windows, singeing our faces and dragging us down to the
depths where, yawning, we surrendered to the good intentions
of the orator. A bee buzzing overhead seemed to be drilling
through several layers of steel, belying its small size with the
deafening roar of several diesel engines combined—at first

smothering the voice of Dr. Ramiz, and then drowning it out altogether.

The first to drop off was Lazybones Asaf Bey, in the back row. In the role of honorary director, I sat just below the speaker, my hands politely poised on my knees as I tried to hide the gaping holes in my shoes—this was supposedly how it was done in Europe (I am referring to the seat I was assigned as director, and not to the shortcomings of my shoes). For a moment it seemed as if Lazybones Asaf, his arms sliding off the chairs he'd been using as his bed, had set his sights on the nape of a woman in a monstrous hat in the seat right in front of him. But then, as his head dove below the hat and out of sight, the divine hum of a thousand angels serenaded by violins rose from the back row. At around the third page of the dream manual, the divine hum and the buzzing bee became a small bay of cool and rippling waters over which the dreams of a young poet in our group might sail, to wage alone the epic sea battles of another age: the ship's hawsers groaned, and the cannonballs roared out in blasts of black smoke as flames spread amid the charges and the battle cries. A woman of forty in the front row took advantage of the clamor to release a dozen ducklings she seemed to have stowed in her pocket, masking herself behind their quacking. And just beyond her someone else did the same and soon the meeting hall had become a draining bathtub insatiably gobbling up air.

By the tenth page almost everyone was fast asleep with the exception of those who'd already left for home to sleep in greater comfort. Once everyone was secured in slumber, each larynx settled into its usual repertoire, its racket and rhythm offering us swift and unadulterated consolation.

Dr. Ramiz fought as hard as he possibly could against this collective mutiny. Never before had I seen the man hold his own with such fortitude. His voice sprang from his chest like the roar of a lion, blowing back the soft grass and undergrowth freshly revived by Asaf Bey's murmurings, lashing out erratically to either side, wrestling with unseen enemies, pouncing upon them, suffocating them once he got hold, and if not strangling them, then causing them to cower in terror.

His face was drenched in sweat, and his hands flew about as if to disperse the snores assaulting him from twenty different mouths. As he struggled to open a way for himself through the clamor, his words left his lips with the sharp snap of a whip, leaping across the room like a fiery temptress and spraying to the right and left like a fireman's hose. But how could a single man struggle with so many enemies at once—enemies so high-minded, so evasive, so adept at hunkering down and metamorphosing?

Obstacles he'd presumed obliterated bounced back to life seconds later, and once again he was forced to set his ambush in the shadows as the ducks kept up their frantic quacking, as burst water pipes hissed like cobras, as the bathtub sucked all the water in the world down its drain, as trucks ground into low gear on insurmountable inclines, and as the noisiest of trains thundered past, one after the other.

But the voice of Dr. Ramiz was ever alert and ever vigilant, quickly tackling whatever crossed its path; it carried on promising, supplicating, threatening, and changing shape, concocting patterns of speech never before heard, to announce its state of siege.

Prying open my ever-heavier eyelids, and with my hands still on my knees, I marveled at Dr. Ramiz's industry, courage, and power.

"Furthermore it is an ill omen if a lady sees an unbridled madman in her dream. Have her repent and beg God's forgiveness."

A young woman in the third row, whom I hadn't noticed earlier, awoke from a deep slumber to release a long and deep "Ohhhhh," before stretching out in her chair. Seizing upon this first sign of hope—and his last chance for salvation—Dr. Ramiz thundered on:

"And if this lunatic is a man, and if he is in the nude, the lady in question will commit adultery. Let her husband beware . . ."

The forty-year-old woman's neck, now a large turtledove, began to coo. The ducklings were nowhere to be seen. Unfazed by these developments, the orator carried on.

"And it is indeed a bright omen if a man finds himself in his

dream among a tribe of sleeping beauties—for he is the absolute actor, so obliged to explain himself to no one."

Availing himself of the freedom evoked by these final words,
Dr. Ramiz lowered his head and fell asleep.

VIII

At the time of Pakize's and my marriage, her thyroid gland was
still healthy, and she was neither moody nor short-tempered.
Knowing nothing about real life, she was happy and good-
natured. Both her mother and father were still alive. Indeed not
a soul could have imagined their days would soon come to an
end, for they were both so healthy and full of energy. Her sisters had not yet decided to come to live with us. My older sister-
in-law's musical talents were as yet undiscovered, while the
younger one had yet to convince herself that a tenacious will
was all she needed to become a beauty queen. I myself had not
yet resigned from the post office in Fener, at the behest of
Cemal Bey (whom I knew from the Spiritualist Society), to
become an employee at the Bank of Miscellaneous Affairs,
where Cemal Bey sat on the board of directors and would later
become general manager. Put simply, I still had a steady job,
and our lives were relatively safe and secure. And I had yet to
fall in love with Selma Hanımefendi.

Yes, all this had yet to happen, which is why we were reasonably happy and snug in our little home during our first year of
marriage, nestled under the tranquil gaze of the Blessed One.
This life was certainly very different from the one I had led
with Emine. My second wife had nothing in common with my
first. Pakize lacked Emine's contentment—a gift of her calm
and generous nature—and Emine's serene beauty. But Pakize
was young and happy, with her own particular way of enjoying
the world; she knew how to live in a world all her own.

She loved just one thing in life: the cinema. Films did not just
educate her: they also mesmerized her. So enraptured was she
by the silver screen, so engulfed was she in its world of fantasy,

that she could no longer distinguish between her own life and the adventures she saw in films.

One day she informed me in all earnestness that she could no longer perform a certain Spanish dance. It was a Sunday morning in the second year of our marriage. Her hair was spread across her pillow, and she was lolling about in bed, waiting for a crane to hoist her out. Standing at the window, I was considering how happy I might have been if I had married a woman who was quicker to rise in the morning and a little more eager to have breakfast. Suddenly she called out to me:

"Hayri," she said. "You know, I think I've forgotten that one Spanish dance number."

I knew Pakize liked to dance, but I'd never known her to be familiar with Spanish dancing. One could hardly expect so much from a person whose great girth made it difficult for her even to walk properly, let alone see where she was placing her feet.

"You don't say. Which Spanish dance is that?"

"I swear to God I can't remember. I tried it yesterday, but I just couldn't do it. How do you forget something you knew just three days ago?"

"I didn't know you knew a Spanish dance."

"But how could you forget, love? Wasn't I just dancing it the other day? You know the one you really liked, at the club? Everyone cheered; then that officer came in and . . ."

Since our marriage we'd gone nowhere but the cinema. It was only later that I realized my wife had confused herself with Jeanette MacDonald, an actress we had recently seen in a film; in fact she'd transformed herself into the woman from the film. A few days later, I found her distressed when she couldn't find her red dressing gown or my riding jacket. She collapsed into uncontrollable weeping when her white satin gown was nowhere to be found. Another morning she threw her arms around my neck and warned me repeatedly to take care on my way to the office.

I cannot tell you how strange it was to be married to a woman who did not just occasionally fancy herself as Jeanette MacDonald or Rosalind Russell but who also took me for Charles Boyer, Clark Gable, or William Powell. One day she even mistook one of our neighbor's daughters for Marta Eggerth.

Beckoning to her from our window, she asked, "Marta, my dear, where in the world are you going dressed like that?"

In truth it was a difficult thing to deal with. Dangerous misunderstandings could crop up at any moment of the day, with one version of events contradicting the next. But there were light moments too, and some of these even proved useful. My wife, as I have already said, was blissfully content within a world of cinema and thus impervious to life's trials. My missing buttons were no longer replaced, as it was well-known that Adolphe Menjou had at least a hundred thirty suits. She didn't even notice when my jacket wore out at the elbows. Everything she saw in films, she saw as ours: castles, diamonds, lush gardens, and noble and courteous friends. So it made no difference to her if we had our evening meal in the kitchen or not at all. In short, she had the key to a quick getaway. But even so, it would have been impossible for me not to worry about her just a little.

What cog had come loose in her brain to keep pulling her back into that world of make believe? Was it despair that sometimes turned her into a child? There had to be more to it than that—something deeply rooted in childhood must have set the stage. After a strong southerly wind had kept me up one night, I told Pakize I was going to take a twenty-minute nap. We had planned a picnic that day, and several of our neighbors were due to come over within the hour. Pakize may have been right to warn me that I wouldn't be able to get up again if I went back to bed, but I protested, "Oh no, I'll be fine. You'll see. I'll wake up right on time." Fifteen or twenty minutes later—well before our guests had arrived—I woke up to the blare of the radio. My wife had turned it up to full volume and was astounded that I had managed to wake up. So, just to say something, I blurted out one of the odd historical tidbits I had picked up from God knows whom: "Napoléon had the same knack for timely napping!" The moment the words left my mouth, I saw a fine sparkle in her eyes and was filled with regret. But it was too late. From that day on, Pakize would compare me to Napoléon. Though she couldn't have had much of an idea who Napoléon was, she knew me inside out, and as the adage goes,

"We may not know Joseph, but we know you perfectly well."
As we sat nibbling stuffed grape leaves under the pine trees on
Heybeliada, and later as we lounged about digesting them for
hours on end, she entertained us with her list of similarities: the
great military commander also relished *sele* olives; he was an
avid fan of cowboy films; he always slept on his right side; and
he snored in the morning just like me. And this was just the
first stage. Three or four days later, she began to look for ways
in which Napoléon took after *me*. She went to the attic and
pulled out my reserve officer uniform, which she had cleaned
and pressed before hanging it first in our bedroom and then in
the guest room. The following day she insisted I put it on, come
what may. "You forget who you are!" she remonstrated. Oh
Lord! How beautiful she was when a silly whim like this overcame her. How her fair countenance would soften . . . Then
finally there was my coronation. She was so excited she could
hardly wait. This was the second, or rather the third, stage. As
time went on she came to believe with all her heart that she
was Joséphine de Beauharnais, and so she adopted her step-
children, believing them the fruits of her first marriage. Yes,
from that day forth she took Emine's children for her own.
And suddenly I was their stepfather. Perhaps those reading
these memoirs will find something to laugh about in all this,
but there is no denying the confusion it brought to my life. No,
there was something not quite right about Pakize. Once I
had come to accept this, I began to see the woman I held so
dearly in my arms—the woman with whom I shared so many
responsibilities—as impaired or only half-there. It was partly
Pakize's doing that I came to obey Cemal Bey so blindly and to
fall so desperately in love with Selma Hanım.

Things changed somewhat after Pakize's mother and father
passed away. And her feet finally hit the ground when my
sisters-in-law came to live with us. But changes in my wife
would always make themselves known in the most awkward
and unexpected ways. It was now her sisters' turn to be the
axis upon which our lives revolved, with my children and me,
and even Pakize, relegated to the background. Pakize took such
pity on these two orphan sisters—thirty-five and twenty-eight

years old—that if anyone deserved pity over time, it was us. And slowly we sank into a wretched and precarious existence that lasted until my fortuitous meeting with Halit Ayarcı. I was being lowered into a bottomless well, every moment sinking a little deeper into the darkness. But I am getting ahead of myself: first I must describe my life at the Spiritualist Society.

IX

The Spiritualist Society differed in every respect from the Society for Psychoanalysis. At our lively and unruly meetings, we found common cause in the world beyond, from which dispatches arrived almost twice a week, and our deliberations on their possible meanings were not without merit. There was, additionally, an abundance of females. Though many were mediums, at least seven or eight attended purely out of interest. I was the association's accountant and secretary, so I got into the habit of stopping by every evening after work, to keep abreast of my paperwork; I used my free time to collect the monthly dues and update the books. It was here—in this association that every day offered up a new surprise—that I first met Cemal Bey.

I can say with authority that the likes of Cemal Bey are rarely seen in a spiritualist association. Such societies exist for those who prefer to find themselves in pleasant circumstances while engaged in the deception of their fellow man. But Cemal Bey took no pleasure in collective lying. For him, a falsehood was a weapon, a means by which to embellish his life or his own person. He had no time for inventions already in circulation. As much as he liked to think of himself as a man of broad and compassionate understanding, he wouldn't tolerate the slightest sign of weakness, and he was quick to unmask anyone so foolish as to lie to his face. He was a spoilsport, pure and simple; this alone can explain why his political life was so short-lived.

Yet he was a frequent attendee of our meetings and séances, and whenever he lectured us, it was always with the same condescending smile. There was no doubt that his interest in certain spiritualist issues was genuine, as was the pleasure he took in discussing them. And of course he was a little bit in love with one of our members, Nevzat Hanım.

No matter how ardent his visits to the association, Cemal Bey failed to attract Nevzat Hanım's eye. After the passing of her husband, this beautiful woman seemed to have closed her heart to love. She lived with her mother-in-law, in an apartment in Şişli, passing her days reading books on spiritualism and contacting spirits. It was a way of life that had adversely affected her health: she often complained of headaches and insomnia.

She herself was partly responsible for the insomnia, for her séances lasted long into the night, and then there was Murat. Murat was a spirit and a regular at Nevzat Hanım's séances. He had all but set up camp in the house; when silence descended, he'd creep out to clean the windows and shake out the carpets, rearrange the furniture and put books back in their place. He could go so far as to tear up tomes Nevzat Hanım had yet to read, sometimes even arranging for their complete disappearance. It was widely known that Murat had once destroyed a rather racy novel Cemal Bey had given Nevzat Hanım the same day. And he would perform such deeds with raucous theatricality.

Another quirk of Murat's character was his unwillingness to speak about his private life. When pressed at the séance table, he would sometimes claim to be a mathematics teacher from Adana, dead for ten years, or a soldier who had died a martyr in the Crimean War; on other occasions, he was an engineer, a man Nevzat Hanım's late husband, Sezai Bey, had known as a reserve officer. But his name was always the same. And whatever mortal form he adopted, this ever loyal and resourceful spirit exuded an independence of mind, a commanding air, and the promise of moral constancy; confronted, as he often was, by a question he found irritating, he had but one livid reply: "Drive such thoughts from your mind!"

Everyone knew Murat was the man of the house now that Nevzat Hanım no longer had a maid; sometimes he even opened the door for the poor woman before she found her keys in her purse. And rumor had it that he did the same for visitors.

This may explain my terror each time I stood at her door, a compass in my hands, or whatever other trifle of a gift Cemal Bey had sent me over to offer her on his behalf. But for Nevzat Hanım it was quite the reverse: she was content with this strange state of affairs, and she sang the spirit's praises. So certain was she of his constancy that she sometimes left the house without her keys. This despite the fact that she had, she once admitted to me, returned home late from a ball and found herself locked out. "What right does he have to be so jealous?" she complained on that occasion. "How can he presume to infringe upon the freedom of a woman my age?"

Some of our friends claimed to have spoken with Murat on the telephone. In the wake of this alarming news, it was perhaps inevitable that other details should come to light—and that these would vary wildly, depending on which adventurous soul happened to be telling the tale.

"The voice was quite muffled. It sounded as if it was coming from far away, through miles of dense fog, but I could still just make out the words, or rather they were inside me. It was a very sad voice. No one in the land of the living could sound so belligerent and aggrieved."

So said a young poet held in high regard by our coffeehouse coterie.

"As I listened to that voice, my thoughts gained the clarity of crystal," he recalled. "When I asked if Nevzat Hanım was at home, he said, 'Yes, but it would be best for you to stay away, as she's not feeling at all well.'"

A rich merchant named Şuayp Bey gave an altogether different account:

"Once the line went through, I heard for the very first time in my life what you might call pure silence. This wasn't silence as you or I have come to know it; it was something else. Then someone intoned: 'Who's there?' I gave my name and said, 'I was wondering if I might ask you about a book Nevzat Hanım was going to give me . . . ?' Until he cried, 'Forget about the book. Go home at once. Your wife's had an accident. Run! And don't stop!' I asked him who he was and he said, 'I am Murat,' before hanging up on me. It was as if the voice was chastising me."

Şuayp Bey then told us that when he returned home he found his wife crumpled in a heap at the bottom of the stairs.

Three weeks later the lawyer Nail Bey gave us yet another glimpse of this Murat who involved himself so intimately in our worldly affairs, who returned from the world beyond to issue reprimands and warnings and wise counsel:

"It was truly bizarre. First I heard this unholy din; there were whistles and bells—you might have thought the world was coming to an end. Then I heard a voice: 'Wrong number!' So I hung up and dialed again. But the same thing happened again. On my third try, the same voice said, 'I don't think you understand, the hanımefendi cannot come to the phone right now. She's busy.' I interjected, 'Fine, but I need to speak to her about the apartment. It's an extremely important matter,' only to have him reproach me: 'Have you no understanding of her character whatsoever? She cannot come to the phone now; she's working, consulting with the spirits. Please do not insist!' Then I asked, 'Who is this?' And he answered, 'You still don't know who I am? I am Murat!' In the background I could still hear cymbals and bells and foghorns. But the oddest thing was the wooden mockery in his voice."

Cemal Bey and I were the only ones who had never spoken to Murat on the telephone, and neither had we met him at the apartment in Şişli. But to tell you the truth, this didn't put me out in the least.

Had I never met Cemal Bey, my time at the Spiritualist Society would have been a pure delight; nothing in this world could have taken me away from it. Who doesn't relish that sweet shiver running down the spine when communing with the world beyond?

But, sadly, I did meet Cemal Bey, and, sadly, I was putty in his hands. In any event, I was in no position to pass up the chance to make a little extra money, even if it was only now and then. One day Cemal Bey cornered me. I should say that he was initially taken aback by my attire, and that he found my personality preposterous. He made no attempt to hide his surprise: "So, such people do actually exist!" he declared, before sending me off on a personal errand. It went on like this until the very end. No sooner had he seen me at the association than he sent me off on some urgent errand. He would begin, "Hayri, my dear lamb, could you possibly . . . ?" But the honey in his voice would never last long. I rarely saw him speak to me without his feet pointing disrespectfully at my nose. And the words themselves were pure horror. What might have been a mere repetition turned quickly into an insult:

"Tomorrow, at eleven o'clock . . . You won't forget, now? Yes, at eleven o'clock, at precisely eleven, you understand?"

He would say all this in a voice so sharp and strident that it made me lightheaded and nauseous; it was as if he took a pocketknife and carved every word into my brain. Then, without warning, a dark curtain would drop over my eyes and I'd be clenching my fists. In moments such as those I would have happily given away half my life for the chance to bash in his chin and rearrange his face—knocking his fat, oily jowls right up into his finely plucked eyebrows, smashing him to bits like a broken old record. But this storm would be short-lived, for now Selma Hanım came to life in my mind, her voluptuous body overflowing like the tide, her fine, supple curves swelling as if her corset had just been loosened, with the modesty of her measured gaze tempered by the sweet tickle of her laugh; until I could think only of the prize I'd be granted for my patience:

"Yes, sir."

Sometimes he'd rattle off the name of a tailor, cobbler, or department store or give me the name and address of a wealthy Jewish merchant I was to meet on the dock before helping him carry his luggage to his car—or rather I'd carry all his luggage myself: he made sure I had all the details of the assigned task. As the strain of work mounted, I'd nearly choke on the rage and disgust I felt for the man. It wasn't enough for him write the names and addresses and the task to be done on a simple piece of paper. He would have me read his lists back to him, as many as ten times over—this to convince himself that I'd memorized not just the errands but the order in which I was to carry them out.

I tolerated all this in the hope of catching a glimpse of Selma Hanım, if not sooner then later. Sometimes, in a last attempt at self-defense, my lips would twist into a smile that was, I hoped, a subtle blend of pride and mockery, as with my eyes I made as if to say, "Can't you see how I'm suffering for this fool? But I'm just having him on—don't get the wrong idea. I'm just enjoying this while it lasts as . . ." It was, I hoped, a glare that drew my cohorts at the coffeehouse into my game, making them my playmates and partners in crime.

But whoever even noticed my furtive glances or pathetic smiles? Cemal Bey was possessed of an autocrat's diminishing gaze: he might have been viewing us from his own personal fire tower; and so blinding was the force of his personality that no one could have seen those changes in my expression, even if I'd held a lantern to my face.

So, no, charm was not Cemal's strong point; the only thing (remotely) bearable about the man was the warmth of his greeting. But his friendly overtures were more difficult to bear than his indifference. Should this man link his arm in mine, to whisper words meant for my ears only, I would shiver so violently one might have thought I'd succumbed to a ferocious stroke. Others suffered similarly. If Cemal happened to sit down next to him on the sofa, Şuayp Bey would withdraw his hands ever so slowly and return them to his lap, and the lawyer Nail Bey seemed to freeze altogether. Yet everyone remained solicitous, respectful, fearful, and anxious to get along. He was the dangerous reptile, and we were his paralyzed prey. With such powers, he could have achieved great things in the underworld. But (as we shall see in due course) he too had come into this world with a certain weakness. It was as if fortune and chance had stripped his will of a clear purpose so as to shield themselves from its full power.

The deeper my own involvement, the more clearly I saw the effect he had on others. One day Cemal's tailor showed me the running tab in his ledger. The figures were astounding. The man looked at me long and hard, and then shook his head as he pointed to the last figure noted: "It was only yesterday that I refunded him two hundred lira. He insisted . . ." And then, as if gripped by sudden madness, he made a terrifying display of tearing up the receipt. Three days later I saw Cemal Bey reprimand the tailor for a crease in the very suit he was wearing— though there was, if you ask me, no crease whatsoever—and I was flabbergasted by the poor man's patience in the face of it. It was the sort of thing you wouldn't believe unless you saw it with your own eyes. As he sank into shame, the poor man was almost swallowed up by his shoulders. And he kept saying, "As you wish, sir," as if he had no other words.

He extracted money from his haberdasher, cobbler, and landlord in the same way. When his landlord finally mustered enough courage to remind his tenant that he owed two hundred liras in back rent, this poor browbeaten man was subjected to a vigorous lecture on a landlord's sacred duties, which ended only when he promised to change the bathroom tiles and install glass around the back balcony. In his shrill Bosnian accent, Cemal Bey kept shrieking, "The tiles, the tiles!" Apparently the bathroom tiles didn't match his madam's nightgown. He made as if this terrible stroke of ill fortune had shaken him to his very core.

There was only one person in the Spiritualist Society who dismissed Cemal Bey's imperial presence, and that was Mlle Aphrodite; in fact she did not even see it. With her smooth, firm skin and her thirty-two teeth flashing like flaming paraffin whenever she opened her mouth, and her suggestive eyes deepening beneath those long lashes like the setting sun, and a light and lilting accent (inherited from her Italian father) whose aftertaste—sharp as mustard—lodged in your throat but still lightened your heart with sweetness, and with her hands darting about without design but, like a spider, stunning all it touched, in wave after wave of warm allure, as she secured her conquest, she was, perhaps without knowing it, the pure embodiment of womanhood.

Every aspect of Aphrodite took the form of a command: she was inspiration personified, though she seemed sometimes saddened to be burdened with gifts she couldn't hide.

On seeing Cemal Bey, she'd bring her hand to her cheek and pretend to shave as she squealed, "Ouch! I've just cut myself!" before taking shameless flight to my office, or to the kitchen, where she'd rest against the closed door to giggle in that mustardy voice. We could forgive her playful provocations, for none of us doubted their intent. We all knew that what drove her away from Cemal Bey was an absolute and insuperable disgust. And she made no secret of it:

"What am I supposed to do? I just can't stand the man. There's something so repugnant about him. I don't know what."

But Cemal Bey, who ignored all this, remained kind and condescending, affecting an air that seemed to say, "Beauty and Youth will always forgive such faults. How could we blame such a creature so pitifully ignorant and uneducated?" But in fact he found her behavior upsetting, grating as it did against the pride he wore like armor. Cemal Bey was a proud man and such pride is always kept close at hand, where it is most visible: it is the rich man's automobile, the general's aide-de-camp, the policeman's revolver, the traffic warden's whistle. No one could engage with him in any way without sensing this pride or thinking about it obsessively or feeling deeply disturbed.

When Aphrodite was twenty, her mother fell gravely ill, after which time the girl spent her evenings at her bedside. One evening she began scribbling something on a table in the room; not finding this odd, she did the same thing at just the same hour the following evening, and the next, without quite knowing what she was doing. When, on the morning after the third night, Aphrodite realized what was happening, she took a closer look at the pages she'd assumed were nothing but thoughtless scribbles, and between the doodles and the crooked words she spied a sentence: "Find a new doctor!" Too frightened at first to breathe a word to anyone, she confided in a friend, following which, and upon the insistence of an uncle then residing in their home, they found a new doctor—and her mother was saved.

From then, all she had to do was sit down at a desk with pencil in hand for a few minutes before starting her involuntary scribbling. At first her writing was no more than disjointed, meaningless words jumbled together into obtuse sentences, but with time they came to focus on a wide range of topics: there were news flashes on current events and personal or family matters, and even commentaries on city life. After testing this newfound talent on several friends, and at the insistence of the society, she came to learn how, by concentrating her powers on particular points of interest, she could find the answers people were likely to accept.

Before long, she would find herself yanked out of bed by an overwhelming force, to be dragged to her desk to fill page after page. She often wrote all night long, but by morning neither the authoress nor her friends could make any sense of her scribbling. Sometimes they found no more than a tangled string of meaningless words, names, and numbers—with the numbers 17 and 153 occurring most frequently. She wrote in a smattering of Italian, Greek, French, and Turkish.

Aphrodite's father was Genoese. An event of major significance in his youth having put his life in danger, he had no choice but to flee to Izmir, and from there to Istanbul, where he married a Greek girl and settled down. He was a fine jeweler and an excellent tenor. He opened a very popular little shop near the funicular in Beyoğlu and soon enough he became a man of means. But he severed all ties with his family because he didn't feel safe, even after so much time had passed. So it was only when he died in 1915 that people found out he was Genoese and had a mother, father, and sister living in Italy. When Scarrechi died, his brother-in-law (formerly his apprentice) took over the running of the business, implementing changes during the Armistice years that transformed the little shop into an enormous shopping center. But by then the high craftsmanship of Aphrodite's father's time was a thing of the past. Customers to this vast and luxurious new emporium that employed the best goldsmiths in the trade still longed for the quality of his craftsmanship, or so it was said.

In the years following his death, Aphrodite and her mother brooded a great deal on the man's early life and his relatives abroad. It was because she was curious to know about them that Aphrodite first undertook to advance her career as a spiritual medium. In the séances she conducted with friends, she concentrated her efforts on this matter in particular, and though its importance waned over time, she came to see that the force rousing her in the middle of the night (compelling her to roll back her eyes and give it voice in the indecipherable automatic writing she produced) was none other than her paternal aunt, who had died in 1923, still waiting for her brother and his family to return to their homeland at long last.

And then the pleas from the other side became clearer and the deceased more direct in applying pressure:

"Why won't you come? Why won't you come live with us in our home? Why won't you come to collect your inheritance?" she scolded them. "I never married. I lived on next to nothing, saving it all for you. Why won't you come?"

Aphrodite's poor mother knew nothing about her husband other than that he had once lived in Genoa, under a certain name, so she was reluctant to accept these ever-more-insistent invitations: it was out of the question, and, anyway, she did not possess a single official document that established her as a member of his family. But soon enough she gave way to her determined daughter and the insistent community to which Aphrodite belonged; when she at last capitulated, she said, "Well, if nothing else, we'll have gone on a journey." Whereupon, following a string of strange and startling coincidences, the matter of the inheritance was settled with some ease.

As it turned out, there really wasn't much of a fortune. Along with a modest sum of money the woman had saved, she'd left behind two houses on a long and narrow street, numbers 17 and 153. Yet the costs incurred by Aphrodite and her mother on their journey came to more than the value of both properties combined. Even so, it was a source of great pride to them that they had succeeded in their quest, and under circumstances that knew no precedent: in this they were a great inspiration to others. They could not help but be impressed by the many sacrifices this relative had made to hold on to these two fully furnished homes for so many years. She'd made her living running a boarding house and tatting her own lace—her legacy included vast quantities of the stuff. But, sadly, the woman's obsession with collecting and hoarding meant the houses themselves were in rather poor condition.

Aphrodite and her mother didn't have the heart to sell these properties that had come to them by such a bizarre route, and as neither of them was willing to follow the old auntie's directive to

resettle in Italy—in any event their livelihoods were in Istanbul—
they oversaw a little restoration work on the houses and left.

From that day on, the aunt was nowhere to be found. Whenever Aphrodite had a free moment she would sit down at her
desk and take hold of her pen with softly furrowed brow and
creased forehead, there to wait as her countenance turned as
hard as marble, her every contour erased, and thus she would
wait for hours on end for her loving aunt to communicate with
her once more.

She never reappeared. It was as if, freed of her heavy burden, this self-sacrificing soul had at last allowed herself to drift off
into the pure sleep that she had been promised. And she deserved
so much. She had devoted her entire life to her lost brother and his
children, though they lived so very far away. In truth, she'd never
known how many children he had or if he had any at all, for that
matter, but all the same she always set aside for them all that she
came to own, with her eyes forever fixed on the horizon so that
she might say to them upon their return, "This is your home, and
here is everything that I have saved for you."

Even in death she remained mindful of her sacred mission;
lost in the eternal void, and bereft of clues, she continued to
search for her brother far and wide, until, after untold years,
she found her way to the bedside of the young girl, Aphrodite.
This alone should have been cause for thanks.

But it was not enough for Aphrodite. Having bound herself
up in her auntie's will—the Spiritualist Society had named her
the Will—she longed for her return, and her continuing absence
plunged the young woman into misery. She hadn't even been
able to thank her properly; not even had she said, "But, dear
Auntie, why so much trouble? If only you knew how very
touched we were by your sacrifices . . ." With time, a certain
sort of sorrow ate into her expressions of gratitude:

"What's it to me, an inheritance? I have my own money.
Why did she go to so much trouble? Why didn't she just get
married? How could someone do such a thing? She did all this,
but why hasn't she come back to me?"

It seemed that all Aphrodite wanted to do was embrace her

aunt, if only just the once, and after thanking her properly, she would have liked to explain how all her sacrifices had been in vain, and perhaps even reprimand her auntie for having abandoned her so abruptly. But try as she might, she couldn't bring herself to understand how a compassionate and determined soul like her aunt could lose faith in her cause so suddenly:

"There's most definitely something wrong. Either she's angry with us or there's been an accident . . ."

She imagined her aunt on the roadside of the wide and heavily trafficked interstellar highways—wounded, paralyzed, and abandoned and more helpless than ever.

"Perhaps she wants us to live in our new homes. But we are from Istanbul. It's the only city we know. Even my father never wanted to leave. And all our friends are here."

At the time when I became a keen regular at the Spiritualist Society (if only to escape the fractious mood swings of my wife and her sisters), Aphrodite had just come up with a new explanation. Every now and then she'd take the lace adorning the edge of her gown between her fingers and show it to us.

"If she loves me, how can she resent me so much?" she cried. "How can she hold a grudge? She must be tired. Or perhaps she couldn't marry in the material world, at least not before she found us, but perhaps now she's found someone in the world beyond and married *him*."

If she could just about convince herself of this possibility, then she could be sure that her auntie was at peace with the world. She would laugh and sing and hug and kiss the men she fancied. But this free spirit could never forgive herself: she was the reason her aunt had never married, and she blamed herself mercilessly for having kept her aunt from living a full life. She believed that women should marry at all costs. Any other course was utter catastrophe, which is why she was delighted when my aunt made her late marriage.

"But of course!" she exclaimed. "Why wouldn't she? We all must live!"

My aunt had remarried for her own selfish reasons, with no consideration for anyone but herself, but Aphrodite chose not to notice how mean and unjust the woman had been to us and gave the union her full blessing. And when Naşit Bey died, freeing my aunt to plan her third foray into marriage, Aphrodite measured one aunt against the other, and, finding a greater exuberance of willpower in mine, she judged *her* aunt to have lost the contest, brooding over her fate thereafter in the way a neighborhood boy might mourn the defeat of his rooster in a cock fight.

Aphrodite had been the most sought-after girl in all of Beyoğlu since she was eighteen. Almost everyone in high society knew who she was; and in both Turkish and foreign circles. Invited to every event of consequence, she'd find herself surrounded by at least half a dozen suitors. Yet she never could bring herself to marry: perhaps her freedom was too dear. It was like looking at someone lingering in bed after waking, unable to shake free of the mood left by a final dream: she couldn't bring herself to give up the freedom she had savored with such outrageous extravagance right up to her twentieth name day. And despite the many changes in her life over the previous five years, she still hoped to carry on as before.

She had suitors of all ages and showed each and every one the same kindness and generosity. They courted her as if possessed, and, suffice it to say, they were all fairly miserable. But after a time they either drifted away from the beautiful young girl, who seemed to have no notion of her gorgeous femininity (never mind its dangers), or they remained at her side, resigned to a life of spellbound intimacy and restless despair.

Aphrodite's adventures were closely followed by every member of the association, male or female. She was as talked about as Nevzat Hanım's Murat. When I first joined the association, hoping only to earn a little extra cash, I was under the impression that it had been founded for no other reason than to discuss the questions of Murat and the old woman, with members either doubting or accepting their existence.

Our official psychic, Sabriye Hanımefendi (who claimed to have been Aphrodite's classmate and intimate at the French lycée Notre Dame de Sion, despite a ten-year age difference and an evident mutual distaste), maintained that the young lady was in no way a spiritual medium and never had been. The truth, according to Sabriye Hanim, was that she had had a passionate affair with a young Italian diplomat who had served two years at the embassy in Istanbul. The romance had captured the imagination of Istanbul's upper echelons. Everyone—the entire foreign community as well as the Turkish elite that moved in the same circles—thought the Italian diplomat devastatingly handsome and rather sophisticated, and they followed each new development with rapture. But the romance took a fascinating turn after the young diplomat abruptly departed for his native land. That was when Aphrodite dreamed up the whole adventure, convincing her mother to travel with her to Italy so she could meet with her lover one last time and perhaps win his hand in marriage. This was why the matter of the inheritance was so quickly resolved. All had been orchestrated in advance. Was it possible that a matter as convoluted as an inheritance could have been resolved so easily, without divine intervention of this order?

Was there any truth in the story that Sabriye Hanım recounted a little differently to each and every member of the association? No one could really say. But this much is certain: had there been so much as a hint of truth in her tale, it would not have found much favor with the association. For, like Nevzat Hanım's Murat, Aphrodite's aunt was one of the little group's life buoys. The association needed its myths, imaginary or real: it was through these myths that its members communed with the mysteries of death resurrected.

The myth of Aphrodite was more than an extravagant and alluring adventure; with its promises and warnings, stern words and enticements, it gave life its meaning and its order. The spirit's proclamations never once contradicted our beliefs, speaking a fluid truth that left its true form unknown. Aphrodite's aunt and Nevzat Hanım's Murat were our eternal companions; their essence seeping into ours. They lived out their lives as we lived out ours; they were real even though they were lies.

Our spiritual leader was not seeking the truth in such matters. She was interested only in facts. Well, for us Aphrodite's aunt was a fact. And that was satisfactory enough! One could be sitting at home on a dark and snowy night when one of these amiable spirits suddenly tapped on the door and shuffled in like a guest, hanging his coat and scarf onto the stove for the icicles to snap and crackle over the heat, guiding us to a world that was so different from our own, unfurling before our very eyes, flaunting its aura for those with eyes to see.

The novelist Atiye Hanım understood all this perfectly, which is why she had no time for Sabriye Hanım and her logic and good sense. With such wild speculation whirling around about, it was useless for Aphrodite to try to deny anything. Deprived of her aunt, the poor girl drifted hopelessly among us, like a forlorn and banished queen fed only by the glory of her past. But perhaps this portrait was itself a product of Atiye Hanım's imagination—for the real Aphrodite wasn't in the least hopeless or despairing. It was simply that Atiye Hanım the novelist chose to see the matter in this light.

Whenever it came up in conversation, Atiye Hanım would change the subject, leaving no opportunity for objections before turning the conversation—I never really understood why—to *Queen Christina*, a film that had created quite a sensation in her youth. Then she would sink into confusion. Atiye Hanım dearly loved the film, representing as it did a turning point in her life as an artist. It had long been her dream to write the story of Kösem Sultan along the lines of this film. For her, Aphrodite became a living example of Kösem Sultan.

But for a long time life would stand in the way, for life had endowed Atiye Hanım with a wealth of material. Her tireless consumption of men had given her enough to fill sixteen rapid-fire romance novels; her current novel in progress dealt with events that had occurred ten years before. Over the last decade she'd gone through at least as many men again, and having suffered dearly for it, she was now bloated with sadness and a profusion of sensitivities. Life for her meant loving, making love, changing lovers, and suffering: she'd need at least another sixteen novels to recount all her new adventures. So her Kösem Sultan novel would just have to wait.

It wasn't that she couldn't believe Sabriye Hanım's various narratives. In fact she was quite convinced of Aphrodite's aunt's need to exist in spirit form. But if it did not, then she had no objections to the young diplomat. As a novelist, she was more than clear on the necessity for at least so much. Moreover, she knew all too well that a person doesn't just up and travel to Italy without a good reason, even if all the aunties in the world—dead and alive—were assembled in one spot. Of course she felt there was no need to relay any of this to Sabriye Hanım. The helpless creature was condemned to suffer lifelong jealousy.

Quite unlike Atiye Hanım, Mme Plotkin, the granddaughter of a Jew who had emigrated from Poland to Turkey during the constitution years, believed everything Sabriye Hanım said. But she was never one to gossip, only voicing her opinions on the matter when the subject came up naturally and even then only among her intimate circle of friends. Moreover, Mme Plotkin valued the truth, and she never withheld any detail she knew to be relevant. A case in point: on a trip to Czechoslovakia a year before, she and M. Plotkin had met the young Italian diplomat and the Brazilian widow he'd married. By her account the diplomat had been very fond of Aphrodite but had in fact found the Brazilian widow more beautiful, more comme il faut, and frankly much wealthier. Speaking of Aphrodite she cried:

"The poor girl has such bad luck. Now she's in love with Semih Bey. But Semih Bey's madly in love with Nevzat Hanım."

Sabriye Hanım sighed and began to explain:

"Poor Semih Bey's swimming against the current. Nevzat will never again love anyone on this earth. Not him, not anyone. But that's just the male mind for you!"

And with her proud and ever pejorative smile, she flashed her eyes at Cemal Bey, who happened to be eavesdropping. Sabriye Hanım's cheeks paled as a strange light flickered in her eyes; then she bit down on her paper-thin lips, shutting them like the lid of a box. But under no circumstances did this mean she'd remain quiet, for surely at such times in her heart she'd say, "Forgive me, my love, but I had no choice but to avenge myself!" Sabriye Hanım was in love with Cemal Bey.

This was why she never succeeded in becoming a medium, though it wasn't for Cemal Bey that she'd joined the Spiritualist Society. The fact is that Sabriye Hanım had joined to indulge her fascination with human affairs. She frequently made the claim—her eyes stretching as wide as her little mouselike face could bear—that from the age of five she'd done everything in her power to uncover the truth behind whatever domestic saga was unfolding at home. Her heightened curiosity was perhaps a byproduct of the jealousy she felt for her stepmother, or perhaps it was simply congenital. And as she grew older, her passion for sleuthing grew and grew: stretching first out to her street and then to her neighborhood and the city and every other aspect of her life. But in thirty years she had learned everything there was to know, and, having set into place a reliable network of informers, she began to take a keen interest in the world beyond.

Just as science had shifted its focus to the stars after fully acquainting itself with the workings of earth, Sabriye Hanım now set her sights on the world beyond. For her, the séances and the Spiritualist Society were windows to its mysteries. And Sabriye Hanım loved windows. At home she always sat at one of the two windows that looked out onto the street. Now she stood before a window that looked out over the vast landscapes of infinity.

Yet it would be untrue to say that any of this caused Sabriye Hanım to sever her ties with the material world. She believed the world beyond was but a continuation of the one we currently inhabited. She claimed hundreds of acquaintances there. Undoubtedly she knew at least one person on the other side (sometimes several) who had something to tell her about whatever affair she was investigating on earth, either through direct involvement in the affair or by witnessing it firsthand. Indeed the two worlds were remarkably close. For instance, in the matter of her neighbor Zeynep's suicide, consultations with those in the world beyond proved vital.

Sabriye Hanım's distress following the suicide was genuine. She'd truly valued Zeynep as a friend. That a woman of Zeynep's noble and courteous bearing could take her life proved that she had been doomed by her fate. She hadn't gone to a good school like Sabriye Hanım, and she had lived a sheltered life, but she was nevertheless an intelligent woman. Her rich husband had loved her. There had been no apparent problem between them. But still, one day she took her life; she found a gun and shot herself. Citing a nervous breakdown as the cause of suicide, the police closed the case. But Sabriye Hanım, who was of the view

that women experienced nervous episodes when they were trying to pester someone into doing something, could never bring
herself to accept the verdict. Two years after the tragedy,
Zeynep Hanım's husband still hadn't remarried. Though
Sabriye Hanım followed his every move, she couldn't uncover a
single romantic affair. He remained the same quiet and well-
mannered man. He didn't seem overly relieved by his wife's
absence. If such a tragedy ever happened to Selma Hanım—
God forbid!—I'm sure that cold-hearted Cemal Bey would
have been rather pleased. But no one seemed in any way relieved
by Zeynep Hanım's suicide, and no one seemed to grieve for
her save, of course, her husband. As for her female friends, they
seemed neither to relish the situation nor to exhibit signs of a
guilty conscience: Nevzat Hanım, though she lived in Zeynep's
apartment building, still assumed a childlike air and a bewildered expression, while Atiye Hanım merely added a suicide to
her current novel—wouldn't any other author have done the
same? Selma Hanım managed to affect only a few tears, for her
makeup had been carefully applied that day, in anticipation of
an engagement later that evening (she'd recently grown concerned about the wrinkles rapidly gathering around her eyes).
Seher Hanım got word of the tragedy only months after the
fact, and Mme Plotkin had been so preoccupied with the imports
arriving from the factory her husband had commandeered in
Czechoslovakia that she wouldn't have registered the event
in the first place. So . . .

What was the reason behind poor Zeynep Hanım's death?
Why did she take her own life?

Countless other affairs remained as unresolved as her suicide. Hundreds, even thousands, of people in that great warehouse that was the world beyond had wrapped themselves up
in their own secrets as they waited in envious silence.

Sabriye Hanım wanted to communicate with them and
encourage them to speak. This was why she was interested in
spiritualism: she wanted to close the unfinished cases in the
banks of her mind, release their mysteries to the light.

But her situation was soon complicated by an unfortunate

decision. Once the séances had begun, it was quickly agreed that Sabriye Hanım was the perfect medium. This, however, was the last thing she wanted. Even in the comfort of her own bed, she always remained, throughout the night, alert to the slightest sound. Now she was going to be hypnotized, and this made her very uneasy indeed.

A medium is never free. And can never ask questions. She is under someone else's control, with yet someone else's thoughts bubbling out of her mouth like water bursting from the spout of a public fountain. The operator-hypnotist asks the questions, and the spirit answers. Sabriye Hanım, however, wanted to ask the questions herself. It was for this express purpose that she'd joined the association. Now the roles were reversed.

But Sabriye Hanım, through force of will, achieved the impossible: she broke the rules. Instead of directly answering questions posed by the spiritual mentor, the spirits speaking through her preferred to address the more mundane issues of the world beyond. If the hypnotist happened to question Sabriye Hanım on the purification of souls, a matter thoroughly discussed by the medium Hüsnü Bey, son of the old sheikh Kadiri, the tenor of a conversation changed dramatically. According to the spiritualist lexicon, the word "purification" described a soul's deliverance from evil passions and its return to innocence, but Sabriye Hanım took the word to mean "liquidation."

"Oh come on!" she cried. "Liquidate the company? Not at all! It's more prosperous than ever before. Company shares have only gone up and will continue to do so!"

But then if the hypnotist asked Hüsnü Bey, "Have you ever connected with a higher being?" The medium might give the following answer:

"It would take at least ten thousand years of suffering to attain that height. And besides, if I ever reached a higher being, I'd have nothing to do with any of you." But if the mouthpiece for that very same spirit was Sabriye Hanım, she might say:

"No, I've never tried. Truth is, I've never even thought of trying. I've been too busy following Rudolph Valentino's latest love affair! If you like, I'll tell you all about it!"

Several times, in the midst of a deep trance, she'd suddenly interrupt the spirit to cry:

"I can't find her. I can't find Zeynep Hanım. I suppose there's an isolated wing for those who've taken their own lives." And apologizing, she said, "I'm new here. Forgive me."

Sometimes when the spiritual mentor asked the same gracious, pious, kindly spirit what needed to be done to make people more immaculate and pure, she would cry:

"Are you all fools? Forget about all this and look at what's right under your noses. Over the last few days, someone among you has been preparing for something that will surely make you quake!"

Sabriye Hanım's success as a medium lay in her ability to leave her body behind and travel only with her thoughts. Once given a task, she would cast off her corporeal form like an old dress and stare blankly, blissfully out the window, running her eyes up over the walls as she described everything she saw in sumptuous detail. This was of course only the most natural manifestation of her curiosity. Once she found the opportunity to quench it, she used every trick in the book to avoid coming out too early, and to avoid returning to our world she would beg and badger the spiritual mentor: "I'll just have one more look to see what's happening on the opposite building's third floor. I thought I saw Suat Hanım, but it wasn't her. The woman was blond . . . and tall. I didn't recognize her." Describing to us everything she saw, this normally unprepossessing woman was transformed: her face lit up as if she had just awoken from a happy dream, and she seemed almost beautiful.

Sabriye Hanım put forward just one condition before she engaged in these séances, and that was that the hypnotist wasn't to wake her up before she took a quick look around Nevzat Hanım's home. Awake and fully compos mentis, she'd exclaim, "What did I say? Did I see anything? You let me have a look around, right?"

The truth was that Sabriye Hanım believed Zeynep Hanım had shot herself after uncovering a secret love affair between her husband and Nevzat Hanım. She also believed that Murat, like Aphrodite's aunt, was a fiction—a fiction invented to cover

up a love affair, a criminal love affair that had resulted in the
death of someone she dearly loved.

The association did not merely disagree with Sabriye Hanım;
it rejected her theory wholesale. Murat was nothing like Aphrodite's aunt. He wasn't the kind of spirit that could be knocked
out in just one blow. So much of the association's quaint
warmth came from this churlish and outspoken but loveable
spirit. Who will ever forget that sudden rush we all felt the evening when a capricious Murat cut the electricity and we all
huddled together in fear? The following week the association
was compelled to ban new members, if only to protect this
dearly loved creature from exposure.

So the promises the hypnotist made to Sabriye Hanım were
never honored: he made every effort to keep her far from
Nevzat Hanım's home. Though she probably could have indeed
conversed with Nevzat Hanım, no one could be sure to what
extent she could actually converse directly with Murat. And no
one wanted to offend him.

Sabriye Hanım's skepticism and her affinity for tragedy were
not entirely unappreciated. But it was never forgotten that she
was a naturally inquisitive character, with a formidable grip on
affairs of the heart.

She was well aware of all this and so reluctant to partake in
hypnotic séances, preferring homelier ways to communicate with
the departed. She often led séances at home or at the club during
which she treated those spirits who'd accepted her invitations to
lectures on the nature of the true torments in the world beyond. It
was hard not to be taken aback by her questions. In séances of
this nature she preferred not to call those spirits who were already
accustomed to the operating styles of the hypnotist or the sheikh.
This was why she chose to fall in league with Seyit Lutfullah,
whose story I had shared with her, undertaking a momentous
collaboration with him, of which more later. I arranged for Seyit
Lutfullah to attend Sabriye Hanım's lecture "Spiritualism and
Social Hygiene" at the association the following week; in the talk
she fervently declared her commitment to her art, going so far as
to explain under what conditions a secret service of spirits might
be assembled, and expounding on the many benefits such an

assembly would afford. We all knew that Taflan Deva Bey was lending her tremendous support in her efforts. This refined and learned man of no small means indeed had an overwhelming passion for social hygiene. I often think how different—and more wonderful—our lives would be had our country's more gifted individuals succeeded in finding their rightful places. I cannot imagine a person among us who, after listening to him for just ten minutes, would not be swept away by the overpowering desire to have Taflan Deva Bey made mayor of Istanbul, or of any other province in the country, for life and to spend every penny he had to make it possible. He was aided by his insight and good manners and his ability to attract individuals from all social strata. What a pity that Deva Bey was only concerned with the social and moral manifestations of hygiene. For him, streets, homes, and the entire cities were themselves always secondary and tertiary points of considerations. What was most essential for him was a society's ability to purge itself of deviant thought.

Thus it was Sabriye Hanım's curiosity that led me to reconnect with Seyit Lutfullah one night, at a time in my life when I least expected to see him. The truth is that I had begun to feel closer to him since joining the Spiritualist Society. No matter how pure the association's scientific goals, and no matter how serious its debates and investigations, he was the true master of the manor! It was as if he were standing there next to me from my first day there. And in certain communications, it was all too clear that he had intervened.

X

My life might have gone on like this forever had I not been pulled out of the Spiritualist Society through the entirely unexpected intervention by Cemal Bey, who offered me an attractive and handsomely remunerated position in his company. My work for him was to be made official. "We're already friends, aren't we?" he said. But to accept I had to be free for work during daylight hours. Not only was I obliged to leave the post office in Fener; I also had to sever my ties with the Spiritualist Society. Enticed as I was by the conditions of employment, I accepted the offer without fully considering the consequences. In Cemal's words, I was at last making a career for myself. And from this rung I would only climb higher. I was an individual with talent, he said—so why had I been content to drift from one menial position to the next? It simply made no sense for me to waste any more time in service.

Life at the Spiritualist Society had worn me down. It was impossible for me to get home in time for dinner. I hadn't been sleeping well at all; the association members had been taking up nearly all my time. The only break I'd ever had from them was when I was off running errands for Cemal Bey.

Before I left the association, I said good-bye to Nail Bey, and once again he listened to everything I had to say on the matter. Then he closed his eyes and intoned:

"Lutfullah."

I cocked my head to indicate I hadn't understood. Assuming he was only having me on, I answered:

"He's in safe hands. Sabriye Hanım's looking after him."

Nail handed me a communiqué that had been distributed the day before. It warned of evil spirits plaguing the association and advised that Seyit Lutfullah was not to be summoned to any future gatherings.

Nail Bey leaned toward me and said:

"Seyit Lutfullah knows too much, he knows as much as Sabriye Hanım. And you've been asking him such misleading questions. So watch your step!"

Only much later did I fully grasp what Nail Bey was trying to tell me. Speaking with him then I was under the impression that I was leaving the association with my old friend Seyit Lutfullah by my side.

The work I was to do for Cemal Bey was simple and straightforward. After five o'clock I was free to do as I pleased. I had a new circle of friends. I no longer had to put up with the masses at the Fener post office or the mounting chorus of moans as they pushed and shoved their way to the one public telephone on a wooden table covered in cigarette burns. My new surroundings were comfortable and refined. I had a telephone that was for my use only. No longer did I need to jump up at the call of a bell. Now there were men jumping up when I rang for them. The first day I rang for the office boy eight times. The first time I asked him about the weather; the second time I asked him for the time; when he hurried up a third time, I asked for his help in putting on my coat; the fourth time I had him take it off; on his fifth trip I got his name; but by then the whole thing had become rather tedious for us both. Calling him up to see me for the sixth time, I offered him a cigarette and asked him to sit with me for a while; and on the seventh buzz I asked him to go away, until finally I rang for him to come back and keep me company.

You might not believe me, but I found it all to be a genuine delight. I had indeed stepped onto the first rung of the ladder!

I started meeting Dr. Ramiz in the coffeehouse in Şehzadebaşı again. But the place had lost its warm atmosphere; four years had passed and most of the regulars had moved on. But this was of little import, as the main characters were still there: Lazybones Asaf Bey, Dr. Ramiz, a few painters, a journalist. My recent exploits had made me a character in my own right. From time to time, the poet Ekrem Bey would come round to fill us in on the latest spiritualist gossip: Nevzat Hanım seemed discontent and hopelessly scatty, and Sabriye Hanım almost never came to meetings anymore.

One day at the office I received a telephone call from Sabriye Hanım. She invited me to a meeting at her home. I invented an excuse but she insisted. She left me no choice. When I told Cemal Bey later in the day, he flew into a terrible rage:

"Out of the question!" he croaked. "Absolutely not. I forbid you to go!"

So naturally I didn't go.

Throughout my time in his employ, my personal relationship with Cemal Bey remained constant. He sent for me whenever there was something he needed; whether I was at the coffeehouse or at home, he would find me. But he was no longer the same man: day by day he grew increasingly petulant and no matter how carefully I carried out his precise commands he would accuse me of botching the job and scold me harshly. I ascribed his change in behavior to various problems that I knew to be causing him anxiety at the time. He was suffering from severe financial difficulties. Whenever we met, he was busy going over his accounts. On several occasions I watched him fish a wad of cash out of his pocket and sort the bills into separate piles before returning the small fortune to his wallet with a mournful look on his face.

"I won't make it through the month!" he groaned.

With the money he had counted right under my nose, he could have sent the entire community at the customs bureau on the hajj. That year he spent the whole winter fretting over his accounts. Then suddenly his situation improved. The same could not be said of the way he treated me: I was still account-able for his misadventures with his tailor, cobbler, haberdasher, his butcher in Karaköy, and his landlord; I suffered them all and paid dearly with my sweat. But his financial woes had somehow disappeared.

It was around this time that something happened that seemed of little consequence. One evening Sabriye Hanım decided to call on us at home, in a car so enormous it blocked off our entire street. Together we revisited memories from the past, and in doing so she managed to squeeze out of me the odd piece of information regarding Cemal Bey's private life. Then, after kissing my wife and my sister-in-laws good-bye, she took her leave.

Her visit had a devastating effect on the family morale. Her fashionable attire had left my wife and her sisters awestruck. In setting out at once to imitate her style, they failed to remember that dressing in such a way required money. To them, it was a simple matter of will; and all three began to tap it most aggres-sively. I had to spend three months' wages in one month. But the spree continued unabated; there was still so much more they had to have. Before saying her farewells, Sabriye Hanım had declared my younger sister-in-law to be rather pretty; swept away by the compliment and convinced of its sincerity, she entered her first beauty contest that very year.

Two months later Nevzat Hanım somehow found my address

and came to visit us, too. She was curious to find out just what Sabriye Hanım had asked me that night, and she was curious to know my personal opinion of Cemal Bey.

The three sisters were quick to conclude that Nevzat Hanım's style was in fact the true embodiment of elegance. Everything— from all their gowns to their undergarments—had to be changed. All their old clothing was sold secondhand, for next to nothing. Thus we burned our way through two more months' wages. To make matters worse, Pakize began to feel jealous; though she couldn't have cared less about him until then, her husband had suddenly become a prized commodity. There had to be a reason why women of such quality would visit me so brazenly. She suspected we were up to something.

How had Cemal Bey heard about Nevzat Hanım's visit? The very next day he was as cold as ice. No longer content to limit his criticism to the way I carried out his personal errands, he began to find fault with my work at the office. Nothing I did pleased him. He flung papers in my face and even shouted at me in front of the office boys. It was no longer the good life but a living hell. With each of Cemal's remonstrations, I swallowed a bed of red-hot coals. And I'd had to sell my own clothes to keep up with the fashion revolution at home. I'd been reduced to wearing a suit covered in motley patches. But neither this sartorial disgrace nor my scraggly two-month-old beard did anything to lessen Pakize's jealousy. I had no choice but to supply her with a running account for every minute of my day.

I have already told you that I am an ignorant man. All my life I've had to learn new words. At almost every stage, I was obliged to renew my lexicon with revisions based on real-life experience—with my own blood and toil. Through my adventures with the Şehzadebaşı Diamond, I came to understand the meaning of the word "absurd." Till then I had understood the word to allude to things beyond my ken. Now it was part and parcel of my life. A fear I had never before experienced took root inside me. I lived each second of the day afraid of what awaited me around the next corner. I knew that within the next half hour either my wife or one of her sisters would come by the office to check up on me, and that Cemal Bey would call me in to chastise me, showing no mercy (all this while my visitors were still there), and that I would wrest myself free of him only to come face to face with one of my creditors.

With every passing minute, I felt degraded in a new way. With every hour, misfortune appeared before me in a new guise. Yet there was no reason for me to be suffering so. In no way had I brought this on myself. It all seemed to unfurl by its own logic.

At around this time, a young woman came forward, claiming she wanted to marry me—though I had made my situation clear. But, then again, it may have been my marital status that piqued her interest. I met all sorts of people by chance in those days, without ever considering the consequences. One of these creatures took to me. And there was absolutely nothing I could do beyond surrendering to her claws. I just couldn't break free. A machine operated by some external hand was now controlling my life; at one point the engine picked up speed only to slow down a little later, and sometimes it stopped functioning altogether. When this happened, neither the saw nor the blade worked; and a fear took the place of my panic and pain. I trembled to think what might, as the saying goes, next be lying in store.

Toward the end of summer Cemal Bey went to Ankara for three days. It was nothing less than heaven. Though anxious as ever, I was spared the terrible burden of the man's company. No longer was I submerged in a deep sea; no longer did I feel that horrific weight on my back or my bones nearly splintering beneath it. And then there was the rest of it: the daily hardships, the concomitant fatigue, pain, and suffering. Thus I came to understand the extent to which a single person can impinge upon the life of another.

Over those three days I couldn't stop thinking about Cemal Bey. In a way nothing had changed. Everyone at the office had adopted his style, so I was more or less exposed to the same kind of treatment. Life at home was ever the same. I felt just a bit more comfortable and more relaxed. Yet this creature known as Cemal Bey still cast its looming shadow over my life; there was no escape.

And he wasn't just a part of my life: he infused all that surrounded me.

My own life had taught me this: mankind's hell is mankind. There might very well be hundreds of diseases that will end our lives, hundreds of paths that may lead to our undoing, but all these pale next to the devastation that can be wrought by another human being.

Now I was to discover that I wasn't alone in this view. Before leaving for Ankara, Cemal Bey gave me a long list of errands. For one of these, I had to speak with his wife. So I stopped by their home. Selma Hanım did not greet me at all warmly; in fact she didn't even seem happy to see me. Everything was just as it had always been. Yet something between us had changed. She seemed more at ease and sure of herself, and she was wearing an expression I'd never seen before. She seemed relieved.

She insisted that I stay for a coffee. She sat down opposite me in the living room, really not that far away, and I watched her fiddle with the folds on her skirt. She too was liberated but, like me, for a limited time only. She had the easy air of a child granted a reprieve from her governess. Or was it something more than that? She called to mind a young girl rescued from an evil witch in one of those fairy tales.

Surely Nevzat Hanım must have been the same. She had a new lightness of being, seemed more at ease.

At one point Selma Hanım asked me if I had seen Nevzat Hanım. To demonstrate my mastery of the intricacies of class distinction, I took care to endow Cemal Bey with the title beyefendi.

"The beyefendi has prohibited my association with her."

At first it seemed that Selma Hanım hadn't understood.

"It seems Nevzat Hanım isn't feeling well. I haven't been able to visit her either."

Then all at once she looked me in the eyes as if she had just come to her senses. She wanted to say something but stopped. She had understood.

And so? What would that achieve? It would do nothing but poison the three days of freedom that chance had bestowed upon her. It was best not to think about it at all. Escape was the only way, to take flight into myself. But was there even such a place to take refuge? Indeed was I even there? This thing called "I" was no more than a mess of desire, pain, and fear.

This was why I was not so very upset when Cemal Bey relieved me of my position the moment he got back. If nothing else, I was finally free. I'd never see the wretch again. I'd never have to suffer his screeching voice. His oafish gestures and the revolting lines on his narrow little forehead would never again haunt my dreams. The nausea would finally cease. Anger and rage would no longer eat away my insides.

Yet I wondered how I'd break the news at home. They were sure to take it badly. What's more, they'd say it was my fault. I hadn't even begun to think about how we were going to get by. That was the next step. Now I had to get through the "first moment." It frightened me like a dangerous underpass. I found everyone at home in a storm of nervous energy and despair. They all had long faces; they were fighting off tears.

So they knew. I wondered who might have told them. Where could they have heard the news?

Calmly, I asked Pakize:

"How did you hear?"

She handed me the newspaper.

Why would my recent dismissal be featured in the paper? I wasn't that important a man. I was a run-of-the-mill secretary. No, this must be something else. I read the section she pointed out to me. Three jury members for that year's beauty contest had resigned. Among them was Sabriye Hanım. My younger sister-in-law was in a flood of tears:

"She promised me. She promised me she'd help."

I tried telling them again and again that it really wasn't the end of the world, and that I'd been laid off, and that we now ran the risk of going hungry, and that this was what we needed to be thinking about. Impossible. They were far too deep into their own troubles.

PART III

TOWARD DAWN

I

Ismail the Lame—to whom I had, the previous night, after a tortuous argument with Pakize and her sisters, consented to give my daughter's hand in marriage—was at the table next to mine, playing dominoes. Assaulted by his pug eyes; his dirty, swollen face; his ropey jaundiced flesh; and a stump of a nose that only served to accentuate his pockmarks, I lamented my ill fortune and the beautiful spring day it had poisoned.

If Zehra had grown up in any other home, if she had received just a little kindness and attention, Ismail the Lame would never have been her one and only suitor. Despite her unkempt appearance and threadbare clothes, she was as beautiful as a fresh spring day. Sadly, my sisters-in-law—the music lover and the aspiring beauty queen—had conspired over the course of twelve years to convince my daughter she was ugly and disagreeable. At first Pakize had tried to soften the ill will they showed my daughter. But then during our darkest days she too turned on Zehra, as if blaming her for our misfortune.

The night before, my older sister-in-law had scolded Zehra mercilessly so as to cover up a misdeed perpetrated by Pakize: for absolutely no reason, she had made Ahmet cry. Though Zehra suffered personal attacks in silence, she did not like anyone hurting Ahmet, so she had kicked up a frightful row with her stepmother. This is what I liked most about Zehra: the way something lying dormant deep inside her would suddenly come to life. She understood things I didn't and could do what I could never dare: she could take a stand against injustice. Unfortunately, this particular act of rebellion did not play out in my favor. In such situations Pakize had but one tactic. For her, conflict with others was but a diversionary firefight behind the front lines, and she saw no need to hesitate in throwing all her adversarial strength against me in one main assault. This was just what happened. The fight lasted into the early hours. The grand finale saw my blanket and pillow hurled onto the living room divan before Pakize pushed me out of the bedroom.

Pakize misjudged the effect this so called sanction had on me. She thought she caused me deep distress whenever she banished me to the divan. But the truth is that, despite her thirty-five years, she still didn't sleep properly. So a night on the divan was a welcome change from my usual nightly struggle to keep my feet from hanging off the edge of the bed.

Convinced that the divan was the worst possible punishment I could ever receive, Pakize refused to listen when I suggested we sleep separately.

"Oh please! Heaven forbid," she would say, dismissing my proposals, "I should sleep in the bedroom while my husband sleeps on the divan in the living room. I could never reconcile myself with that. Just the thought of you suffering such discomfort . . . I wouldn't be able to sleep at all."

But the most uncomfortable spot was right beside her. In her waking hours, my wife was so very calm, sweet, and listless—save when she was arguing or out at the cinema—but the moment she drifted off to sleep she became an acrobat, her legs and arms and hands multiplying to enhance the feats to be performed; as she lay facedown, her body would jerk in fits and starts, like a spider striking a wild variety of poses, swirling from modern dance into African ritual as her ever-growing limbs came flinging at me from all directions, poking and pushing and clinging to my body in the strangest formations before brutally thrusting me away.

If you add to this the restless snoring, snorting, and mumbling (all consequences of her malfunctioning thyroid gland), you might just begin to have a sense of the mad festivities I was obliged to endure each night.

Pakize also liked to jolt me awake in the middle of the night to give me passionate accounts of her dreams. That was how I came to learn that she experienced in her dreams all that she lacked in her waking hours. So no matter how wrenching an argument, I quietly rejoiced if it ended in my sleeping alone.

So I was sleeping in the living room. After everyone had gone to sleep, my daughter tiptoed into the room and told me she had decided to marry Ismail the Lame. Her eyes were full of tears. "I can't take it anymore," she said. "I'll take Ahmet with me—maybe the family can care for him. Ismail's mother will be here again tomorrow. Every day she asks me if I'll marry him. This time I'm going to say yes." Muffling her sobs, she tiptoed out of the room as silently as she had come in.

And now Ismail the Lame sat there before me. I saw him in all his ugliness. I saw how his vile disposition had eaten through his gross form, seeping into the depths of his mortal soul. He bore all the unsavory traits recorded in the science of phrenology: His forehead was so narrow it was hardly even there, meaning he was vain; he had gangly arms and stubby fingers, and the palms of his hand were deep, coarse, and crimson, as if they were festering wounds; his jutting lower lip and his eyes' sideward glances showed him to be a cruel, moronic trickster and a liar; his voice grated like a steel brush, in itself enough to confirm that he was uncivilized and utterly lacking in social grace; and he had yellow, crooked teeth, all mashed one on top of another, a testament to his miserly nature and unfortunate fate. That he possessed every human flaw imaginable was clear beyond doubt. What business did poor Zehra have with such a man?

It was getting harder and harder to keep calm. Every moment I felt like packing up and leaving the coffeehouse. But I was waiting for Dr. Ramiz and so was forced to endure the poisonous presence of my future son-in-law.

His chin and upper lip twitched like cogs in a watch; his Adam's apple jerked back and forth in his neck as he played cards. Worst of all were his hands: those thick, gnarled fingers, untouched by profession or trade, seemed to have been made expressly for crimes too egregious for a civilized mind even to contemplate.

"I'll take Ahmet with me," Zehra had said the night before,

as if to console me, but now the words horrified me. We were to sacrifice two people instead of just one. I brought my hand to my forehead. "Come now, Hayri İrdal, pull yourself together," I thought. "There is no way you can care for this boy. It's out of the question." But what difference would it make? My fortune would stay the same, I thought, even as disaster loomed.

Twice I tried to force myself to get up. Each time I was pushed back into my chair as if directed by my future son-in-law's curses. How foul tempered and evil. How ugly and crude. No, sir, I was not going to give any daughter of mine to that man. Oh, and the way he played cards—such gruesome avarice. The game more than just a pastime playing itself out in the physical world: it took over his body, operating each part separately, pecking at this and probing at that. His right foot (inside a poorly patched shoe that exposed his shredded sock) pumped up and down like the pedal of a sewing machine; his Adam's apple bulged now in this direction and now in that; his hooklike fingers were either grasping at things or hanging from them; he wheezed in air between his teeth as his chin jutted forward as if to spit out whatever had just been sucked in; as he struggled to befoul all around him, he let out the most preposterous snarls.

"Vile, I tell you, sir, utterly vile! Vile and moronic, moronic and beastly . . ."

A hand fell onto my shoulder.

"Daydreaming again?" asked Dr. Ramiz. He was smiling broadly. Next to him stood a man, probably forty-two, forty-three years old, tall, with light wheat-colored skin, smartly dressed, rather flamboyant, indeed a rather handsome man.

"Allow me to introduce to you my good friend Hayri Bey," Dr. Ramiz said to the man. "He's quite an interesting fellow. Don't be fooled by his attire!" And then, turning to me, he said:

"Halit Ayarcı, a friend of mine from school." There followed the usual polite exchange. As the doctor continued to quiz me about this and that, his eyes kept drifting to the empty table beyond me.

Humans are such strange creatures. At the time I thought it

unfortunate that Halit Ayarcı had chosen just this moment to arrive: his appearance had made it impossible for me to ask Dr. Ramiz for the few liras he owed me. How could I have known then that this man accompanying Dr. Ramiz to the coffeehouse was the harbinger of my good fortune? He brought with him the prosperity of my children and a future for my wife and her sisters.

"What an arrogant man," I thought. "He sizes people up as if he might buy them." Thus my anger toward this stranger was doubled. Yet his eyes brought no discomfort; his gaze was like no other's; I could find in it not the slightest hint of contempt or mockery. He studied people with the same detachment he might accord an object. He wished only to understand the thing before his eyes, nothing more.

We were preparing to part company; I was sinking into my chair, ruefully aware that the chance for demanding those liras had come and gone: meanwhile Dr. Ramiz was turning toward the table he'd been eyeing in the distance, even as he went through the usual motions, giving me a thorough looking over while slapping my shoulder, pinching my cheeks, and chucking my chin (this being the standard routine in the coffeehouse at the time, no one ever took his leave without first taking a thorough inventory of my attire). Then he stopped and said to his friend:

"Weren't you having problems with your watch? Why don't you let Hayri Bey have a look at it? He's quite remarkable with watches and clocks."

With the passing of the years Dr. Ramiz was ever more inclined to excessive chatter.

"I'll have you know the man's one of a kind, a truly magnanimous soul. He might not have his own shop, but he most certainly has a keen grasp on watches and clocks, yes, sir . . ."

In a high-flown voice he added:

"Won't you join us, Hayri Bey? Let's all have a coffee together."

And then, to show Halit Ayarcı just how much he cared for his old classmate, despite the stark differences between us in education, manners, station, rank, wealth, and well-being, he embraced me from behind, throwing his arms right over my hunchback.

This is how it had been for five years. My old friends felt compelled to demonstrate their lasting affection, in spite of all that had passed. And Dr. Ramiz was the most pure-hearted of the lot. We made our way to the empty table, where the doctor began to enumerate my talents, at the same time subjecting his teeth to a vigorous cleaning, sucking individually on each one in his mouth.

"What is there Hayri Bey doesn't know? The science of physiology, phrenology, alchemy, numerology, cleromancy, arithmancy, divine wizardry . . . You name it—he knows them all, not to mention the ancient sciences. Why, just the other day he put forward a diagnosis that surprised even yours truly!"

The truth of the matter is that I had been making ends meet for five years by recycling material from Seyit Lutfullah's repertoire.

As he listened to Dr. Ramiz, Halit Bey sized me up with an expression that said, "If I come into some money, I'll definitely swing by and purchase this creature, now that I know where to find him. But how could I make use of him?" Except when interacting with others, Halit Bey seemed almost absent. This was why his gaze never disturbed. To him people were no more than objects occupying space.

Suddenly, he asked, "Do you really have such experience with timepieces?"

I knew as much about alchemy, cleromancy, and the ancient sciences as I knew about timepieces, and I was no more magnanimous than a member of a secret religious sect, though I did have a certain look of the dervish: I wore a scraggly beard and my hair had recently turned white. But I had grown accustomed to lying. There was no other way for me to survive this meager silver piece I called my life. This was how people wanted me to be. I was a liar. Was there any other choice but to say I knew all there was to know about watches? But there were at least thirty-five different ways to say this. I could say the same thing quite differently to Cemal Bey or Dr. Ramiz, Selma Hanım or Sabriye Hanım, or Lazybones Asaf. I paused to look at this Halit Ayarcı. But no, the time had come to act. In the calmest manner I could muster, I said, "Let's have a look, then."

From his pocket he pulled a small gold watch, which he placed in my hand. It was missing its chain, but it was so finely crafted that I felt as if there were a little sun in my palm. No, I wasn't lost entirely. There were still things in this world that I loved.

Fearful that the watch might elude my grasp, I closed my fingers around it as Halit Ayarcı explained:

"It's hasn't been working for two months. It's a family heirloom, passed down to me from my father, which is why it's so dear to me. What do you think is the problem?"

"There's a problem, yes, and a grave one at that. Of course it isn't ticking. A watch without a chain is like an animal without a halter, a woman without an altar. If someone truly cares for a watch, he will first and foremost attach it to himself with a chain."

I uttered these words to buy myself a little time and also to take stock of my companions.

Halit Ayarcı studied my face carefully:

"You're absolutely right! I've dropped it not once but twice."

"How unfortunate," I replied. "For it's a magnificent piece, and extremely rare nowadays. English make, middle of the nineteenth century. A masterpiece, as I'm sure you know."

The watch was truly beautiful. I nearly forgot all about my troubles with Ismail and my daughter. It had been years since I'd touched a watch of such beauty. Not since I'd repaired Selma Hanım's watch had I seen a piece this fine. I was in heaven.

"But I don't have any tools here. If I can just find my penknife . . ."

And after thrusting my hand into the first pocket, I quickly retracted it in shame. My penknife was with Ali Efendi, the peddler in the Malta Bazaar. This state of affairs had become quite common of late. Whenever we needed something at home and couldn't find it (and that meant just about anything in the house save those things that belonged to my sisters-in-law), we were at once reminded of the Flea Market, or rather the

Malta Bazaar. Or even worse, we were haunted by the peddler's face, with its snub nose and maddening, greedy leer. This
grotesque vision rose up to haunt us relentlessly—in our beds
and at the dinner table, as we dressed, undressed, and conversed. Each absent object had its own story, but all were
replaced by a single face that refused us any hope of peace.

Dr. Ramiz opened his briefcase and removed his penknife.
With a mournful expression, he studied the sorry state of his
fingernails before handing the knife over. A slight smile lit up
Halit Ayarcı's face. Yes, indeed, this man knew not just how to
look but to see.

I opened the watch. There was no need for a magnifying
glass, nor did the watch require any intricate treatment for
repair. It had merely become magnetized.

Halit Ayarcı was looking on with such fixed attention that
one might have thought I was examining his child.

"Oh, there's nothing at all to worry about," I said. "The
watch has become magnetized—that's all. By no means have it
dismantled. There's no need. There's a particular instrument
for just this sort of thing, which any serious major watchmaker
should have. It would take no more than half an hour to fix."

Nodding his head, Halit Ayarcı asked, "How could they not
have identified the problem before?"

"They tend not to. Or rather they don't pay attention to such
things. A timepiece is like the human body. Doctors look for
the illnesses that are most common. But there's a difference
in treatment. In the human body, organs sometimes cease to
function, and not all can be replaced, whereas the parts of a
watch or a clock can be."

Dr. Ramiz was beside himself with joy, so much so that he
looked deranged. I had risen to heights he had never dreamed
possible: I was speaking clearly and concisely, and receiving
due respect.

"Have they actually replaced a part in this watch?" Halit Ayarcı
asked. "I can't believe it. I've known that man for years . . ."

Was the sixth sense that the spiritualists always talked of
finally coming to life inside me? Or was I simply trying to capture this man's attention? Perhaps I had tired of the coffeehouse;

perhaps I wanted to reach out and embrace this most humane of new acquaintances. I spoke with all the eloquence I could muster:

"You must go back to the man and first have him replace the stone that was removed from this spot here, or at least have him find a replacement of equal weight. This might not seem of great importance, but you have to have a balancing weight here. The craftsmen who made this watch would not have set a lentil between two ruby stones. Then have him demagnetize the piece. And finally have him replace this wire."

Halit Ayarcı was silent for several minutes. I clasped my fingers around the watch as if it were the key to my fate. Indeed I was no longer even looking at it.

Meanwhile the argument at the table beside us gathered force, and there was a sudden outburst of punching and slapping before chairs flew up to smash into each other in midair. With his face a bright shade of yellow and his hair standing on end and his Adam's apple twitching like an eagle eyeing its prey, my future son-in-law lashed out at the men who were restraining him as he sputtered every curse in the book.

"Good God," I thought to myself. "Good God, he's going to kill someone, and maybe not just one. You can tell just looking at the brute's eyes, at his teeth. He'll be hanged or get life at the very least! Dear God, it's hopeless. My daughter will be left with no choice, no choice but to live with us forever."

How I regretted having disregarded, disdained, and even toyed with the golden chance that had fallen on our doorstep.

"You never liked the man? Well, then leave it to God. He will have the brute in prison for the night and hanged before the week is out. Your daughter will become a widow before she ever marries. The poor girl, God knows she'll be devastated when she hears the news."

How could I have predicted the punishment I would suffer for the thoughts that had flitted through my mind only minutes before this fracas? But such is the lot of the poor. The office charged with our affairs in the palace of the preordained never errs, never neglects its responsibilities. We allow ourselves to be distracted by a scenario that is as unlikely as it is innocent, and we are made to pay for it; we dream vaguely of violence and repudiation and are called to account.

On this occasion, it seemed my future son-in-law had decided to refute the sciences of physiognomy and phrenology. No one was killed. In fact, he never managed to land the slightest blow. On the contrary, he received two resounding slaps to the face before I could ask his attackers to desist for the love of God. Then a premium-sized fist tickled his upper lip before one of the sturdier wooden chairs in the coffeehouse landed flat on his head. Later a progression of relentless kicks unhinged him from the earth, sending him soaring into the air before he collapsed in a heap on the pavement just outside the front door. Dear Lord, what a joy to behold!

Oh yes, it was truly exhilarating. First of all, he didn't kill anyone. So he wouldn't be imprisoned or hanged. Naturally, if my daughter hadn't been involved in the matter, I'd not have felt the slightest remorse. But she was involved. He wasn't to be hanged or imprisoned, and so I could, if I wished, still accept him as my son-in-law.

Then there was the thrashing he'd received before my very eyes. No longer would he be able to strut about in front of me like a rooster. Now when he said, "What's up, old geezer?" I could volley back with "Not too bad, Ismail, my boy. I was just at the coffeehouse. You know, the one where you got thoroughly trounced just the other day? I'm just coming back from there." Or I'd just shout, "The coffeehouse! The chair! Sabri the proprietor!" and carry on my way. Or better yet, "Ismail, my lamb, have you reimbursed the coffeehouse for that chair? Goodness, my dear boy, you really must be more careful with such things. Your skull smashed it to bits, after all. That's no fault of the proprietor, now is it? Why should Sabri suffer such a loss on your account?"

There was a third reason to be happy. After his thrashing, Ismail would be out of commission for at least three days, and if nothing else, his mind would be far from the subject of marriage. That gave me time to think. Some people spend their lives making good use of time, but in my life it has always stuck a foot out in front of me. I have tripped over time.

But why had I sat quietly through the pummeling? Why hadn't I jumped up to applaud the people who had given the miserable brute his comeuppance? Why had I not kissed their foreheads?

"You scoundrel," I might have cried. "You cast your greedy eye on my pearl of a daughter and then you grin at me with such impertinence, stare at me so vacantly, like some moron. May God bless the hands that struck you!"

Halit Ayarcı interrupted my musings.

"Would they be able to fix it so quickly?"

"An hour at the most. They'll have to find the stone first and then remount it."

He turned to Dr. Ramiz.

"Off we go then, Doctor! Let's be off to settle this straightaway! And you, good sir, will have everything done in just the way you have described it to us. That is, of course, if it isn't too much of an inconvenience. Then afterward we'll spend some time together . . ."

"But, sir, in such clothes . . ."

It was not really because I was ashamed of being seen with them in such clothes that I objected. At the time I had no choice but to accept my sorry state and the clothes and possessions that came with it. Matters of honor, glory, and attire are of no consequence to a man who has— however fleetingly—considered giving his pearl of a daughter away to Ismail the Lame. I hesitated in the hope that they might pity me with a few liras if I stayed behind. All too often I'd been sent away from those places to which I had been so exuberantly invited and obliged to walk home by foot. But how could Halit Ayarcı have known what I was thinking at the time?

"But what's the problem with your clothing? People understand who you are from your face."

So he understood. I already knew that my fate was inscribed on my face. Allow me to say that Halit Ayarcı never considered my clothing: unlike all the others, Halit Ayarcı considered only my face.

They hailed the first taxi they could find. I stepped toward the front door, as I planned to sit beside the driver; surely that was where I was expected to sit. But, taking me by the arm, Halit Ayarcı pulled me away and, opening the other door with his other hand, he seated me in the back of the car. He sat Dr. Ramiz down next to me and took the place beside him. What a strange man. Even his courtesy came in the form of an order— the man's great girth gave a certain weight to his words, and he had no qualms about using his hands if necessary.

How many years had passed since my last jaunt in a private car? It was a winter evening and I was taking Selma Hanım her ball gown; not a moment passed without my kissing and caressing the cardboard box that never left my lap; I might have been bearing the cloak of the Holy Prophet himself. That was perhaps the happiest night of my life. Selma Hanım invited me upstairs and offered me a coffee; after donning the gown for which I had searched high and low, from four o'clock to nine, she came and sat beside me. Cemal Bey was on a business trip, and Selma was waiting for the friends who would accompany her to the ball. She had never been so cordial: she had forgotten the distance between us. At one point she said, "Hayri, why don't you come along too? It shouldn't be any problem. Cemal Bey has so many suits . . . You'll just have to shave." Then, as if mindful of the panic in my eyes, she said, "Oh never mind, then, but on one condition: remember that I must attend this ball, and if my friends don't show up, I shall have no choice but to go with you." And I began to pray for her friends to come late, for them to not come at all, for them to come as soon as possible, for them to save me from the ache of ecstasy. That night I came to understand that there was more to Selma Hanım than just style, elegance, and a well-chosen dress; she was more than the height of grace and more than just an intoxicating flurry of laughter. That night I came to understand that she also had a body, a very fine female body, a ship that could take a man on the world's most alluring cruise. Her back held more delights than a palatial mirror; her arms were like moonlit silver streams.

Perhaps it was the delight of seeing my future son-in-law mangled before my eyes that had led me to revisit this rare moment of bliss.

However hard I tried, I could not put the great thrashing out of my mind: the more I went over it, the more I recalled. There was a particular snort every time his nose suffered a blow that I am quite sure I will treasure for the rest of my life. Only a nose as vile as his could have performed so well. I could not let my sweet memories of Selma Hanım distract me from this fortuitous beating and the bounties it had brought me. What might have happened had I not been in the coffeehouse to witness it? How differently life would have played itself out. Had I only read about his getting pulverized, or killed, in the paper, had someone from the neighborhood just relayed the event to me with disingenuous concern, while secretly relishing every detail, I would have said, "Oh, what a scoundrel," and moved on. But now the memory of that day would, like Selma Hanım's intoxicating compliments on that other night, stay with me forever. I could return to them whenever I liked, recalling the spot where each sweet blow had landed, and where he had collapsed on the floor, and in what position, and how he'd got up, his face smeared with blood, and how he'd again fallen, face first, onto the ground. And ah, how he looked at me when he finally left the coffeehouse—he knew just what I was thinking, the lousy wretch, the miserable cretin, the lowly brute. For I knew he had suffered far more at that moment than at any other during the entire affair. He was the sort of man who had come into this world to be punished. And the most devastating blow was to be trounced before my eyes. Humiliation coursed through every fiber of his being. The accursed scoundrel! How dare he take a fancy to my daughter? Had he no idea just how low he had sunk?

Arriving in Beyazıt Square, I fished about in my pockets for my watch, as usual. But of course it wasn't there. I'd sold it eight months earlier. I looked up at the clocks in the square. One had stopped at half past three and the other seemed to be racing like a train that had been running late since eleven o'clock the night before, desperately trying to get back on schedule by evening. Just to make conversation, I said, "These clocks never tell the correct time."

Having just cast off the memory of my future son-in-law like a dead snake, I felt comfortable in my own skin, so I added, "Do you know that no two city clocks ever tell the same time? If you like, just have a look at the clock in Eminönü, and then we'll compare it with the one in Karaköy."

No one replied. Both men seemed to be daydreaming. I shrugged my shoulders. What did I care? I was no longer under any obligation to give Zehra to that brute. Nothing else mattered. But, dear God, however was I going to provide for her?

To dispel my grief, I turned my thoughts back to the thrashing of Ismail the Lame, but to no avail; then I tried thinking about Selma Hanım, but that didn't work either. The heaviness prevailed. Dr. Ramiz finally spoke when we reached Eminönü.

"You're absolutely right, my good man. A difference of twenty-five minutes."

In Karaköy, Halit Ayarcı added, "And here we're half an hour ahead!"

The watchmaker was a rich Armenian obsessed with faux politesse. There was no way you could look at the man without marveling at his shirtmaker, and what a barber! As for the shine on his shoes, the scoundrel clearly slept in his footwear. Upon seeing Halit Ayarcı, he greeted him in a splattering of French, but his words went unnoticed. Taking out his watch, Halit Ayarcı turned to me and said:

"Would you kindly explain the matter to this gentleman, Hayri Bey?"

Agop Horlogian betrayed both compassion and contempt as he inspected me from head to toe, finally settling his fascinated eyes on my shoes. Surely if I had presented myself to this man in any other circumstance, he would have dismissed me, without a moment's hesitation, as a beggar.

This was perhaps why I mustered my most imposing voice as I explained the condition of Halit Ayarcı's watch.

"First of all," I said, "you've dismantled this watch most brutishly on three occasions. These watches are delicate mechanisms that cannot sustain such crude handling. Look at the back of this piece. This wasn't made on a factory line. It was painstakingly crafted by hand! It's a letter from one master craftsman to another, but clearly it wasn't written for you!"

And I pointed to the designs engraved on the inside of the front cover. Then I slowly pursed my lips and said: "It truly grieves me to see a craftsman's place usurped by a merchant."

Oh Nuri Efendi, my saintly master, may you rest in peace. You should have seen the state of the poor man as he listened to me. The victory was yours. Hearing just one of your words of wisdom, Horlogian's eyes were released from my shoes, as if he had suddenly grasped that they hadn't come to see him all by themselves, that surely they must have a master; it had finally occurred to him that the miserable man standing before him must also have a head, even a face.

No, I'll never give my daughter to that hound!

Having thanked him with an almost courteous smile for having remembered to look up at my face, I continued.

"It seems your apprentices have misplaced this one particular stone while repairing the watch. So if you would attend to this . . ."

Nervously rubbing his hands, Horlogian muttered something unintelligible, but by then I had lost all my patience.

"You," I cried, "will do what I say. Everything that I say! First you will demagnetize this timepiece."

Then I turned to Halit Ayarcı and said, "Once upon a time this kind of work wasn't done for mere financial reward. It was done by those who were apprenticed to the trade and by people who truly loved the work."

I could almost hear Nuri Efendi's voice echoing in my ear: "Bravo, my son."

Had I not been so racked with other worries at the time, had I not felt swept away on a sea of misadventures, with only five liras in my pocket to feed my family that night, I doubt I would have been so sharp with the watchmaker Horlogian. At one point I looked the poor man in the eye. I was ashamed of my behavior, but I thought to myself, "Let him get what he deserves. He's not worried about finding food for dinner tonight . . ."

By God, a man can be so snug behind a well-paid job. He can take on the entire world. Within a minute, Horlogian had pulled himself together. He could have handed us the watch and chased us out of his shop then and there.

Instead we stayed for an hour and a half. And over that time the grace of God and the spiritual presence of my master allowed me to bestow upon the watch merchant a precise and highly constructive lesson in the maintenance of a timepiece. When he replaced the stone, reestablishing the correct weight so as not to disturb the mechanics of the watch, I paid particular attention; the man's face was drenched in sweat.

Finally I warned the merchant against using too much oil when working with timepieces of this caliber.

"You're not roasting an eggplant! You're repairing a watch. Stop using this kind of oil! These days it's easy to find very light bone oil."

Halit Ayarcı's eyes were riveted on me the whole while. By the time we left the shop, Horlogian seemed to have forgotten his French. Feeling compelled to pay me a compliment, he asked, "Is the esteemed gentleman from Switzerland? Or perhaps just educated there?"

"Why would you think that?"

"It's just that you have such an impressive understanding of timepieces."

My answer was brief.

"I love them," I said, "very much."

Then I wished I hadn't berated the fellow so harshly: he might have taken me on as an apprentice.

Dr. Ramiz and Halit Ayarcı were engaged in a lively dispute at the shop entrance. Where would they go that evening? Or, rather, where would *we* go?

Finally Halit Ayarcı announced, "Off we go then up the Bosphorus. And Hayri Efendi is to honor us with his presence. We'll drink rakı together, won't we, Beyefendi?"

"That makes four," I said to myself. "In just one hour I have been addressed as beyefendi four times. What's more, Ismail the Lame was beaten to a pulp before my eyes. And perhaps for that very reason he would never again ask for my daughter's hand in marriage. And then, after that, I had ruffled the feathers of one of Istanbul's eminent watchmakers for an hour and a half. And all this was happening to me. My family was at home, starving, and I was now riding in a car whose make I would never be able to divine, not even if it were mine. And to top it all off, we were on our way to Büyükdere to drink rakı.

My last visit to Büyükdere had been to attend the funeral of a relative of Selma Hanım. I will never forget how exhausted I was that day. My devotion to this woman was such that I nearly carried the casket on my back all by myself. And by the end I was on the verge of throwing myself into the grave with the deceased. What people won't do for love . . .

My worst memory from that day was locking eyes with Cemal Bey; he was having a private laugh about the state I was in. He had pouted throughout the entire ceremony, as aggravated as if his shoe were pinching a painful corn on the bottom of his foot. His demeanor had set me so on edge that more than once I had considered shoving him into the grave as an escort to the deceased before making my escape. After which I would climb to the top of Hünkartepe and sing that folk song to the cool breeze, "My Lover at Sea." Why not some other song? I don't know. But naturally I'd done no such thing. To make matters worse, he'd asked me to take his arm on the way back, and I'd more or less had to carry the brute myself.

"Why is it that the poor and the downtrodden always get beaten? Take Cemal Bey, no one would ever dare lay a finger on such a man."

I had picked up the habit of speaking to myself aloud. Dr. Ramiz turned to me with a teasing smile and said, "Again? What do you expect from the miserable man?"

Then turning to Halit Ayarcı, he said, "Hayri Bey simply cannot stomach Cemal."

My face flushed to hear my secrets so baldly revealed, so I turned to the window.

"He's absolutely right!" Halit Ayarcı said. Then he turned to face me. "It's not like I haven't thought about doing it once or twice myself. But in the end I was a bit frightened by the thought of it. I realized that once I started I'd never stop. Just imagine . . . If someone actually planted a slap on that face, he wouldn't be able to stop at just one!"

I shot a glance at his enormous hands, saddened to think that nothing of the sort had ever occurred.

On the ferryboat returning from the funeral, Cemal had never once left my side. Practically every five minutes, as if to remind me just how tired I really was, he said, "Hayri Bey, you seem all puffed out! I'll never forget all your help today. She was such a strange woman. More of a nut than that aunt of yours, but the same sort of person . . . Of course Selma never liked her. And she harbored no goodwill toward us either. But all the same, she was a relative. We were under obligation not to neglect this last responsibility of ours. What to do? That's what I asked myself this morning. I asked Selma and she said, 'Don't worry. Once Hayri Bey reads about it in the paper, he'll be over in no time.' As it happens, all those extra details in the obituary were added just for you. But the truth is, you really have overextended yourself . . ."

Yes, that was just how it happened. I had volunteered for the job.

Cemal Bey couldn't openly call me an idiot or an incurable moron. He could only repeat the story to me ten times over, to hammer home the fact that I was indeed a fool. "No, Selma never loved that woman. She'd been mistreated by her on many occasions. But still, she's ever so grateful to you for all you've done."

Every time he opened his mouth I felt the ground shift beneath my feet. To think of how I'd gone to sit at the head of that grave without even having made my ablutions, to wail painful prayers for this relative they had never liked.

And oh, the fantasies I played over in my mind. One took me forward to the day after the funeral, or perhaps a week later, when I'd run into Selma Hanım, who, after greeting me with her most charming smile, would say, "Oh, Hayri Bey, Cemal Bey told me all about your devotion to my aunt. I can't tell you how touched I was. I am so grateful for your unfaltering friendship. But I knew, Hayri Bey, I always knew that you were my very best friend!" And she would carry on with similar flatteries, and I'd be so flustered that I'd begin to stammer until, finding nothing to say, I would throw myself down at her feet and, with a voice even sweeter than before, Selma Hanım would say, "No, no, I know everything . . . Don't do this to a miserable woman imprisoned by her true feelings!"

I had endured all the hardship as I kept imagining that scene straight out of a Turkish film—but of course Selma Hanım would never speak with that nasal voice our actors affected. But every five minutes Cemal Bey said something else, wrenching me from my sweet reverie.

At some point I drifted back to listen to what Halit Ayarcı was saying.

"It's simply not possible to know Cemal, even superficially, and not want to kill the man. I thought about it on more than one occasion when we studied together at Galatasaray Lycée."

After that funeral I hadn't uttered the name Büyükdere again. But rakı was another matter altogether. My bond with the drink was stronger, deeper. But even the drink reminded me of the man. In fact, I had experience of rakı with Cemal Beyefendi himself, an episode that cast him in an unfavorable light. One day I paid him a visit and found him just settling down to drink at the dinner table; he promptly sat me down and offered me a rakı. As he took his first sip, his face contorted into such a miserable wince that I lost all my appetite, but, just to show the man how to drink rakı, I threw back eight glasses, one after the other, and left the house swooning. Thinking back now on all my experiences with Cemal Bey, I wonder if I wasn't actually right to feel the way I did about him. Clearly there was nothing, nothing at all, about the man I liked, save his wife . . .

The second time I found myself without a job there was a period when I was drinking a considerable amount of rakı. I owed a few liras to every little drinking hole from Şehzadebaşı to Edirnekapı that reeked of bitter beans and burnt olive oil. And my tab at the corner shop grew with the number of forty fives of rakı I begged the shopkeeper to give me every evening; he only allowed me such credit because he had his eyes on the derelict plot beside our old house. Sometimes I didn't dare take the bottle home; I would knock it back then and there, right next to the counter, oblivious to the impertinence of the shop boys and Yusuf Efendi's insinuations about the state of my home and all my debt, not caring a whit for what they might say behind my back; and then, doing my best not to look them in the eye, I would say, as I stared off into space, "Put this in a corner for me. I'll come by tomorrow evening and pick up where I left off."

So I was familiar with both Büyükdere and rakı. Both evoked infinite memories. It was only natural for the two to come together. And of course there were those who drank rakı in Büyükdere. But how had I ended up in this scene? This was the strange part: me, rakı, and Büyükdere. No, that wasn't it. Büyükdere, rakı, me—no matter how I imagined it, the combination was still something my mind of two hours ago would never have accepted. And even more incredible, the me in this scenario had been addressed four times as beyefendi.

Hayri Bey, Hayri Efendi, Hayri my son, Hayri the Fortuneteller, Hayri l'Horloger, the orphan Hayri, the wizard Hayri, prodigal Hayri, Hayri the Tippler, the Addict, husband to Pakize Hayri, the brother-in-law to his wife's sisters Hayri—and now Hayri Beyefendi.

"Hayri Beyefendi, won't you have a cigarette?"

"Why, thank you, Beyefendi."

That was how people should speak. It was something I would have said six or seven years ago. It was one more thing I had forgotten. In a rush I felt fire spreading over my lips and gums; it had been a while since I'd had a cigarette. When I heard the fifth "beyefendi," I nearly leapt up from my seat in joy.

The car soared like an arrow cleaving the beautiful misty spring evening and pushing it to either side. In the fog over the hills of Çemberlikuyu, that evening unfurled like a ribbon whose colors ran from wine dark to golden, ever gaining in beauty, in a verdant lushness that stretched out as far as the eye could see and that was soft as fresh grass, timid and frail as wildflowers. It was as if we were at the end of that ribbon, rushing forward, collecting the many reflections around it.

Rakı, Büyükdere, and I, and the "I" in this equation was a beyefendi. And the car was soaring at seventy kilometers. And I was as elated as if I were a child all over again, speeding off to a holiday fair!

"You seem rather lost in thought, Hayri Beycfendi!"

Praise God that Dr. Ramiz was there. I never felt I had to speak when addressed in his company. He answered for me.

"Hayri Bey's always like that!"

Hayri Beyefendi, our Hayri, your Hayri, Hayri plunged in thought—there were so many different Hayris. Oh, if we could only drop a few of them off along the way. I could be just one person, just myself, like everyone else.

The car sped down the coast, pulling the trees out of the earth and tossing them over our head as we passed. Everything was as soft as the hair of a young child. My first child who died of neglect six years ago had hair like that. What could be wrong about running this old fellow down? He's more bedraggled than I—obviously not all quite there. Bravo, cabbie! You swept right by him without a scratch. Now he'll know the dangers around him and take better care. Perhaps he'll dream of it tonight. Perhaps he'll be torn from his loved one as abruptly as if he'd been in a car accident after all. But why did I keep thinking of Selma Hanım and Cemal Bey? I suppose it was being in a car.

"My dear Hayri Bey, could you come over and see us tonight? Selma's expecting you. Yes, around six or seven . . ."

On the phone Cemal Bey sounded like a child rocking back and forth, desperate to pee.

"Right away, sir," I replied.

I felt disgusted just talking to him, so I hung up the phone, knowing all too well that my face was bright yellow with rage. He always wanted to hang up first.

I waited until seven to knock, but I had been at the door since six thirty. The maid flashed me an oily smile when she opened it. She was drenched in the most revolting perfume in the world, and there was a nasty flicker in her eyes. Despite the light in the foyer, it seemed like she was leering at me through a dingy darkness. Her hand clutched onto my jacket. But why get upset? Weren't we both serving the same people, in just the same way? Shouldn't there be some sense of common cause? No, I wasn't angry. I was merely in a hurry.

The blinds in Selma Hanım's bedroom were drawn, and a single lamp gave off a piercing light that gave the room the aura

of a cave by the sea. The bed was swollen in the dappled light—
a gigantic seashell with Selma Hanım stretched out inside.

Was she ill? My daughter, my little girl, was ill at the time.
She'd been poorly for the last ten days. Dr. Ramiz had not managed to stop in to see us yesterday. But Selma Hanım's illness
was of a different nature altogether, relegating all else to the
background: I suddenly forgot all about Ahmet's chest problems, Zehra's sinusitis, my wife's thyroid gland, even her slight
fever. Silk undergarments were strewn about over an armchair
and a chaise longue. Cemal Bey had collapsed into an armchair
and sat there waiting for me in his dressing gown.

"I wish you the swiftest recovery, madam." Blood throbs in
my temples. I want to say more, but what? That morning my
daughter's temperature spiked to thirty-eight degrees and her
face looked so terribly strange. But this is of no concern to Selma
Hanım. I should be home right now. But I'm happy to be here.

"My dear Hayri Bey, I've put you to so much trouble yet again.
But there really is no one else we can count on to help us."

She's so beautiful, so charming. Her face reminds me of the
sweet shops of my childhood—or the window displays of the
florists today, flashing with color and light.

I hear Nuri Efendi's voice echoing in my head: "Man's only
fortress is patience."

I listen to him inside my fortress. But in this particular room
its defenses are thin.

"We must have a gift delivered. And as you can see, I'm not
well. I simply cannot get rid of this cold. Cemal Bey wanted to
go, but he had a touch of fever this morning. I was worried that
one of us might take a turn for the worse."

And there it was, the slap in the face. Nothing involving
Cemal Bey could ever bring me happiness. But such were the
workings of a woman's mind. What could she do? Being beautiful was enough. She went on:

"Besides, he's already made other plans for the evening, so
the task must fall on your shoulders. The woman's a relative of
ours . . . in the maternity ward . . . in Şişli. We were always
close friends. And there is just no one else we can call but you!"

Undoubtedly her malady makes her more beautiful. A simple

sneeze and she's more charming than ever. Ah, if only I could take her away from here and suspend her over the head of my bed like a chandelier. She fumbles for something in her bed: "Please, a tissue from over there . . ."

"But, hanım, you could catch a cold . . ."

"No . . . The room's quite warm."

The room's warm, but still, please cover up. Cover your arms, your neck, and your chest. Let your figure disappear beneath the covers. Cover yourself up so this dogged fidelity can survive. For if not, if not . . . Yes—oh, why must she hide herself from me? How lowly is the station from which I gaze up at her . . .

"The gift is ready. It's there on the chair. I have just one other request. Ayşe will give you one of Cemal's suits to wear. The complete suit. I'm sure you'll understand—they're wealthy people. The gift must be delivered by an old and faithful servant of the family. I'm sure you'll look absolutely wonderful."

She laughs again. I want to take that with me too. But where would I hang it? It isn't enough just to serve her? I also have to convince her friends and family that I was born in their home and lulled them to sleep as babies in their cradles. I have to look sharp and clean! And beyond that, I have to be seen wearing one of Cemal Bey's suits! So that people will notice and say, "They're looking after the man well enough, that's for sure. Wasn't Cemal Bey wearing that very suit just the other day? He's got quite some girth! That's true nobility, with the air of a well-mannered man."

"You won't be angry with me, will you, Hayri Bey? Besides, I know how much you care for me. You'd never be angry with me, would you?"

So she knows I love her. Oh joy! I am overwhelmed with joy. She buries her face in her pillow. Her hair is a mess. Like a beach of soft sand the bed takes the shape of a woman sleeping facedown under the covers. The covers softly undulate over the form of her body. If only I could just take the gift and flee . . . but she rolls over and flashes me the same capricious smile. Clearly I am the only one for her. But evidently she is preparing yet another impertinence:

"Ayşe will give you money. You'll take a car!"

Ayşe has prepared the brown suit I had seen Cemal Bey wearing just three days ago. I undress in a narrow nook in the kitchen, with Ayşe standing just outside the door. She opens the door, and there before my eyes are Emine, my children, Pakize, everyone. Why do they all insist on swarming around me at moments like this? Only Selma Hanım isn't there. She's curled up in her bed like a sly cat. If she appears too, if I can't get her out of my mind, I won't be able to go through with this. But shouldn't I be the one catching Ayşe unawares?

Both of us feel knots in our throats, and then we swallow. Her arms are nothing like Selma's. Nausea strong enough to turn all the stomachs in the world seizes me. No, I am not the kind of man to fancy someone like Ayşe. But Selma Hanım only gives me tips, secondhand suits, and errands. I dangle in a void between the two of them. I need to grasp onto one side so as not to fall. But how to manage such a feat?

A transformed Hayri steps out the front door with two packages tucked under his arms. I'll leave one with the tobacconist; I can pick it up on the way back. But if I do go all the way to Şişli, how will ever I get back home? By tram, I suppose. There's no other way. Ayşe's not like me; she works for money up front. But, then again, so do I: how many times have I had cash advances on my monthly wages—first from creditors, then from friends, and finally from any old stranger who happens to be around?

I have to get the money out of her somehow. But why don't I like her? Ayşe, Pakize, Selma Hanım, Emine—I can't even think of them anymore. I'm no longer worthy of them. I can't rid myself of the nausea I feel when I think of her corpulence. How could I have stooped so low? To betray such a beautiful woman—and with her own maid! And both Selma Hanım and Cemal Bey making fun of my very thoughts . . . "Cemal Bey has a bit of a fever today."

The car came to an abrupt halt in front of the restaurant. The mullet in the display window glittered red and blue, reflecting the last remnants of our journey up the Bosphorus.

"After you, Beyefendi."

"Oh no, please, sir, I insist . . ."

The proprietor greeted us in the courtyard and took Halit Ayarcı by the hand. So this was the custom. I'd do the same if I had money. But not like that, no, I couldn't. How could I ever be so confident? This was not just a greeting at the door of a restaurant—it was more along the lines of regal conquest. If shaking hands like this had been the custom in their day, then surely Alexander the Great would have done the same in Egypt, and Darius in Greece. The restaurant seemed to expand with our every step. Or perhaps not, for at the same time it was narrowing its focus, galloping toward us en masse. All eyes were fixed on us, except for those of a rather attractive woman in the corner who had buried her head in her plate. If only I could have seen her face just then. But I was just a little too late. I couldn't tell if I knew her or not. But I understand why Halit turned his back to the sea—he didn't want to disturb her. But who is she? He had me sit down opposite him. The woman lifted her head up from her plate, her face stripped of joy.

Beyond us the sea and the night—a rich blue night that swims through a man like a fish from a dream whose silence has settled inside him.

"Soon the moon will rise just over the opposite shore."

Halit Bey ordered like he was firing celebratory gunshots at a wedding.

"Rakı—but not Kulüp. One of those . . . You know, the ones I brought the other night!"

Another brand apart from Kulüp rakı! But why not? There are premium grades of everything. Weren't women the same? First Selma Hanım, then Nevzat Hanım, Pakize, and last my older sister-in-law, even though she is Pakize's sister—they were all different grades. And then so many more. The universe is like a huge head of cabbage, layer upon layer.

The headwaiter gave us the menu.

Halit Bey turned to me and said, "Do us the honor of selecting the meze!"

I pulled myself together.

"You are more familiar with this restaurant than I, Your Grace. I am only familiar with stuffed mussels. I once sold them in the Balıkpazarı . . ."

I could have gone on: "I'm a poor man. If you hadn't brought me here, I could have done no more than walk past this establishment's front door. Perhaps they have dishes I wouldn't even know. I am Hayri İrdal, the man whose youngest daughter was carried to her grave by the cemetery guard just five years ago. You must understand that I am a miserable wretch. And tomorrow I'll give my eldest daughter to Ismail the Lame, the very scoundrel who had the impertinence to receive that thrashing before Your Excellency's very eyes."

But what good would all that have done? Why ruin an evening that had started out so beautifully? That night fortune made me Hayri Beyefendi. Best to make the most of it.

Crossing my legs, I looked about the place with studied nonchalance. Or at least I think I did. Perhaps my face seemed racked with confusion, because (as I am sure you are already aware) I am like any other wretched soul, trundling about this world with my mortal burden borne on the hump of my back.

The headwaiter waited patiently. Good God, he gazed upon Halit Ayarcı with such compassion, such love! It was as if joy itself had attached Gabriel's wings to the waiter's torso. And when his eyes were graced by the gaze of Halit Ayarcı, it seemed he might fly through the window, over the sea, and up into the sky still holding the tray of mezes, maybe even taking the entire restaurant with him. But no, he wouldn't make it so far; for he would be absorbed into the windowpanes, like the angels in the frescoes of the domes of the Hagia Sophia. And from there he would cry out to Halit Ayarcı: "Ah! the blood in my veins! Oh! the light of my eyes!"

"A toast to you, Doctor! And you too, Beyefendi."

The customs of such places were second nature to him. His voice was made for giving orders. I wondered if he didn't have a bit of the actor in him. But no, this wasn't acting; this was on another scale. He is so comfortable in his own skin. He has never suffered defeat.

"Some ice? Just a bit more? Now, we will down the first few glasses in haste, and then we'll slow down. And so we'll be able to enjoy ourselves for as long as we like."

Sitting at this table in a restaurant was far more pleasant

than standing behind the counter in my corner shop. There was time to drink rakı with due attention. The melting ice turned a milky gray, swirling down my glass like liquid marble. This must have been how God created light on the second day. Then the pleasure of the second sip. I pressed my tongue against the roof of my mouth oh so gently, to taste the hint of mastic. What a change from those forty-fives I used to drink! With the second sip and the third, a weight bore down on me, a lid slamming shut, and a strange new warmth coursed through each and every fiber in my body. I felt myself in the echoing inner chamber of a hammam. My fourth sip emptied the glass. Was it right to be drinking so quickly? Shouldn't I have savored it? This evening would never repeat itself: never again would I enjoy such food or drink!

Halit Ayarcı refilled my glass. Ah, if only everyone loved his watch as much as this man does; if only they all could be friends with Dr. Ramiz . . . The ice in my glass turned the rakı into veined marble.

"Aren't you eating, Hayri Beyefendi?"

I'd lost track of how many glasses I'd had. There was no use trying to remember. "No, thank you," I said. When all the food was laid out on the table before me, I suddenly felt full— that's just the way I am. Dr. Ramiz is another story. He was devouring the food as if he'd no memory of all the advice he'd given me about polite eating whenever he'd invited me to eat at that little *meyhane* in Şehzadebaşı. Plates kept circling back to him as if he were the official checkpoint. And as I viewed him through a huge and melting cube of ice, I fancied myself behind a vast pane of glass.

"Psychoanalysis is the most important discovery of the age."

Halit Ayarcı's voice suddenly went sharp.

"Enough of your psychoanalysis, Doctor. For God's sake! We're drinking rakı."

Dr. Ramiz dropped the subject at once, turning his attention to his lobster. To tell you the truth, I'd spent ten long years— our entire acquaintance—longing to tell the doctor just that. But whenever we'd gone to a *meyhane*, psychoanalysis had been the only topic allowed.

"You really taught Horlogian a good thing or two!"

"Perhaps I went a bit too far. But the man did deserve it."

"He did indeed. Very much so, I would say!"

Once again Halit Ayarcı was looking me over as if deciding whether to buy me.

"Hayri Bey, just where did you learn about watches and clocks?"

"As a child—when I was still a child—I met an esteemed religious time setter by the name of Nuri Efendi. He was a friend of my father's . . ."

I was unable to finish my story as a procession of ten or more people poured into the restaurant. Everyone turned to watch them. At the head of the party was a lavishly dressed, large man—the kind whose photograph often appeared in the newspapers; from across the room he waved to Halit Ayarcı, who returned the greeting by half rising to his feet in a most dignified manner. Extra tables were pulled out and chairs swung into place. Waiters ricocheted about the restaurant like billiard balls. Then the lavishly dressed man came over to see us, while the others in his party stayed behind, talking and joking among themselves as they waited for their table to be set. Though they seemed reasonably relaxed, they each kept an eye on the man approaching our table, while giving the same attention to the seat he would soon occupy at theirs, as if resigned, on such occasions, to suffer split vision.

The newcomer placed a firm hand on Halit Ayarcı's shoulder, as if to keep his friend from standing, and in an affectionate voice, he said: "So how are things, Halit Bey?"

Now this was a voice! Powerful, confident of its authority, deep with suggestion—it was far superior to Halit Bey's. It was a voice both personal and distant, a voice that embraced you while keeping you at bay, towering over you even as it took you by the arm and walked beside you. It took the man no more than three or four words to work his magic. This was the moment when we grasped Halit Ayarcı's true importance, for here was a man of even greater importance paying his respects: this alone made him a hundred times more important in our eyes. It wasn't an ordinary conversation we were witnessing but a mounting multiplication of regard and respect.

"So kind of you to ask, sir."

"Who are these friends of yours?"

And with this gesture we were born anew. Dr. Ramiz and I cowered in shame and wonder before this Adam newly created in God's image. But Halit Ayarcı showed no surprise. After introducing Dr. Ramiz, he turned to me.

"One of my dear friends, Hayri İrdal Bey, our country's most renowned master of watches and clocks. An unrivaled individual indeed."

From the manner of his introduction I understood that Halit Ayarcı was the kind of man who saw both his future and his past through the prism of the present; he had presented me as an old friend. And the grandee seemed delighted to have made my acquaintance. His face lit up with a childish smile. It was while he was preparing to express his delight that the dish of red mullet on our table distracted him. I could wait, but red mullet could not. They'd go cold, and cold red mullet was of no use to anyone. He picked one up with the hand that had been resting on Halit Ayarcı's shoulder and with that same childish smile he popped the entire fish into his mouth. But he hadn't forgotten me, and by way of proof he put his left hand on my shoulder to direct the same smile my way. Clearly he had taken a shine to me. His attention and respect drove me an inch and half deep into the wooden floorboards beneath us. He kept staring at me, and with such tender constancy. There was no need to talk; we understood one another. He had taken to me, and I to him. Oozing confidence, he extended his right hand to the table as if to caress a lock of hair, and soon another mullet was nothing but a pile of bones casually tossed to the wooden floor. He repeated the operation two or three times. There was no need for a fork—a fork would have been far too cumbersome. He was not a man to put on airs. He beamed at me with genuine sincerity. Why should he not give the red mullet the same consideration? Who could expect the man to mediate his affection with a fork? Besides, a fork was for real food, not for simple snacks like red mullet!

He looked at me after his fifth red mullet and I could see that his compassion for me was now a hundred times stronger, as if I had created those fish with my own hands or at least caught or cooked them; with his eyes still locked on mine, he said:

"Divine, absolutely divine . . . and cooked to perfection. Height of the season, you know!"

Applying his full weight to my shoulder, he gave his final order:

"But please, help yourselves! It's the season for red mullet."

With this he released his grip on my shoulder, and as he turned toward his table, his eyes left me too. We had become brothers over red mullet. Was there need for anything more? Then a tray of fresh almonds on ice caught his eye: now here was a new treat. As he sampled the nuts, he exchanged a few last words with Halit Bey, but what a strange conversation. For as he feasted on the almonds, he wasn't really listening to Halit Bey, and naturally he couldn't speak himself, not when he was so busy with those nuts; this was a man who did not like to see time wasted, who left it to his entourage to do the talking.

At one point Halit Bey said to him, "I suppose I'll come and bother you with this one of these days."

The answer was brief.

"Most certainly, and why not tomorrow? We can have lunch here."

With some reluctance he withdrew the hand that had found its way back to my shoulder, softening the betrayal with one last tender, heart-shattering glance, whereupon he took his leave, enchanting us with his smile and his sparkling spectacles, and assuming the fatherly air of a man who was, despite his evident superiority, determined to indulge us.

We all sat down. Dr. Ramiz's face was flushed with joy. If not in seventh heaven, I was at the very least embracing Jesus Christ somewhere in the fourth. And why not? Not even a stone could have resisted flattery this sincere. I looked down at my left shoulder. He had gazed down at my shoulder as if it were bathed in light, as if it belonged to one of those Assyrian gods we read about in our schoolbooks. How could it be that I, Hayri İrdal, I, a miserable waste of life, could be showered with such attention? It was beyond comprehension. Dear Lord! Your glory is truly great!

Only Halit Ayarcı seemed unaffected. The moment he sat down he turned to me, and in a decisive tone of voice that told me an important matter had been settled, he said, "Yes."

I gathered that he wanted me to carry on with what I had been saying before being interrupted by the new arrival. But I didn't exactly understand what he wanted me to say. And I felt so far from Nuri Efendi.

But as soon as Halit Bey pronounced his decisive yes, Dr. Ramiz began his babbling.

"Truly a great man," he exploded. "How fatherly, and so noble. I never would have thought of him like this."

"Is he always like this?" I asked Halit Ayarcı.

"Yes," he answered absentmindedly. "He is always like that. Always friendly, always hungry."

Then he shrugged his shoulders and, with a sly smile, continued. I had truly taken to this important man. I had warmed to him, I felt bound to him, I had taken a shine to him, I was soldered to him—or whatever the expression is—and I begrudged Halit Ayarcı's belittling him; but do allow me to add that at the time I had just barely made the acquaintance of my benefactor.

"Of course when he isn't in power . . . He's a little different when he has a position. And I don't mean his appetite; that is constant and never changes. But in this he is not alone: it is the same with his predecessors and successors. That is to say, it runs in the family. I'm referring to his affable manners and easy flattery. In any event, no one ever meets him in person when he's in power; then you're more likely just to see pictures of him in the papers, and when he falls from power you see just . . ."

He pulled the evening paper out of his pocket, flipped it open, and pointed to a picture on the first page:

"Here's the man who took his place. I ran into him here a month ago, and because we were the only ones here we sat together and talked for hours. At the time your gentleman's picture was the one in the paper. Strange, isn't it?"

I listened to him with my mouth wide open in surprise.

"But he didn't seem at all bothered to have lost his position,"
I said.

"He wouldn't . . . because he's the very embodiment of
power. Or, better said, power embodies him. They walk
together arm in arm."

My eyes were glued to the photograph before me.

"It's strange though," I said. "They look so similar."

I stuttered a little out of fear.

"Indeed they do. What the two have in common is the power
they exude. It is a matter of multiple incarnations: I am in you
and you are in me . . ."

He gestured as if to say it was difficult to explain.

Dr. Ramiz winced when he heard this and kept his eyes fixed
on the politician's table. He challenged Halit Bey:

"But he is a perfect gentlemen; everything about him speaks
of greatness."

Halit Ayarcı shrugged and raised his glass. "Let's drink!"

"Cheers."

And we drank. From the moment the politician had placed
his hand on my shoulder to look me in the eye, a strange change
had come over me. Suddenly my appetite had returned, sending
ripples of warmth through my body; swept away by a calm
beatitude, I ate and drank and laughed and joined the fun. The
drink had opened new doors to my flights of fancy. With each
sip, and indeed with each new glass, I saw the woes that had so
oppressed me taking flight, as the daybreak call to prayers
might startle a murder of crows from the treetops in the mosque
courtyard, dispatching them to far-flung lands, never to return.

This lightness of being, this ebb and flow of the heart—as
my troubles scattered, as I drifted without fear in a most peculiar sea of bliss, I did not for a second forget that I owed it all to
the weighty and glorious hand that had rested upon my shoulder, to those eyes that had latched onto mine like magnets.

It was beyond my comprehension. In my childhood I had
been taken to see so many holy tombs and mausoleums of Muslim
saints and to meet countless holy men whose very breath could
remedy all ills. From Eyüpsultan all the way to Yuşa Hill, and
on to Selamiefendi in Kısıklı and Fatih, Aksaray, Hırkaişerif,

Edirnekapı, Ayvansaray, Topkapı, Yedikule, Kocamustafapaşa, Türbe, Sirkeci, and Eminönü, I knew where every tomb, grave, or mausoleum of any saint or miracle worker could be found in almost any neighborhood in all Istanbul, both within and outside the old city walls, and from time to time I'd visit them to pray and implore and collect stones from their graveyards, and if I couldn't find anything better than cloth to tie to the tomb, I'd rip a piece of lining from my coat and tie that to the fence. Yet never had I been as deeply affected as I was now.

Each time, I'd return from my visits to these tombs a little more despondent and distraught and deeper in despair. Neither Bukağılı Dede, nor Elekçi Baba, nor Üryan Dede, nor Tezveren Sultan, not one—not even those who slept in the coolness of holy springs, nor the Christian saints drooling in their sleep on the high windswept hilltops of Heybeliada, Büyükada, and Kınalıada among the Princes' Islands—not one offered any balm for my wounds, not one ever lifted a finger to ease my pain and suffering as I struggled to put food on the table.

Yet these sacred men are far removed from worldly affairs, and for them material possessions are of no value whatsoever; they gave away all they owned, to live in circumstances more abject than my own, and there to discipline their minds and strengthen their souls.

Seyit Lutfullah lived in his run-down *medrese* and Yılanlı Dede, who supposedly had been mentored by Seyit Lutfullah, though I never saw them together, lived in a cellar in Çukurbostan; Karpuz Hoca took refuge in a derelict house in Sütlüce; and Yekçeşim Ali Efendi spent all his time wandering around the cemetery in Edirnekapı. The eminent Sheikh Mustafa of Altıparmak, Deli Hafız, Sheikh Viranı—they were all the same way. While I was bemoaning the fact that I didn't have a clean shirt to put on in the morning, Dede the Shirtless was busy violently tearing up his in the middle of the street—shirts that had been given to him as gifts.

Clearly such personalities could not help me solve problems that stemmed from my worldly concerns. Furthermore, the dead ones never even looked me in the eye, and the ones who were still alive only counseled patience and contentment.

Among these people there was Emine of the Seven Brides, one of our neighbors; I hounded her for three years, begging her to intercede with her blessings for my lottery tickets, when finally one day she reached out and touched my ticket with her blessed hand and said, "All right, then, you've begged me for so long that you've made my heart heavy. I have prayed for you and, yes, you will win a little money back! But don't ever ask this of me ever again. Don't force such sins upon me!"

Yes, but why was it a sin for a miserable creature like me to win back a few of the pennies I had gambled away on the lottery? I just couldn't make sense of it.

I pleaded with Emine of the Seven Brides so passionately that I threw myself at her feet: "Just a little more than what I've put in, oh blessed one!" I cried. "If nothing else, just refund me the total that I've lost over the last ten years playing this useless invention." Was that so much to ask? I didn't think so. "Well, then just give me back everything I lost this year! That comes to about ten kuruş. Please, that's the least you can do for me!" I begged. But she was stubborn as a rock. It was the intractability of a saint, simply said. So I returned home in utter despair. I waited out the entire month, thinking, "Maybe she's right, but certainly after so much groveling she'll work something out for me!" But no use—the holy woman's prophecy came true. Amid the big money prizes that literally drowned their recipients with sums as staggering as the fortune showered upon sultans during their accession to the throne in olden times, a single lira coin, dry as a bone, meandered back to me like a goat let out to graze.

The politician was in a class apart; he was not the kind of man who would subject himself to misery and pain just to temper his mind and soul, a man who blunted the edge of his fortune, ready to dismiss the bounties of this world for eternal happiness in the world beyond. He was in every way the opposite: for he belonged to the society of men who snatch, seize, devour, and smash whatever takes their fancy, only to look for something new when they finish, becoming bored and restless until they find it. It was clear that he had never flirted with the ascetic life, nor was he the type of man who would sacrifice his diet, even when struggling against the gravest illness. The way he looked down at our table, his manner of complimenting others, the celerity with which he zeroed in on the mullet, the split second it took him to notice the bit of fried mussel dangling on the end of my fork, his falconlike attention to the bounties the table promised, and the swiftness with which he swooped down to claim what was rightfully his, even if it happened to be in the hands of another . . . No, he was forged of a different sort of steel. He was born for this life. Consider for a moment: he did not hesitate in relieving Hayri İrdal of the mussel dangling before him in midair because Hayri had spent his whole life in the corner of a coffeehouse, scrounging for food day in to day out, and now that he was sitting in an elegant Bosphorus restaurant in Büyükdere he couldn't bring himself to eat it; this man was gracious enough to savor it on his behalf. With this gesture he had propelled Hayri İrdal into celestial bliss, while his old friend Dr. Ramiz watched on with envious desire.

To meet such a man, to look him directly in the eye—this was without doubt an auspicious event and a great source of happiness. And naturally it promised an abundance of good fortune (as indeed it did). My life's orbit and its very meaning changed the next day; in fact it started to change that very night.

It began when the aforementioned weight on my shoulders was lifted and I first felt the new lightness of being to which I have already alluded. Then slowly but surely my patterns of thought began to shift. Indeed my very perception of the world began to alter, as did the manner in which I perceived objects and understood humankind. Of course all this did not occur in just one day; it happened incrementally, and not without some growing pains. Indeed on many occasions the transformation negated the man I had previously been. But, yes, in the end it all happened.

That night Halit Ayarcı heard the complete story of my life. I told him all about Nuri Efendi, Seyit Lutfullah, Abdüsselam Bey, Ferhat Bey, Aristidi Efendi, Naşit Bey, and the treasure of the emperor Andronikos, although I lingered perhaps a bit too long on the topic of turning mercury into gold, explaining that the preferred method was a combination of numerology and consultation with spirits via a medium. I could still feel the weight of the politician's hand on my shoulder turning the wheel of my fate; perhaps I was calling on all my oratory skills with the hope that I might plant in this esteemed and wealthy individual's mind the passion to pursue the treasure so he might then acquire the secret powers of the universe. Indeed I even disclosed certain details to him that I had never told anyone.

"All the treasure—silver and gold inlaid with jewels and pearls—is under a tent raised by twenty-seven golden poles. And chest after chest overflows with gems and jewels, gold and silver bowls, ladies' ornamental jewelry, rings, chains, evil-eye talismans . . ."

Halit Ayarcı laughed and said, "Impossible. The Byzantines didn't have evil-eye talismans. Those are particular to the Turks."

I had to think that over for a moment. What was the infidel's equivalent? The word *maşallah* was definitely ours, most certainly.

"Yes, but surely they wore some sort of evil eye for good luck and to ward off evil spirits. Seyit Lutfullah told me that such tokens were normal gifts in the Christian states, which were then passed on to us and became true talismans with magical properties. That was what I was referring to."

But Halit Ayarcı wasn't interested in Seyit Lutfullah. He was far more interested in Nuri Efendi. He had little curiosity about the calendars and the astronomical tables my late master had intermittently published, nor was he interested in the chemical formulae he had unearthed in old manuscripts. He was concerned only with his horological works.

So there was nothing to do but move the conversation in that direction. I conveyed to him all the adages of my late master that were still fresh in my memory. Halit Bey rejoiced after nearly every sentence:

"Unbelievable. We need such a man among us. *Mon chér*, this man is a true philosophe, and just the kind we need—a philosopher of time. Do you understand? A philosopher of time is a philosopher of work, and you too, Hayri Bey, are a philosopher, indeed a true philosopher!"

But I wasn't listening to him. I was standing up, pointing at the politician's table.

"Do you see what's happening there? The plates, everything is moving. Dear God!"

The plates on his table seemed to be rattling as if they were being buffeted by a strong southern wind. But the remarkable thing was that no one at the table seemed frightened, no one was whispering prayers, and not one of them was darting away from the ruckus; rather, they were all holding on to their sides in uproarious laughter. It was as if they were all possessed by evil djinn. And the terrible thing was that after my declaration their laughter intensified, and the plates on the table rattled with even greater vigor. They were all looking at me and laughing.

Halit Bey said reassuringly, "Don't mind them. That's just our friend Faik. He always does magic tricks at these places. He loves entertaining the crowd with such parlor games."

"No, no," I said. "You're pulling my leg. I'm drunk. Just a moment ago I could have sworn I was looking at the treasure of the emperor Andronikos at the bottom of the sea. There's something wrong with me. Please, I need to go home."

By then I really did want to go home. I had tired of this life that really wasn't mine; all this fun had worn me out. I wanted to go home; I longed to be surrounded by the things of my life: my own troubles, my own poverty.

"But no, let's all go together. As for your being drunk, you can very well see for yourself that you are not—far from it in fact. And even if you were, you'd come round soon enough. How could you think of abandoning the evening so abruptly? Now, please do sit down and explain to me this idea of a letter written from one master to the other. But before that, let's drink."

And Dr. Ramiz echoed him: "Yes, let's drink."

We drank more. I felt ill at ease. Yet still I did the best I could to satisfy Halit Ayarcı's curiosity.

"Old watches were crafted by hand. Those who made them were masters of metallurgy. That is, they were jewelers in the highest sense of the word. As they were the great artists of their field, the watches they created were adorned with sublime

details, with engravings and flourishes and so on. Oftentimes
the most beautiful, indeed the most important, of these were
engraved inside the inner cover—that is to say, on the inside of
the back lid—a place that is only ever seen by another watchmaker. This was why the late Nuri Efendi called them letters
from one master to another. Take, for example, the engraving
on the inside of the cover of your watch. You know, the woman
with the helmet and that fantastic goliath of a man with his
hand on her shoulder. I once saw a watch resembling this one
while working with Nuri Efendi.

Halit Ayarcı identified the scene: "Why, you mean Hercules
and Athena!"

Then returning to the topic he said, "But you're absolutely
right. Only a watchmaker would see them."

And Halit Bey raised his glass once again. "A toast," he
exclaimed. "To you in particular, Hayri Bey, but not if you
continue to wear that glum face. That you are unemployed and
entangled in all sorts of trouble must not stop us from having a
good time."

"If only I had your point of view . . ."

"One day you will. But first tell us about your present situation. Let's just review the various positions you've held."

So I told him about my life at home: about my wife and her
sisters and about Ahmet and Zehra. He listened to everything I
had to say, with Dr. Ramiz interjecting now and then to elaborate a particular point. Then he looked me straight in the eye
and said:

"The most common predicament in the world: First, you
have no money. Then, you find yourself living with three young
women who need to be married off. And, finally, everyone
at home is suffering from poor health. It all boils down to
the same fundamental problem. Simply said: it's a matter of
money."

It all seemed so easy if you took each word at face value:
money, three weddings, and plenty of food and drink. I expected him to carry on and suggest that we enact a few new
laws to allow for the swift and easy settlement of my affairs.

"But how could I ever give my daughter to Ismail the Lame?"
I moaned.

"Naturally you'll do nothing of the sort. According to what
you've just told me, you have a daughter who is both charming
and good-looking. Of course you won't give such a girl to that
man."

But it was the same old cul-de-sac.

"Well then, whatever will I do if I don't?"

"You will find the right match. He will come to you without
any intervention on your part."

"And the others? My sisters-in-law—especially the older
one, the fanatic *musicienne*—who would ever marry her?"

Halit Ayarcı thought for a moment.

"From what you have told us, she isn't quite the type to be
snatched up. But you never know. For example, first a little fame
on the radio, and then perhaps she becomes a famous singer in
a club, or maybe a professional vocalist . . . And presto! You see
there's a solution to any problem. Just a few minor adjustments
to your life balance, a little entreprencurialism, some elbow
grease, an ever so modest change in perspective—and voilà!
Everything has been changed.

"I must confess that I never thought of it that way. I assumed
the only solution was a natural disaster or an epidemic that
would wipe out the entire household. I was just biding my time."

"A mistake, a miscalculation . . . Don't you expect something from these miserable people at home, from yourself?
Now, from what you've said, these are ambitious individuals,
obsessed with getting the most out of life. This means they
already have success inside them and suffer for lack of an out-
let. They're not the kind of people to settle for a humdrum
existence."

"No, certainly not. My wife thinks she's in Hollywood, and
her elder sister is convinced she's a renowned singer. And the
younger one . . ."

"But of course. Of course this is what they think! And they are
all a little angry with you because you don't understand them."

I lowered my head. I thought he would at least try to see it from my point of view. I had spent the last six hours with this man, I was captivated by his every move, but clearly he was insane. He didn't have to suddenly throw his hands around my throat or remove all his attire and cartwheel in the open air to make this clear. He continued:

"Yes, why wouldn't these people be a little frustrated with you for not understanding them? What could be more natural? But don't begrudge them, for you have had no experience with life and humankind. You are like an army convinced of its defeat before entering the war. Instead of stepping onto the bridge of the ship, you've taken cover down in the hull."

This diagnosis of my illness, or rather this identification of my discontent, left me nothing to do but drink. And thank God there was plenty of rakı. I could celebrate this happy event as much as my heart desired.

But still he carried on:

"Especially your attitude toward your eldest *baldız*—a true artist. The way you deny her . . ."

I put down my glass. Once again I was determined to interject—in the name of logic, in the name of reason—come what may. After I did so, I'd be content to hold my tongue.

"But please, Beyefendi," I implored. "An artist? A *true* artist? In my modest opinion, her voice is wretched. She simply has no talent. And then, of course, she knows nothing at all about music. She has no understanding of Turkish *makams*: she can't tell the difference between a Mahur and an Isfahan, a Rast from an Acemaşiran. No, impossible. Perhaps she possesses other merits. Perhaps she's pretty—what do I know? Well, actually, no, she's not, but perhaps I just haven't noticed. But to enjoy music rendered by such a voice! Out of the question. She has no ear, sir, none at all. She's entirely tone deaf. She can't distinguish one pitch from the other."

Halit Bey offered me a cigarette. Then he took one for himself and looked out over the moonlight, still shimmering over the sea in all its glory. After a moment, when it seemed as if he was listening to an argument at the opposite table, he shrugged his shoulders, turned to me, and said:

"Well, we've determined, then, that she isn't beautiful, for

you would know, as you have the eye of an ⌐
learned your life story. And I know that you unders⌐
in a woman. But you don't understand art, at least no⌐
of our times. First of all, it is a question of the masses. W⌐
do they love and what do they reject? No one really knows.
This question also touches on the desperation of the masses.
You know very well that this exalted ideal known as good
taste comes with many counterparts that range from our deepest desires to whatever comes to us most easily. It is when we
lose hope in the notion of taste that we surrender to these counterparts. It's all rather confusing, so we lose hope in taste.
When we speak of music, people first inquire as to the genre;
once such a question is posed, the matter of taste or style is
eliminated. Then there is the matter of the public's untrained
ear. We live in the age of radio, and we listen to music all the
time. The radio has become the natural companion to rheumatism, the common cold, penury, the possibility of war, and the
trials of just getting through the day. And if you add the masses
to all this . . . No, I am quite sure that this hanımefendi of
whom you speak will conquer Istanbul within just a few days,
in a startling rise to fame. But look at it this way: the task
would certainly be far more difficult if your sister-in-law had
taken a passionate interest in Western classical music, as such
music requires years of rigorous training indeed."

He looked at me for a moment. I was truly flabbergasted.

"No one ever really takes these things seriously anyway . . .
without realizing it of course. Can't you see this side of the
picture?"

"Not seriously. What do you mean? Then they're simply out
of their minds . . ."

"Of course. They only want to lend a little emotional color to
their lives with a few exceptional moments. Everyone seeks to
fill the void inside them with a little sentimentality, to dress up
their lives as they please, but as they understand absolutely
nothing about music they can only really enjoy songs for their
lyrics alone. My poor Hayri Bey, you are an unusual man
indeed. Your criteria are the stuff of the past. They are, as you
said earlier, like letters passed down from one master to the

...ned by that traditional mode. Today ...trying to distinguish the Isfahan from ...ne, which singer does she aspire to be?" ...as singers. But always with the same voice, ...interpreted in exactly the same way."

...is a true original! It's solved. Unique and ne... here! I mean new, new in capital letters! For when it ... of the new, there's no need for any other talent. Now we ...ed only choose which direction to take: folk music or classical Turkish music, or folk music with a hint of *alafranga*, or perhaps *alafranga* with a hint of folk? But of course we can't really decide on such things here at the dinner table. Yet it seems to me that, according to all you have said about her talents and skills"—here Halit Ayarcı screwed up his face and made a crinkling gesture with his fingers as if he were testing poor-quality fabric—"she would be more successful with certain local folk songs with a hint of the *alafranga* . . . Yes, that's my guess. But why doesn't she try a Turkish tango! Or there are some songs . . ."

He looked absently into my eyes.

"Yes, that's the problem. You lack entrepreneurial spirit. You're an idealist. And you fail to comprehend the reality around you. In short, you're old-fashioned. A shame, what a terrible shame! If only you had a shred of realism in you, just only so much, a wee bit. Oh, then everything would change."

This time he'd gone too far.

"I'm not a realist? Would I have told you all I have in the manner that I did if I weren't a realist? Have I spoken to you about my sister-in-law with any inkling of hope? Have I changed anything about her for you? Have I dressed up any aspect of her? It seems to me that I am the only one who sees things for what they truly are. Indeed I am too much of a realist, I'll have you know—so much that it pains me."

Halit Ayarcı smiled. He'd been gesturing the whole time to the people at the next table. He took a sip of rakı and turned to face me.

"Let's end this conversation and join the other table. It seems this evening might not turn out too bad after all. I might even

say promising . . . Look now, Hayri Bey, I have already decided
on it. From now on we shall work together. This is why we
must agree on certain things. Being a realist does not mean seeing the truth for what it is. It is a question of determining our
relationship with the truth in the way that is most beneficial for
us. What do you achieve by accepting reality as it is? What will
that offer apart from a slew of petty decisions that are neither
meaningful nor valuable on their own? You can't do anything
but draw up endless lists of what you need and do not have.
What difference does that make? If anything, it only leads you
away from your true path. You become permanently settled in
pessimism and eventually you are crushed beneath it. To see
the truth as it is . . . is to admit defeat. Yes, it is the very definition of defeatism, for it is its very genesis. You, Hayri Bey, are a
man poisoned by words, which is why I said you were old-
fashioned. But the realism of today's man is something else.
What can I make with the material at hand, with this very
object and all it has to offer? That's the question to ask. For
example, in this instance your greatest error is in your misper-
ception of your dear sister-in-law's problem—in your starting
with the abstract concept of music. If you were to tackle the
problem from your sister-in-law's point of view, the matter
would be altogether different. If Newton had considered the
apple that dropped onto his head as nothing but an apple, he
might have deemed it rotten and tossed it aside. But he didn't.
Instead he asked himself, just what can I do with this apple? He
asked just what its maximum benefit might be. And you should
do the very same! My *baldız* wants nothing but to be a successful musician. So I have two factors: my *baldız* and music. As
the first factor cannot be changed, I have no choice but to
change the second. Just what kind of music does my *baldız*
like, then? This is what you must consider. Or will you stay forever in your cul-de-sac? Why of course not."

I thought of myself sitting on a stone in the Kamburkarga
cul-de-sac just behind our home, with my sister-in-law singing
her heart out as she hacked away at her oud.

"Of course not. A thousand times over, no!"

"Can you change her?"

I jumped up out of my seat.

"Not one bit! Impossible! Entirely out of the question!"

"Then you'll do what I just told you. Remember that in this day and age, and especially with matters of this sort, all you need to do is desire the change. Life goes on, Hayri Bey. As you go on your way, stymied by words at every step, life discovers something new every day. Consider how just four or five hours ago I discovered you—and now I am discovering a singer, your sister-in-law."

"May God make it so, sir."

What else could I do but thank him. He had discovered my *baldız*. Grace upon her! Since I was born, people have taught me to look through the wrong end of the telescope. But I simply never could. I was stubborn. Why bother? My entire life was absurd. So why wouldn't I just give this a try?

Nevertheless, I garnered my strength for one last act of resistance.

"Ah, but if you could only see her, or rather listen to her, singing there right before you like a great barrel wobbling on her crimson high heels, her sweat streaming like a fountain as she snaps along and sings, 'If only my love would come join this joyful scene . . .'"

Halit Ayarcı looked at me warmly.

"So she snaps her fingers does she, eh? How nice. That's perfect, but, my good man, this is a success all on its own. Think about it for a minute: she won't be one of those singers who twirls a scarf around her finger while she sings, unable to ever unwind it, nor will she be one of those who tear up napkins as they go along. What more could you ask for? She'll have both hands free, she'll be able to wave to the crowd and blow kisses, and she'll receive thunderous applause in return! You possess a veritable treasure, and you don't even know it. Let's try to sum up, then: You say she's ugly, so from a contemporary perspective she's sympathetic. You say her voice is wretched, which means it is emotive and conducive to certain styles. You say she has no talent—well then, without a doubt she is an original. I will see to your *baldız* tomorrow. And soon she'll be on the stage. She'll be famous and her name will be in all the papers."

This is as much as I can remember clearly from that night. In fact I have the vague recollection that following Halit Ayarcı's final words to me I thought something to the effect of, "You and your promises . . . You'll forget all about it tomorrow morning." And the rest is just a blank—though toward morning I did find myself belly dancing with someone from the next table. It was a soft, gentle morning shrouded in mist. A breeze rushed through the open window, bringing with it the putter of motorboats and swaying the still-lit lamps. We carried on with our belly dance through the break of day and into the beautiful morning. I was overcome by the most blissful sensation of lightness imaginable. I still didn't know if Halit Ayarcı's promises of that evening would come true, but he had already shown me which end of the telescope I was to look through from here on in.

II

Yet Halit Ayarcı kept all his promises. Within a week, my sister-in-law began singing in a small club; both Halit Ayarcı and Dr. Ramiz attended the premiere, along with Pakize and the rest of our family. It was indeed a triumph, though I had the feeling that Halit Ayarcı provided both the venue and its audience simply to fulfill his promises of that night. Every time my sister-in-law committed an error in style, she was met with maniacal applause. With every passing moment, I sank deeper into my chair with shame, but in the end the poor girl was hailed as the star of the evening, and cries of "Brava!" were followed by hysterical screams erupting from her sisters and aunts. From time to time, Pakize turned to me with a look that said, "Didn't I tell you?" Halit Ayarcı watched the entire performance in silence. But as we left the club he said to me:

"Yes, just as I expected. The hanımefendi will be a great success indeed. You need to believe in life, Hayri Bey. But you have more belief in the Acemaşiran *makam* than you do in life itself! Didn't you just see how well she was received? This is the impact a living human being can have on others. There's simply no way on earth your classical *makams* could ever achieve such success. It's smooth sailing from now on. Oh, you'll see what she can do."

And this wasn't all he did. It was around this time that Halit Ayarcı opened the little office that would become the nucleus of the Time Regulation Institute. One fine morning I stepped through the front door of that little office near the municipality building, wearing a suit Halit Ayarcı had sent me the night before. I was ushered inside by a wise and elderly servant. Nermin Hanım, our head secretary, who was also a relative of Halit Ayarcı's, jumped up at the first sight of me, as delighted as if she had just set eyes on an old friend. She showed me my desk. She even stopped knitting to do so. That day I learned that Nermin Hanım was always either knitting or talking; she never did anything else. Or, rather, she talked unless she was alone, in which case she knitted.

She was unlike any woman I had ever known. It took no more than a second for her to make a new friend. She had no secrets and no interest in silence. And she never held a grudge: She had even succeeded in divorcing three different husbands without resentment or rancor. Indeed she was still on rather good terms with them. She launched right in:

"The suit looks good. From what Halit Bey told me about you, I figured it would be perfect on you. But really, your shoes do need shining. And you must find another barber. This one seems to have no idea how to cut hair. I can't tell you how happy I am to have found a friend like you here. I did worry a bit when my uncle first asked me to stay on here. The idea of an office can be so unappealing. I said to myself, if anything, there'd be all sorts of strangers there, and I wouldn't know what to do. But I felt much better when he said we'd be together, especially after he told me what you were like. We're about the same age, so I knew we'd be good friends. And my husband's not a jealous man. Besides, in this day and age a wise husband's never jealous of his wife. Today's family is an institution founded on friendship—though the men in this country haven't reached that level of maturity. Oh, but I'm tired of it all. In the past it was such a cinch getting divorced, but now it's so difficult. The judges keep trying to get you reunited, and they stall the trials. I divorced my first husband without even really knowing how it all happened. For the second one, the trial lasted a year, and then they wouldn't allow me to marry for a whole year after. Then, the third time, it was practically impossible. Anyway, we're no more than secretaries, you and I, but once my uncle has the organization all stamped and approved, you'll be assistant director and I'll be head secretary! My uncle Halit is a great organizer. And he's already organized this whole exciting project. We live nearby, in Şişli, so I'll be bringing my own lunches, and if you do the same, you won't waste any time going out for lunch. But, then, come to think of it, there's no need for you to bring lunch. I can bring yours too. My mother-in-law's a wonderful cook. And she'll make us tray upon tray of all sorts of food just to make sure she doesn't have to see me. But to tell you the truth, I was trying to get her to work here as a secretary too. But my uncle said it wouldn't do. This is a modern institution, he said, and we need young women. But, then again, you never know who's young or old anymore. You shorten your skirt and cut your hair short and, well . . . And then if you wear a beret . . . One of my friend's husbands was a little too interested in young girls. The poor thing didn't know what to do. Finally I had to intervene. I said, 'Sister, all you have to do is throw on a middle school uniform and get one of those caps.' At first she said, not a chance, but now the silly man never leaves home. Oh, it's so nice to have you here . . . I thought maybe you wouldn't be able to find the office this morning, and I was just about to send a car for you. Then I was worried I might disturb Mrs. İrdal, so I changed my mind. My uncle said you are quite good at reading coffee grounds. Oh, I was so excited when I heard that! You'll read my grounds every day, won't you?"

That was Nermin Hanım. The most surprising thing of all is that she was the one who wanted to divorce each of her three husbands, whereas—considering the monologue she'd just delivered—one would have imagined it would be her unfortunate ex-husbands who were desperate for divorce. Indeed she was the kind of person who spent all twelve waking hours chattering.

The office consisted of two adjacent rooms. My desk was in the first, directly opposite Nermin Hanım's desk; and this room led to Halit Ayarcı's office.

But allow me just to say in advance that these humbly furnished rooms bore no resemblance whatsoever to the quarters of what was to be Istanbul's most advanced and modern institute. Indeed the difference between them wasn't even a question of degree. They were two different worlds altogether.

At one point I asked Nermin Hanım just what it was we were meant to be doing. After a prolonged exposé of the habits of her first husband and his extended family, she told me that there was nothing to do for the time being and that we were to wait for Halit Ayarcı's arrival. And so we spent our first month there doing just that. Every now and then Halit Ayarcı would telephone and check up on us, telling us to keep up the good work and always reminding us to replenish the stationery supplies. Curtains and typewriters arrived toward the end of the month.

In the middle of the second month, Halit Ayarcı came by the office. Together we compiled a list of almost a hundred slogans based on what I could remember from my time with Nuri Efendi: "Metals are never regulated on their own," or "Regulation is chasing down the seconds." Sometimes Halit Ayarcı added his own, more meaningful, creations: "Shared time is shared work," "A true man is conscious of time," "The path to well-being springs from a sound understanding of time," and so on and so forth.

After that came the task of having them printed. We printed a thousand copies of every slogan and distributed them throughout the city. One morning toward the end of the third month, a joyous Halit Ayarcı announced that the preliminary work on our institute was complete. Then he set out to compose the official terms of institutional justification. Little by little our once calm institute came to life.

Those three months were unlike anything I had ever experienced. I shall never forget them. It was a strange and confusing period in which I fluctuated between elation and fear: there was the pride I felt in having achieved something at long last, and there was the fear of losing it. I had to keep reminding

THE TIME REGULATION INSTITUTE

myself I was employed again, with a regular income. After a long and heavy sleep, I was living life to the fullest. I no longer dashed from one coffeehouse to the other in search of a familiar face. I was freed from that terrible question, what should I do now? No longer was I despised by my family for being unemployed; no longer was I obliged to recount my misfortunes to all and sundry. Because I now spent all day in the office, I no longer had to suffer acquaintances turning away to ignore me in public places. I was starting my life all over again. I was an ordinary citizen of the world. Endowed now with a surging sense of purpose, I felt I could move mountains.

But there was a problem: I had a job but no work. This new job was unlike any other I had known. It seemed to have nothing to do with people or even life itself, for that matter. I believed, for example, that I had done real work for the Spiritualist Society—if that doesn't sound too absurd, bearing in mind that all I'd done was report to a group of people who delighted in lying to one another and to themselves. But there wasn't even that much to be found in my new employment. It was an undertaking born of a few words. It had the logic of a fairy tale. I mentioned this to Halit Bey, but he was only interested in the problem of unsynchronized public clocks and cognizant of the fact that he wasn't engaged in a major project at the time. Other people had put their faith in his idea. And just around then, a very important man missed the funeral of another very important man because the city clocks weren't synchronized. Thereafter, in the space of ten days, a budget was earmarked to provide us with our reasonably well-furbished office space, and as if that were not enough, they undertook to supply us with any other office equipment we happened to lack. Could such a job really exist? What was its purpose? And why?

The most confusing thing of all was that Halit Ayarcı was almost never to be found at our offices. If for no other reason, he could have stopped in more often because his presence alone would have made us more secure. And perhaps, had he graced us with his presence, he might have drummed up some work for us to do. But he rarely did; he was out of the picture almost entirely. He did no more than to call in now and then to see how we were getting on or to give us orders that seemed of little importance.

But we were treated to continuous updates on the institute's shiny future. Nermin Hanım was always babbling on about the new structure and the tremendous staff it would house. While I continued to view my days in our humble little office as somewhat absurd, she would ramble on and on about the new branches and departments and ideas her so-called uncle Halit Ayarcı had in store for us. I found it all rather disconcerting. I could not see our office even attempting an expansion along such lines. Better to remain as inconspicuous as was practical. The most sensible course would be for us to surface at the beginning of every month, just long enough to collect our salaries, and in the interim to remain invisible. But that's not at all how it happened. After some time had passed, Halit Ayarcı began flooding us with draft versions of documents and letters to be sent all over the city, and he petitioned to have the office refurbished in a manner befitting its station, at the same time instructing us to order additional stationery. But there was more: he became so preoccupied with my attire that you might have thought he was outfitting me for the stage.

One day, while dictating one of Halit Ayarcı's drafts to Nermin Hanım, I nearly burst into tears of despair. The letter began by describing the Time Regulation Institute as something along the lines of "an invaluable institution" that had not yet been granted the status it deserved and went on to insist upon a reappraisal of the budget to give the institute sufficient funding to allow for a full staff to run it, as well as an accountant and an additional secretary.

But how strange that three days later we received a response that, after tabling objections to our proposals on many different counts, stated that our situation would be taken into consideration. Not a day went by without a new shipment of furniture arriving at the doorstep of our humble little office. First they redid the linoleum floors, and then supplied me with my own telephone, as if the one only fifteen steps away from my desk wasn't good enough. The following day we received half a dozen desk lamps. Then they replaced our desks. Halit

Ayarcı received a first-class American desk, mine was only one notch less commanding, and Nermin Hanım's was so finely varnished you would slide right off it. Halit Ayarcı knew exactly when all the new furnishings were due to arrive and gave instructions over the telephone as to where they should be placed. He explained to me just how I was to arrange my desk lamp, black writing pad, and penholder.

All of this could mean one thing: without a supply department or some kind of warehouse, our office would eventually have to be liquidated and we'd all go hungry. I didn't care that much if I was promoted to assistant manager or not, but I was keen to hold on to the salary that was the equivalent of three office boys' combined. Just the thought that I might lose it was enough to drive me mad.

Once I tried to convey these feelings to Halit Ayarcı over the phone, and after listening to all I had to say, he replied: "My dear Hayri Bey, we keep coming back to the same old point. Be a realist!"

And he hung up.

Naturally this harked back to what he had told me in Büyükdere, but this time he seemed on the verge of laughter. He called back an hour later.

"Hayri Bey," he roared. "Still afraid of losing that little wage? Stop entertaining such nonsense and be realistic!"

And he hung up on me again.

I no longer concealed my concerns from Nermin Hanım. When she actually allowed me to speak, or rather to finish what I had to say, I tried to explain to her as best I could why this job had no future. But she had complete confidence in Halit Ayarcı.

"Impossible!" she cried. "Uncle Halit's never wrong. He's a man of action. He'd never take on a job he didn't completely believe in. You still don't really know him."

"But why doesn't he ever come to the office?"

"He'll come . . . But only when everything is in place. He's going to Ankara tomorrow to discuss the project!"

What else could I do but quietly pray that he wouldn't actually explain anything to anyone.

Perhaps my paranoia began to get to her, because Nermin Hanım began to worry too:

"I really don't need the money," she said. "But I certainly don't like the idea of shutting myself away at home again, right under my mother-in-law's nose, strapped with all those household chores. She's a good woman, but she never opens her mouth. She just scurries away. How can anyone live with such silence? But, you know, ever since I got this position my mother-in-law's completely changed, and she's doing all the housework herself."

Even so, Nermin Hanım was nothing like me. Her manner of speaking could not have been more different. She leapt from one thought to the other like a sparrow prancing from one branch to the next; by the time she reached her third sentence, she had left her original point far behind to dive into a subject that had nothing to do with it. Her life was governed by her tongue and her two lips. No sooner had she begun discussing the travails of being pent up at home with her mother-in-law than she was expounding on her first husband with some fury, and then, before you knew it, she was delving into her childhood in a family kiosk somewhere near Küçükmustafapaşa, only to stop in midflow to ask if you thought the hat she had recently purchased truly became her.

All this was amplified by digressions both major and minor. Each began the same way: "Maybe you know . . ." She could have been referring to at least twenty different people, and if I told her that I didn't know the person in question, she would seem temporarily undone, but then she'd rally, supplying me with such descriptions as to make the individual worthy of my notice; but then, in the middle of her description, the man's daughter or wife would be mentioned, and it was back to the beginning.

One encounter was enough for Nermin Hanım to adopt a new friend, and to each new friend she related her life story, in installments. The man who put in our linoleum floors, the electrician, the upholsterer, the porters, the public notaries who came to sign our accounts—each had at one time or another listened to some saga from her life. But she was beginning to suspect that perhaps this job wouldn't last for much longer. Eventually her idle talk, previously content to flutter from one branch to the next, came to hover around one central point.

Soon our office assistant, Derviş Efendi, was also infected by our concerns. The poor man had truly warmed to the new office, even though there weren't many visitors, and not much in the way of tips. But he was comfortable, and no one bothered him. He wasn't made to wait beside the door or anything like that. He sat in a chair next to Nermin Hanım's desk, listening to her stories and praising her hats—there was a new one every day and each one deserving of a *maşallah*! If he ever bored of her conversation, he could always leave with the good intention of making Turkish coffee.

Surely this job was the easiest he could ever find. Thirty-five years working as an office assistant, and suddenly he'd found himself in an office managed the way an office should have always been managed. But he too wasn't sure what work we were meant to be doing; he was more than a little surprised that an entire company had been formed just so he could watch me tinker with watches until nightfall and listen to Nermin Hanım's life story as she knit sweater after sweater. He never tired of us, or told us to do anything else; he was content enough, but it simply did not make sense. One day he came to me and said rather sheepishly:

"Sir, I too am a little confused by this job. I'm beginning to feel a little suspicious about the whole thing. Sometimes I even wonder if I've died and gone to heaven."

Until then, it had never once occurred to me that these creatures called office assistants might conceive of a paradise designed to fit their lifestyle. But why couldn't our ideas about happiness comply with our standards of living?

Our fragile peace was disrupted toward the end of the third month by a great upsurge of activity. One morning Halit Ayarcı arrived at the office with the mayor of Istanbul and one of his assistants. Nermin Hanım was engrossed in knitting Halit Ayarcı's third sweater, and I was busy regaling everyone with tales of Seyit Lutfullah's romantic adventures with his beloved Aselban. Needless to say, we were thrown into a great confusion by this unexpected visit, and we sprang to our feet at once. Before I could begin to think of how to welcome a man of the mayor's stature, Halit Ayarcı was already introducing me:

"My most valuable assistant, Hayri İrdal Bey. We are so fortunate to have him working on the project with us."

Then he added:

"Do you know, Beyefendi, that for the sake of the institute Hayri İrdal is working here more or less as an honorary member?"

The mayor grasped my hand as if to say, I shall never let go of this—our only chance to bring success to our institute.

"His remuneration is truly shameful. Something to be ashamed of indeed . . ."

My dear benefactor spoke as if he might weep over the injustice I had to endure. The strange thing was that even the mayor seemed truly concerned; he lowered his head and stared at his shoes.

"There's no other way this will work, Halit Bey."

And then he shook my hand more firmly than before, as if to thank me from the bottom of his heart for all my sacrifices.

"Of course the current situation is temporary. When, thanks to his efforts, we finish organizing everything, Hayri Bey will be appointed our assistant manager."

This bit of good news seemed to revive the mayor. He lifted his head from his shoes to look joyfully into my eyes. And for the first time in my life I beheld a man who was happy for the happiness of another man.

"Nermin Hanım is our head secretary. She's a top-flight intellectual. Hers is a different sacrifice altogether, as she left her blessed home to be with us."

Nermin Hanım blushed bright red, like a young schoolgirl who was wearing for the first time a dress she had brought with her on holiday. When asked if she was holding up well, she flashed a sweet smile, as if she were sucking on a candy.

"So we've stolen our dear friend right from her home . . ."

To show how much he was tickled by this idea, Halit Ayarcı said:

"Yes, very much indeed. Stolen right from her own home."

Looking rather pleased with his line, the mayor made an even brighter observation, in a way never before expressed:

"But oh, we've triumphed in the name of life! What do you say to that, Hayri Bey?"

And with my approval, this little foray into social niceties came to a close.

Halit Ayarcı:

"If you please, shall we take a little tour?"

What was there to see? From our room you went right into Halit Bey's. But experienced men see these things differently. The mayor knew how to turn the few steps to the next room into a journey lasting a full half an hour. He took the time to examine each empty entity in turn: over and over he inspected the filing cabinet, the receipt cabinet, the typewriters still in their cases, the large black leather-bound ledgers that had sat unopened on their desks since the day of their arrival, the still bulbless desk lamps that promised long and uninterrupted nights of labor, and then of course the drapes. After which, with his hand resting on the doorknob and already facing the next room, he made a U-turn, to inspect the same room all over again! I saw how very mistaken I had been. For visits and inspections of this nature, you didn't need much space at all, and neither did you need too many objects for inspection. The important thing was to make the decision to inspect something and then to do so. The mayor would linger a few moments before a most mundane object, indicating to us that he was thinking of something, but he said nothing, and just when he seemed to be opening his mouth to speak he stopped and, swaying back and forth, rested his hand on Halit Ayarcı's arm.

Casting his eye once more over our room from the doorway into Halit Ayarcı's office, he said:

"Those curtains really are quite nice."

He gave the same attention and care to Halit Ayarcı's office. In fact he even drew open the tulle curtains and looked for some time out over the street he'd known for so many years. Then he inspected the furniture once again. No, he wasn't entirely pleased with the furniture:

"Well as for your friends, I suppose it will do, but yours is rather sub par. And in such an important institute . . ."

Smiling, Halit Ayarcı responded:

"For now, let's focus on the conditions of our colleagues hard at work. In any case, we shall have to move to new quarters soon. We'll never fit here! We can upgrade the furnishings when we move."

The mayor had his assistant make a note of this. And so the first step toward finding a new building was taken. Just before he left the room, the mayor noticed the diagram Halit Ayarcı had had us hang on his wall the evening before. He stared at it for some time:

"So that's it, then, eh!"

"Yes, sir, it gives particular attention to the regulation of time in cinemas and during lunch hours. Of course the chart is incomplete. Hayri Bey is delving into the matter more deeply. Regulation varies dramatically by occupation."

"A textbook study of social behavior . . ."

"Is that not our very aim?"

I hadn't the slightest notion of time regulation by occupation, and not once had I considered the possibility that we might be conducting a study in social behavior. All the same I was delighted to be the author of one.

We went back into our room and once again the mayor spent a little time looking over the empty files, the typewriters asleep in their cases, and the large black ledgers on the desks. Then he read the slogans on the wall:

" 'Regulation is chasing down the seconds.' An important saying indeed, Halit Bey!"

"Indeed, sir."

Halit Bey showed no modesty, though he did tell the mayor, without once mentioning Nuri Efendi's name, that the watch and clock repairmen of the past composed this sort of meaningful adage and that men such as they were well versed in the social questions and work ethics of their day, and that one of our institute's aims was to introduce such paragons to the public.

"That task will fall to our publishing department."

The mayor cast a sideways glance at his assistant, and the man quickly jotted down in his notebook the need for a publishing department and the important task that would be its responsibility. Then the mayor noticed the desk lamps. Turning to Halit Ayarcı, he offered his solemn congratulations.

"So then, you'll be working nights too! A tremendous sacrifice, an enormous success . . . Thank you, I am very pleased. Allow me to extend to you my thanks and congratulations."

With a magnanimous and fully endearing flourish of the hand, Halit Ayarcı motioned to discount his involvement in the project. And thus were accorded to him all the unknown future successes of our files, typewriters, cabinets, and lamps; of our new curtains, though they accentuated the office's dirt and unpainted walls; and having been granted recognition, even for feats that Nermin Hanım and I had yet to achieve, Halit Ayarci promptly returned it all to the mayor:

"Oh, but please, sir, the success is all yours. For it's you who has made all of this possible."

Oh, how much he resembled Yusuf Kamil Pasha just then! When Sultan Abdülaziz visited the pasha's home for the first time, he was given not only the deeds to newly constructed kiosks but also the most beautiful manuscripts to hand and a great heap of precious jewels atop a golden platter and all of his wife's fortune!

"The success is yours alone. Please take it for your own. For myself and all of us here are in your service . . ."

But apparently the mayor was no less courteous than Sultan Abdülaziz himself.

For the sultan first accepted the platter, which is to say all of Zeynep Hanım's wealth, and then chose the one thing that was most fitting—a manuscript of the Holy Koran—before exercising great humility in returning everything else to its rightful owner. It was in much the same manner that the mayor accepted his success with a carefree and courteous smile that said, "Oh, but that was just what I was expecting!" before saying, "Oh no, we've only done our part. The real success is due to you"—thereby returning the success to Halit Ayarcı, and a little to us too, for he shot us a sideways glance as we stood watching through the crack in the door. Indeed Nermin Hanım looked very much like Zeynep Hanım, who had no doubt stood in the same way, in her headscarf, patiently waiting for the final decree from the great ruler.

But Halit Ayarcı wasn't listening. He was convinced that the success of the operation depended entirely on its success being attributed to the mayor. But it was simply hopeless; his interlocutor was equally insistent.

"Yes, precisely what I was saying—it is our duty to provide support to those working on the project, but the true success is all yours. I have only laid the groundwork, using all the possibilities afforded to me." And the platter came right back to us.

So this was how it was done. First it is determined that this thing called success has been achieved, and then the author of this success is sought out and duly congratulated, after which the author claims that the success belongs to the man who just congratulated him and promptly returns it; and he, after setting his share of the success aside, returns the rest to the original author while uttering a few meaningful platitudes. After witnessing a prolonged routine of official transfers and returns, who could ever doubt our future? The success of our institute was thus confirmed. When this official routine had come to a close, I could at last relax.

Following the consensus our joint success and a rigorous analysis of the status of both parties involved, the mayor flopped unceremoniously into Nermin Hanım's chair.

Halit Ayarcı sat down in the chair next to hers, while the mayor's assistant found a perch on the table in the middle of the room; we found other chairs for ourselves, thus completing the ring. Once we were all settled, we began discussing the matter of personnel for the Time Regulation Institute.

Halit Bey pulled a little notebook from his pocket, flipped it open, and, referring to his notes, explained his ideas. The institute had been established to study social behavior using avant-garde methods, he explained, and so it was only natural for an institute of this scope to require fixed personnel, among other things.

"We have a director and an assistant director. Additionally, we'll require a publishing division, an administrative head, an office supplies manager, and a head of office operations. For now, these positions will make up our Absolute Staff."

The Absolute Staff was to be supported by a technical team structured to reflect the workings of a clock; it would regulate itself in much the same way clocks regulated our everyday lives: the Minute Hand, Pin, and Spring Departments would complete the first division, while the second division would include Social Coordination and Labor Statistics.

"All of these teams will be led by highly qualified specialists. Hayri Bey will be in charge of Labor Statistics. And I will be managing the Social Coordination group myself. In fact this is where we believe our main revenues will come from. In this way we can ensure that the director's and assistant director's salaries will not exceed the salary scale as set by law. Naturally an institute of this scale would never fit into this building. It would be best if we had a new building that was purpose-built."

"We've already made a note of that, Halit Bey. But don't you think we have one department head too many? I mean, along with the staff you've mentioned—as you say, the Absolute Staff."

"That's right, sir. Each department will have its own team working under it. A kind of organizational or organic skeleton."

"I had no idea. How clever of you to come up with this idea of a permanent staff. It's just that an administrative head seems unnecessary. In fact even a head of office operations seems a bit much."

For some time Halit Ayarcı insisted on these two positions, explaining that the work would be too taxing otherwise. But finally he sacrificed the administrative head, and once he had made this concession, the principle of an Absolute Staff was officially accepted.

It was impossible to be unmoved by the mayor's sensitivity to all the issues. There was not a single sacrifice he wouldn't make for the smooth operation of our institute, while he was clearly doing his best to slim down the budget. At one point he asked for my opinion on a matter. Halit Ayarcı jumped in on my behalf.

"Hayri Bey is always ready to sacrifice himself for the nation and for public service."

By now I had a grasp on how all this worked and so I finished his thought:

"In other words I am ready to tackle the job."

My enthusiasm was met with effusive thanks from the mayor. Whereupon Halit Ayarcı added:

"Ah, but if not for you, never in the world would I have charged myself with such a lofty endeavor."

And so, after being forged in a man's imagination piece by piece, I had become the axis around which this great organization revolved. Surely this was what our forebears knew as valor and esteem—such words allowed for matters to be seen in the most favorable light. Ah, I thought, if only it were possible, if only I could read the entire history of the world.

When it became clear that we were all more or less agreed, the mayor expressed his final reservations.

"Where will you find so many specialists?"

"That's the easy part. Hayri Bey and I will see to that. As a matter of fact, Hayri Bey has an extremely effective plan for this. We shall train our own personnel. In this Hayri Bey is absolutely right. In making this effort, we shall ensure that they are much more reliable in their work."

But now I knew what to say: I'd had plenty of time to practice thinking like Halit Bey when hunting flies in the office.

"Perhaps foreign specialists could be engaged?"

Halit Ayarcı rejected this idea outright.

"This enterprise on which we have embarked is most delicate. Our dirty laundry will be exposed for all to see. Oh no, we can't have foreigners here. They'd ruin the whole exercise—make a mess of it. They simply wouldn't understand."

The mayor seemed both pleased and taken aback.

"Frankly, I don't want foreigners either. One, it's difficult just to make yourself understood; and, two, their finding everything so strange is simply unbearable. They simply cannot adapt, not even to the most natural situations."

Halit Bey didn't even bother to listen. It was his way or the highway.

"We've no need for foreigners. This isn't the kind of work they would understand. We shall train our own specialists from our own people."

He spoke with such decisiveness, showing no regard for what the mayor or anyone else might think. What if the mayor wanted but a few foreign specialists to set an example? Had I been in his shoes, I would have acted more cautiously; I would have given due consideration to the mayor's ideas. And I'd have continued to mull them over afterward. Whenever I am engaged in official proceedings, I acquire a tired and bedraggled look and become evasive, allowing my interlocutor his full say on the matter and deciding for myself later on, because in such situations the actual decision isn't what really matters but, rather, how people shape it. Man is not a noble thing for naught.

"I'm of the same mind. But will the public place sufficient trust in us? We've become so dependent on foreign specialization that—"

"And just for that very reason we shall not include them. What have we become? Must we learn everything from them? Will the young boys of our country ever attain positions of any real import? Halit Bey's system has promised us so much. We shall see this to the very end. And the public will soon see that we do."

The mayor clapped his hands and cried:

"Now, here's where I disagree. For I am no longer of an age when I can relish things that make life any more difficult than it need be."

Ever magnanimous and realistic, Halit Bey chose not to take the comment personally.

"If only we could be sure of their making a real difference," the mayor continued, "we might just be willing to make sacrifices . . ."

Halit Ayarcı suddenly became stern:

"No, sir. Our own people must train our personnel. Did we march all the way to the gates of Vienna with foreign specialists? In those days everyone was a specialist, because we had faith in ourselves."

Ah, such lofty language, such irrefutable analogies! Whatever could the mayor say in the face of Süleyman the Magnificent and his army of who knows how many hundreds of thousands, not to mention their armor, their cannons, their guns and spears? His only hope was a proud retreat.

"Yes, the very heart of the matter."

"In fact we have many people. Hayri Bey has just completed the list."

The mayor still seemed to have his hesitations.

"It's just that, as we all know, in these kinds of affairs . . . To find such a diverse staff so suddenly . . . I mean, people will gossip and soon they'll claim favoritism."

Halit Bey dismissed his fears with a simple wave of his hand:

"We've already thought of that. Unknown entities and applicants without proper references shall be refused admittance to the institute. In this respect our principles are quite sound. Half our staff will be made up of people from our own families and people we know personally. And the other half will come to us on the recommendation of esteemed individuals in whom we have complete trust. Thus we will nip all gossip in the bud. Each and every employee will enjoy a public guarantee."

The mayor seemed quite pleased with all this.

"I had never thought of this before. You do indeed find all the shortcuts, Halit Bey. This principle will clear a good many obstacles. This means, then, that you will have an entrance exam?"

"Oh no, no such thing."

"A diploma of sorts?"

"Oh no, sir, nothing of the sort. Those are the requirements for run-of-the-mill civil servants, whereas this line of work delves into life itself. We need specialists, not civil servants. And by taking this route, we can extricate ourselves from the legal requirements of pay scales."

As they both nodded, they looked meaningfully into each other's eyes.

The mayor paused for a moment. He had more to say.

"You have presented me with a flawless system, and I simply have no objection."

Halit Ayarcı flashed a modest smile. "Thanks to you, we have been able to make the necessary preparations."

"In that case we must make due preparations on our end, which means finding you qualified people."

"I was going to ask you the very same. It's just that for now let's try not to generate false hopes."

"Quite true, yes, you're right indeed."

Halit Ayarcı once again looked down at the notebook he was still holding. Just then I took the opportunity to stand up, as I wanted to see just what was in Halit Ayarcı's miraculous notebook. Apart from a few figures, I saw only a few block letters.

"Eventually we'll need typists and office boys, and later on controllers and suchlike, to see to secondary office affairs. But we shall appoint these people as and when we need them, and only after we have established our permanent staff. What we do need at once is another secretary. That will be our first concern."

Then he turned to me:

"Perhaps your own Zehra Hanım would accept the position? There would of course be a modest remuncration. She'd feel quite at home at the institute. It would be something like a second home to her."

Then he turned to the mayor:

"Zehra Hanım is Hayri Bey's daughter."

In the face of this sound evidence and support, the mayor had but one reply:

"May God grant it so!"

Three days later Zehra began work at the Time Regulation Institute, under the supervision of Nermin Hanım—meaning she came to the office with her handbag full of toiletries and the wool she would use to knit Halit Bey a thank-you sweater.

But allow me to add that, within just a few years, Halit Ayarcı came to own what may be the most extravagant sweater collection the world has ever known. There was hardly a typist in the office who hadn't knitted him one or two. The most beautiful were undoubtedly those made by Nermin Hanım; they were genuine masterpieces: replete with all the colors of an *arc-en-ciel* and adorned with motifs suggesting timepieces, they sparkled like crystal in sunlight.

The mayor now returned rather abruptly to a previous point,

asking if we genuinely needed a head of office operations. He was really quite pleased that we had sacrificed the position of administrative head. If we were to make this additional sacrifice, he would be entirely satisfied.

"I have always been sensitive to such particulars. Later on you'll be able to promote someone from the auxiliary staff. And the name itself is rather unseemly: head of office operations. In fact it's rather unfortunate to have to besmirch the institute with such a name. This is an era of pure and unadulterated Turkish."

Halit Bey seemed to me to have been outplayed by this last objection.

"Well if you say so, sir . . ."

The poor mayor seemed as delighted as a child to have scored a victory in the name of the public good. Then suddenly he remembered:

"Naturally you'll be submitting a memorandum of justification."

Halit Ayarcı smiled:

"Don't worry about that. It's long since prepared. We've been working on this for the last two months. Just the other night I went over it once again with Hayri Bey. This morning I made a few alterations before consulting you, but they are really not so important, one or two minor points, and then I will send it on to you."

As he uttered these final words, he looked in my direction.

"If you like, I could just go over the main points, or better yet I'll read them to you."

And he made a motion to retrieve something from his jacket's inner pocket.

A glum expression settled on the mayor's face.

"By all means," he said.

And he closed his eyes as if surrendering to whatever torment was in store for him. But the mayor was just as clever as Halit Ayarcı and not one to be taken off guard. So with a glance at his watch he suddenly leapt to his feet and cried:

"Oh my, it's lunchtime. Why not leave that for some other time. We've achieved so much today already as it is."

Then he looked at all of us.

"We'll all eat together, won't we?"

Nermin Hanım and I both protested and Halit Ayarcı said:

"They're fine. Who knows what Nermin Hanım has brought in today for lunch. As I mentioned before, she's a wonderful housewife."

He was right. There wasn't anything the poor woman's mother-in-law wouldn't do to ensure Nermin Hanım's comfort at the office, sacrificing any amount of money or time just so she wouldn't have to endure her nattering on all day long at home. Derviş Efendi went to their home every day around eleven in the morning and returned with ample provisions.

Upon leaving the office with Halit Bey, the mayor paused at the door and asked me to think a little more about the future staff:

"It's a good thing we cut those two management positions. We might be able to cut even more!"

Halit Bey answered on my behalf:

"Hayri Bey's even worse than I am, sir. I might be willing to make the slight cut here or there, but as the primary specialist in the institute I don't think he would be ready to sacrifice much more."

Like a baby swallow on its first flight, I leapt into the conversation:

"In an enterprise like ours, the best approach is the one that achieves the highest efficiency."

Oh my Lord, if only I could tell you how much I longed to be facing a mirror at just that moment, to catch a glimpse of my hungry reflection. For the first time—yes, perhaps for the first time in all of my life—I had uttered words of true importance.

They left the office arm in arm. Nermin Hanım and I escorted them as far as the stairwell, where, for the last time, the mayor extended his thanks to us both.

Having returned to the office, I sat down, took my head in my hands, and set about rubbing the top of it with great vigor. I had been doing this ever since our famous night in Büyükdere. I felt as if I'd been walking on my hands ever since, with my two feet waving in the air; everything seemed upside down, obeying a logic I did not recognize.

Nermin Hanım was entirely charmed.

"Isn't the mayor just the most delightful creature? Once I finish this sweater for Uncle Halit, I'll start working on one for him."

Before I could come up with an apposite reply, Derviş Efendi stepped in, holding an enormous tray of food.

And so it was that I came to understand why the institute was a success and how its staff was to be organized. But when it came to the organization of our statistical studies, and in particular the graphic representation of such studies, I was quite the tyrant. It took Halit Ayarcı no more than three or four days to fill in the gaps. I found him, one morning, working in front of my desk. He'd taken off his jacket and hung it on the chair behind him. He'd rolled up his sleeves and was leaning over a large and almost completed chart. You could see from his face and shoulders that he was engrossed in the work at hand. I went over to him and said:

"May your work come easily, Beyefendi."

Without looking up at me, he replied:

"Yes, that's it! The regulation of time will always vary according to occupation. For example, just have a look here: laborers, menial workers, civil servants, and clerics are more exacting in their regulation of time, and teachers are the same, whereas businessmen, housewives, and in particular servants—in other words, those who in fact don't really work, which is to say, those with no work apart from their actual work . . ."

I was baffled by this last expression: "those with no work apart from their actual work."

"In other words, those people who don't do anything save the work they have been instructed to do, or, to put it another way, those who devote all their time to one particular job. For example, a woman who knows how to read and write and who enjoys music will feel the need to finish with her domestic duties quickly, because she has other things to do. So for such a person time is a valuable commodity; the same goes for a housewife who works outside her home, as well as for servants who work day shifts, but as for the others, the concept of time is less pronounced."

Halit Ayarcı bent over his diagram.

"The colors are wonderful, aren't they? Nermin Hanım did them. I explained the method to her, and she prepared all this in just one night. Now it's up to me to find an occupation for every colored column."

This was perhaps the strangest thing I had ever heard or seen. I tried to object:

"But, sir," I said, "shouldn't this be done in just the opposite way? That is to say, first a survey is conducted, and then the figures, or rather the results, are collected. Then columns that represent these results are arranged accordingly. At least that's as much as I know about—"

Halit Ayarcı looked at me as if for the first time.

"The old method," he said. "Obsolete and absurd, and it gobbles up a terrible amount of time, offering no conclusive evidence. This method is far more reliable. Here the margin of error is reduced as there's no possibility for any verification. For example, have a closer look at this little yellow column between the red one and the purple. It's shorter than all the others. Nermin Hanım may not have consciously considered this, but she made it this way all the same. And so there must be a reason. I asked her about it this morning, and she told me that she really didn't know, and that it just came to her like that. So it was a flash of inspiration. And inspiration is never wrong. So then it falls to me to assign a function to this column, and I've been racking my brains for half an hour trying to do precisely that: I cannot imagine a mathematical equation capable of uncovering a more suitable occupation than the one that will eventually emerge from my cudgeled brain. Numbers are deceptive. They lead us to absurd and faulty results. In any case, it's impossible to count anything properly. I'd believe in statistics if human beings were one-dimensional. But humans are complex beings, forever in a state of flux. And if that's the case, then why get bogged down in tasks so arduous? I'm setting aside this yellow column for patients with grave illnesses, as they are less concerned with the regulation of time. The fact that it is six times smaller than the columns next to it attests to this discrepancy. And this single black line shows that the dead are no longer concerned with time."

"Yes, I see—but is it really necessary to include that in the diagram? It seems only natural . . ."

"I believe so. In fact it is vital that we include it in this diagram. If we don't, how will we teach the public to understand that true consciousness in a human being derives from the relationship between timepieces and time? But how strange, it's as if you've forgotten the very reason our institute was established. We are challenging the order of society itself. We are here to serve the common good. Or did you assume I haven't got anything better to do?"

"I don't know about you, but for me there's nothing more important. And never has been. Of this I am convinced."

He made a few final changes on the chart and then turned to me.

"Forget about such questions. You'll get used to these things in time. One day they'll be like second nature. What you said to the mayor the other day was entirely and absolutely wonderful."

"Oh, but it was what *you* said that was truly admirable."

"We're old friends. We went to school together and we've been close ever since."

"It's just that . . ."

"Yes?"

"That whole discussion about our 'success' rather surprised me. We haven't done anything yet!"

"Well, you're wrong about that, Hayri Bey. Just to start is success in itself. Think about it: we have established ourselves in this little office, and we have managed with these conditions, sacrificing ourselves to do this vital work. Is this not success?"

Suddenly he stopped; looking me directly in the eye, he asked, "Hayri Bey, don't you believe in what we're doing?"

I glanced at the personal effects I had arranged around the edge of my desk. I thought it might be time for me to collect myself and my things and leave. When he realized what I was thinking, he smiled as if to reassure me.

"Don't worry. I don't intend to let you go. There's still so much work waiting for us at the institute. But still I'd like to know why—why don't you believe in what we're doing?"

"It's just that we don't seem to be engaged in meaningful activity."

"What do you mean by meaningful? Are the meanings we share not plucked from the air at a moment's notice? Take a porter, for example. There's a piece of furniture, and he has to carry it from one place to another."

"Is that all?"

"But to your mind, or rather your logic, everything and anything can be refuted! Thinking about any kind work for ten minutes, no five, even three, can render it utterly absurd. You need but ponder something closely to extract it from any system of logic."

For more than a moment he was lost in thought. Then he leaned back over his diagram. Then he got up to have a look at the chart from a distance. Wheeling around to face me, he declared:

"My good man, first there was man and then work. Work was created by man to be executed by man. And we have created this. Are you suggesting that because no one ever thought of such a thing before, or approached the idea in such a way, our endeavor cannot be construed as meaningful work? We are indeed engaged in work, and work that is vital. Work is a matter of mastering one's time, knowing how to use it. We are paving the way for such a philosophy. We'll give our people a consciousness of time. We'll create a whole new collection of adages and ideas, and spread them all over the country. We shall declare that man is first and foremost a creature who works, and that work itself is time. Is this not a constructive thing to do?"

He really seemed rather distraught just then. He was nearly out of breath, and panting as if he'd just put down a heavy load.

"I sense that you limit yourself to timepieces and neglect that which lies beyond. A clock is an instrument, a tool, albeit a very important one. Progress begins with the evolution of the timepiece. Civilization took its greatest leap forward when men began walking about with watches in their pockets, keeping time that was independent from the sun. This was a rupture with nature itself. Men began following their own particular interpretation of time. But that's not all. For a timepiece is time itself, we mustn't forget that!"

The best I could do was fall back on my usual refrain.

"Sir, as you know, I'm an ignorant man. And all that I do know—or rather whatever I manage to actually hear, whatever my ears manage to pick up—comes from Nuri Efendi, Dr. Ramiz, and you. So how could I know about such things?"

Halit Bey laughed.

"Don't make yourself out to be so naive. I'm quite convinced there are a many good things you do know. You're intelligent enough. You just don't believe it. You lack faith. You are in pursuit of an absolute. How strange to see a watchmaker— a man who concerns himself with relative notions such as time—in pursuit of absolute values. I just don't understand."

He seized my shoulder and shook me.

"You're going to change, Hayri Bey, change. But above all else, the Time Regulation Institute needs you to believe."

With that he sprang to his feet, dropped to his knees, seized one leg of his chair, and raised it high into the air; and without bending his arm, he stood straight up and marched around the room holding the pose. Then, tilting his head back, he placed the chair leg square on his nose and, opening his arms wide open for balance, he resumed his slow tour of the room.

With a deep breath, he returned the chair to the floor. Until this moment I hadn't noticed quite what a splendid body he had. He was a good-looking man, and nimble too, with muscles rippling across his chest.

"But why didn't you cheer? You were too surprised, weren't you? I have nearly eighty different tricks like this up my sleeve. I could easily find work for myself in a circus, if I wanted to do such a thing of course. But I have chosen to regulate clocks."

And he slammed his fist down on the desk.

"And regulate them I shall! We shall regulate them together."

Returning to his own desk and chair, he gestured for me sit down opposite him.

"We've forgotten about Dr. Ramiz. We need to find a position for him. I will elect the doctor to be a new member of the staff. Whom will you recommend?"

"I've no idea," I said.

I truly didn't know what to say, as I hadn't the faintest idea what he was talking about. It was all beyond my comprehension. I was, in addition, suffering from the sort of headache that comes with seasickness. With great patience, Halit Bey continued:

"Allow me to explain. Half of our staff will be made up of people we know. Isn't that what we discussed the other day? One from their side, and one from ours, and as there are two of us, whenever I offer someone a post, you earn the right to suggest someone too. Now, I've just suggested Dr. Ramiz."

I felt a little more at ease. We were playing some kind of family game. Halit Bey had put forward Ramiz.

"Lazybones Asaf Bey . . ."

"Very good. For which position? I must say I do like the name. Dr. Ramiz's profession requires that he be appointed to the Labor Statistics and Social Coordination division. What would be suitable for Asaf Bey?"

"One of the branches. For example, the Gear Branch . . ."

"Can he handle that?"

"He was a dentist once."

"But he's not anymore?"

"No, not since a patient bit his hand. Besides, he has an aversion to work. He enjoys sleeping most of all. If a patient ever came to his office while he was dozing in the coffeehouse, or carrying on with people there, his assistant would send word and he would take his time preparing himself for the job. Most times he'd come right back, as the patient couldn't be bothered to wait. I suppose he'll refuse the offer."

I thought Halit Bey might find the story amusing, but he didn't seem ruffled at all. With perfect composure, he said:

"An interesting fellow indeed. There's certainly something about him . . . And I am certain we'll find him a job that he'll perform with great success. But he may not be the best one to start off with. We'll consider him later. Can you think of someone else to recommend?"

"The poet Ekrem Bey. We're fond of one another. He's in his thirties."

"Now this sounds promising. What's his occupation?"

"Really nothing at all up until now."

"I see, a young man, a fresh talent. Agreed. We'll get back to Asaf Bey later on. Any other recommendations?"

"I haven't mentioned Zehra Hanım, because she counts for Nermin Hanım."

"Our current staff is by no means our complete staff. And I shall not submit a proposal for a final staff until our institute has been approved, because I am obliged to keep the staff as large as I possibly can. Institutions that are up and running offer a sense of security. This is why I want the institute to be a living organism in the full sense of the term, so that our time can itself be made visible through our staff's expertise. Everyone will gain a clear understanding of what we're doing! So we must recruit personnel who will agree to the task given to them, whatever the situation."

"Would it not be wiser to begin with a slightly smaller team?"

"Out of the question."

"The organization could expand when the need for more personnel arises."

"Oh no, you're proposing we set sail on a ship with nothing but a rudder and a funnel. No, a ship is a unified entity: It has an engine, a prow, a stern, a bridge, and cabins and whatever else. All this forms a whole, from the captain all the way down to the rats! Find me a crew for my ship and the passengers and the rats! Do you understand? Working with a small staff means not working at all. An institute is a living organism, with arms, legs, and a stomach—we need them all. And I shall go one step further and say that we are compelled even to employ extraneous limbs."

I mustered all my courage.

"And just why is that?" I asked.

"To discharge them when the need arises. Surely you are aware that all the world is jealous of an institution that has the official or semiofficial blessing of the state? You can see it everywhere. There's always talk of reducing costs, and decisions are made accordingly. And what will we do when external pressure is brought to bear on us and we have no choice but to take action? Are we to sacrifice our closest friends and relatives? Of course not. I plan to have several scapegoats on hand. You know whereof I speak, do you not? Every year the ancient Jews would transfer all their sins to a goat and then chase the creature out into the desert. When the need arises, we'll do the very same. We must have all this mapped out in advance. Once the institute has been in place for two years, talk of extravagant spending will begin. So we shall need at least two or three people we can comfortably sacrifice, if we are to show the public that we have nothing but the best intentions. And what shall we do after that? Draw straws? Well, perhaps we could, but . . . In any event, we shall take the necessary precautions now so as to have a few people ready, the kind of people any institute can do without, in fact the kind we could take legal action against, the kind of person who has aroused suspicions from the start. And of course we shall keep some personnel in reserve, to run our time regulation stations."

He was pacing frantically about the room.

Regulation stations were small roadside posts where ladies and gentlemen could stop in to adjust their timepieces. There fashionable young ladies, handsome men, strapping young lads, and citizens both young and old could have their watches regulated for a modest fee, after which they would be issued with a receipt. They were placed along the busy boulevards of the city's most fashionable and affluent neighborhoods, and over time they penetrated deeper into the backstreets and other, more modest, parts of the city. Our first stations were in Nişantaşı and Galatasaray.

An undertaking this ambitious would require a large staff. We would need young, sharp-witted, and personable employees who could explain the Time Regulation Institute's mission to customers and applicants while they tended to the regulation of their timepieces.

Sadly I felt compelled once again to put forward an objection:

"But who would go into a shop for such a simple thing, as if he were just popping in to have a shoe shine? And then of course there's the fact that modern life has been slowly destroying our most dynamic local businesses, not to mention the local barbers and corner pudding shops. People passing by will just pop their heads into the station and adjust their watches themselves."

Halit Ayarcı replied:

"Now, there you've got it wrong, for just the opposite will occur: people will come running. Our stations will be so stylishly designed and run by such charming staff that they'll be busier than the busiest shops in town. Just trust me!"

Only four months remained before our personnel request was to be certified. This didn't bother me overmuch. I was assured four months of relative peace of mind, after which the matter would pass into God's hands. But, I thought to myself, if all this is to end in four month's time, I better take precautions for the future. That was the least I could do.

Fortune had not given me the opportunity to live the life of an ordinary man. And so, if I was to succeed, I had to be that much more courageous and enterprising, while exuding a resolute nonchalance in my dealings with others. Perhaps Halit Bey won't manage to pull this one off. Though clearly his courage would never falter—he would remain the same man. Should I follow in his footsteps? What if I tried, for example, to overtake him in this matter of the regulation stations? And so I made my first deliberate (and not insubstantial) proposal since the opening of our institute.

"Will the personnel have a distinctive uniform?" I asked.

"I hadn't thought about that."

"You know, I'm not sure it would be favorably received, but if we want the institute to catch on, I believe it's a must. A uniform that will bring out the best in a man's body and that will conceal, if necessary, a woman's age, while highlighting a beauty beyond sexuality, something sharper and more striking—a uniform to suit the silver screen. If anything, some kind of cap, and if for no reason other than to give it a more masculine air!"

"Why is that?"

"To draw attention. What would the public think of a motley mass of people?"

Halit Bey thought it over for a moment and then cried:

"It's done, then. You win! We will issue uniforms. Better yet, we'll have something for our entire personnel, managers aside. We'll design a little badge for them. A rosette at the very least! Our entire staff will be decked out in special attire, which means we'll have a unique look that is sure to appeal to the public!"

"What's more," I said, "we shall need to give special attention to the manner in which employees address the clientele. The latest trend is all too clear—there's no limit to what people are calling each other these days. Daddy-o, brother man, Uncle Tom, big boss, foreman Joe, sister Jane—it's gotten out of control. It's as if they've created this singular extended family!"

Saying this, I couldn't help but recall the tram conductor who had harassed me earlier that day: "Hey, Daddy-o, you asleep?'

Halit Ayarcı was beside himself.

"An excellent idea!" he cried. "Also accepted. Anything else?"

"We'd draw more business if our staff were to speak in sweet and measured tones whenever they interacted with customers, and even more so if we were to teach them to be deferential, polite, and professional. If they could learn to speak about the institute and timepieces in a uniform way, relaying exactly the same information every time, and with the air of a serious professional, without adding extraneous information, and, perhaps most important, if they themselves behaved like timepieces, constructed to do this very job, saying only what was needed, speaking with a seriousness of purpose that might seem strange coming from the mouths of employees of certain ages, and then falling silent."

"A kind of automaton, then? The greatest weakness of our age is its greatest strength. The foundation, the very backbone, of a new, hyperorganized Middle Ages, as we prepare to enter a new period of enlightenment. You're right, Hayri Bey. Better said—you're an absolute genius! You've made a remarkable discovery. People will be just like alarm clocks, speaking when fixed to do so, and then remaining silent when they're not on duty, isn't that it? The human being on vinyl. Fantastic!"

He threw his arms around me.

"Congratulations, Hayri Bey! You've stumbled upon the primary psychological problem of our age. But this won't be easy. Just how can we do this?"

"I know someone who can," I said. "A woman, to be exact, for only a woman could really handle such a job. Someone who can mold anyone to just the shape she's looking for. Sabriye Hanım could not only teach our staff—she could oversee its development."

I told him about Sabriye Hanım. He already knew a little bit about her. My friends from the Spiritualist Society were always on my mind.

"There's no time like tomorrow—we'll write a letter inviting her to come visit us here. I'm quite sure she'll be the one for the job. She can be a little cantankerous, but she's sure to take the offer! And she'll be especially good in the follow-up."

He thought for a moment.

"If you ask me, I say we restrict the personnel in the regulation stations to women and young girls. Let's not post any men there. From what you're saying, the only ones to whom we'll be able to teach such manners and etiquette are young girls. We'll have to find something else for the men to do. Why would we need to turn a whole army of men into automatons! We wouldn't be able to do it anyway. Today's women can get on with young and pretty women just as well as men can. It's obvious from the way they admire all the new movie stars."

If nothing else I was quite sure that there were just as many brainless men as there were women. No, I thought both should receive the same training, but I didn't insist because something else came to mind. We would definitely need a fashion advisor, regarding dress and uniforms. I wondered if we couldn't employ both Selma Hanım and Nevzat Hanım. I brought this up, and my face blushed bright crimson. He agreed with me in principle, but he was hesitant about the persons in question. So, trying out my new approach, I called his bluff.

"As manager of the institute, your grace suggested Sabriye Hanım, and I accepted. So I in turn shall choose Selma Hanım as she is a close friend of mine."

Halit Ayarcı thought this over for a moment and then began laughing.

"Well if it must be a matter of principle, then agreed. But what will we do about her husband?"

"We'll take him as one of the scapegoats."

He looked me over in silence.

"There's more to you than meets the eye!" he exclaimed. "Indeed you even know how to mount a counterattack. All agreed, then. Nevzat Hanım included. But don't forget that we're splitting the selection staff. Let's have a few recommended people come and then we'll decide. I don't mean Selma. Get in touch with both these ladies and have a word with them about it. I'm quite busy these days. And it seems you've gotten the knack of things. Let's not rush into anything with Cemal Bey and Nevzat Hanım!

Leaving the building, he said, almost as an afterthought, as if the matter were of no import:

"Ah, yes, I almost forgot. The mayor has raised your salary just a touch for the interim period, while we settle the new staff. Starting this month you receive three hundred liras!"

First I thought of throwing my arms around him and kissing his hands, but in the nick of time I recalled my recent decision. I was going to catch up with this man; I would use him as my model. It was my only hope, so I held myself back.

"Thank you," I said.

And in the most serious voice I could muster.

"But I believe the most important matter is the success of our institute."

We stared at each other for a moment.

"Yes," he said. "That's most important."

Two years later I stopped in at one of the time regulation stations whose fundamental principles I had discussed with Halit Ayarcı. A young girl dressed like an airline stewardess flashed me a syrupy smile and, like a spider, spun a web all around me. She adjusted my wristwatch before I could even take it off. Of course, the adjustment was incorrect, as she set it according to her own. And all the while she droned on about timepieces and their role in society, saying things a hundred times more idiotic than I had ever heard, always with the same saccharine smile plastered on her face; she even answered my questions and went on about the regulation of cosmic time, making a point of never allowing the conversation to move toward any topic that didn't have to do with watches or time. As I left she stuffed into my hand a pile of prospectuses about the institute that I had written myself. And she suggested that I go visit the institute's new building on Freedom Hill as soon as possible. And as if all this wasn't enough, she sold me a one-year regulation plan and three editions of the calendar published by the institute.

On my way out I paused in front of my photograph, one of many decorating the walls. It was my best photograph, taken as I made my selection from the fashions that Selma Hanım had brought in for my approval. Smiling at the young girl, I asked her if she recognized me. First she told me that my question was very personal, adding that there was no article in the regulation station manuals requiring her to supply me with an answer. But I insisted and she said:

"Of course I recognized you—I just didn't want to disregard Sabriye Hanım's instructions. We must always smile, but never look a customer in the eye for too long. We must be personal so as not to be too impersonal, and talk continuously about watches, as if we know it all by heart, thus providing essential information about the institute in the clearest way possible."

So I hadn't been wrong in selecting Sabriye Hanım for the job.

"All right, then, so you know me! Now, what do you think we should do?"

She glanced at the clock on the wall:

"I'm off at seven," she said. "Then I'll be able to listen to you."

Zehra didn't stay very long at the institute itself. She preferred working at the regulation stations, where she met her future husband. Naturally, just after the wedding we made her husband a specialist and manager in chief of the Minute Hand Department. I couldn't just leave my son-in-law out in the cold. My younger sister-in-law was appointed to the position left open by Zehra. Then there was a young man who came to us seeking employment but without any references; realizing there was but one way to join our set, he promptly proposed to my sister-in-law. This gave me the idea of establishing a separate management department for conjugal affairs operating within the institute. But Halit Ayarcı rejected this perfectly sensible proposal, fearing that such a department would detract from the seriousness of our mission.

Two days after my discussions with Halit Bey, I went to visit Sabriye Hanım in her home. She was simply thrilled to see me. She spoke of the past with such tenderness and melancholy, showing me she truly had a heart. When I brought up the job proposal, she was thrilled with the idea of a mutual collaboration. And she was pleased that I now had a job with real responsibility, and was wearing proper clothes.

"The Spiritualist Society has disbanded," she said. "I've been terribly bored. You know I was looking for just this sort of job. I am at your disposal."

I told her that we still hadn't organized our official personnel list, and were still awaiting official approval, but were hopeful it would come through soon.

"Give it some thought. You would be charged with forming groups of five to ten young girls, whom you would train to carry out what might seem to be a somewhat meaningless task. The entire success of the venture rests on the demeanor of these girls. They alone could be the very reason why the institute takes off. Why are we doing this? I can't really say. But it must work. First and foremost they should be as pleasing and unobtrusive as possible—by no means should they make people feel uncomfortable. I suppose we'll add additional duties to these stations later on. But for now the job is to train these girls."

Sabriye Hanım pursed her lips and listened to me intently.

"If you hadn't told me you were working with Halit Ayarcı, I would have guessed as much. This is just the sort of thing he'd dream up. He never was one for the ordinary. For him, work must first be an adventure. An expedition to the North Pole, smuggling contraband—anything's possible. But he won't settle for just any old thing. To be worthy of his interest, an undertaking must be bizarre and perhaps impossible. It should be startling, even frightening! But then there should be actual work. This is why he never could stay very long in the civil service. He's friendly with all the powerful people. And there was a time when he was one of them. But he just never warmed to the work—it was never enough of an adventure for him. Even so, there has to be some part of a project in which he truly believes. I imagine you don't take all this too seriously, but I'm quite sure that Halit Ayarcı starts his projects with firm conviction. And I'm quite sure this goes for the Time Regulation Institute. Once again he's thought up something wonderful for society, but he's dreaming an impossible dream. Being useful isn't enough to make it great. Like I said, he always needs to surprise everyone or rile them up or just make a lot of noise. As a matter of fact, I could tell right away that you were using his own words to explain the institute's objectives to me. So in a word, comrade, I'm in. You'll see just how much fun it'll be!"

I knew I wouldn't even have to ask Sabriye Hanım a question to get her talking.

"How could I ever turn down such an opportunity?" she said.

As I sat in Sabriye Hanım's living room, drinking tea, I couldn't help but think about how much my life had changed. Five years earlier I'd come over to visit her quite often, and I'd sit opposite her, just like this. But though she was kind to me back then, it came in the form of coddling, a righteous and smug caressing of my heart. Later on I was in such a state that I wouldn't even dare ring her doorbell. So something had changed since then. How was I to cope with this change, to make the best of it? How in the world was I going to keep it all going? It was more than just a new job. It was something else altogether. As if reading my mind, Sabriye Hanım abruptly changed the subject.

"You know, Hayri Bey, you've really changed."

"God forbid. Is that so?" I said.

"Why yes, and very much so! Don't take this the wrong way. I'm not saying this to offend you or belittle you in any way. You seem more at peace with yourself and your life. Yes, that's it. You've made peace with your life. You know this is Halit Bey's influence. Halit Bey is comfortable in his own skin.'"

So that was it. Halit Bey was comfortable in his own skin. It wasn't a question of money. It wasn't just a surge of self-confidence, which under normal circumstances would occur naturally. This was something else. He played with life as if he were playing with a toy he'd picked up somewhere. And once again I realized that since I'd met the man I had, without realizing, entered his frame of mind. I had even begun to imitate him. Nothing Sabriye Hanım told me about Halit Ayarcı's secondary characteristics could pale the light of this fundamental truth.

"Almost everyone who works with Halit Bey adopts his manner, insomuch as they are able. Halit Bey isn't fond of me, perhaps because I know him a little too well. But, myself, I am very fond of him."

I told Sabriye Hanım that Halit Ayarcı was also thinking of hiring Nevzat Hanım, Cemal Bey, and Selma Hanım. She smiled when she heard Selma Hanım's name, as if she had been expecting as much.

"Selma Hanım will agree," she said. "In fact she'll be quite tickled that you thought of her. I imagine she needs the work too, but for reasons different from my own. It seems things aren't going very well for Cemal Bey. His financial affairs are in a terrible state, and he's burdened with all sorts of other problems too. But I'm not too sure about Nevzat."

"Why's that?"

"Nevzat isn't the old Nevzat anymore. You'll find Selma Hanım very much changed as well. Nevzat's become more and more detached of late. She's cut off all contact with her friends. She lives as if she's atoning for a sin. She's become deeply religious. She does nothing but read the Koran, from morning till night, and she prays five times a day. In fact she's even stopped all communication with the spiritual world."

"What's happened to Murat?"

"He's disappeared. Like I said, she's no longer the same Nevzat Hanım."

Then she quickly changed the subject.

"Why, do you know who I recently befriended? Your aunt. What a wonderful woman, so vibrant and alive, and what vigor for her age! To be honest I feel bad you two have drifted apart, for your sake that is. Such an open-minded, clear-sighted human being . . . And do you know she has a keen interest in Sufi mysticism too? In fact she's even written several ecstatic love poems. Tomorrow I'm invited to her house for tea."

It was clear that the conversation was going to get boring, and so I left the house, promising Sabriye Hanım I'd telephone her as soon as I could.

I was really quite moved by what Sabriye Hanım had said about Selma Hanım. That's probably why I called her from the first corner shop I could find. I planned to hang up if Cemal Bey answered. Just to hear Sabriye Hanım say just those few words about Selma Hanım had set me alight, though I hadn't thought about her for the last five years, and could hardly recall her face, on account of all that I had suffered, and it had to happen now, just as my life was just starting to get on track and I had entered into a sort of second honeymoon with Pakize.

Selma Hanım picked up.

"And where have you been hiding, old friend! I kept asking Cemal Bey about you and he'd say, 'Oh, who can tell with Hayri Bey. He resigned and never came back.' I begged him to look for you, and I assume he asked around everywhere he could. But to no avail . . .'"

Her smooth, crystalline voice was infused with a childlike exuberance. So that's what happened, then. Cemal Bey had told her I'd resigned. I was an unreliable character. He'd looked all over for me, did he? But somehow just couldn't find me.

I told her about my current situation, and I asked her if she would be willing to help. She loved the name:

"The Time Regulation Institute. What does that mean, my dear?" she asked. "This must be a joke. Really, is this some kind of lark? "Well, then, tell what it's all about."

I did my very best to explain the institute to her, and then I told her what we were asking her to do. She agreed to come the next morning. This was when Zehra was still new in the office, so I decided to meet her in Halit Bey's room. Straightaway I noticed that many things about her had indeed changed. She was elegant and beautiful as before, and completely in control of all her movements. But although her smiles lit the room like a fireworks display, there seemed to be something wrong with the launching device. She had lost her usual good cheer. It was clear she had gone through some ordeal. It was as if she were speaking through sorrowful, dark thoughts and perhaps even a fear we couldn't know. There was something sad or thoughtful in her voice that I had never noticed before, perhaps even fear. I had lived with fear all my life; I knew the viper all too well. Once it's coiled up inside you, your soul is at its mercy. But what was she afraid of? Why did she seem so ill at ease? I just couldn't understand.

First she asked me to describe the job. And she kept saying, affecting an air of childlike innocence, "Oh, how could little old me manage such a thing?" And her gestures were so enchanting that I spent the rest of our conversation waiting most impatiently for their return.

"It's not quite what you may be thinking," I said. "You'll just offer suggestions to the institute. There's nothing to it really. And you can do this better than anyone, as you have such impeccable taste."

Finally she agreed, figuring that it would be an entertaining job. Fashion was just her thing, after all. All that remained was to consult with Cemal Bey.

"Perhaps he'll say no," she said. "So I can't promise anything right away. I don't want to create problems."

"Problems? Of course not. I can't imagine Cemal Bey objecting to anything you really wanted to do!"

I made a point of saying this, and she nodded.

"Cemal hasn't been his usual self lately."

This woman who was usually so self-contained was on the brink of tears. I felt a knot in my stomach.

What shocked me was to see Selma Hanım's entire life behind these words. So she'd never understood Cemal Bey and never doubted him; she'd been hopelessly blind. All her life she'd seen him as a paragon of maturity and loved him for it. And that wasn't all—she was attached to him. She was under his command. She loved him, she was jealous of him, and she feared him. I had loved this woman until then, but at one remove from her life. I'd known she was married to Cemal Bey, and I'd accepted that. But I'd never thought very much about their relationship. In my mind I could never link Cemal Bey to Selma

Hanım, nor did I feel compelled to do the reverse. She suffered her husband in very much the same way she might suffer a chronic illness.

Now that I realized I was indeed jealous of him, the situation suddenly changed. Till now I had simply despised Cemal Bey. I'd harbored untold rancor toward the man, but I had never been jealous of him. Now suddenly I was jealous. Blood racing through my veins, I said, "Well then, ask him. I hope he doesn't refuse."

The true catastrophe that day was the harsh reality I had to face: this woman I had loved so dearly now seemed just like any woman moaning about her life. But there was something even stranger, even absurd in all this: Once I'd freed myself from my troubles I'd simply gone and replaced them. Just after finding myself in a new job, I'd gone right back to my obsession with Selma Hanım; I was like a swimmer who loses focus after lifting his head above the wave to look at the opposite shore. "Why should I be surprised?" I thought to myself. "I'm just slowly reverting to my old self."

After we'd discussed her employment, Selma Hanım was curious to know about the last five years of my life. First she asked me why I had resigned from Cemal's service.

"You know, in those days Cemal Bey was always saying he planned to raise your salary."

For a moment, I stared blankly into her face. I was about to tell her everything. But why should I rush into such things? Perhaps she wouldn't even believe me. Or I'd just be adding yet another sorrow to her life. Best would be to wiggle out with a white lie:

"I was out of Istanbul," I said.

"But people saw you here . . ."

"Well, that's not to say I didn't come back from time to time while I was staying in Izmir."

Selma Hanım raised her head and looked into my eyes.

"Why won't you tell me the truth?" she said. "I know that Cemal was lying to me."

Another silence.

Slowly she said, "Or rather I suspected so much. But now I'm sure. Your tone just now said it all . . ."

I did everything I could to soothe her, but she carried on.

"No," she said. "This whole thing isn't as simple as you might think. It's really rather complicated. I don't care what he hides from me. But finally he understood that I was fond of you. You always went out of your way to help me. We were such good friends! Perhaps he kept it from me, thinking that I would be upset, which is perhaps kind but still unforgiveable, because there were just too many lies. But why did he go and fire you when he was the one who brought you there in the first place?"

"Perhaps the others insisted that I go . . ."

"Impossible! If that were the case, then he wouldn't have lied to me. But even so, how could he have let such a thing happen? No, there was definitely something else."

Then she fixed her eyes on mine.

"Who knows how much pain and trouble it has caused you."

"Don't worry yourself about that," I said. "Everything's fine now. Don't worry about me. There's no need to make an issue out of it. In fact forget about our offer. Perhaps he would be displeased to see us together. I would hate to inconvenience you!"

Selma Hanım rummaged about in her purse for a tissue.

"I'm already inconvenienced!" she whimpered.

Such is fate. No one can remain a star forever. It is sure to descend from its place in our imagination and find a new one among the masses.

"All the same, I'm very pleased we were able to meet again. As for the job, let's think it over. I'll call you."

We walked down the stairs together.

Outside she said: "It's just so surprising. How can anyone tell so many lies?" And she left.

Surprising indeed.

III

Two months after the mayor's visit to our office, a far more important and powerful figure—I might go so far as to say an absolute power—paid us a visit. But we were no longer in the old office: we had relocated to larger and more comfortable premises.

And our staff had expanded. Nermin Hanım, Zehra, and Ekrem Bey, and I made up the core staff, and we had more work than ever. Halit Ayarcı came every morning and dictated all sorts of things to Nermin Hanım or Zehra. My daughter's poor typing didn't seem to bother him at all, and he was slowly getting Ekrem Bey used to the idea of the institute having a business plan.

The unexpected visit didn't fluster Halit Ayarcı in the least. On arriving, he spent a few minutes at the entrance, detailing the institute's fundamental aims for the mayor and the esteemed personage who accompanied him. But there was a clear difference between this visitor and the mayor: At first the esteemed personage did not speak but only listened with his eyes fixed firmly on your own, and if necessary, he approved what you had said by lowering his lashes. After the briefing he asked to have a look around. He was charmed by the maxims posted on the wall, declaring that they should be distributed, not just across the city, but throughout the country. In response to his suggestion, Halit Ayarcı only said, "We are planning to do just that, sir."

But the mayor gave a different answer:

"Above all else there's the matter of funding. Such a thing is just not feasible, considering the institute's present financial state, even if we were to consider the entire budget for this fiscal year. But Halit Bey is doing all he can."

Strangely enough, our roles had changed. I was now Halit Bey, while the mayor had become Halit Bey. I was the fourth man down the ladder. Yet Halit Ayarcı wasn't going to leave me in the shadows. His questions to me were crystal clear, and clearly shaped to indicate the expected answer, which he fielded with his own particular style.

The esteemed personage turned to the mayor.

"Naturally," he concurred, "but not everything depends on money alone. Human willpower can overcome material limitations."

Oh, how much I prayed for him to carry on speaking just then. If I could only learn the secret behind this matter of willpower, everything would fall into place. But he stopped there. Clearly he expected us to solve this knotty problem on our own.

The mayor had no objection whatsoever. Thus bearing this

accepted truth in mind—for he too seemed to have been able to overcome material restrictions through the application of will-power alone—he continued to remind the esteemed personage, in the most amenable manner possible, always acknowledging his interlocutor's ideas as true, that a project as expensive as this could never be realized without financial support, and that, as it was willpower to be expended in the process, it would be a very expensive project indeed. In my opinion the mayor was right. When unemployed, I'd had to spend so much of this prized commodity—that is to say, my willpower—just to get by, so much so that my reserves had long since gone dry. Perhaps this explains why for months I was like a football bouncing around Halit Ayarcı's feet.

Halit Ayarcı remained detached throughout this exchange. Perched on the corner of his desk, he looked about the room with calm indifference, as if taking pity on the time wasted in such frivolous debate. I never knew that boredom could be so lofty and noble. He waited for the conversation to finish as another might wait for a cloud of dust blown up by a gust of wind to settle. His look seemed to say, "I know just when to intervene. But first you'll have to decide for yourselves! I can't help you overcome your personality flaws. I can but sit here hopelessly and find a way to tolerate them. In any case, you'll eventually come around to where I've been all along." No one could have displayed such patient understanding with greater poise.

At last the esteemed personage made his decision:

"There's no need to worry about the finances. We have already taken the first steps, and now we must make all necessary sacrifices. I would only like to emphasize the importance of being as economical as possible."

The mayor thanked the great man for his simple wishes with a sentence that observed the meandering rituals we had first noted in his exchange with our own leader on the occasion of his first visit. Halit Ayarcı chose this moment to rise from his desk, abandoning his role as observer to say:

"When we do attain greater capacity, we plan to publish a very important work that is already written!"

Oh no, there was no way I could ever be like this man! There was no way I could ever attain such mastery.

"So you have something ready for publication? So fast!"

"First, we have quite a substantial study. A book my friend Hayri Bey has devoted most of his life to. It is a source of great happiness to us!"

The quick-thinking mayor took this opportunity to introduce me properly.

"No one knows more about the history of our watchmakers than our friend Hayri Bey. He has a capital understanding—not just of timepieces but of the philosophy that underpins them."

Now all eyes were on me. By any legal definition, this was a classic case of deliberate misrepresentation. Caught red-handed at the scene of the crime . . . Oh, good God! If only I could escape. But why? Never before had I been the subject of such rapt attention.

"What is your book called, Hayri Beyefendi?"

The question sent me tumbling down a hill in the dead of the night, grasping anything and everything to stop my fall, until Halit Ayarcı answered on my behalf:

"It is a study of Ahmet Zamanı Efendi—*The Life and Works of Ahmet the Timely*."

"Ahmet the Timely? Never heard of him . . ."

"The eminent seventeenth-century scholar. He lived during the reign of the Mehmed IV, our golden age."

"What was his claim to fame?"

"He was the most important clock smith of his time. In fact they even say he discovered *rabia* calculations before Graham. Hayri Bey was the pupil of Nuri Efendi, a man who came directly from the school of this clock smith and religious time setter."

Once again all eyes turned to me.

"Have you finished writing your book?"

Now it was my turn to speak. It was the least I could do. Halit Ayarcı had taken me this far. The rest was up to me. I knew what I had to do.

"To be honest, no, not yet. That is to say, there are a few remaining issues, but it's nearing completion. In fact it's practically done."

Once again Halit Ayarcı shook off his indifference:

"I imagine we'll have it ready by this coming April."

Then turning to his guest, he said:

"This April will be the hundred and eightieth anniversary of the death of Ahmet the Timely."

He did the calculations in his head.

"Yes, that will make exactly one hundred eighty years."

"That means we could mark the occasion with a ceremony worthy of it?"

Halit Ayarcı left the ball in the mayor's court.

"That is Halit Bey's intention, sir," the mayor said. "Though it could prove difficult for Hayri Bey."

"An opportunity not to be missed. We can make it part of the institute's official opening, can't we, Hayri Bey? It would only add to the magnificence of the occasion."

Halit Ayarcı rejoined the conversation once more.

"I had anticipated an opening ceremony in the new building," he said.

For the first time both parties objected.

"Oh no, no, it'd be too late then. Besides, we can always have a ceremony for the inauguration of the new building. The more such ceremonies the better!"

The esteemed personage looked at me again:

"Hayri Bey, this book must be finished by the end of February. I want the completed book from you by then, and this is an order. It's just not right for us to have neglected such an important person from our past. Recognize the importance of the work you are doing and work accordingly. And remind me of the matter of publication . . ."

"Right away, sir. It's already in my project submission."

And Halit Bey added:

"It's just that the actual name of the work isn't specified. I'll add it to a supplementary list."

I had never known anyone by the name of Ahmet the Timely. In fact this was the first time I had ever heard the name. Oh, dear Lord! Why didn't you just give me a meager salary instead of turning me into someone else's lie? Indeed this was what I now was. I had become a confabulation and the term of my sentence was indefinite; my life was presented to me in daily installments like a serial in a magazine.

The great man kept returning to Ahmet the Timely.

"An important discovery," he said. "But how can it be that he's still unknown?"

I answered without haste, in the most persuasive voice I could muster, so as not to appear to be making it up on the spot.

"It's a known fact, sir, that our predecessors perceived fame as a catastrophe. And the sage of whom we speak died at a very young age—he was forty-two or round about there, I suppose . . ."

"Split figures way back then . . . Discovered by one of our own?"

All at once I couldn't breathe. I was flush out of inspiration. The facts such as they were seemed self-evident. But Halit Ayarcı was in the room:

"And why not, sir?"

But instead of continuing he looked down at the enormous palm of his hand firmly pressed down on the glass tabletop.

"That period, was it an extremely important time? We know so little about our forebears . . ."

"The age—it was an extremely important age. There was of course a tremendous interest in the mechanical. Almost everyone was busy inventing things, in ways great and small. People were flying from one minaret to the next."

His eminence turned to me once again.

"What kind of man was he?"

Halit Ayarcı was fiddling with the buttons on his jacket. This meant it was all up to me now. I rallied all my courage and strength. "Well, he was a patron saint!" But who was the patron saint of liars? I wondered.

"He was a tall man, fair but with a brown beard and black eyes. He had a slight lisp when he was a child, but they say he overcame the impediment with the application of willpower. Well, that is to say, that's what my late master Nuri Efendi told me. He had a number of peculiar quirks of personality. For example, though he grew a variety of excellent fruit, he ate nothing but grapes. And he didn't eat either sugar or honey. He was a member of one of the Mevlevi Sufi lodges, the son of a rich man, but very well received in his lifetime, being opposed to the custom of taking more than one wife . . ."

"So he was a modern man! Practically one of us!"

"More or less . . . He loved the color yellow. Indeed my master Nuri Efendi told me he wore a yellow robe and a yellow fur coat, though it was not the fashion at the time. 'Yellow is the color of the sun,' he would say, or so they say. I have done research into this, but I still haven't tracked down the source of his conviction."

The mayor and the esteemed personage beamed with delight as I said all this. Ah, the magic of little details . . . Just a few personality traits, a few snippets of conversation, and there you have a full life before you. This could explain why our ancient forefathers read only poetry!

"Did he have a profession or something of that sort?"

I couldn't stop here, and it was too late to turn back; I had to carry on whether I liked it or not, dreaming up new details as I went along.

"He was the muezzin in a little mosque in Çengelköy. But they drove him out because of his ideas about marriage, so he created a *selamlik* in his own home and invited people to come for evening prayers. He recited the call to prayer directly from his own window!"

Halit Bey turned back to me:

"Didn't you mention that he corresponded with Western mathematicians through a Venetian contact?"

"That's right, but nothing has been proven. If only that tome hadn't been lost by the Nuruosmaniye Library . . ."

The great man was flabbergasted.

"Truly an important discovery . . . A man of such . . ."

In an expert intervention, Halit Ayarcı made the story a little more believable.

"It seems to me that he must have been a disciple in the Çelebi circle—there's really no other possible explanation."

This explanation satisfied both gentlemen. Pleased that the matter had been settled so smoothly, the mayor suggested a tour of the office.

This was more or less the same tour he'd taken two months earlier. Yet now our office was a little larger, and as the esteemed personage was far more important than he, the mayor was careful to reflect that fact in his degree of fastidiousness. The tour lasted two hours. The man paused in front of nearly everything in the office and picked up almost every available object, turning it over and over again in his hands, inspecting each piece from all angles before replacing it. He peeked into each and every one of our empty notebooks, almost meditating over the diagrams on the wall.

At one point he turned to me, as he tried to unsheathe one of the typewriters, and asked:

"Do you know how he died?"

"Unfortunately not, sir . . . but . . ."

"Shall I venture a guess? Let's see if I get it right. Diabetes," he said. "I've got it too, so I should know."

Of course no one asked why both men should be afflicted by the same illness. Why would we? Indeed why even doubt such a thing at all? Everyone eventually died of some type of mortal affliction, so naturally Ahmet the Timely had died of one too. What difference did it make if he died of diabetes or a bout of boredom? It was much more important that the esteemed personage should show goodwill and a collaborative spirit. All of us accepted his idea as highly possible, without a moment's hesitation. I even went so far as to give it a mild stamp of approval:

"Yes, sir, it's highly likely, considering the man ate nothing but grapes."

Then he looked at his watch. It was a beautiful, gold-encrusted Longines. "I'm tired," he said. We were all tired, which is why the coffee Derviş Ağa brought in for us, as we stepped into Halit Ayarcı's office, was so well received. In fact the great man seemed not at all bothered that it contained almost no sugar.

After coffee we went on to discuss the matter of personnel, in much the same way we had done previously. Then came the ritual of congratulation. This time the golden platter passed back and forth between the mayor and the great man until Halit Bey abruptly raised his arms and popped it onto the latter's lap, like a baby boy in swaddling clothes. My dear benefactor then closed the matter:

"Had I not put my trust in your kind favor, I'd never have

considered such an undertaking. I couldn't possibly thank you enough. And I am delighted that you have offered me the chance to serve you in this capacity."

This was what he did throughout the entire affair: he spoke only at the most crucial moments, coaxing all in attendance to accept his wishes, without actively seeking acquiescence; and now he was saying that the very foundation of the enterprise was in fact the great man's, thus making it clear that any further discussion was pointless.

But a man of his experience would never be so foolish as to leave this great institute entirely in our hands.

"I've had this institute in mind since the very beginning. It's as much mine as it is yours . . . Of course the mayor will be here to assist you . . ."

He complimented me once more as he left:

"I'd like a copy of the book. You will finish it, Hayri Bey?"

And pinching my cheek, he spoke once again of his high expectations. Leaving the office, he reaffirmed his previous command:

"Distribute those slogans! As soon as possible, and with as broad a reach as you can manage."

At the top of the stairs, he turned to the mayor, whereupon I heard him whisper, "Just what are these 'split figures'?"

Halit Ayarcı turned to me after they left:

"I don't suppose you'll doubt our work anymore."

"I suppose not," I said. "So the institute will be officially established. If only we knew what we were to do."

"How can you still not know? Why, we're going to regulate watches and clocks."

"Yes, but how? With such an overstaffed organization . . ."

"We'll find a way. Everyone will have to come up with work based on the name of the position we give them. Once we're all set up, I'll send a memo to all our friends asking them to do just this. And naturally they will. They won't just sit there idly . . ."

With his hand on the doorknob he asked:

"When will the book be done? I mean, how long will it take you to finish?"

"How will I ever write such a book?" I cried. "And about a man who never even existed!"

Halit Ayarcı furrowed his brow. It was the first time I saw him truly angry.

"What do you mean, a man who never existed? You were just talking about him. Didn't he live during the reign of Mehmed IV? Didn't he like the color yellow? 'The color of the sun,' as he used to say . . . You even know that he was a member of the Mevlevi lodge. It is widely accepted that he worked on the Graham calculations and that he died of diabetes. Oh no, my good friend, I will not brook this sort of sabotage. This institute will be a success. Everyone will uphold his responsibilities. And this is your first!"

"That's all well, but all this is nothing more than nonsense. I made it all up!"

He suddenly grabbed me by the lapel:

"You will write the book! Otherwise you will step inside and write your letter of resignation! I shall not be betrayed by my closest friend at this institute in which I have so much vested time and effort. You yourself were just speaking about the man, and now you're saying he never existed?"

"I never said the name Ahmet the Timely."

"But you said Nuri Efendi. What's the difference?"

Then suddenly he laughed, perhaps because of the sour expression on my face.

"Anything with a name exists, Hayri Bey!" he cried. "So, yes, Ahmet Efendi the Timely exists. He exists in part because we want him to. Indeed our illustrious friend desires the very same. Don't worry. Just get to work. Now, what progress have you made on the personnel issue? They're giving us free reign. Where's your list?"

A little disgruntled, I said, "I hardly know anybody."

"Well, find them, then."

"I have no relatives."

"Everyone has relatives."

"Perhaps, but none that I know. I don't know where they are. Should I advertise in the papers?"

He smiled again.

"Ah, Hayri Bey, Hayri Bey," he said. "You are truly wearing

me out. I just haven't been able to accustom you to these things. No, there's no need for an advertisement. We'll just wait a little and see. They'll come. I suppose it's time now to invite Sabriye Hanım and Selma Hanım."

When I stepped back into my room, I saw that Zehra was there waiting for me. She wanted to ask me if she could leave. She looked so happy and beautiful in her new dress. She'd decorated her room in our new apartment so tastefully. At last she was getting on with Pakize. There hadn't been a fight at home since my wife started treatment for her thyroid gland. Ahmet had put on six kilos in three months. I told my daughter she could leave and that she could take tomorrow off if she wanted to. Instead of thanking me, she simply curtsied and left. I put my head in my hands and began to think things over. No, there'd be no letting up. Even though I was safe now in this labyrinth of lies, I still knew that everyone could see the undeniable and overwhelming truth. The Time Regulation Institute had saved my life.

Halit Ayarcı had brought prosperity to our home. As I was thinking all this over, the telephone rang. It was Halit Ayarcı, speaking in a calm, collected voice that gave no hint of our tense discussion earlier.

"Tomorrow I'll bring you a few history books—these should help you with your work on Ahmet the Timely. You'll see just how easy it's going to be."

"Thank you, sir."

"We'll have it done in a couple of months."

"I suppose so, sir. You'll help, of course."

"Wait a little before you invite Sabriye Hanım and Selma Hanım. I'm going now, if there's anything, call me at home."

"Yes, sir."

IV

The press had taken an interest in the institute since the day it opened its doors. The closer we came to obtaining official permission to extend our personnel, the more the newspapers wrote about us. We were literally the talk of the town. The institute's organizational structure, its aims, objectives, and modus operandi—all these were heatedly discussed in the press, and naturally the personal lives of the manager, assistant manager, or other staff members were considered fair game. Some of the dailies were charmed by Halit Ayarcı, while others were shocked that a project this important and ambitious should have been entrusted to a businessman of his ilk. Others posed the question, "Just what does this institute intend to do?" Halit Ayarcı read each and every piece with care, laughing away all criticism with good humor.

"But of course—anyone undertaking a job of this scale and importance should be prepared for criticism!" he bellowed. "The important thing is to get people talking."

He was particularly pleased with the way one journalist had chosen to interpret the Time Regulation Institute's mission, its mode of operation, and even its name: to him we marked an important new development in the history of bureaucracy.

"Whoever wrote that piece truly understands what we're doing. An intelligent man indeed! Above all else he understands our modern age. It's been given many names, but first and foremost it is the age of bureaucracy. All the philosophers, from Spengler to Kieserling, are writing about bureaucracy. I would go as far as to say that it is an age in which bureaucracy has reached its zenith, an age of real freedom. Any man who understands is a valuable figure. I am in the process of establishing an absolute institution—a mechanism that defines its own function. What could be closer to perfection than that?"

As the date of our public personnel announcement grew closer, the news coverage gathered force, abruptly setting its focus on individuals; after a fortnight of playing with Halit Bey, they dropped him and set their sights on me.

It might not have been entirely unjustified to see Halit Ayarcı's hand in this, seeing as the change of tack brought all discussion of the institute's legitimacy to a sudden halt. But this much is true, I was much more likely fodder than Halit Bey, as the public could not have failed to have been delighted by the many misfortunes I had suffered. Thus began a brief but discomfiting interlude. Almost every other day, a journalist would print my picture in the paper, and there would be heated debate about my personal life, as well as questions raised as to my suitability for the post. A swarm of conflicting interpretations whirled around the century-old story of Ahmet Efendi the Signer and his mosque, the Şerbetçibaşı Diamond, my childhood neighborhood and all the people I knew from that time, and my employment record, not to mention my years of unemployment.

For some people, I was the all-in-all favorite. As they saw it, I had devoted my entire life to timepieces and time. They saw everything I did before the establishment of the institute as laying the groundwork for this new endeavor. I had been Nuri Efendi's last student. It followed, then, that I was the heir of all knowledge—progressive and mystical—about Sheikh Ahmet the Timely.

Just around this time, the time setter Nuri Efendi's tomb in Merkezefendi underwent a thorough restoration—surely another one of Halit Ayarcı's discreet manipulations—the result being I was catapulted onto the front page. During my speech at the ceremony unveiling the restored tomb, and on the insistence of Halit Ayarcı, I made frequent references to Ahmet the Timely, and in so doing I succeeded in capturing the public's imagination. Not only did the press laud my intelligence and powers of perspicacity, but I was also praised for my unique mode of delivery.

The following week there appeared the strangest headline I had ever seen: "Hayri İrdal: The Apprentice Years." According to this article, clocks and time had fascinated me since the age of three. As a small child I was always asking my father about the inner workings of the Blessed One, the great grandfather clock in our home. This article, a true masterpiece, concluded with the following words: "From morning till night, his father would remind him that this rather large grandfather clock—the only genuine piece of furniture in their home, this heirloom passed down to them from their noble and devout ancestors—was the very symbol of the universe. Thus did fortune prepare the scene: even before his birth, it had been ordained that Hayri İrdal would spend his formative years in the company of this clock." A week later another writer described me as "our undiscovered Voltaire," making preposterous comparisons between me and the French philosopher, who had supposedly amassed a small fortune through watchmaking. The author of a third piece cast aside Nuri Efendi, my father, and Voltaire to argue that my life was an experiment, a vehicle for the study of our society and society in general. "Since childhood, Hayri İrdal has been preoccupied with matters of the mind," he intoned. "So it is only fitting that the day should come when this, his life's work, would bear fruit."

Naturally Dr. Ramiz could not resist involving himself in the commotion. Not to be outdone, he even presumed to analyze my mind, an article he later expanded into a full-length book. His central claim was that I had a love-hate relationship—a father complex!—with this clock that was to have stood in a mosque that was consecrated but, due to lack of funds, never built. He mentioned Seyit Lutfullah, as well as the dream manuals and fortune-telling guides, and he praised my intuitive understanding. To him I was a kind of Ebu Ali Sinan. "Yes," said the doctor, "Hayri Bey is nothing less than a modern reincarnation of this Eastern Faust. In much the same way as the latter performed calculations in relative time, Hayri Bey performs calculation in living time. Our dear friend Halit Ayarcı should be praised to the skies for unearthing this precious and momentous truth!"

The most frustrating thing about all this foolishness was the way Halit Ayarcı smiled under his mustache every time I complained about it: never once did he think to ease my troubled mind.

"Of course," he said. "Of course, my dear friend, when an institute of this importance comes into being, those caught up in its glory should expect a little noise. And what exactly were you suggesting I should do about it? Step out and say, 'No, these are all lies'? That would destroy our work before we've even begun. Just let it all pass. Think of it as a wave that will soon have crested and dispersed."

At other times he said:

"Am I to blame because you resemble Faust or Voltaire? Or because others happen to think you do? People say such things because they want to see something special in us too. Do you think it's easy for a civilization carrying so much history on its back to catch up in just fifty years? A little exaggeration along the way is only natural. A novelist will be likened to Zola, and you will be compared with this or that philosopher. Truth is, I am shocked by this attitude of yours! You should be glad that I'm not jealous of you, but instead you're angry with me, even aggressive! If I were you, I'd stay quiet and focus on my work ahead. You need to pull yourself together and write your book, and then come up with new ways to expand our institute! These are all such simple tasks—they'll soon be second nature, as you'll see. What I am saying is that you're there already. You were in a rage last week when you read that article that was so critical of you. But to me it seems there is nothing to get so riled up about. I mean, if what you are telling me now is true, why then, you should have welcomed this article with open arms. For that journalist was describing your life as you yourself have explained it to me. But the piece angered you, and that can only mean you were pleased with the others!"

The critical piece was not, however, so easily forgotten. Beginning with a discussion of "what a mistake it had been to hire a man known by all of Istanbul to be mad," it ended by dismissing me as a common swindler who had managed to evade the hand of justice: "Yet another hoax? And when the fiasco of the Şerbetçibaşı Diamond is still fresh in our minds?" But it placed the blame on both me and Halit Ayarcı, casting him as a profiteer—a businessman playing games with the public—and me as his puppet!

After the esteemed personage's visit, Halit Ayarcı made me controller of his timber factory, awarding me a wage of one hundred liras—though there was no actual work to be done—and in the wake of that harshly critical article I was given a similar post at his soap factory. To me, this only served to confirm that I had every right to be angry about that cruel article.

"Well, of course that article made me angry. If people speak

against me, why shouldn't I be angry? You know I was innocent in the diamond case!"

"No," Halit assured me, "you were upset about the word
'puppet.'"

"But I wasn't, for that I can't deny!"

With the same cool and collected manner, he said:

"You really are a very strange man. You have no idea what it
means to collaborate. It's so very clear that you have always
lived in your own world. You have never managed to adjust to
public life. Only people unaccustomed to the company of others would think to question personal freedom. First you say
they shouldn't criticize you, and then you say their praise
should be kept in check. What sort of thing is that?! It's too
good to be true . . . No, my good friend, everyone is free in
their own particular way!"

He wasn't entirely wrong. I did appreciate my favorable
reviews. What angered me were the exaggerations that even I
could not believe. Not long after Dr. Ramiz published his article, a journalist interviewed my wife. And so in the end everything came out. As if to make up for ten years of indifference,
as if to compensate for her condescension and neglect and in
effect the sum total of all the mistakes she made during our
marriage, she spent the entire twenty minutes singing my praises.
But Pakize was not the sort to take an interest in watches,
clocks, psychoanalysis, or higher knowledge of any sort. She
was a modern woman who adored the cinema, who saw the
world through the silver screen. So whether I liked it or not,
she was going to recast me as her new matinee idol.

In this, the film version of our lives, my wife truly loved me.
We'd loved each other since childhood. Following a series of
misadventures, I had been obliged to marry Emine, and so Pakize had married her first husband. But she'd never forgotten
me, nor I her. I was given to understand that I had spoken to
her on the day before my wedding and told her that I'd had no
choice. My first wife had been a good woman, though she'd
lacked in sophistication and so had not really understood me,
which was why, with her at my side, I'd never achieved success,
let alone come to understand my true nature. After Emine's

death, Pakize had left her husband and sought me out, knowing that like all great men I was reserved, proud, and a little
absentminded where women are concerned. It was only then—
thanks to Pakize—that I had set off on my professional career.
"He even left his post as a civil servant so he could follow his
vocation. For seven or eight years, we survived on the trifles my
family had left me. But in the end we spent all we had." During
the interview, Pakize never once complained. As the wife of a
great man, she'd known she would have to make significant
sacrifices. And my private life? Naturally I was a little eccentric. But when I wasn't lost in my work, I was cheerful enough.
I was not a poor equestrian, a magnificent swimmer, and I dabbled in tennis. "He had penchant for gambling but he gave it up
for me!" I knew all about women's fashion and the meaning of
true elegance. My younger sister-in-law followed my counsel in
her attire. And what were my favorite things, apart from
watches and clocks? Music of course: both *alafranga* and *alaturca*. I played the piano and the banjo too. My older sister-
in-law owed her success to me. "Oh, don't you know? My sister
sings every night at the Crystal Waterfall Music Club. If you
happen to be there at half past eleven . . ." I enjoyed chatting
with my family at home. I drank juice every morning with
breakfast. One particular quirk of mine—I was always falling
in love, but my wife had turned a blind eye to this. "As they're
women worthy of his status. And you know what women are
like—they just never leave men alone." As for my wife, she had
once wanted to be a dancer, but, "When you marry someone
like Hayri, you get used to making sacrifices with good grace.
Before the inauguration of the Time Regulation Institute, or,
rather, before its foundation, I'd received two offers: One from
Hollywood . . . Yes, that's right, from Hollywood . . . a film
about the East . . . ," while the other had come from a large
Swiss watchmaking firm. She couldn't furnish the name. She'd
been so busy with her housework that she couldn't remember
all the details. "In fact his early career was in acting. We're a
family of artists. He was a thespian in his youth. And recently
he had a role in a film!" Indeed in my years of unemployment,
I'd been an extra in two different films. My favorite food?

"Boiled vegetables, grilled meat, and so on." According to my wife, I loved to eat but was careful with my diet. My greatest shortcoming was that I worked so hard I forgot to take care of myself. Clearly I was not one for nightlife, and so we rarely went out, but we did sometimes go to the cinema. From here the interview moved on to discuss my favorite movie stars.

Now, if such an interview didn't put both my wife and I in jail for perjury or pack us off to the mental asylum—irrespective of judge or court of law—it was sure to lead to a hasty divorce. I could not believe my eyes. "He works at night, goes to sleep toward dawn, and sleeps but half an hour." But this was only when there was a pressing job to finish. Other times I'd sleep for twenty-four hours. But I just couldn't fathom why I would enjoy sleeping naked on the floor. Now that my rheumatism restricted my equestrian activities, I was limiting myself to gymnastics. I had been cruelly treated by my relatives, but Pakize didn't linger for too long on this. She was even open about not wishing to speak of my aunt. "Hayri forgave them for everything some time ago."

The following morning Halit Ayarcı read the interview to me in the office. Ignoring my rage, he burst out laughing at every sentence.

"This is wonderful," he cried. "Wonderful! There couldn't be a more perfect interview. The first thing for me to do now is to bring out a paper with your wife as editor. *Tea Time*! Yes the name shall be *Tea Time*. Can such a talent be ignored? She's captured you perfectly! Exactly as you are."

"Better to say she made an absolute fool of me. What has she captured? It's nothing but drivel from start to finish. I've been disgraced for the entire world to see."

His face suddenly darkening, Halit Ayarcı assumed a serious air:

"She has reformed you, reorganized you, and recast you as a loveable person. Why must you always see the dark side of things? She's done this out of love for you. She's given you your true identity."

"But it's nothing but lies from top to bottom!"

"That's what you think. Everyone will love this. Take just

this part here: 'He puts my shoes on for me. It's just his favorite thing to do!'"

"She doesn't even own a decent pair of shoes!"

"Well then, that's your fault now, isn't it? The husband of such a woman should, above all, consider her happiness and comfort. So go out tomorrow and buy half a dozen pairs of new shoes. Then there's this trip to Switzerland! "My husband's never traveled. Last summer he sent me to Switzerland, to visit the factory that had offered him a job. And to be honest, the idea sounded wonderful. I love traveling, but—what can I say? I just can't leave my husband. I asked him, 'Why don't you like traveling, Hayri Bey? It'd be such a shame if indeed you really don't. Perhaps it's because you get a bit woozy on the ferry or train . . . But, then, you do ride horses . . .'"

I stood up and cried:

"This woman is a raging lunatic. What's more, she's a liar. How could we have loved each other in our childhood? She's sixteen years younger than I am!"

"A simple error in chronology. We all make such mistakes! And so what? Let's suppose that all of it, from beginning to end, is untrue. Would you be any better off if it were? Let's say you really don't like walking in the snow, but what do you gain from everyone believing this?"

He stood up and took me by the shoulder.

"You're changing, Hayri Bey, you're changing. And this should be a source of happiness. A new life, a new man . . . And there's no other choice, as you won't be coming back a second time. If I were you, I would try to be the man my wife wants me to be. Consider the interview a road map and follow it devoutly!"

"So I should sleep naked on the floor, is that right?"

Halit Ayarcı thought for a moment, stroking his chin:

"I suppose there's a slight slipup there. How can I put it? A simple fantasy! Don't worry about that one."

"But I should take up playing the banjo and singing American folk songs?"

"Well, why not? I've got one at home. I picked it up when I was in America. I'll send it over to you this evening. On second thought, I'll bring it over myself. You can start practicing. Not a bad idea at all in fact! And you do have a nice voice . . . Get cracking! Haven't you had enough of your Eastern *makams*, the Acemaşiran and all that? Don't you feel for anything beyond a longing for the things of our past?"

I picked up the phone before answering his question, but he stopped me.

"No," he said. "There's no turning back now. What's done is done. It wouldn't be right to upset such a thoughtful woman. Don't you see how much she loves you? Now it's time for you to be worthy of her love."

Just then Zehra came into the room, holding that day's paper. She threw her arms around me.

"Oh, Daddy!" she cried. "I always knew you were a man like this! But you kept it all a secret from us. Could there be any other explanation? God bless Mother."

Halit Ayarcı smiled and looked intently at my daughter.

"I'm of the very same opinion," he said. "Your mother's a wonderful woman! I haven't read anything quite so wonderful in a very long time!"

I was losing my mind.

By the late-afternoon prayers I'd come face-to-face with the first clear reverberation of this wonderful interview. Dr. Ramiz, Lazybones Asaf Bey, Halit Ayarcı, and I were all chatting in Halit Bey's office. Or rather Halit Ayarcı was chipping away at my various points of resistance. Dr. Ramiz had been led out onto the open road by Halit Bey's enthusiasm and was driving his horses into a full gallop. It was no longer just as matter of Ahmet the Timely. Now my reaction to my wife's interview in the paper was a crime in itself.

According to Dr. Ramiz, I was a man in denial of his full powers, stubbornly closing his eyes to the movements of the age, and because I had limited my worldview, I had created a whole range of needless shortcomings, so as to inflict my responsibilities on those around me.

"Others can see you for who you truly are, but you somehow cannot! You've imprisoned yourself in a web of baseless fears and paranoia. How can you tolerate it?"

To him, my continuing doubts about the existence of Ahmet the Timely and my rejection of my wife's picture of me as a banjo-playing equestrian were all symptoms of the same malady.

"Your wife has presented you as the ideal modern man and still you doubt and deny it all!"

"My wife is insane. Since we've been married, she's gone to bed every night assuming that I am the lead man in the film she saw the evening before, and in the morning she jumps up out of bed in a frantic search for the pearl-studded slippers she wore in *The Thief of Baghdad.*"

I saw Dr. Ramiz's jaw drop, but Halit Ayarcı went on unruffled:

"Of course his wife's crazy, and I'm a liar and a snake charmer . . . Well then, what's your daughter, Zehra Hanım?"

"Zehra has been swept away by the whole thing. Just the other night she said, 'I'm so pleased with my life. It feels like I'm in an operetta or a vaudeville play. At last I'm getting a taste of life!'"

Dr. Ramiz replied:

"But can't you see? This only means that she too accepts your artist's soul. She even said as much this morning. 'Daddy,' she said, "I always knew you were a man like this!'"

By now Halit Ayarcı was quite cross with me; addressing the doctor, he said:

"Give up the ghost, good man. Leave him to wallow in his stubbornness and skepticism. Life marches forward. One day, when the caravan leaves him behind, *then* he'll understand. Today we live in what is called the modern world! And look at the state of those who deny it! We can't change them by force. May they be blessed with common sense. We, however, are in pursuit of real life!"

Dr. Ramiz suddenly softened:

"I only pity him because I know his strength. This is why I am speaking in such a way, applying pressure . . . Why else would I bother?"

"I don't pity him at all! I only have time for the institute."

Roused from his nap, Lazybones Asaf stuck his open hand out into the air as if trying to capture a fly.

"And I was also just thinking," he said. "We'll have to buy a refrigerator for the summer, don't you think? And a fan . . ."

Halit Ayarcı pursed his lips to keep from laughing out loud.

"The most difficult thing is to work with a man who doesn't believe."

By now I was truly dispirited.

"I do everything you tell me to do. Isn't that enough? Why must I believe?"

"Don't do, just believe—that's all we ask of you."

Now it was Halit Ayarcı's turn to be indignant.

"Because what I need above all," he railed, "is belief—a true belief in the importance of our work here. You people are the run-down, threadbare spirits of another age. It's quite impossible to work with people who have no faith in life. You don't even believe in Ahmet the Timely!"

"Well, that's because there's no such man. He's simply not there. There's not a trace of such a man in all history! Show me one single document, just a mention of the name—that's enough."

Dr. Ramiz interjected:

"That way of thinking is antiquated. History is at the disposal of the present. I can show you hundreds of papers on hundreds of topics, and they are all lies, so what's the difference? If he hadn't existed, you couldn't have known the name, you never could have spoken of him. It all boils down to this: you see yourself above and beyond your own age. This is intellectually arrogant. In effect you are trying to say, 'I am in command of all truths!' No, my dear saint, such power is beyond our ken. No man can be omniscient, it's simply not possible."

A sudden scuffle outside the door kept me from answering. First I heard Derviş Efendi. The poor man was frantic:

"Impossible, madam, impossible without asking first! They're in the middle of an official meeting!"

A sharp voice responded in a barbed retort:

"I know all about their meetings—out of my way!"

Apparently Derviş Ağa was imploring her.

"I said out of my way, you brute!"

Now there was no doubt left in my mind: It was my aunt. It'd been twenty-four years, but I still recognized her voice. I was pinned to my chair. There was no way out.

The door flung open and my aunt stormed into the room, clutching a pile of papers and a great suitcase of a purse under her arm, furiously brandishing her umbrella above her gray head, itself embellished with such extravagant black plumes that it was more ostentatious than an eagle. She seemed more awesome and otherworldly than when she returned from the cemetery in Merkezefendi. Her heavily powdered face was contorted by rage, and her kohl-lined eyes flashed like lightning. Jewelry dangled from her wrists, her fingers, her neck, her ears. Her beige raincoat—an Ottoman cloak by another name—billowed as she entered, as if she were flying. If not for the circumstances, I would have burst out laughing. We all rose to our feet—that is, all but Halit Ayarcı, who remained calm and still in his chair, blinking at her as if to say, "Well, what have we here?"

"A meeting, now, is it? A meeting about what, then?"

Then she saw me.

"You miserable good-for-nothing! You slovenly bag of bones! As if what you'd done before was not enough, you let them claim in the papers that I am a relative of yours? Hah!"

I dodged the first blow of her umbrella, which crashed down instead on Lazybones Asaf's shoulder. The second smashed the enormous crystal top of Halit Ayarcı's desk, breaking the umbrella, too.

"You shameless, impertinent trickster! So your strumpet of a wife says she forgives me, eh?"

"Please, Auntie . . ." And before I could say "for the love of God," the lower end of the umbrella landed directly on my nose.

I felt warm liquid run down over my upper lip. Inspecting it with my fingers, I saw it was blood.

"Serves him right! Oh, just you wait and see. Oh, that's nothing . . ."

And just as she was about to descend upon me, she stopped—shaken, perhaps, by the sight of blood, or maybe because she had used up all her strength. She was trembling and seemed on the verge of collapse.

Halit Ayarcı slowly rose to his feet. Quietly he stepped around the table, as if receiving a newly arrived guest, and, placing his hand on my aunt's shoulder, he gestured for her to sit down in the seat next to his. He placed her purse and papers on the table whose glass top had been shattered into a million pieces.

"May I assume I at last have the honor of meeting Zarife Hanım?"

My aunt was deathly pale. But her anger had not yet abated. With spittle spraying from her lips, she barked, "That's right. Zarife Hanım, aunt to this good-for-nothing!"

Maintaining his cool and genial air, Halit Ayarcı said, "And I am Halit Ayarcı! The director of this institute."

This was enough to send my aunt back into a rage.

"Aha! So all these tricksters have a ringleader, eh? And tell me, then, what exactly does this institute do?"

And looking me straight in the eye she added, "Not that it surprises me to see a slovenly creature like my nephew involved in such nonsense!"

Halit Ayarcı turned to me, and my aunt continued:

"Like father like son. The man did nothing but scrounge after this and that. But what more could you expect from a man addicted to gambling? And now he rides horses and plays tennis! Oh please, he can't even tell a horse from a donkey! And then you go and allow them to print my name in the papers! Since when has this oh-so-forgiving man been married?"

She turned to Halit Ayarcı.

"But you, sir, you seem like a decent human being. How did you get mixed up with a lowlife like him?"

Still exuding graciousness, Halit Ayarcı replied: "You are speaking out against an official organization! What a shame! We are working to the best of our abilities to provide a public service."

"Service? And just what kind of service is that? You're going to regulate clocks, now, are you? You think I'll believe that? I am Zarife the Veil Shredder, not one to be so easily deceived by such words!"

Suddenly she stopped to look about the room.

"Why should I care about your work anyway? There was a time when I too busied myself with such projects. But I've put all that behind me. I came to see the man whose wife says she's forgiven me. Look at the wretch—he doesn't even wipe the blood off his nose! And then all these high-and-mighty words . . ."

I slowly pulled out my handkerchief and wiped the blood off my face. Had she not blocked my exit, I'd have exited the room at once.

Halit Ayarcı rang the bell. Derviş Efendi looked entirely changed when he stepped into the room. His forehead was swollen and his collar was torn. He made an extra-long loop around the room, staying as far away from my aunt as possible.

"What will you be drinking, then, madam? Coffee, tea?"

"Coffee," she ejaculated. "I'm a connoisseur, so make it good. Doctors have been telling me to stop drinking it for the last twenty years, but I don't listen. But if this dolt is making it then forget it!"

"Derviş Efendi makes wonderful coffee. I'm sure you'll be pleased! We'll have coffee too, Derviş Efendi."

But before Derviş Efendi left the room, he added:

"But first someone bring me a bucket or something of the sort so I can clean up all this glass! What a shame if someone were to come in now."

And he kicked a piece of broken umbrella under his desk.

"After all, this is an official establishment, madam!"

My aunt seemed rather put out.

"I wouldn't have come, but I couldn't find him at home! It seems they've moved and nobody could give me the new address. So I had no choice but to come here."

Flashing his sweetest smile, Halit Bey comforted her:

"No harm done, madam, not at all . . . Such things happen in families. In fact we would have come to you if you hadn't come here yourself!"

"To me? But whatever for?"

"Well, of course!" he answered. "We were just talking about it now. Here, allow me to explain: we need to establish a group that can support the efforts of the Time Regulation Institute, so as to acquaint the public with its ideas, a group that can in fact oversee the publication of our material. And this is why

we decided some time ago that we should establish the Clock
Lover's Society. Today we were discussing its founding delegation. This is why we were having a meeting. My friends and I
feel that there must be more female members than men. And,
in particular, its president must be a woman, an esteemed
individual . . . We've been thinking this over since morning,
and we just couldn't come up with an individual worthy of
the post. And then finally Hayri Bey says to us, 'I've got it!
My aunt would be the ideal person for the job. Above all, she
is respectability incarnate. The woman could lead an entire
army. She is experienced, and she is well loved by all who
know her. What a shame that she's so cross with me. I couldn't
offer such a post to her. She'd drive me away if I even tried
speaking to her!' Upon hearing about you, we'd unanimously
decided to offer you the post. And at just that moment, you
honored us with your presence! Please take my seat if you
would accept the presidency!"

For a moment my aunt stared at Halit Ayarcı, then at the
empty chair beside her. She looked both perplexed but
tempted, like a young girl who'd been asked to dance for the
first time.

"I just don't know if I could I do such a thing. And at this
age . . ."

Halit Ayarcı smiled.

"How could you not? We've already seen you in action!"

Eyeing me sternly, my aunt said, "Oh that was nothing. Wait
till I get my hands on your wife!"

Halit Ayarcı let out an easy laugh. "Oh no, Pakize Hanım
isn't to blame here. Of that I'm quite sure. You'll love her the
moment you see her. She's not that kind of woman. Those
details were the embellishments of the journalist. Apparently
there were a few misunderstandings. Surely you noticed that
most of the photographs were not even of Hayri Bey!"

Indeed most of the photographs in the paper were not of me.
The one of me riding a horse had clearly been taken somewhere
in the English countryside. Never in my life had I seen the place
that was meant to be my library. And my collection of watches
and clocks exceeded my wildest dreams.

There was a moment of silence. Then Halit Ayarcı rose to his feet and said to my aunt, "If you would accept our offer, please take your seat and we'll start the proceedings!"

Without a word, my aunt stood up and strode to the head of the table. Halit Bey sat down in the chair beside her.

"If you would be so kind, Dr. Ramiz, to take minutes for the meeting."

Dr. Ramiz sat down at the table and flipped open a legal pad. Ever the woman, my aunt launched into her complaints:

"It always happens like this, the real work always falls to me. This will be the fourth time I've headed a society. It's been like this ever since the days of the Committee of Union and Progress."

But Halit Ayarcı lost no time; he asked my aunt her opinion on the first order of business: identifying members for the board.

"There will be myself, Hayri Bey, and the doctor, but the remaining members must be women."

My aunt wasn't pleased. Perhaps it was only appropriate for us to have a place in the Clock Lover's Society, but there had to be a few young and sympathetic souls under the president's charge. Halit Bey suggested the poet Ekrem Bey. Then we began to think about possible female members. My aunt put forward a few names. Halit Bey proposed Sabriye Hanım and Nevzat Hanım. Zarife accepted the former but not the latter.

"Sabriye is such a nice girl," she said. "She remembers everything she hears and expresses herself well, but what can I do with the other one? She's a dreadful whiner."

Then my aunt recommended Selma Hanım. And so, after jotting down a dozen names, the meeting was adjourned, with the next meeting to be held in a week's time, at my aunt's home. As she was leaving, Zehra stepped into the room, whereupon Halit Bey turned to my aunt:

"Do you know this young lady? She's your nephew's daughter!"

After casting a malicious glance in my direction, she uttered a few kind words about Zehra. Judging by the look on her face, she didn't seem at all pleased to meet yet another relation. But when Zehra left the room, my aunt followed her with her eyes and, after a moment of reflection, she turned to me:

"That one must be from the other wife, the one that never understood you. I see no resemblance to the current strumpet."

At our next meeting, we drew up the statutes of the Clock Lover's Society. Within two weeks, we'd gotten through the official red tape and everything was in place. One day Halit Bey gave me the news:

"We've reached an agreement with your aunt. She has donated her plot of land on Freedom Hill to the institute. That's where we will erect our new building!"

A few days later, I learned that my aunt had donated yet another even larger plot of land, beyond Suadiye, to the Time Regulation Institute—providing that its value would be returned in installments. Halit Bey was in quite a jolly mood on the day he gave me the news.

"Don't you see? How could you ever be angry with your wife again? A woman as intelligent as Pakize Hanım! I saw her at your aunt's place just the other day. You wouldn't believe how well the two are getting on. 'If this woman isn't elected member of the society's management board, I'm packing my bags,' were your aunt's very words."

Pakize had already told me all about it. As for Zehra, she hardly ever left my aunt's house.

"Great," I said. "That's wonderful—all very good. So then I'm the only one who's out of step! And it seems I always will be."

"No," he said. "You don't understand, and you're not trying to do so. But that's not important! Just finish your book."

V

Halit Ayarcı's banjo still hangs on the wall in my study; one of his servants brought it to my house the evening of that fateful day when my aunt swept into our office in such a fury. It is, if ever it catches my eye, a painful reminder of how naive I've been at certain points in my life. Perhaps it was wrong to have caused my dear benefactor so much grief? Some are born with the light of truth inside them. For me, it was quite the opposite. Even my aunt was nothing like me. Despite her age and abundant life experience, she accepted Halit Ayarcı's invitation before my very eyes, and after just two hours of discussion and debate. And no sooner had she agreed to become the president of a society about which she knew nothing, than she invited everyone to her home for the following meeting. But I was forever arguing with Halit Bey, never fearing that I might be offending this man from whom I expected so much.

When I saw Halit Bey's servant at the front door, holding the bizarre instrument, I very nearly flew into a rage. Instead I put it down on the sofa, as Pakize and Zehra jumped up and down with excitement. "Come on now," squealed my wife, "let's hear you play!" That was very nearly the last straw. I still hadn't spoken to Pakize about her interview; I hadn't yet asked her what had possessed her to humiliate me in that way. I was wary of where such a conversation might lead, while my wife went out of her way to avoid it. Meanwhile she preened like a cat who has mothered seven kittens in one fell swoop. Her lack of sensibility tested my patience even more. But a minor intervention on Zehra's part put an end to my rage:

"Dad," she said. "Do you know who I saw today? Ismail the Lame. Right outside the office. Oh, he was so very surprised to see me! His face went white as ash. Then he let out a long whistle and hobbled off. But how ugly he was! I can't believe I was on the verge of marrying that man. God forbid! Whatever would I have done with such a miserable creature?"

My anger suddenly subsided. Just then Pakize cried:

"Hayri, you still haven't thanked me. Halit Bey told me I would never be able to understand my husband! 'Do you think you could you ever really understand the importance of such a man?' he said to me. In fact we even bet on it. But oh! I won— didn't I ever! If only you could have heard how he thanked me on the phone this morning!"

So that was how it had happened. Halit Ayarcı had thought

it all through in advance, encouraging Pakize to lampoon me for the pleasure of my friends and enemies alike. I thanked my wife:

"That's just wonderful," I said. "But how in the world did you come up with the story about me sleeping naked on the floor? Couldn't you have come up with something else? You know very well that I never go to bed without my nightcap and sweater!"

Taken aback, she cried:

"I couldn't remember the word for hammock! Halit Bey told me that throughout your entire childhood you slept in a hammock. But I just couldn't remember the word."

Having dealt with these trivial irritations, she handed me my benefactor's gift.

"Come on, play for us, just a little, please."

I took the instrument in my hand and tapped on it here and there, my point being to prove to them that I had no idea how to play. But I was dumbfounded by the transformation on Pakize's face. She was transported. Tears welled up in her eyes. But Zehra had vanished. And Ahmet wasn't there either; apparently he was busy working in his room. There was no mention of my performance over supper.

I saw Zehra before I went to bed.

"How was it? Do you like my banjo?"

Zehra fixed her saucer eyes on mine and asked, "Do we have any other choice, Dad? It's just that I'm really so worried about Ahmet."

But I had more urgent concerns.

"Did you really see Ismail the Lame?"

"No, but you seemed so angry and frustrated that I had to say something to stop you. And he came to mind."

Toying with a button on my jacket, she looked me straight in the eye:

"Was that such a bad thing?" she asked. "You were going to have an argument over nothing at all. I'm fed up with all the fighting. My whole life I've had to listen to you two squabbling. You have no idea how much I've suffered. The shouting terrifies me so much! And the way your faces are transformed by anger, becoming so very different, it's so hard to bear that. There's nothing worse in the whole world, nothing more horrid."

"But you get angry sometimes too," I said.

"Not any more! I'm more relaxed now. If I can't love the people in my life, I don't feel comfortable. It's like everything's turned upside down."

Zehra was in a talkative mood. Just like any other young girl, she wanted to talk about herself. And I had no idea how much truth there was in any of it. But I was pleased that she was opening her heart to me.

"Besides, we can't even really argue," she said. "You're like me. How can a man really argue if he thinks that everyone else is right?"

"Whatever do you mean, my girl?"

"Isn't that how it is?" she said. "Isn't that the way you are? Even if I haven't done anything wrong, I still can't forgive myself for meddling in other people's lives!"

"Well, are you at least happy now?" I asked.

Her face suddenly lit up.

"Of course I am," she said. "We're no longer living on top of one another. Everyone has their own life. But, then again, the work we're doing—it seems so strange. I keep thinking to myself, where's it all going? And another thing, everyone's changed so much that . . ."

She was right. Everyone had changed.

"Only Ahmet's the same. He's still closed off to everyone, always so serious. We did something without telling you. Ahmet sat for the state exams and passed."

So that was it. That was reason for the secretive air at home over the past month.

"Why didn't you tell me? There's nothing wrong with that."

"He didn't want to tell you till after it was all done. He wasn't going to tell you if he didn't pass."

For a moment I wondered if Zehra and her mother would have gotten along this well if her mother were still alive.

"You're not angry, right?"

I couldn't believe that my children still loved and respected me. Even Ahmet wanted to protect me from needless pain. This was undoubtedly something he had inherited from Emine. I felt a jolt of pain in me. If Emine had lived, I wouldn't have found myself in such a predicament. How wonderful it would have been to pull the burden of life together, like two carriage horses harnessed side by side, one forever keeping an eye on the other. I remembered my elation upon stepping into the courtyard of our old home on the day I was released from the Department of Justice Medical Facility.

I sat alone in my study until late that night, at a loss for what to do. I just didn't want to go to bed. The memory of Emine was so overwhelming that I couldn't bear the sight of Pakize, even though she was asleep. Still, I knew I was being unfair.

That evening the weather was oppressive. At around half past one, thunder and lightning shook the sky. The curtains in the room billowed dramatically, one after the other, before fading into the green glow beyond. Then the sky was rent asunder and released a violent rain. Pakize was afraid of thunder. So with a heavy heart I crept into the bedroom and lay down beside her. Sensing my presence, she instantly awoke. Mumbling coyly, affecting a voice she must have assumed intimated tender compassion, she said:

"Up working late again? Hayri, you really should go easy on yourself."

Not even the stilted female voices in radio commercials were as cold as her voice. At first I thought she was making fun of me. If only that were the case, but, no, she was serious, even though she knew very well that I hadn't actually been working, that I didn't do any work. She was merely playing the role of the sensible, well-intentioned wife thinking only of her husband's health. She threw her arm over my neck, and my body went cold. How was she any different from a wind-up clock or an automaton? I considered how steadily her interest in me had grown since I'd started work again. Indeed her attention made me feel as if I'd been living in a refrigerator for half a year. I almost missed those days when Pakize thought me spineless and slovenly, indolent, moronic, and clumsy, only acknowledging my existence when she was sexually aroused. At least then she seemed more herself.

At first I felt an overwhelming urge to leap out of bed. But then she'd wake up and start talking. The best thing was to stay in bed but entirely still. Slowly I extricated my every limb from hers, shrinking up against the wall where, eyes still wide open, I listened to the rain and thunder as I waited for morning. I kept asking myself, is she an idiot or just a liar? She was both. Perhaps she lied out of idiocy. Or perhaps it was something far more horrible than just that. She simply didn't have a personality. Occasionally the rain subsided and I heard her breathing. "If nothing else," I thought, "I hope she's more herself in her dreams." At one point I sat up and stared at her face. Her lips were parted and she seemed to be smiling. Her face seemed contracted, as sometimes happened when she was emotionally overwhelmed. As if she was no longer of this world! Yet how beautiful she was like that: with her eyes shut, lips slightly open, her breathing shallow and—most emotive of all—her selflessness. But why was she always so happy in her sleep? Why and for whom was she smiling? This was no ordinary smile. It spoke of bliss. So she was happy, like Zehra. Perhaps she had attained this peace of mind because she felt she was doing her part. Or perhaps in her sleep she could escape everything and everyone, to take refuge in a corner all her own. So she too had a secret. She was happy and she was beautiful, even though she was absent from her body. For a moment, I felt envious of her wholeness. I was about to disturb her, break the spell. But what would that do? Within minutes she would have become the person I knew, the same old stone statuette.

With this thought in mind, I shrank back against the wall. Toward morning, I drifted off to sleep. The dream I had then may go some way to illustrating my frame of mind.

I dreamt I was in the living room of our old home. I was studying my reflection in a vast mirror, muttering to myself as I studied my face more closely: But this isn't me? Could this be me? It's simply impossible . . . And indeed the face before me wasn't mine. Every moment it changed—changed so dramatically that I could hardly capture it in my gaze. Then I heard my aunt cry, "Come on, we're late," as she tugged me. We were hurrying quickly through narrow backstreets. But with every step one of us lost a shoe, and we had to stop and put it back on before racing off again. "At last, we're here!" she cried. And I found myself all alone in a rather large square where some kind of celebration was underway. I could hear horns and drums, and suddenly I was on an enormous merry-go-round made of layer upon layer of overlapping rings. With every turn, I saw someone I knew, and we waved to each other as we laughed and laughed. Then slowly the rings started to turn faster and faster, and the ring I was riding together with Halit Ayarcı, Selma Hanım, Cemal Bey, and my aunt snapped abruptly off its axis, and, still spinning, rose up to the heavens. Terrified that I might die, I threw my arms around the neck of the animal I was riding: it was Seyit Lutfullah's turtle. Holding on for dear life so as not to fall, I fixed my eyes on my aunt. She was no longer mounted on one of the merry-go-round animals. She was flying all by herself. I woke up to Pakize saying, "Come on, wake up! It's nine o'clock! You'll be late to work!"

VI

Snug in her armchair, my aunt was telling her entourage what sort of man I was.

"Sister, you have absolutely no idea. He's completely unpredictable. My late brother should have named him Misfortune, and not Hayri. He didn't pay me a single visit in twenty years. But I always wondered what he was doing, what would become of him. Was it easy for him? He's the last in the family. And of course I love him. If not for him, the dynasty of Ahmet Efendi the Some Timer would vanish from earth. Then at last I saw his name in the paper, and I said to myself, well, at the very least, I said, I should go and see him. Not a small feat for a woman at my age, I'd say."

With a black shawl over her shoulders, a petite Japanese fan fluttering in her hand, and her entire person shimmering in a sea of jewelry, she thus aired her complaints to Selma Hanım and the other ladies. I sat on the other end of the sofa, a mere

ornament to the scene. I had fallen into a jar of jam; I was sinking in a swell of sweet reproach never before tasted.

"At one point I heard that he had lost his life in the war. For
months, my late husband and I mourned his loss. For three
years, we went to his grave on the anniversary of his death and
said prayers and recited passages from the Koran. But somehow I always felt that he was still alive—that one day he would
come back to us—and that's exactly what happened."

She was telling the truth. Just around the time I was discharged from the army a friend of mine went round to see my
aunt and found the house teeming with people; and to his surprise he heard my name recited in their prayers. And so my
friend had said to my aunt, "If you're praying for Hayri, your
nephew, why, then you have the wrong man, for that Hayri is
alive and well." And in response she had cried, "So yet another
lie from the scoundrel, eh! I could only expect as much from
the son of that good-for-nothing! He's never to set foot in this
house again. Never! Oh and if does, there'll be trouble!"

Now the very same woman smiled as she sang my praises and
spoke of my late father. No doubt she would have feigned shock
if someone tried to explain how my father had died of hunger
while I was serving in the army and how I was nearly locked up
in a madhouse after her husband's exploitation of my story about
the Şerbetçibaşı Diamond; she would have denied it all.

But she knew I wouldn't bring up such things, that I wouldn't
remind people of the past. I was now a reserved and well-
mannered man, who towed the line. Now I had a good friend,
Halit Ayarcı, who had turned my life around, and I had a serious job.

It was the first time my aunt had come to visit us at home.
The Clock Lover's Society held its first public meeting that day
and this was the reception. She continued:

"What more can you expect from someone in this day and
age? Families will look after their own, won't they? So be it.
But my dear Hayri isn't like this at all. God bless his wife and
daughter! They came to me and . . ."

Just then I heard Zehra flirting with three young men on the sofa near the hall. Pakize was in the inner living room with another group, Halit Ayarcı and Sabriye Hanım. My older sister-in-law was playing the celebrated artiste, stomping around like a restless racehorse as she waited to be summoned to show off her renowned musical talents. My aunt continued:

"But to tell you the truth, I never expected the Hayri I knew when he was a child to become such a modern man! And his job is so pertinent in this day and age. It seems that he is the one who came up with the idea! He was a calm and quiet man. But oh, how he loved watches and clocks! Do you remember how you went to work on my dining-room clock when I was ill? And then you lost the pendulum!"

For a moment, I was afraid she might say, "Now you will either find that pendulum or never let me catch sight of you again!" But no, she was too busy rewriting the past, indeed even embellishing it. And why not? What more can we do than create the environment for ourselves to live in? Especially as we can't just accept the sharp blade of the present.

"I always wished my stepdaughter had been more like Zehra! But, oh no, she turned out to be a strumpet."

There was a glimmer in Selma Hanım's eyes. She had divined my aunt's reason for joining our coterie. Her situation was the opposite of mine; while I was now inundated with activity, she was lonely. My aunt wasn't getting along with her stepdaughter and son-in-law. But how could Halit Ayarcı have known this? And why did he have to arrange for her to come in such a roundabout way? How could he have been so willing to risk everything for such a person?

And my aunt finished her monologue, confirming my thoughts.

"I'm so pleased with myself for not giving Hayri her hand in marriage. Of course my relationship with my poor late husband, Naşit, suffered dearly for this."

What could anyone say? Everything had changed, and I had no choice but to accept everything as it was, or, rather, however it was on any given day.

"Oh, my son! You certainly are a lucky one."

Ekrem Bey appeared, and my aunt quickly moved on.

"Aha! Here's another unreliable one. This one doesn't even

come to the meetings, even though he's a member of the board. Come now, dear Ekrem, shall we not mingle a little and see how the other guests are getting on?"

But poor Ekrem was looking at someone just behind us. And Nevzat Hanım, squirming to free herself from Cemal Bey's clutches, also stepped away to mingle with my aunt. A few others tagged along in hope of finding more amusing company.

I asked Selma Hanım what she thought of my aunt. Instead of answering directly, she only said, "She loves you very much. She talked about no one but you for the past hour!" I told her about my various adventures with my aunt. At first she laughed and laughed but then she turned serious, murmuring:

"Men of greatness rise out of strange circumstances."

I looked at her in complete surprise. What could I say?

A little later Sabriye Hanım came over to us. She had spent the entire day working at the regulation station that was soon to open in Taksim. "Those three girls have been trained exceedingly well," she said. "We've been rehearsing since morning! Everything is just the way we want it to be. It's just that we still don't have the uniforms." Selma Hanım said she could start work herself whenever we wanted. A little later Cemal Bey came over to collect his wife. I asked Sabriye Hanım:

"Did Selma Hanım ever ask Cemal Bey if she could work with us?"

"There's no need. They're getting divorced," she said. "But that's between you and me, for the time being. Cemal Bey was caught embezzling, and the company is on the verge of bankruptcy. It's a terrible mess. Haven't you heard?"

"But Cemal Bey doesn't seem worried at all." He'd been comfortably carrying on with Nevzat Hanım.

"Cemal would keep his composure on his deathbed," she said. "But none of this really matters. How is your aunt? Wonderful, isn't she?"

"Yes," I said. "But I don't understand any of this. Did she really make peace with me? And why? Was all that nonsense my wife spouted to the paper just a setup, to attract her to the institute? I can't be sure of anything anymore."

"You don't understand Halit Bey, that's why. You assume

that he acts according to some master plan and that he ensnared your aunt because she's rich. But no, he merely wanted to promote the institute through you, and just then your aunt turned up and so he seized the opportunity. Halit Bey's a casual fellow, but he's clever. And he plays fair—he's no opportunist!"

The Clock Lover's Society boasted a whole host of beautiful young women and handsome, courteous young men. It became quite an attraction in its own right. Yet most of these people were from the Spiritualist Society, the coffeehouse, or Halit Bey's own circle of friends. At one point we were visited by the exalted politician I'd first met at the restaurant in Büyükdere. I was with my aunt when he stepped in. When I told him I was her nephew, he was all the more delighted with our enterprise. He showed a keen interest in the institute.

"How is work?"

I was preparing my answer when a waiter stepped in between us, offering caviar canapés. The politician looked me in the eye, and then down at the tray. With a great show of indifference, he told the waiter to set the tray on the table beside us. A while later whiskey was served. With a tumbler of whiskey already in his hand, Halit joined us. "We're creating quite a substantial cooperative, sir," he exclaimed. "To our personnel!" As usual, I was catching up with plans I'd not been told about. Moreover, Halit Bey informed me later that evening that I was also going to be involved in a project to establish Timely Banks. So whether I knew it or not, I was now enjoying a certain success in life. But what had I really achieved? Save my frustration with this strange and incongruous crowd, what else had I achieved?

VII

From the moment of its publication, *The Life and Works of Ahmet the Timely* was met with great acclaim. The public immediately warmed to this important historic figure—a figure created by Halit Ayarcı in the space of a moment. No one seemed to question the likelihood that such a figure could have anticipated Graham's calculations two centuries before the fact. At the insistence of Halit Ayarcı, I had described in great detail the fascination our forbears had for mathematics at that time, so much so that they must have assumed Ahmet the Timely's discovery was derived from a mathematical equation. Yet as the book neared publication, I felt absolute terror. "What if no one likes it?" I wondered. "What if they discover it's all a lie?" Fear made my every moment agony. I couldn't sleep. Halit Ayarcı simply laughed to see me so anxious. He took every opportunity to assure me that my fears were ungrounded:

"My good friend Hayri İrdal," he said. "My dear friend, you'll see that your book will be adored. You seem to be under the impression that it contains untruths. But that's not so. There is nothing you have done that is not true. Today's Ahmet the Timely is not a falsification: he is the very embodiment of truth. Do you know what would make him a falsification and a disaster? If he had actually lived at the end of the seventeenth century, if he'd entertained the ideas we've attributed to him, well, then that would be a lie. He would be in the wrong age. He would have had to travel through time, which is, of course, impossible. In matters such as these, there is no set truth. It is a question of working with the century at hand and making him a man of his time. Our age needs Ahmet the Timely Efendi. And it is only at the end of the seventeenth century that this need can be filled. That's all there is to it. He is truth incarnate. We all heard what your aunt said last night. You may recall her tracing the lineage of Ahmet Efendi the Some Timer back to the age of Fatih Sultan. Did anyone challenge her? No. Everyone was quite pleased to accept it as the truth. And why not? Her assertion is proven by two living entities: you and your aunt! In acknowledging that you exist, they accept her line of reasoning. What could be more natural than these two dear individuals tracing their lineage that far back? Had your aunt said such a thing twenty years ago, everyone would have been ashamed of her, and that's because in those days you two were not the same people. People would have cried, 'Oh God, please! Could there be anything more ridiculous than people of so little consequence tracing their ancestry back to the age of Fatih Sultan?' It's just as the saying goes: the blasphemous man builds his casket out of firewood. A pack of lies. Would their manners not be more noble and graceful if it were really true? Today, on the other hand, they say nothing of the sort. Here's another example: When your aunt became aware of your success, she changed her mind about you and also your father. And what did she say about your father that night? Was she lying? No. She was simply giving her present opinion a place in the past! Very good of you to discover that Ahmet the Timely participated in the Ottoman siege on Vienna. A man of his importance would not have been far removed from that momentous occasion. I can't begin to tell how you much I enjoyed this discovery of yours. It calls to mind Goethe's military involvement in the French Revolution and at the battle of Valmy. Great men ride the currents of the age. That said, it is good that Ahmet the Timely never saw glory on the battlefield—that shows you to be balanced in your judgment. No one can do everything! Be there at the event but have others perform the heroics! Indeed if such a great deed had ever happened—let's say Ahmet the Timely conquered such and such a castle—it wouldn't have escaped the eyes of a historian. It really was a stroke of luck that you happened to read his *On the Mores of Conjugal Ceremonies and Bonds* when you were young. For if you hadn't, this important work would have been lost, and it would not be here for us to enjoy today. Just imagine the public grief had that work—or his treatise on horology—disappeared. Quite good that you jotted down these two titles from one of the old manuscripts in the Nuruosmaniye Library. Ah, and here we see how important it is that you appreciated the importance of old ink. My dear friend, you have written a magnum opus!"

On another occasion he said the following:

"As important as creating a movement is maintaining its momentum. In extending our movement to the past, you have intensified its forward momentum. In addition you have shown that our forbears were both revolutionary and modern. No one can begrudge his past forever. Is history material only for critical thought? Can we not stumble upon someone from the past whom we love and enjoy? Oh, you'll see how pleased everyone will be with our work!"

Unfortunately a handful of armchair academics tried to spoil the fun, being so impertinent as to suggest that such a figure had never actually existed and dismissing the book as a complete fabrication.

Had I finished the book in my original frame of mind, I might have taken pleasure in their criticism. "Oh, thank God!" I would have cried. "How could I ever thank you more? If anything, now I know that there are sensible people out there! They won't tolerate these lies. What could be more felicitous than this?" But sadly I was no longer the same man. Over the six months I'd spent working on the book, I'd come to see the world through Halit Ayarcı's eyes, so much so that I found any objection to my work intolerable. It was now, after all, a question of an author's pride. And I had grown very fond of Ahmet the Timely. To doubt his existence at this late date would be far too troubling. I had, in effect, come to see Halit Ayarcı's notion of relativity as my own.

By way of illustration, allow me to describe two unrelated matters that caused me considerable trouble at around this time. First there was the individual whose family had lived in Çengelköy for five or six generations who claimed to be Ahmet the Timely's direct descendent. He filed for his family name to be changed and went so far as to ask me to attest to the veracity of his connection in a court of law. Unfortunately he was unable to support his claim with the original deeds, or indeed with any genealogy reports. All he had were copies he'd written out himself. In the name of truth, I was obliged to deny the veracity of the documentation. My decision was vigorously applauded in the newspapers. They marveled at my scrupulous attention to the niceties of the case. And after this the book grew even more popular. Halit Bey was amused by my fine show of resilience. Only Zehra was a touch upset: "Perhaps the poor man really was the Timely Efendi's great-great-grandson," she whimpered. I silenced her, saying:

"He might very well be a Timely, but he can't be related to our Timely, as such a man never really existed!"

The second test came from the Spiritual Society, where one of my friends succeeded, after struggling day and night for a month, in summoning and communicating with the spirit of Ahmet the Timely. Ahmet the Timely took this opportunity to challenge certain points in my book: He denied ever stammering or speaking with a lisp, and he offered up new information on his dervish lodge as well as the extent of his influence. The papers picked up the story, after which the book became more popular still. The strangest thing about it was that—before taking his leave—he asked the summoning spiritualists to extend his gratitude to me. This may well have been the first time an official message of thanks from the world beyond had ever been reported in the media, and it was given the full appreciation it deserved.

And then there was Cemal Bey—now Selma Hanım's ex-husband. He had always been hostile toward me. He was beside himself upon hearing I had become more intimate with his ex-wife. Using the book as a pretext, he launched an assault against both me and the institute. Born liar that he was, he could not stop at denying Ahmet the Timely's existence; he went so far as to try and replace him with a fictitious character of his own.

And so it was that Cemal Bey came to insist that there had never been an Ahmet the Timely, but at the same moment in history there had indeed been a man known as Fenni Efendi who had been passionate about flowers, interested in mechanics, and who moved in influential circles. According to Cemal Bey, it was this man who had occupied himself with timepieces and time. We had done no more than to attribute the work of Fenni Efendi to our fictitious Ahmet Efendi. And the reason for this was clear: The name Timely best suited our institute and so was easily used in promoting our endeavors. Thus in an effort to generate effective publicity for the institute we had distorted the historical truth. Sitting at the heart of this absurd affair was a paradox: while Cemal Bey claimed the book on horology had been falsely attributed to the fictitious Ahmet the Timely and was in fact the work of Fenni Efendi, master of science, whose existence could be verified, he went on to claim that its criticism of polygamy had no basis, concluding that we must have written the entire book ourselves.

It was a masterstroke. It was to land a more decisive blow that Cemal Bey had given credence to our lies. So instead of launching yet another dead-end debate as to whether such a man could have existed, he had laid claim to one small part of the lie and waged his war on us from there. The moment his outlandish attack was made public, doubts about Sheikh Ahmet Zamanı the Timely began to circulate. Despite Halit Ayarcı's prompt press conferences and my own written responses to these charges, we were not able to dispel the suspicions. The book's reputation had been severely compromised.

I was with Selma Hanım when I first saw the article. In fact she had the morning's paper with her when she arrived for our rendezvous at the pied-à-terre where we'd been seeing one another regularly.

"Just look at this, the viper's little sting!" she said, and when my eyes fell on an old photograph of myself next to a likeness of Cemal Bey, I flew into a rage.

Cemal was doing everything in his power to bring me down.

The article began: "A charlatan and trickster through and through, Hayri İrdal once served at my firm as a lesser clerk, but I was forced to dismiss him for egregious moral turpitude and perjury." And it finished: "But the individual truly responsible for this man's corruption of the good name of a historical figure, his life and his works, a man who can hardly do simple addition let alone lead a discussion on *rabia* figures, is no other than Halit Ayarcı Bey."

For a moment, the whole world and everything in it seemed to be crashing down around me; it suddenly became clear to me that I would never be able to find my way back along the roads I'd traveled over the past year. There could be no fate worse than this. The miracle of my good fortune—the money, fame, and status that had come to me unbidden, throwing open doors and revealing new vistas—would be gone, all gone! Most terrifying of all was the glimmer in Selma's eyes, which had become so strange and timorous since we'd begun to see each other more intimately.

I would now say that it was only after tasting that fear that I began to take my work at the institute in earnest, embracing it with open arms. No longer did I waver between fact and fiction. To be or not to be—that was the question that drove me. I took care to remind myself that certain thoughts were mere whimsy: that they served only as window dressing, to be accepted as read. Unless I took care, I could go back to being a man without a future, without anything. I might even end up on the streets. I could find myself back in the old days, which, after this blessed interlude, could only be harder and more painful to bear. The loneliness, the humiliation, the self-doubt! The beautiful woman seated before me, half-naked and smiling, took on the air of a distant dream. On that spring morning I looked out over a misty sea and reminded myself that this warm and pleasant apartment, this trysting place, this intimate seclusion, and my real life hovering outside—all this could vanish in an instant. Selma had brought spring flowers that morning and arranged them in a vase between us. For one terrible moment, they seemed to wither before my very eyes.

Suddenly the telephone rang. To me, with my shattered nerves, the sound was as terrifying, as intolerable as if it were ushering in the end of the world. As in truth, it did. For the ring was a summons from the outside world, an assault on our secret haven. And I knew that it was my enemy. Fearfully I picked up the phone. I was somewhat soothed to hear the teasing tones of Halit Ayarcı.

"Have you seen it?" he asked.

"Yes, I've just read it. We're ruined. What do we do now?"

His first reply was in jest:

"Yes, the sky's falling, so just enjoy!"

But then more seriously:

"Pay it no mind," he said. "But we do need to get a bit more serious now. You must write a careful response to this man as soon as possible. As for me, I shall seek out his Achilles heel and apply pressure. That should keep the masses busy for a while, but what's most important is for us to orchestrate a counterblow that will astound them all. You know what I mean? Something new, entirely new . . . Something, my friend, to astound our enemies and friends alike! An institute such as ours will always fall under public scrutiny. Remember this and proceed accordingly. And never forget—you must always rely on your luck!"

"Nothing but words," I said. "Just words! It's all over. They'll take you down with me. There's no hope. We've nothing left to do but pick up the pieces and go."

Once I had finished, Halit Ayarcı let loose one of his loudest guffaws.

"There will be no plundering, my dear Hayri, no packing up and running! I shall stay put and so shall you! People like us, we who embark on bold pursuits, it is not for us to surrender to our enemies so easily."

His cool confidence was infuriating. For a moment, I wondered if my good benefactor had his wits about him. Was he aware of the gravity of the situation? As if reading my thoughts, his voice grew more serious:

"Of course," he said, "the man dealt us a magnificent blow. I never saw it coming. Cemal Bey does indeed know how to wage war with an untruth. Only an untruth can challenge an untruth. Had he attacked us in the usual way, by charging us with invention, he would have come across as a mere crank. Instead he's turned our own artillery against us. But there's nothing to worry about. I have faith in my good fortune. See you this evening!"

Halit Ayarcı had assessed the situation correctly. But he was wrong on one count: When it came to Cemal Bey, however could I trust in my luck? Wasn't he the antithesis of good fortune? Until I'd had the good fortune to meet Halit Ayarcı, hadn't I spent years down in the ditch, as a direct result of the blows Cemal had dealt me? And now, just as I was getting back up on my feet, I was face-to-face with this man all over again. How strange is the human soul: as I pondered all this, I somehow forgot that it was this man's wife who had half her body

draped over my shoulder as she nibbled on my ear, awaiting my
love and attention. Yet I had played no part in Cemal's separa-
tion with Selma. Though of course our liaison upset him.

The phone rang immediately after I hung up. It was Cemal
Bey. His voice sounded the same as ever: polite and proud and
cold enough to freeze a polar cap.

"Hayri Bey," he intoned, "would you be so kind as to have a
look at the paper today, if of course you could spare the time?
There's an article that might tickle your fancy!"

"No need, Cemal Bey, no need at all," I replied. "An old
friend brought me the paper this morning."

And I hung up.

Although Cemal Bey had indeed divorced Selma, he was still
jealous. He had learned of our trysting place. He had followed
us; we were his overwhelming obsession.

And now Cemal Bey had swallowed me whole. Selma raised
an eyebrow, lost in thought.

"I don't understand it at all!" she said. "Not one bit. You
cannot begin to appreciate how much rancor this man has
toward me. He thought I was small and helpless. At home he
would call me an artificial flower and never let me leave the
house without an artificial flower pinned to my chest or coat
collar. 'You should carry one,' he'd always say, 'because that's
how I have to carry you around with me!' If anyone thought to
compliment me on my fake flower—oh, how he loved it! Oh
that malicious smile . . ."

It goes without saying that Selma was not just my lover. She
was also my revenge against the monstrous thing called my
past. It was thanks to her that I could turn to the dark days I'd
left behind and say, "So there you have it! What have you got
on me now? I am presently in the arms of the one person before
whom I was so cruelly humiliated. What more could I ask for?"
It was strangely pleasing to see my former boss so jealous, and
it only added to my sense of well-being. This woman was the
amulet who protected me from my past.

Both Halit Ayarcı and I responded to Cemal Bey's attack. In
my written responses I assumed the air of a man unjustly
treated. It could have happened to anyone. But I was the

victim. The injustice was clear. I did not expect Cemal to furnish any proof of perjury or any evidence of an ethical breach. I was a man with inherently good moral values, whom he had dismissed after accepting that he couldn't corrupt me. In my second statement, I continued as I had begun, assuming the same victimized tone, but this time taking care to disclose inside information about his company. Halit Ayarcı was a little more vindictive in his meetings with the press. And in the official statement released by the Clock Lover's Society, the fury was positively volcanic. But Cemal Bey was undeterred; he carried on with his offensive. We needed something else, something new, something that would erase all memory of the matter and absolve us forever. I cannot remember a time I cudgeled my brains more desperately. But it was hopeless: neither Halit Ayarcı nor I could come up with any idea that might swing public opinion back in our favor. We were floundering in a void. We could not manage a single step beyond the ordinary.

Meanwhile Cemal Bey was paying close attention to my affair with Selma. Wherever we met, we almost always received a telephone call from him. And Pakize received countless anonymous letters.

It was just around this time that I thought up the cash-punishment system I brought to the reader's attention at the beginning of these memoirs; the idea came to me one evening, while I was watching Halit Ayarcı play a round of backgammon with my wife, but when I first blurted it out, it was only to underline the hopeless intractability of our predicament.

"I've racked my brains and that's all I could come up with. Could our situation be any worse?"

But Halit Ayarcı had already thrown down the dice and was on his feet. There was a strange stillness in his eyes.

"Now, just say that again, will you?"

And before I could finish, he threw his arms around my wife.

"We're saved! A clear victory, Hayri Bey—a resounding triumph," he cried.

Three days later we had finalized our cash-fine program, complete with an elaborate system of bonuses, lotteries, time

agreements, and reductions. Halit Ayarcı announced my innovation in the Hollywood method par excellence, and within a
few weeks everyone had forgotten all about Ahmet the Timely,
and the Time Regulation Institute was garnering unprecedented attention and growing steadily in prestige. On the heels
of this new success, the Clock Lover's Society succeeded in setting up Time Regulation Teams in the villages across the country. The number of Time Regulation Stations had already
multiplied. The city was ours. An army of young girls and boys
donning uniforms designed by Sabriye Hanım and wearing our
rosettes on their collars were soon to be found throughout the
city, to the delight of all who saw them.

And so everything was back on track. Once again we were
the champions of the day, more powerful than ever before. I
was indulged like an uncle. With every passing day, I received
more praise for my eccentric past, my knack for invention, and
my sincerity. There wasn't a circle of society that didn't seek
my company. And to be honest, I wasn't shy in making the best
of my newly acquired fame. Everything was designed to com-
plement this success: my spectacles, my umbrella, my hat that
never sat just right on my head, my suits that were a little too
baggy, my fatherly airs—even the prayer beads I twirled in my
fingers. Wherever I went, I was the center of attention; I was
quizzed on every topic under the sun. I was loved because I
lived in a manner that never disturbed the balance set by public
opinion.

Yet Cemal Bey still dogged my life, as ever the ambassador
of my ill fortune. One day he would rear his ugly head, and it
would be all over. When I told Halit Ayarcı of my fears, he lost
his temper and reprimanded me:

"You're only thinking this way because you don't really
believe in your work. If a person undertakes a job for no reason
other than personal gain, and if he thinks of nothing else, well
then, surely he will blame himself in the end, just like you are
doing now!"

"That's all fine and well, but isn't this a little different?"

"No, not at all. If you didn't have this worm gnawing inside
you, then you wouldn't fear Cemal Bey or anyone else, for that

matter. Your fear stems from your lack of self-confidence. You're a cynic. And you're only working for money, pursuing your own personal happiness and nothing more. Weren't you this way when the institute first opened? Weren't you afraid of your office boy's wages being cut? Didn't you take every opportunity to remind me?"

Once the dust had settled, my good benefactor reverted to his usual tone, speaking now of our lofty ideals. He wasn't entirely incorrect. He was the play's producer. He had to act accordingly.

But for me it was a different matter. Cemal Bey was an ache from the past. He was part of my life; waiting inside me, ready to lash out at a moment's notice, like a cancer in remission.

VIII

And that's just what happened. My final encounter with Cemal Bey caught me entirely off guard. Yet this last surprise encounter didn't spell the end for the institute, nor did it generate any undue financial strain or alter my station. Nevertheless both Selma and I remained profoundly affected for many months to come.

I saw the story the moment I picked up the morning paper: Nevzat Hanım and Cemal Bey had been murdered by Zeynep Hanım's ex-husband, Tayfur Bey, who, following the double murder, took his own life. The suicide note revealed the mystery Sabriye Hanım had been so assiduously, if also hesitantly, trying to solve for all those years. Sabriye Hanım was right. Contrary to public opinion, Zeynep Hanım hadn't committed suicide; she'd been murdered by her own husband, Tayfur Bey, who was desperately in love with Nevzat Hanım. The police had just discovered the diary he had been keeping for all those years, or so they said.

As tragic as these three deaths were, they carried another significance for me. Cemal Bey had been a repulsive, temperamental, supercilious, and utterly unbearable man; wherever the beast went he acquired a host of new enemies; he scrambled in and out of human society like a scorpion wagging its poisoned tail; but he died the hero of a love story, an ending that no one on earth deserved less than he. It was so absurd, so needlessly preposterous. Perhaps fortune had arranged this fate just to mock him, to extract a revenge for his pride at presuming himself above human frailty, for his unshakable confidence and self-possession. It was impossible to think of Cemal Bey in love, or Cemal Bey dying for love, or even knowingly playing a part in such a love affair. But I know he would have been the first to laugh at this overblown drama, had he not known it was at his expense. "Me?" he would say, pursing his lips. "Impossible!" Cemal liked to squeeze his victims in his tongs, drive them in his filthy and invisible yokes, poison them with his serpent's tail. He would have it no other way. Yet the manner of his death had so changed his public persona that even those who had known him were easily deceived. And as for those who had never known him, who had only come to know him through the story of his death, he lived on in their minds as a man of pure fiction. And so it was that the mysterious wheel of fortune allowed Cemal to die a well-respected man, and a generous saint of the community, at least in the minds of those who first made his acquaintance when reading in the papers of his death. Murder, of course, is a terrible fate. Yet if indeed it was Cemal's inescapable fate to be felled by the hand of another man, well then, he should have been killed by the first person he came upon for no other reason, save the fact that he was Cemal Bey: with his stub of a nose and that narrow, wrinkled brow above his plucked and polished face, and his cloying, stuffy voice, and those little glimmering raptor's eyes darting about the room; yes, by rights he should have been struck down long ago. But that's not how it happened. Somehow he managed to weasel his way into a tragic novel, lurching from one misunderstanding to the next, to become the cause of the untimely murder of a lovely, bashful, but unhappy woman who had never managed to learn how to express herself. This simply didn't make sense. It boggled my mind when I considered how lucky this man had been in the manner of his death, a man who had, when he was only five, profited from the inattention of his mother during a visit to a friend, plucked fish out of an aquarium, poking out their eyes with his fingers before tossing them back into the tank, only to laugh as he watched them suffer. This was Cemal's life in its essence. In adulthood he had never actually poked out anyone's eyes, but he might as well have. In one way or another, he manipulated everyone. Selma only really started to live after she left him; she was so very beautiful, but her years with him were spent in vain. The day Cemal died, the well-mannered and well-versed lawyer Nail Bey was instantly cured of asthma. Nail Bey never told anyone what had happened between him and Cemal Bey. Even our mutual friend Sabriye Hanım, ever alert to such affairs—indeed I had learned quite a lot about Selma Hanım from her, never asking her directly, of course, but by eavesdropping on various conversations—knew nothing. But on the day we paid our last respects to Cemal Bey, Nail Bey and I found ourselves in the same car, and I found him a changed man. A man reborn! At one point he turned to me and said, "I'm so ashamed!"

The perpetrator of these reprehensible deeds had imposed himself on a young and beautiful woman who should have shunned him, and now he had been embraced as a tragic hero by hundreds of thousands of simple souls who had never known the man, who knew nothing of romance either. He had played his part in Nevzat's death, just as he had in Selma's tumultuous life.

I'd seen Tayfur Bey once or twice. He struck me as cold and calculating, and inclined to self-reliance. His urbane manner might have concealed any number of character flaws. He was clearly capable of murder, given the chance to prepare. He hadn't seemed the kind of murderer who could have hacked his victim into pieces without difficulty. Yet he'd done such a job on Cemal Bey as to render him virtually unrecognizable. Many thought it strange that Cemal Bey had been stabbed mostly in the face. But this made perfect sense to me. Although he'd been sufficiently clearheaded to leave behind a detailed confession, the killer had clearly lost his mind at the sight of that horrific face. Indeed he said as much in his suicide note.

Cemal Bey was a man who forced himself on people. And

that was just how he had insinuated himself into Nevzat Hanım's life. He was a man who sought his death in other people. But Nevzat Hanım's life story was truly absurd, enough to drive a man to perdition.

Could anything be more natural than for our good friend Ekrem the Poet to nurture a love for this quiet woman who lived cloistered in her own little world? But he played no part in the Nevzat Hanım affair. For in all her life Nevzat Hanım had only ever really known one man, her husband. As I mentioned earlier, the woman's very face had shut down on the day her husband died. Her earlier life had been plagued by Tayfur Bey, who was so bent on marrying her, and so zealous in his efforts to remove all obstacles, that he'd even murdered his wife. And then, to make a bad business worse, Cemal Bey, who was somehow privy to all this, began pestering the poor woman too.

Nevzat Hanım had spent her entire life oppressed by those around her. Jealousy, love, obsession, egotism, persecution, womanizing of the basest sort, paranoid possessiveness, and compulsive curiosity—she excited the soul's most cruel passions, reducing this blameless creature to a shadow of herself. Smothered by attention, she was understood by no one.

In childhood her temperamental and less-attractive older sister had envied Nevzat Hanım. After this sister was married off—their father was rather wealthy—Nevzat Hanım at last had room to breathe, but almost at once her own future husband, Salim Bey, entered the picture. A feeble, cowardly, arrogant, and even irascible man of no distinction, he, having convinced himself that he was in love, had managed, after years of stubborn insistence, to convince the innocent girl to love him in return, or rather he had contrived to convince her that she was in love. But by the second week of their marriage, the young woman had already discovered that she had never loved her husband and never would. Salim Bey was a man devoid of character and, above all else, mean. The truth was that he had never really loved his wife either. Indeed for him love was nothing more than a needling obsession. He was concerned only with possession. There were times when he might have experienced something like love, but only if he feared losing his possession.

In spite of all this, he had a rather lofty opinion of himself. As is often the case with those who lack a clear sense of themselves, he lived in the world but was not of it. When Nevzat came to see their marriage as untenable and suggested divorce, his response was clear: "Out of the question! What will my friends and everyone else say? Do you want to make me a fool in their eyes? In any case, how could I ever live without you?" It went on like this for three years. Then one night Nevzat Hanım's father, who had been suffering from serious heart problems, died of a heart attack. The man had loved his daughter deeply, and he had known she was unhappy. According to what her family said afterward, the two had spoken briefly a few days before his death, and it was agreed that it was the daughter's unhappy marriage that had caused the father's fatal attack. Poor Nevzat Hanım was thus caught in the crossfire. In the third year of this risible and indeed unconscionable marriage (in which she had remained only out of fear of what her husband's relatives, her neighbors, her friends, even the doorman of their apartment building might say), Salim Bey died in active military service, in an accident that was no one's fault but his own. It was rather unfortunate for Nevzat Hanım in that—three days before her husband died before his entire battalion as a result of his own cowardice—she received a letter from the front, in which this man who had taken no pleasure from his life with her, who understood neither women nor love, who showed his wife affection only in response to jealousy or fear, confessed to despair and thoughts of suicide. But those who had witnessed the accident said it couldn't have been premeditated. The horse Salim Bey had been riding at the time was one of the calmest training horses, not known for being particularly skittish. If Salim Bey hadn't been so frightened when the horse jumped, it wouldn't have bucked so furiously. Had Salim just allowed himself to fall, the animal would certainly have calmed down. Another rider even tested the horse and found that it quickly stopped bucking if the rider kept calm. At the end of the day, Salim Bey's accident was not an accident: he had provoked the animal through fear and lack of experience.

But the fiction of the accident persisted. While Nevzat Hanım, mindful of his last letter, remained convinced that her husband had committed suicide, Salim Bey's relatives were of the same opinion, as they too had received disturbing letters from the front. But these were quite different in tone; his complaints were of another kind: for in them he named the very source of his discontent.

To make matters worse, Salim's mother, who had never loved her son, finding him spineless, tightfisted, and altogether useless, took advantage of his death and moved into the widow's home. It nearly gave Nevzat Hanım a nervous breakdown. It wasn't long before Zeynep Hanım—already terribly distraught—suspected that her husband, Tayfur Bey, was in love with Nevzat Hanım. Indeed hopelessly in love with Nevzat Hanım, Tayfur Bey was driven to murder his wife, Zeynep, in the hope of marrying Nevzat Hanım, and, stranger still, he confessed his crime to his beloved, in the belief that she would be left with no choice but to marry him. So poor Nevzat Hanım had to bear the burden of three deaths, of which one was her own father's. We had always thought of Nevzat Hanım as a woman undone by the oppressive weight of her dreams, when in fact, beneath her quiet and well-meaning smile, she'd been struggling with a bitter fate. Though it was no fault of hers that people died, and even killed one another, she was burdened with the blame. If only she'd had the wherewithal to exercise her will, if only she'd been a bit more selfish or better at defending herself, she might have found the strength to cast off her burdens and find a modicum of freedom. No one understood why she'd not told the police the truth about Zeynep Hanım's suicide.

When I first heard the news, I could not help but think of something my daughter had said to me, something I in fact mentioned earlier in these memoirs. When struggling to understand the madness that had descended on our home, she had mourned the fact that we were the kind of people who bore the blame. And that, I believe, is the crux of the matter. Nevzat Hanım was the kind of person who blamed herself for things she never did. Perhaps this came from her strict family upbringing or a childhood discolored by her elder sister's jealousy. According to Sabriye Hanım, it had all begun with her sister staging a suicide attempt when they were young. At no point in her life had she been properly protected.

But more than anything else, she blamed herself for Salim's death. It was his death that had drawn her to spiritualism. Murat was but a fiction, conjured up by a mother-in-law who did everything in her power to isolate the young widow. It was she who had answered the phone as Murat. In fact I'd been quite startled by her strident and oddly familiar voice on the occasion of our first meeting. Trumpets and foghorns were but remote figments of the auditory imagination next to this awesome voice. Throughout my life I have seen how lies are propped up, not only by those directly involved with them, but also by people with no particular reason to perpetuate them, which is why Sabriye Hanım's explanation of the affair didn't surprise me at all.

Later on, Sabriye Hanım, who was on intimate terms with Zeynep, joined forces with her, using her spinster wits to engineer a double blackmail that almost led to a police investigation, for she believed that there was indeed a serious relationship between Nevzat Hanım and Tayfur Bey: this served only to increase the stress and strain on the young widow. And then there was Cemal Bey.

But this much is clear: while Nevzat Hanım's mother-in-law was still alive, Cemal Bey, Tayfur Bey, and Sabriye Hanım could never have gained easy access to Nevzat Hanım's apartment. In fact the pseudoséances held at their home served no purpose other than to perpetuate the Murat story. But with the death of the old woman, all impediments were removed.

According to Sabriye Hanım, Cemal Bey was after Nevzat Hanım's money. Cemal Bey had been thrown out of his own firm for embezzlement and had only barely managed to cover his debt by dipping into Selma Hanım's inheritance; now he wanted to marry Nevzat Hanım for her money. And this being his last and only hope, he was relentless in pressing his claim.

Though Selma did not deny that money may have played a part in the affair, she also claimed that Cemal Bey had indeed fallen for Nevzat Hanım. "Cemal was a ladies' man, and he always enjoyed a challenge. Most likely Nevzat's monastic lifestyle had a certain appeal," she said. In fact, and this again according to Selma, Cemal Bey had entered into a similar affair with Zeynep Hanım.

As for Tayfur Bey, he had never understood Nevzat Hanım. He'd assumed that his young wife had surrendered to Cemal's unctuous entreaties. For, yes, indeed, there was a letter Tayfur Bey wrote before he died in which he made only the briefest mention of his love for his wife, devoting most of his energies to expressing his jealous and aggressive hatred for Cemal.

Nevzat Hanım's sorry fate was to have been overwhelmed by these four men; just one of them would be enough to ruin any life.

IX

I assumed that the matter of personnel would be a tiring affair, not to mention their remuneration, and so I wanted to begin with as small a group as possible. Yet expansion was inevitable, given the exponential growth in the number of our own handpicked candidates, and in those recommended to us by our friends. We received several applications almost daily. The two office lines—Halit Ayarcı's and my own—never stopped ringing. By the end of the first month, I came to understand how wrong I'd been to complain about not having enough friends or relations. I was amazed to discover just how large my family was. I was likewise impressed by the loyalty of old school friends and the continuing affection that my old neighborhood acquaintances still had for me. My quota had long since been exceeded in the applicant ledger. Most were people who had been sensitive enough to stay at arm's length during the years when my spirits had been so dampened by misfortune; now they had entered into an all-out war as they struggled to give me the chance to prove that I too felt compassion for my friends and relatives.

When I asked Halit Ayarcı what he thought I should do in the face of this barrage, he gave me the following answer:

"My dear Hayri İrdal, in matters such as these there are two methods: either you put the whole affair out of your mind or you separate the applicants into prearranged categories and then choose one from each group. As I'm in the same boat, why don't we ponder the two options together? If we agree to leave the affair to fate and fortune, we'll have no choice but to draw lots. But I imagine the result would not necessarily turn out in our favor. And if word ever got out that we'd availed ourselves of such a method, then we'd almost certainly meet with stiff criticism."

"So shall we create categories!"

"Yes, but what will we use as our criteria?"

"We'll select those with experience. For example, those people who have more or less worked for a certain period of time in a particular field."

"Oh no, never that. It seems you haven't understood the true meaning of 'experience.' To be experienced means to be run down, frozen at some fixed point, and stuck with stagnant ideas. Such people are of no use to us."

There was no other choice but to choose from the inexperienced.

"Well then, we'll choose those without experience," I said.

Halit Ayarcı paused for a moment. He was scrutinizing a new chart on his office wall. Taking me by the arm, he pulled me over to it.

"I designed this chart as part of a study evaluating the love children have for watches and clocks. But certain points don't seem entirely right. This dark-blue column should have been assigned to the children of literate families! But I assigned it to timepieces given as gifts. No, we'll have to move them to this smaller yellow column here . . . Could you kindly have this corrected for me?"

I made the adjustments as requested, but I couldn't help but ask him what use there was in doing so. He looked at me with a grave expression on his face.

"To know is to be one step ahead."

We returned to the matter at hand.

"How will you know which applicants have absolutely no experience?"

"Well, for example, those who have never held a job before."

"But such people will have the experience of inexperience.

They will be more difficult. Managing such people is bound to be difficult. Impossible."

"Then?"

"There remains but one solution: a list of applicants, a list for everyone save those we've already accepted. Better yet, a list of applicants that follows no particular order—if it skips around then no one will see it as coincidence. This will also increase our chances. Do you see what I mean? You accept the first in your book, then skip the second, then accept the third, and so on . . . In fact we could have variations: for example, after the third person you'll skip the fourth, fifth, and sixth, and then accept number ten. Who was your first choice again?"

"Asaf Bey, as you already know. Now he's receiving casual remuneration, but he hasn't been assigned a position yet!"

Halit Ayarcı scrunched up his face.

"Asaf Bey's a sloth of a fellow," he said. "I don't take well to lazy people. At an institute such as ours, which likes to assign predetermined positions to its staff, which champions personal freedom and expects its employees to increase their range and efficacy through exercise of their own creative powers, the lazy are always dangerous. Does he come in every day?"

"He is always the first to arrive!"

And it was indeed the truth: Asaf Bey came to work the earliest and was the last to leave.

"What does he do?"

"Right now, nothing. He just reads the papers. As a matter of fact, you yourself ordered him to do so!"

"Well, is he reading them?"

"No, but Nermin Hanım is reading them for him."

"Have him carry on, then."

"Fine, but we'll have to move him to the permanent payroll once the budget for temporary salaries is exhausted."

Halit Ayarcı paused to give the matter more thought.

"Find a job that suits this friend of ours," he said. "A job that doesn't require work, that will suit this lazy creature perfectly, and that will benefit the institute. Then the problem's solved."

"Isn't it a little strange to set aside staff for such a job?"

"No," he said. "In fact I really don't know. I have no idea whatsoever. But I imagine that within such a vast institute such a position can be found. Perhaps an office to which we can transfer all work that needs to be deferred. Indeed I have no doubt that, given your dear friend's affinities, we shall see certain jobs not just deferred but never done at all!"

"But what about the name? What would the title of such a post be?"

"Is there any need? Ah, such formalities . . . They give those who are actually trying to get things done no room for maneuver. How is one meant to work under such tight restrictions, such rigid formalities?"

He paced up and down the room, and then stopped just in front of me.

"Do we really need a name?"

"I would think so."

He let out a mournful and despairing sigh.

"My dear friend Hayri Bey, if one day I must walk away from this institute I created with such passion, and so dearly love, be sure that formalities such as these will be the sole cause. This isn't just about the name of one particular position. I made arrangements for that some time ago. But why waste our time on such trifling matters? This is what truly saddens me. To waste so much precious time, and in a Time Regulation Institute! Now, that is a terrible tragedy . . ."

Then he rang the service bell. Derviş Ağa stepped into the office:

"Please tell Ekrem Bey to report to the Ping-Pong Room! We'll play a set. And you'll join us too?"

Halit Ayarcı, who loved playing Ping-Pong, had arranged a room on the top floor for just this purpose. As I was often up there, I'd had a separate table set up, so that I could play solitaire if I was bored.

"Yes, sir," I said.

Putting his arm in mine, he almost yanked me out of the room.

"Yes," he said, "we waste far too much time. We can budget

our time more carefully just by circumventing obstacles such as these. I'll draw up a chart. Don't forget that we've been invited to your aunt's tonight."

"Yes, of course . . . But the name?"

"Ah, yes! The Completion Department! Do you understand? That's where we'll transfer all the work we want to put on hold. Two secretaries will suffice. But please, let's not appoint too many people there."

"In fact one should be enough!"

"No, let's say two. One is a young man who has already been recommended by your aunt, and the other is a very refined young lady of my own acquaintance. But if you like, we could transfer the young fellow that your aunt recommended to another office and send in the woman instead. Two women together would make a more industrious pair. That's to say, they would feel more at ease."

The matter settled, we left for the Ping-Pong Room, there to while away our time, for that was how things worked in the Time Regulation Institute, whose sole and earnest aim was to find new ways to economize on time.

X

I loved watching Halit Ayarcı and Ekrem Bey play Ping-Pong. They were both handsome men, and despite their age difference they both had the same agility and athleticism, not to mention a certain grace. Devoid as I was of such attributes, I never failed to be surprised by the harmony of their movements as they together formed a shape while still remaining separate. To watch them afforded me a strange pleasure, as if I were taking revenge on my own body—though I did feel the odd pang of jealousy.

I had always been extremely fond of Ekrem. Like me, he was obliged to rely on other people and what they had to offer him. His affection for me over the last seven years had been constant. He'd shown me kindness even in my darkest moments and always treated me as a friend. He never charged me with ignorance or poor understanding. If ever he found me in one of my more temperamental moods, he would just give me a strange smile. I was quite pleased to have found a job for him at the institute, one that I recommended he leave at the first opportunity. I wasn't frightened by Halit Bey's affection for him. For Halit Bey lived in a world that was far beyond our ken; we both knew we had no chance of ever influencing him.

Ekrem was playing quite badly that day. He wasn't himself. He was what they call a changed man. His movements were awkward, he lacked concentration, his responses were slow, and his timing was all off. With every attack it seemed his hand was a little too far ahead of his body, hanging hesitantly in mid-air. His thoughts were clearly with Nevzat Hanım, and he couldn't coordinate them with his body. Who knows just what he was thinking then? The terrible pain of losing a loved one forever, the gruesome manner of her demise, and the agony he and the community had had to bear—his grief had undone him.

He had seen Nevzat Hanim as a being remote from the real world, a being content in a sphere of her own making—but now, alas, she must have taken on a new meaning in his mind. At long last he had begun to fathom that fixed smile of hers. It was the kind of smile you saw on the lips of a trapeze artist as she leaped into the void with her arms extended toward her partner, knowing all too well that the success of such a feat was measured in millimeters and that any miscalculation meant plummeting to her death. It was not an empty smile; it was heroic. Throughout her life, it masked her suffering. Poor Ekrem: in contemplating her smile, he might have at last understood that Nevzat Hanım was not just the shadow of the woman he loved and read about in books, but a human being. And perhaps this was why he seemed so full of regret. For her quiet smile seemed now a cry for help, drawing his attention above all others.

For it had been Nevzat Hanim's quiet smile that had led Ekrem to believe her to embody the aesthetic he'd expound upon at length in the days we spent together in the Şehzadebaşı coffeehouse. Though he had pilfered it from the annals of an outrageous, if not downright ludicrous, English author whose name now escapes me, he called it his aesthetic of poetic purity. To the mind of Dr. Ramiz, women had absolutely nothing to do with poetry, pure or otherwise. When he was in the right mood, Dr. Ramiz was given to analyzing the objects of Ekrem's desire, most of them dead, more often than not by their own hand, and if ever he happened to be playing the part of a medical doctor, he would diagnose the root cause as anemia. Ekrem Bey never paid much attention to the doctor's ramblings, which he dismissed as incoherent hogwash, and it was, perhaps, because I was a most compliant listener that he spoke to me at such length about his precious aesthetic, which though it offered the illusion of simplicity, was utterly impenetrable, drawing as it did on seven or eight poets and philosophers whose names he was inclined to confuse.

You can probably imagine how much sense I made of my conversations with Ekrem Bey. But this much is true: the day I first met Nevzat Hanımfendi I said to myself, now here is a woman Ekrem Bey could love for a lifetime. There is a point in life when we have so accustomed ourselves to the slings and arrows of fate that we seem to carry their sadness inside us. Ekrem Bey had prepared himself for his romance with Nevzat Hanım by reading enough books to fill a library. But the manner of our formation does not always suit the shape of the lives we end up living. At the very moment when Ekrem Bey believed himself to have discovered his aesthetic in the flesh, he was confronted by a triple homicide.

And no longer was Nevzat Hanım's smile the emanation of a splendid soul, glimmering like a distant star before the naked eye, no longer was it a work of art casting its light on the world from above; it was not the solution to all Ekrem's woes. Behind that smile was a woman entrapped by hopelessness and all manner of oppression. It was only now that Ekrem could see her desperation.

I spoke with Nevzat Hanim that evening at my aunt's soiree (which I mentioned earlier). Somehow she'd managed to escape from Cemal Bey's clutches. The truth of the matter is that my aunt had captured Cemal Bey for herself, and Nevzat Hanım, profiting from the freedom that this brief interlude allowed her, had retreated to a window in a far corner, to watch the world go by. For just a moment, she had dropped her light mask of sweetness. The lines on her face were deep and even animated. She was perhaps more beautiful than ever, like a loaded gun. Slowly I approached her, and with the courage that came from playing the uncle, I said:

"You seem so sad here all alone! Look—Ekrem is waiting for you just over there. Why don't you say something nice to the poor fellow? He's been waiting for years."

Her face suddenly softened, losing its chill, but it did not revert to the one we all knew; it lingered somewhere in between.

"Ekrem Bey," she mumbled. "If he'd been just a little stronger, none of this would have happened."

Then I put to her perhaps the most idiotic question in the world:

"Shall I tell him this myself?"

Her face grew tense again.

"Of course not! What use would that be? Such things must happen on their own accord. Don't misunderstand me. Perhaps the fault's all mine. I'm just so disgusted by everything that . . ."

Then she took my arm.

"Don't worry about me," she said. "I'll be all right. Please just leave me alone. You remember when you were close to Sabriye Hanım. Oh, how I hated you then. You were always poking around, hoping to win her favor . . . but then you disappeared."

She closed her eyes and leaned her head back as if in search of a pillow.

"But you came looking for me at home."

"I know. I wanted to know what Sabriye said about me. If possible, I would have teased it out of you. Anyway, that's all behind us. Now you're back on center stage! So is everyone else. Do you know what it means to be in such crowded company?"

She paused to look at me, and then she cried:

"Leave me! And please don't speak about me to anyone."

And with firm steps she made to lose herself in the crowd

gathered around Halit Bey. Our conversation that night weighed heavily upon me. I knew just how far I had compromised myself to be a part of this enterprise, to be treated like anybody else. But I had never fully grasped how much others had suffered for the same privilege. Nevzat Hanim had a place in my heart that she shared with no other, and now I saw the world through the eyes of a woman I had only wanted to help.

A fortnight after our conversation, I had a second encounter with Nevzat Hanım, this time at the home of Seher Hanım. I was with my aunt. When I first heard Nevzat Hanım's voice floating in from the living room, my first instinct was to turn back. But I couldn't. We sat opposite each other for two hours. She didn't say a word to me. As we were leaving together—my aunt had offered to take her home—we found ourselves alone for a moment and she whispered:

"I offended you that evening . . . Forgive me."

"I'm not angry with you, but with myself," I replied.

Whenever I saw Ekrem after that, I would remember what Nevzat had said, and I could not help but pity the young man. He seemed to be half-missing. At one point it looked as if the game was turning in his favor. He went for three full minutes without offering Halit a single chance to regain the upper hand. Then he faltered and never came back. His life was no different. What could I say?

Then Sabriye Hanım tapped me on the shoulder. My entire body went stiff. It had been like this for days. It had gotten to the point where I would cross the street to avoid her. But I was the one who had invited her to come and work with us! Seeing that I had no desire to talk to her, she moved away, walking around the Ping-Pong table to sit down at a small desk and fiddle with a pack of cards. She pursed her lips; her body was as stiff as mine. Her face was strangely pale.

For a minute or two, Halit Bey tried to lure Ekrem back into the game, but he soon gave up hope and brought the match to an end. Ekrem Bey mopped the sweat off his brow. In my mind was the image of Cemal Bey's body, chopped into pieces. How much longer was this going to last? On our way downstairs we peeked into Asaf Bey's office. The future head of the Completion Department was struggling to get his arms around the unfortunate Gülsüm Hanım, our fifty-five-year-old office assistant. It was such an absurd and unexpected sight that we couldn't help but burst out laughing. Halit Ayarcı took me by the arm, and we tiptoed away from the door.

"What do you say, sir?" I asked. "Perhaps we should begin with the second name on the list!"

So I had quite the knack for choosing them: Ekrem had sunk into depression, Sabriye Hanım had become a miserable witch, and Asaf Bey was going senile.

"Thank God you know Dr. Ramiz."

Throwing on his coat, Halit Ayarcı replied:

"The Completion Department will come together just fine. In fact it's already looking rather promising, but could you please have those young girls I suggested for the department work as assistants to another friend. Or better yet, let's pool together all the women who type. As for you, my dear friend, there's no need to worry. Be sure that you wouldn't have selected those friends of yours if you were in the state you are in now. You are under the impression that their affection for you is inspired by pity, while in fact you have provided them a safe haven."

"And Sabriye too?" I asked.

"No," he said. "She wanted to use you. That much is clear, but still, you can never be sure."

On our way out, he told me how frustrating it was to play Ping-Pong with Ekrem these days:

"I have always avoided love. I've never loved anyone. Perhaps it's a shortcoming. But I don't lose any sleep over it. The problem with love is that, in the end, its pleasures come at a cost: one way or another you end up having to pay. That aside, there's nothing more gruesome than a needless entanglement . . ."

And true enough, I had started to pay. Poor Selma was now a hopeless wreck. She couldn't stop thinking about Cemal Bey and Nevzat Hanım. She'd wake up in a cold sweat in the middle of the night.

But who could ever forget such a thing? I had no pity

whatsoever for Cemal Bey. Had he not come to such a violent end, I would have rejoiced just to be free of the man. But still there was something gnawing away at me, and I couldn't pretend things were as they had been. Try as I might, I could not chase away the image of Nevzat Hanım's head leaning back in search of a pillow, nor could I forget the words we had exchanged that night.

Just as we arrived at the door of my aunt's office, Halit Ayarcı grabbed my arm.

"And we've found a job for the musician as well. Macit Bey, isn't it? The one who always dreamed of conducting? Oh yes, and a hall that fits a hundred—all the young girls poised at their typewriters, and towering above them on a pedestal with his baton in the air will be their maestro! They'll all work under his baton, pounding out their As and Bs and Cs in perfect time! My dear, things seem to be shaping up after all. Just think, a moment ago you were bemoaning the fact that you had chosen Asaf Bey. But consider the sheer originality of this idea—consider it a gesture of consolation. Yes, all our secretaries will work together in one tremendous hall, save of course our personal secretaries. Modern work for modern times!"

When we arrived at the house we found the foyer and both salons bustling with people. I had never seen such a crowd before in my life. Milling alongside our friends and acquaintances were foreigners from all four corners of the globe—from north and south, the Far and Middle East. For the first half hour, it was either Halit Ayarcı or my aunt with a tight grip on my hand, whisking me from here to there to introduce me to our international guests. And before long nearly everyone knew who I was. At one point I managed to sneak off to a corner. That was when I realized every wall in the house had been decorated with slogans and charts pertaining to our work at the institute. Toward eight o'clock the lights went off and a short film was shown. The official opening of our very first regulation station was officially announced! And so everyone there had the chance to watch yours truly, Hayri İrdal, standing before a ribbon, a pile of papers in his hand, first to deliver a speech before a great and distinguished audience, and then to shake a lovely young lady's hand. Oh Lord, what a sweet smile she had! Why hadn't I ever noticed? After the inauguration of the institute, there was a second film. But this time I was in Halit Ayarcı's shadow. Had anyone of import neglected to attend? No—everyone who was anyone was there. How to explain, then, why Halit Ayarcı outshone them all that evening? No sooner had the lights come on than our guests began dashing between Halit Ayarcı and myself. Unbeknownst to me, Halit Bey had arranged the evening so that everyone of consequence was there to meet me. All the most important presences in my life—the Şerbetçibaşı Diamond, Seyit Lutfullah, Ahmet the Timely, the Blessed One, and Nuri Efendi—rained down on me like confetti. With every glass of champagne, they showed more curiosity and enthusiasm for our work.

That night I spoke more than I had in perhaps my entire life. I told almost everyone in attendance almost everything I knew, and whenever I found myself with someone who spoke a foreign language, I found a translator muttering mysteriously just behind me. Halit Ayarcı had thought of everything. At one point I signed almost one hundred fifty good-sized photographs of grandfather clocks. A little later I realized why. In the other room I found my aunt introducing guests to a grandfather clock; it was rather larger than our old clock, and, although replete with rococo flourishes, it had at some later date been bordered on all four sides with ivory panels adorned with Arabic script. The odd thing was that everyone seemed to be marveling at the clock as if they knew it. Hundreds of eyes were upon it, bespectacled and otherwise, as if in anticipation of an official introduction. This was one of the rare grandfather clocks made in Germany at the beginning of the eighteenth century, the golden age of mechanics and automatism; a tall, finely crafted, stately clock, which—if it were properly set and maintained by an experienced master—would reveal its full range of capabilities. But the crowd was so vast, and the ceremony so bizarre, that the clock itself was hardly visible.

My aunt looked more outrageous than ever, with lace rippling over the front of her low-cut black gown and a black shawl thrown over her shoulder; her hair was dyed, and her face heavily made up, and she shimmered with diamonds and pearls; brandishing her cane in one hand, she used the other to introduce the imposter to guests passing by, first giving the name of each newcomer before grandiloquently announcing, "And this is the Blessed One, our family clock," and then adding something to the effect of, "He's staying with us for the time being."

At one point the clock began to chime. I think it must have been the quarter hour. Though it was a sound far more beautiful than that of the actual Blessed One, there was such a commotion in its wake that I could hardly hear it: The door on the front of the clock swung open, and an old Sufi dressed in dervish attire, a character right out of one of Osman Hamdi's paintings, leaped out of the clock and cried, "Welcome!" before disappearing back inside; and without batting an eyelid, my aunt introduced him to the crowd:

"Sheikh Ahmet Efendi the Timely!" she declared.

And the room fairly roared with applause and cries of surprise and admiration. The strangest and indeed most ludicrous thing to behold was the puzzled look on Dr. Ramiz's face as he marveled at how much the Blessed One had changed, for of course the doctor knew the clock all too well, having spent whole days in its company, and he was only too aware that I had sold it. Unable to bear his agitation any longer, he pulled me into a corner to whisper:

"My good man, the Blessed One seems very much changed. How can I put it . . . He seems far too done up!"

I handed him my glass of whiskey.

"You're right!" I cried. "Money, prosperity, the drive to earn more and more—it's changed us all."

"But there seems to be more to it than that!" he said. "He was much more beautiful, and pure. Couldn't you have a word with your aunt and get her to stop?"

"There's simply no way. There's nothing we can do now, and we shouldn't . . . I've tried giving my advice on the matter, but she won't listen."

"But we must find a solution. If nothing else, we should convince her to have that medal removed from his chest!"

"You can try if you like. She says Sultan Abdülaziz gave it to her, and that's all she'll say. Haven't you seen my aunt? Are those the kind of clothes a woman her age should wear? That's our family for you—the older we get, the more depraved we become. But, then again, he is part of the family. To tell you the truth, I don't have all my wits about me."

But my dear friend reassured me.

"No," he said. "You have nothing to fear as long as I'm here by your side! And besides, I was the one who cured you."

Before I could thank my friend, I was again surrounded by my aunt's guests. A woman adorned in nearly as many evil eyes, bells, chains, and rings as a pack mule (and nearly as old as the Blessed One itself) asked me if our ancestors were descended from Ahmet the Timely or the Blessed One. I turned to the interpreter and said, "Please tell the madam that the Blessed One is our grandfather!" Another woman asked me if the Blessed One often changed places, visiting each family home in turn. I told her that visits of this sort were naturally quite rare and possible only with the doctor's permission. So they asked me who the doctor was.

"Well, of course a man of his ripe old age has more than one doctor, but our current doctor is Dr. Ramiz," whereupon I pointed to my dear friend.

I was quite sure that the doctor would be more than pleased to carry on from there, and as the crowd descended upon him I wiggled out to the entrance hall.

How strange it all was. We were all puppets, with Halit Ayarcı pulling the strings. He brought us to just the place he wanted us to be, and then we acted our parts from memory. I had such mixed feelings for the man: my anger and even my rage were tempered with admiration.

Seated on a large sofa to the left of the entrance was Zehra, holding court amid the billowing skirts of her new dress, swinging a glass in the air as she conversed with the young gentlemen gathered around her in a language she didn't know—or perhaps in the one language they all knew only too well. The granddaughter of Ahmet Efendi the Some Timer was truly beautiful that evening, and those around her looked awestruck. As I watched her little hands darting here and there, I admired her finely etched chin; she looked genuinely happy. She was the image of her mother. One of the young gentlemen handed her a plate of food; holding it on her lap, she began to pick at it daintily. It cheered me to see that our changed circumstances had caused her to forget one particular family tradition. As recently as two years ago, that was just how we'd eaten our dried bread.

Then Pakize came over to see me. She too was finely dressed. I hadn't the foggiest idea when she'd had all these dresses made, but I seemed to recognize the fabric. As I cast my eyes over her brightly colored scarf and her little handbag and that smug smile on her face, I couldn't help but wonder which movie star she thought she was that night. Still beaming, she took my arm and said:

"Ah, Hayri, if you only knew how happy I am! I only expected so much when I chose you as my husband."

"How nice of you to say—though I do believe I was the one that chose you, or have the customs changed?"

"The moment he sees me, he reverts to his old ways. In any case, I'm happy now. And when I saw the Blessed One here—oh, I cannot begin to tell you how very pleased I was! You know how much I love him. I'd always go to kiss his hand every holiday"

"So you're enjoying all this, are you?"

"How could I not? This is just what I've always wanted. And you wanted to postpone it!"

Standing behind my wife, I noticed a brute, the spitting image of a bulldog, holding two drinks and making no secret of his eagerness to take my place the moment I moved away.

"Who in God's name is that insolent creature there?" I asked. "Couldn't you find anyone better?"

"He's a member of my fan club. He keeps asking after you. It seems he's a journalist!"

Then she whispered:

"This evening's a resounding success . . ."

Then she noticed that I was studying the fabric of her gown and she said:

"You recognize it, don't you? You remember, we never could sell it because no one would give us anything for it. It's the outer lining of your father's fur coat, dear! I had the moth-eaten sections repaired. Oh, but it was frightfully expensive."

So those golden stars glistening on that green fabric were once moth-eaten pieces of fur.

As the bulldog interjected—"May God make it so!"—I left my wife in his charge, thinking, "Well, one thing's for sure, at least. He can't devour her whole." Just near the front door I heard someone say hello, and I turned to see my younger sister-in-law. Dressed in an unbecoming scarlet gown, she was teasing the men around her, like a dagger nearly drawn. She wore heavy steel earrings thick as horseshoes, and for a moment I regretted all the broken ones we'd thrown away in the army. What a fortune we could have made, pandering to today's fashions! She abandoned her admirers to come to my side, leaning up against me with all her weight to say:

"You are the most handsome man here tonight, my dear brother-in-law!"

Pakize's sister had recently developed a penchant for excessive flattery. It was most likely a by-product of the treatment she was receiving from Dr. Ramiz.

Slowly detaching myself, I said, "Enough of all that. Run off and have fun! But next time try another perfume!"

Without taking the slightest offense, she brought her little kerchief to her nose, and after naming the perfume—I couldn't say what it was and I doubt I could have done so even if my life depended on it—burst into laughter.

My other sister-in-law was sure to make an appearance any time now. Her performance at the club finished around eleven. And the moment she arrived she would no doubt feel obliged to sing a few of the songs that had made her a star. I went back into the living room and then stepped into the back room, where it was relatively quiet. Seher Hanım, Sabriye Hanım, Nermin Hanım, and a coterie of gentlemen had gathered around a handsome wood-burning stove of the type you used to see in

AHMET HAMDI TANPINAR

old houses, and—just as Dr. Ramiz had taught them, as if they were participating in some kind of Bektaşi ceremony—they toasted one another and sipped their rakı, covering half of the glass with one hand. They shoved a glass into my hand. I told them I didn't drink rakı; I only drank whiskey, and the Blessed One didn't allow for it to be any other way. A young man almost Ahmet's age staggered to his feet, swaying to the left and to the right, and handed me a flask he'd managed to retrieve from his back pocket. I couldn't help but think of my son. "The poor fool," I muttered under my breath. "Who knows how much the poor child is suffering, fighting for his integrity under a dim light at school. If only such integrity were possible! If only he could learn to accept that we all must make concessions! But was this ever possible?" I returned the bottle to the young man. It smelled like carbolic acid. With a barely audible "But where are you going?" uttered from behind an old crone who had collapsed into his lap, Dr. Ramiz sent me on my way.

Meanwhile servants were busy shuttling back and forth with enormous platters laden with a meat pilaf and wooden spoons. Scrambling in the wake of these great platters was a horde of men and women bearing smaller plates of pudding. A courteous Frenchman smiled at me and uttered a few words, perhaps assuming that we must understand each other, being more or less the same age. And indeed it wasn't too difficult to make out what he had said: "Attack the pilaf!" I looked aghast at this miserable creature who seemed so ignorant of modern times. But he misread my surprise; pointing instead to the bar where they were serving champagne. Arm in arm, we walked across the room. "Perhaps this will help," I said. Sooner or later someone in this crowd will do me some good, and after that I'll have no trouble blending in. I had no choice but to adapt to my surroundings. I could bear life in no other way.

The champagne refreshed me. I looked about the room, wondering what had become of Selma. I thought how wonderful it would be if she had come too. But there was no sign of her. My beloved had been in ill health since Cemal Bey's death. Then I noticed Ekrem. His gaze was fixed on something across the room, his entire body in rapt attention. Then I realized he was staring at the sofa directly underneath the photograph of Naşit Bey: it was here where—just a month and a half ago—he had sat with Nevzat Hanım. It was all so ridiculous, so absurd. This too soured my mood.

Returning to the hall, I stepped into the late Naşit Bey's office, which was just to the right. It was the first time I'd been in the office of this man I never could find it in my heart to love. But once, while my aunt was showing me around the house, she'd told me there was an especially comfortable sofa in this office. I closed the door behind me. The room had been elegantly furbished. The walls were covered with pictures, but the focal point was just opposite the armchair: an elaborate panel of weaponry, boasting an array of hunting knives and rifles that gave one to believe that Naşit Bey had actually hunted deer and even larger and more dangerous game. And square in the middle of the panel there was an eagle that reminded me of the one that had perched in Aristidi Efendi's pharmacy window, hovering over the two embryos with drooping eyelids, who were locked in a philosophical discussion in their jar of greenish liquid, and despite its faded feathers poised for flight. "What innocent lies we told each other back then," I mumbled to myself as I drifted off to sleep.

When I woke up, it was nearing sunrise but the party was still in full swing. Opening my eyes, I saw Halit Ayarcı standing above me.

"So what do you think?" he said. "Extraordinary, isn't it? I've been looking all over for you. How can you leave a night this wonderful in midswing?"

His relaxed and soothing voice rendered me speechless.

"Your aunt was magnificent. Well, isn't she always . . . And you didn't behave too badly yourself! So get up, then, and come meet a friend who has traveled all the way here to meet you. Van Humbert, a first-rate intellectual!"

As I stretched in the chair, I asked, "Isn't the party over, Halit Bey? They're still going? Won't it ever end?"

"No, my dear friend, we've only just begun. We are as new-born babes."

"That's fine, but exactly where is this game going to lead us? Just tell me that . . . Everything was going along according to plan. Do we really need all this nonsense?"

Halit Bey sat down at Naşit Bey's desk.

"Everything's working just right. But we're alone. We're all alone in this world, and there is nothing I loathe more than loneliness. Do you understand me? Such a magnificent and invaluable institute should have counterparts all the world over. That's what I want. And I am sure you want it too."

XI

Our conversation continued no further, for Dr. Ramiz had burst into the room. My dear friend was in fine form: his hair was in a state, his shirt collar was hanging to one side, and his necktie was flung back over his shoulder. With both hands, he pushed aside the enormous woman who had nearly crushed him at the aforementioned Bektaşi ceremony around the old-style stove. It was truly surprising to see what a close resemblance this poor woman bore to the doctor's late wife, who had given her fortune to further his scientific career—and all the wonders of her 130-kilo body for his private enjoyment. Though she left the former to the doctor, she had taken the latter with her to the other side, to find refuge in that better world untainted by the strains of married life and where lovemaking was never subjected to psychoanalysis. Seeing us, the doctor threw his arm around his new lover's midsection, as dashing as a film star of the first order, and, wresting his chin from its resting place on his right shoulder, he made as if to speak. But Halit Bey brought his finger to his lips and signaled for quiet, gesturing toward the woman who had passed out on the sofa:

"Do come in, Doctor, but please try to keep quiet," he said. "This dear child's feeling somewhat unwell."

Then he pointed to the armchair I'd just been sleeping in.

"It's quite a comfortable chair, and we're just leaving, so make yourself at home!"

I was captivated as ever by his cynical smile. A man who achieves a cynicism of such perfection can accept the world as it is until the end of time, for to be this cynical is to deny all humanity. There is nothing a man with perfect cynicism cannot do, providing he hasn't been poisoned by loneliness that just might settle inside him.

Taking me by the arm, he pulled me out of the room.

"See how the doctor manages to enjoy himself?" he said. "He's not like you! You've no sooner arrived than you've started hunting for something to disapprove of, something that might cause you pain or suffering—and then you wander about the room as if someone were holding a bunch of nettles under your nose and you're trying to get rid of them."

Hoping to change the subject, I interrupted him:

"Judging by your appearance, it seems you haven't had too much to drink!"

"I had just a few," he said. "I wanted to have my wits about me this evening. But now I'll drink. That is to say, I shall allow myself to drink. There's still more champagne! Your aunt is the perfect hostess. Her generosity knows no bounds. I know this may not please you, but now that you are no longer a man in need, I don't mind telling you. She has clearly no intention of leaving this world behind until she has spent every penny of her fortune!"

People were still dancing feverishly in both the main living room and the entrance hall. The air had turned into a thick paste of powder, essence of lavender, perspiration, bare shoulders, sweaty armpits, lipstick. At one point my younger sister-in-law caught sight of me and tried to wend her way toward me; thank God her young chaperone, built like a racehorse, didn't give her the chance.

The Blessed One's room was somewhat calmer. But it was now home to the champagne table. And the crowd swarming around it called to mind an anthill. Halit Ayarcı took me by the hand and led me to Van Humbert, who was conversing with my aunt and my wife. The amiable scholar was drinking a fruit juice spritzer, while my wife and aunt had made the more humane choice: they both were sipping champagne. When I saw my aunt, I could not help but think, "Will her fortune last till the end of her days?" I shrugged my shoulders. "No need to worry, we have money now," I thought. "In fact, her former maid has stopped working altogether. And why shouldn't my aunt just do the same. It would be a little hard but we would manage. With an aunt like her, you can tolerate anything." Indeed it was hard not to love her. She exuded life as abundantly as a field of grain.

Van Humbert seemed a robust man of around sixty-five years; he was of medium height, composed, with the body of a young man and the face of a child. Indeed he had such a young air about him that his bushy beard looked like a disguise. Before Halit Bey had finished introducing me, he asked:

"How was it, then? Were you pleased with the conference? I so wish I'd been here to see it. But the lady and her gentleman friend here refused to let me in."

Before I had time to express my confusion, my wife leaped into the conversation to sing our guest's praises.

"What beautiful Turkish he speaks, don't you think?"

Brushing aside Van Humbert's polite *estağfurullah*, my aunt explained:

"Yes, the evening wasn't without a few minor problems, and I'm truly saddened you were unable to attend. Yet what else were we to do? My nephew had already promised to speak at this family gathering."

Oh dear! So I'd just been at a conference. I hadn't fallen asleep in Naşit Bey's office, staring at the eagle with faded feathers, after all. And this conference was nothing more than a family gathering. That seemed to make sense. You can't just up and deliver a public speech at eleven o'clock at night. Suddenly my life seemed easier than I had thought. I really had no right to complain. A slight twitch of my shanks, a jerk on the reins, a flash of the whip, and I was on my way. Naturally there would be someone kind enough to tell me what my speech should cover. And if not—well, I'd come up with something all the same. But this was a little dangerous. Best was to stay patient. For now there was nothing to do but to look into Van

Humbert's eyes and smile and shake his hand, or rather wait for my fingers to be released from his vicelike grip. Oh, how I would have shown him if I only could have readjusted my fingers.

No sooner had my aunt finished, than my wife jumped back into the conversation:

"My dear Hayri, I hope you were met with wild applause? I'm so sorry I wasn't there at your side, but I couldn't leave our new dear friend behind. I couldn't allow him to tire himself needlessly. What a delightful man! And such charming stories he told us . . ."

Turning to our guest, she added:

"My husband does better with his speeches when I am at his side."

And with that impudent smile on her face and that strange gaze she saved for social occasions, she turned to the poor foreigner and waited for the compliment she felt she deserved. And his Turkish did not let him down: it was with genuine enthusiasm that he declared:

"But of course, madam, provided he is in the company of such a muse as yourself."

Van Humbert must have been overjoyed to find occasion to show off his Turkish. He had probably found our word for "muse" in a dictionary. He seized my hand as quickly as he had seized upon the word, and again he crushed my fingers and the palm of my hand with his vicelike grip. "Mark my words—we'll meet again. And then you'll see just what I'll make of your hand," I told myself. Having been served her compliment, my wife turned to me, as obsequious as a lapdog delivering its master a handkerchief dropped to the floor by a lady guest.

"I hope I didn't mix up the order of your notes."

By this she meant "pull yourself together." I was to play my part. With considerable effort, I managed to wrench my hand free of Van Humbert's grip; holding on to a moist towel wrapped around the neck of a wine bottle, I tried to ease the pain.

"Oh no, dear, nothing of the sort. I simply forgot them at home . . . so I spoke from memory."

Halit Ayarcı let loose the first guffaw. Then we all joined in chorus. Looking at my muse, Van Humbert said:

"It's much better that way. The same thing has happened to me on several occasions. But, you know, you speak much more naturally that way."

With this word of assurance, my wife's anxiety subsided. She smiled sweetly at both Van Humbert and me.

"Where's that chimpanzee of yours? Or I should say bull-dog?" I asked.

Halit Ayarcı slightly furrowed his brow to show his distaste for my crude humor. I got the message straightaway and turning to my guest I asked:

"And how was your trip, sir?"

"But of course, sir, of course. The ticket you arranged afforded me the most luxurious cabin on the ship."

So that meant that perhaps my own signature had authorized the invitation to this silly jackanapes. But the others were keeping quiet on the subject of my speech that night. So, what did I care? Seeing that I spoke from memory, I'll just make something up. I'll say I made changes!

Halit Ayarcı took the opportunity to ask Van Humbert his impressions of Istanbul. We were given all the right answers. The automobile we had provided was very comfortable, and he was quite pleased with the bathroom in his hotel. Though the man who was showing him about town knew no Dutch, his German was rather good.

"Yes, sir, the Grand Bazaar—the Bedesten—and the copper makers . . ."

But alas the old man didn't linger for long in the covered bazaar and quickly moved on to the subject of Ahmet the Timely. He had obviously gone over my book with a fine-tooth comb, and I was soon bombarded by questions. What a difference compared with our critics! It was as if he lingered on every word for particular emphasis. Even Cemal Bey's criticism amounted to nothing next to what this fellow came up with off the top of his head. At one point he pulled a large wad of paper out of his pocket: a list of questions he had prepared in advance! Such a thing was unbearable at that hour of night. Why in the

world had Halit Ayarcı arranged all this without informing
me? Why was he always thrusting such situations upon me by
force majeure?

The first few questions were easily deflected. But as they pro-
gressed I became entangled in a strange act of mental gymnastics. "Not to worry," I said to myself. "After ten minutes I'll
just pretend I've had too much to drink." But how to get
through those ten minutes?

Halit Ayarcı was the first to come to my rescue. Handing a
freshly filled glass of champagne to our guest he said, "Your
stomach must be feeling better now."

Van Humbert looked first at his list of questions, and then at
the champagne. Clearly there was a civil war raging inside his
head. Was he to be a hero or a human being? But the world of
illusion prevailed. Flashing one of her famous smiles, Pakize
asked Van Humbert if he liked dancing, and by the middle of
her next glass she'd expressed sorrow at not having yet been
asked to dance. The old dog Humbert nearly leaped for joy.
Halit Ayarcı threw his arm around my aunt's waist, who toppled enough personal effects to fill a suitcase onto my lap before
letting him sweep her away. Halit Bey had managed to smooth
things over without giving me even half a chance to convey my
anger.

I drained my glass of champagne and, with her shawl, fan,
and operetta binoculars in my arms, went off to listen to my
older sister-in-law sing, or rather bellow at the top of her lungs,
in the second drawing room.

Ye Gods, what a display of steely self-confidence! What unearthly screeching! And how very pleased she was with the
noise she made. The more she wailed, the more hysterical the
crowd became. On catching sight of me, the histrionics rose to
new heights. Prancing about the room in her purple gown, she
seemed even fatter and uglier than ever, yet somehow oddly
charming as she teetered over the audience in her high heels—
no doubt a consequence of her corset's grip on her great
frame—snapping her fingers as she sang. Finishing the song,
she left not a moment to relish the applause and launched
directly into a *semaiye*, a solemn dance number she'd still not

mastered despite many years of effort. Like a fine piece of Indian cloth in the hands of an ordinary tailor, the poor *semaiye* was filleted before my very eyes. This wanton display was applauded by her admirers with equal enthusiasm. And because I had handed over my aunt's personal effects to Ekrem Bey, who happened to be standing beside me, I too could contribute to the applause. After the *semaiye*, she massacred one of Dede Efendi's more beautiful compositions. An entire battalion couldn't have done worse. But the applause continued unabated. Then she began a rather mournful *maya*. But this was no longer music! It was like listening to the ululations of a pack of hungry wolves. As a soldier on Satan's Mountain, I'd listened to both—the *maya* songs of that region and the howling of its wolves. The *maya* folk songs gave the soldiers in my company a way to converse with the stars. As their manly voices were overwhelmed with grief, nature itself was rejuvenated. But when my sister-in-law sang the selfsame songs, they brought the grief back home. It was as if the party had become some kind of wake. This was probably why she quickly left the *maya* for a livelier dance number. She seemed to know no limits. Most of the dancers were now clustered around her. They were clapping. I stood there, open mouthed, watching my sister-in-law invigorate the crowd that was seething around her; forgetting Van Humbert and even myself, I let my mind wander back to that first encounter with Halit Ayarcı in Büyükdere. Toward the middle of the dance number, a young woman no longer able to hold herself back began belly dancing—except she didn't know how. But what difference did that make? Everyone was happy. Soon she was joined by a middle-aged man who was no doubt her husband or lover and who couldn't bear to leave her unattended.

Slowly I pushed my way through the crowd. I left with the intention of finding my wife and our dear guest. But to my surprise, I discovered a new scene unfolding around the jazz group in the other room. And once again our family had taken the lead. In the middle of the room I saw my younger sister-in-law dancing frantically with a young American. Better put, the torture and cruelty they were inflicting on each other in the name of dance knew no limits. She'd taken off her shoes and socks—didn't she think she was short enough already?—and with one hand in her partner's and the other holding up her skirt, she was bouncing up and down furiously on the varnished floor (the carpets had been pushed aside). And now she had collapsed on the floor, but before I could race to her rescue, she bounced back up to her feet, threw her arms around her chaperone, thrust her belly about in the most bizarre manner, and thrashed an invisible enemy with her head before throwing herself to the floor again.

Oh, my oh my. What heedlessness on my part! And I thought I knew my wife's family. Oh, these miserable creatures were nearly bursting with their imprisoned talents! And how little I knew my wife! I might as well have been blind. The poor woman was foolish and absentminded because she'd lived such a constrained life. Wasn't it just the same for everyone? The city's most renowned jazz group struggled to keep pace with my younger sister-in-law. It seemed like the drummer had nine hands, but no matter how frenzied his handwork he still lagged behind. In the other room, my older sister-in law had half the city gathered around her and was leading a wild hora dance from the Black Sea. Suddenly my wife had become the world's most gracious hostess: I'd had no idea she could converse with a man with such aplomb.

My aunt gestured to me from across the room, and with tremendous difficulty I made my way over to her through the crowd. In her old ghostlike voice, she said:

"You silly man, you've seen your sister-in-law? Now that's what I call a human being! And your wife! Shame on you indeed!"

"Yes, you're right, Auntie. How could I have married anyone better?"

"Come now, you weasel. Just admit that you have good luck. If you'd had a real choice in the matter, who knows what kind of miserable creature you might have married."

"My wife, well, yes, all right, then. But what about my daughter? How do you find her?"

She stared at me.

"If God doesn't grant me the opportunity to spend all my money before I croak, I swear I'll leave what's left to her! You understand?"

Halit Ayarcı came over to us and said:

"I just looked in on Dr. Ramiz. He's sleeping like a baby."

"Is he alone?" I asked.

"Oh no," he replied. "He's with his chosen one. Everything's going well. Let's go have a drink!"

We went back to the bar. But no one was there. Still, we managed to find a server who opened a bottle for us. To the detriment of my daughter's inheritance, my aunt ordered a caviar sandwich. No fortune could keep pace with such extravagance. "She'll crawl back to us and expire in my arms," I mumbled to myself. Turning to Halit Ayarcı, I asked:

"Do you think those jewels are real?"

"Of course, but those aren't the important ones," he said. "They are in the bank. It's an incredible fortune really, but don't worry. It won't be too easy for her to go through it so quickly."

Then he changed the subject.

"You managed it all quite well really."

I suddenly lost my head.

"Why didn't you warn me?" I cried. "Am I forever to be forced into situations not of my own making?"

He looked at me, smiling.

"My dear friend," he said. "My poor dear friend! But really I should say poor me! For I am in fact the one to be pitied in this affair. I have just now managed to find a way to express my good intentions. You should have come to understand at least some of this by now. There's no one here forcing you to play a role. And there are no faits accomplis. There is only a man who respects you and who believes in you. I only want you to accept my dreams as second nature. If I were to inform you in advance, I would infringe on your personal freedom. Only then would you indeed be playing a part. But when the evening began, you had no more idea of what might happen, in much the same way that you don't know whom you might bump into when you head out into the street. So you came tonight not knowing quite what to expect, and we have lived through all this together. There's nothing forced about it."

"But I might have put a foot wrong, and everything would have been ruined."

He let out a laugh.

"And, so what if you had? In such circumstances there's no such thing as a mistake. Don't forget that! Imagine that indeed you had committed an error! We'd simply shift from there toward the truth. Mistakes only exist for those foolish enough to try to fix them. But we are different! Once we have accepted an error, we rise above it. But, no, Hayri Bey, oh no, there's no such thing as a mistake and there never will be. It's all a matter of solid preparation and faith in man's potential. I am well aware of your powers, for I was the one who discovered you!"

What did he mean by that?

He refilled our glasses and downed his in one gulp.

"Managing people is incredibly difficult and it takes time. The important thing is to set the stage. Humans then live what they have been given. The trick is to give humankind a chance to be creative. I don't like the theater. I am a man who likes life to unfold naturally!"

"Didn't you tell anyone here what they were to do tonight?"

"Of course I may have made a few hints to a few. You were sleeping. Then Van Humbert came, so I simply said that you were in a conference and would be coming along soon. The rest happened all on its own. Look, if there's anything that's difficult in all this, it's choosing the right people. And there you're absolutely right—I always pick a good team!"

"No, if nothing else, you were wrong in choosing me, because I don't believe in what we're doing. You know this all too well. And I'm suffering for it."

"That's all the better! This is precisely why every step you take, every move you make, is a success. Instead of behaving like all the others—like automatons—you live your life like a man made of flesh and blood!"

At this point Pakize came in alone.

"Where's our guest, then?" I asked.

"With Zehra. I left him in her hands. She's teaching him how to dance the *zeybek*. I'll just have a drink, and then we'll go and watch!"

Refreshed drinks in hand, we went off to do just that. Now, this was a spectacle beyond anyone's wildest dreams. It was nature stripped bare. The jazz group had struck up a feverish *zeybek*. And in the middle of the room, where my sister-in-law had just been displaying her talents, my daughter and Van Humbert were performing the strangest and most unfathomable *zeybek* I had ever seen. All around them were wide-eyed with shock. And for a while we watched Van Humbert's arms dangling awkwardly in the air as he bent down on one knee and struggled to his feet again.

Halit Ayarcı whispered softly into my ear:

"Now this is something else."

I was the chairman of the most spectacular family in the world. With this thought in mind, I nudged my wife, getting even with her for her flirtatious elbow jabs earlier.

Then Halit Ayarcı added:

"What do you think? Does it meet your approval? Set aside paternal pride—aren't you astounded by the success of our women? Did you ever even dream of witnessing such a scene?"

With one eye fixed on the obscene and dangerous contortions that my daughter had forced on Van Humbert's large and shockingly clumsy body, I said:

"How could I have imagined this? Not ever in my wildest dreams. And my own daughter . . ."

"You're right. Such rapid progress is quite unprecedented."

"If only they were just a little more aware of what they're doing. If, for example, my daughter actually knew the steps to this dance, and if my sister-in-law had the faintest idea of what she was just doing, thrashing around on that dance floor, and if the older one didn't go after musical compositions as if she were smashing a chandelier with a chair . . ."

In the politest way possible Halit Ayarcı yawned.

"The same old story. Rather, the same old stories! My dear friend, you are an incurable malcontent. Knowledge is secondary in such matters. Action, action, and action alone!" Then, as if talking to himself, he added:

"Knowledge holds us back. Indeed it offers neither an end nor an aim. The main thing is to do, to create. If only they knew, if only they knew . . . But if they knew, they wouldn't be doing it. They'd never achieve the same innovation, the same excitement at spontaneous discovery. Knowledge would stifle it all. Your daughter has made the evening. With what? With her ability to create. For creation is life. We are living individuals. We are people who choose life. You can scowl at us all you like!"

"I'm not scowling. I'm simply speaking my mind."

"Keep your thoughts to yourself, and feast your eyes on this magnificent spectacle!"

It was indeed a wonderful sight to behold. Van Humbert was now dancing without my daughter's assistance. Executing one outrageous twirl after another, he rose up from the floor only to fall once more. The applause was thunderous.

"Look, my dear friend, study that man's willpower! What effort, such a life force—it's the very joy of living! What is knowledge in the face of such power?"

Then he leaned over and whispered into my ear:

"Yes, my dear friend, that's how I would like to see you."

For a moment I imagined myself in our guest's position.

"Oh, please have mercy!" I groaned. "Next you'll send me to the insane asylum?"

Halit Ayarcı graced me with a delicate smile.

"What a strange idea you have of an insane asylum, sir," he said. "You would send every one of us there, with of course yours truly at the top of the list. But, then again, there is nothing I've done that you haven't participated in!"

I'd offended him. Although I had no desire to bring a sour end to an evening that had begun so brilliantly, there was no turning back.

"You were fully aware of the state I was in when you first met me!" I replied.

"Yes I was. Indeed you never concealed it from me. That's just the way you are—everything is out in the open. The truth is this, my dear friend, no sooner had you settled into your

comfortable new life than your former life comes back to haunt
you. And you find it unnecessary, even extravagant, to think of
letting go!"

"No, I just miss my old self."

"Then go back to it! If you are longing for it, then go back!"
Then his voice suddenly changed.

"But you can't. You just did the calculations. I read what was
going through your mind a few minutes ago: 'I've made peace
with my aunt and things are working out well. Why should I
walk away from it all?' That's what you just told yourself, am I
right? But then you relinquished the idea. You're afraid of the
future!"

He had read my mind perfectly. He placed his hand on my
shoulder and led me into the inner drawing room. People watching us would have assumed we were merrily chatting away.

"Let me tell you your version of the truth. You can't turn
back now because you aren't willing to give anything up.
Despite all your criticism and self-deprecation, you have a
beautiful, forward-thinking wife and a mistress with whom
you are madly in love. And I'm quite sure that you would make
any sacrifice for the welfare of your daughter and son. What's
more, you enjoy notoriety, and you like being busy, even if it
means being engaged in work you dismiss as absurd. At the end
of the day, you're an octopus, with your eight arms wrapped
around the world! And you can't release your hold on anything. How could you ever go back?"

"I don't want to go back," I said. "I just want a more reasonable . . ."

He laughed again.

"Reasonable! Reasonable!" he said, shaking his head. "No,
you're not looking for reason. You're not such a fool. If indeed
you are of the belief that reason operates on its own, well, then
that's different. But, no, you're after something else."

"I'm after the truth. Or rather I want it, or at least a
piece of it."

"Truth is either whole or not there at all. My good friend,
these unassailable truths you're speaking of are there for one
who is content to live with nothing but the shirt on his back

and the odd piece of bread. They are not for someone like you, who wants it all and straightaway! An individual who is pure and complete seeks first of all to meet his own needs."

With one stroke he had thrown me out of myself.

"But I really don't want that much," I said.

"So now you're negotiating. But such matters are nonnegotiable! At this table the man who wins one and the man who wins a thousand will always bet on the very same thing and play till nothing's left. You might chance upon a win, but when you lose, you lose it all, and forever. Once you've entered the game, you have lost. Bargaining with virtue gets you nowhere. This is why our forbears accepted human nature the way it was. You know the old adage: 'Words are clear but man's nature is . . .'"

Then he darted to the drinks table and filled two glasses. The bogus and outlandishly adorned Blessed One seemed to peer across the room in awe.

"In this world no account, no attachment comes free. They all require the same sacrifice. And there is but one step between the absurd and the sublime. Are you up for the task or will you fold?"

I thought for a moment.

"No," I said. "I know I won't. But why are you speaking like this?"

Halit Ayarcı refilled his glass. With a delighted look in his eyes, he glanced first at his glass, then the Blessed One, and then at me.

"I don't know," he said. "Perhaps I'm drunk. Perhaps I am just trying to settle the score with myself. The best thing, of course, is to rise above the matter altogether."

"No," I said. "You're not settling accounts with yourself. You're still trying to break down something inside me. And you're even doing it brick by brick! But why?"

"I'll tell you: Because we've both traveled down the same roads. I am very fond of you, but I'm also at war with you. You remind me very much of myself. Oh no, now don't flatter yourself too much here! I was never like you. I was never confused and downtrodden. But there's a side to you that . . ."

And his laugh was like crystal.

"Have you ever in your life laughed like that?" he asked. "Your soul has never been as pure as mine because I have always remained above and beyond all these matters."

Then suddenly he embraced me.

"But you have taught me to love life!" he cried. "The state you were in when you whiled away your time in that coffee-house in Şehzadebaşı: that ridiculous despair, your hopeless grief, those burdens you could never shake off . . . Your astonishment at the restaurant at Büyükdere, your timidity, your flights of happiness . . . That world in which you lived, small as an olive pit, all of this taught me to love life again. Had I done no more than pass a discreet five-lira note into the palm of your hand that night—how happy you would have been! Yes, you made me love life again. You are a most wonderful foil!"

My face went bright red with shame.

"I wish you'd done just that!" I said, wrenching myself free of his embrace.

"Now, what a ridiculous thing to say," he said.

He smiled again and raised his glass.

"Be as you like, then," he said. "In any event I never wanted to change you altogether! If that were the case, then we would no longer need each other. It's just that you needed mild alterations here and there. At least that way you won't disturb those around you, who are simply living out their lives!"

I paused for a moment. I was lost in doubt.

"You don't believe in anything do you?" I asked.

He took a sip from his glass and then wiped his forehead with the handkerchief he'd taken out of his vest pocket:

"Enough already," he said. "Look, our friends are coming this way. Long live the Time Regulation Institute! Long live the TRI!"

And with this toast, he saluted my entire family, including my aunt, who had taken Van Humbert by the arm.

Van Humbert's delight knew no bounds. You'd think he'd just won a great victory. He congratulated me on my wife and my daughter and invited both of them to Holland. He said he would teach them how to ride a bicycle.

"Here we all ride the carousel together," I said.

Halit Ayarcı looked at me reproachfully. It was clear something had changed between us.

Van Humbert stayed in Istanbul for one month. It would take far too much time for me to explain all the adventures we shared together, but allow me say just this: he left us quite pleased. Years later he described his visit to Istanbul in a series of articles. He never forgot his *zeybek* with my daughter, or Halit Ayarcı's kind attention, or the yogurt kebab we feasted upon in Çamlıca on the day we visited the tomb of Ahmet the Timely.

I'd thought this man to be thoroughly pleased with me, and so it was a shock to see him turn against me. I can only think of the old saying, "A fallen man has no friends," which was first uttered many years before my encounter with Van Humbert. And so I harbor no anger against him, nor dreams of vengeance. I just think it would have been so much better if he'd never come at all. But let's not forget: Van Humbert suffered dearly for his involvement with us. In particular there was his book on ancient Turkic folklore; he'd based it on information gathered from my wife and my older sister-in-law, and it was savaged by the critics. Yet in his subsequent articles he continued to speak fondly of me. He concluded one with this sentence: "Hayri İrdal and his family know all too well how to reach a man's inner essence. No matter what may happen between us, I'll never forget the time I spent with them during my visit to Istanbul. As happy as they might be with the carousel, if they ever come to Holland, I shall keep my promise and teach them all how to ride a bicycle."

PART IV

EVERY SEASON
HAS AN END

I

Halit Ayarcı's prediction came true. Within just a few months of my aunt's cocktail party, we had received telegraphs from several agencies informing us that independent chapters of the Clock Lover's Society had been established in six South American cities. It was not long before those groups were in direct communication with our own Clock Lover's Society, requesting information on our charter, official rules, and regulations. Similar requests came in from all parts of the Middle and Far East, as well as from several countries in Europe. In the space of just two and a half years, three institutes and more than thirty Clock Lover's Societies were established abroad. It was strange to see how, in countries ill disposed to such institutes, the authorities felt compelled to supply the public with clear and concise reasons for their opposition. In almost all cases the announcement was in fact the same: "Our industries are developed to a degree as to preclude the need for such an institute."

And so it was that—whether or not they had an institute—all countries were united in viewing it as a necessity. Following each official telegraph to this effect, Halit Ayarcı organized a press conference at which he again emphasized our institute's importance. When he was occupied elsewhere, the task fell to me. My aunt, meanwhile, became a storm of industry. She did not miss a single one of the International Clock Lover's Society's frequent congresses. For a time, she kept her packed suitcase ready in her bedroom, only to decide that it would be easiest to simply leave it ready in the entrance hall. On most of these trips abroad she was accompanied by my daughter and also (on occasion) her husband. When passing through customs in Istanbul, she was among those who could count on being recognized. She renewed her passport every year without fail. In addition to the ornamental treasures and jewels left to her by the street sweeper's trade guild, she was awarded medals by seven or eight foreign powers. Meanwhile we were just as busy. With the capital raised from our twofold penalty system, we constructed our new building on Freedom Hill, and, in partnership with the cooperative established with support from Timely Banks, which received generous aid from the International Time Trust, we brought into being a unique residential development for our personnel, which came to be known as the Clock Houses.

Aside from the aforementioned cash-penalty system, my most notable—or, rather, most taxing—contribution to the institute was its new building. Though our cash-penalty system attracted a great deal of notice, it was, in my estimation, nothing next to the attention accorded to the erection of our new building. It was this edifice that led to my election as honorary member to the International Society of Architects, but in the beginning I had very little to do with it. As with all other affairs of this genre, we opted for an open competition. After I had composed the rules for this competition, Halit Ayarcı insisted on adding the following requirement: "an original and new style in harmony with modern-day realities and the institute's name." Perhaps out of anger—or perhaps because I wanted to ridicule him—I made a slight change to the last part of his (in my view entirely unnecessary, but in the view of Halit Ayarcı all-important) addendum: "and in a manner that embodies its name inside and out."

This final condition—that the building should comply with its name, both inside and out—was what kept me working on the project for many a long month.

When the competition rules and regulations were published in the papers, they were generally accepted as reasonable. We are cursory readers at best. And, sadly, our overuse of terms like "modern-day realities," "harmony," and "inside and out" has led to their becoming worn phrases stretched way beyond their original shape. Thus the competition entries were nothing more than designs for commonplace buildings with a few stock innovations. It was a surprise to us all that a man like Halit Ayarcı would cling to his words till the end, refusing all others the chance to interpret their meaning. Yet he rejected every last entrant, and each time he justified his decision by referring to the clause that I had included out of obstinacy and a taste for irony, saying that the proposal in question did not comply with the idea inside and out.

"What part of this facade resembles a clock?"

That was his first question. And the second came right on its heels:

"And in what way did you express the essence of timepieces, or of time and regulation, in the building's interior?"

The architects who had entered the competition were unable to answer these questions to his satisfaction, and so they were asked to leave. Never before, and not even during the days of liquidation, had so many pieces critical of the institute appeared in the press. These architects would storm out the front door, with their blueprints stuffed under their arms, and head straight for a newspaper office. Article after article cropped up in the daily papers. We were quick to jump to action and rebut the charges. Halit Ayarcı held one press conference after another, and the message was always this: "Modern man does not engage in idle talk. We shall not tolerate ambiguity. We shall respect the rules and regulations of our competition in their entirety."

A number of those entering the second competition did warm to the idea of a building that reflected the clock theme both inside and out, but still the architects limited themselves to rectangular buildings. Almost to a man, their prospective structures suggested alarm clocks or grandfather clocks, using either additional ornamentation or a narrow foundation with extra floors. Some went further and arranged their second- and third-floor facades to suggest the face of a large clock. Such conceits called for the concentration of windows in the middle of a largish circle. Halit Ayarcı took a dim view these proposals too. To some he said:

"Such ornaments can be tacked onto any building. What's

modern about these designs? I see nothing modern here and nothing pertaining to clocks."

Other proposals he rejected by saying:

"These are all fine as far as they go, but what happens when we have to renovate? Will we be obliged to remove the clock-face altogether? The windows will draw our eyes to the regularity of the floors, and what will be left of our clock?"

Naturally the answers varied. A building could never actually be a clock. A clock has a particular face and a structure all its own. In this sense it already resembles a building. In the face of opposition Halit Ayarcı would either tap on the relevant sentence in the competition rules, which he had written out in block letters and placed under the glass on his desk, or he'd have applicants write out the sentence themselves before pointing to a panel on the opposite wall that read, "Inside and out."

One applicant took the idea further still by making the windows that looked onto the second- and third-floors light shafts resemble clockfaces. And what's more, his design set the entire building to rest atop four substantial pillars. But Halit Ayarcı rejected this one too.

"All too forced! A window's a window. But this isn't a window at all! If I simply rubbed off the designs on the sides, it would look just like Gothic stained-glass. No, we're looking for something else. We want the concept of a timepiece to be embodied in the very structure of the building. They should be as one! We don't want motifs soldered on. We want to see our programs and goals manifested in the building itself."

It was these very words (I must confess) that alerted me to the central problem. "If the concept of a timepiece merges with a building's structure," I thought, "then that building loses its identity as a building." And I nearly burst out laughing, out of pity for my poor friend. But the following morning I arrived at the following conclusion unassisted: "A building that has renounced its very essence as a building, and in so doing denies a building's fundamental principles, should be quite capable of planting the concept of time within man!" I shared my idea with the first architect I met that day. Unprepared as I was, I was unable to furnish an explanation worthy of the idea. Yet this conversation left me with the idea of "mass." "I can make this happen," I thought, "if I can liken a building to a clock in such a way as to annihilate the concept of mass."

It was one of those nights when Ahmet happened to be at home; a quiet dissenter in all things pertaining to the Time Regulation Institute, he usually only came to see us on holidays. We discussed my dilemma. He supported the architect's opinion: "Before it can be anything else, a structure is by its very nature a mass." The following day I dismantled a clock and then reassembled it. No, it was impossible. This wasn't the way to make it work. Perhaps I could make use of its internal structure, but I would still have to do something about the exterior. Halit Ayarcı didn't like the idea of designing the entire facade in the shape of a clockface. So I'd have to come up with something else.

Meanwhile I stayed in regular contact with Halit Ayarcı; I pleaded with him to save himself and the institute from so much pain and suffering, assuring him that just about any structure would fully suit our needs. But he was adamant.

"Until now the Time Regulation Institute has done everything it has promised to do," he said. "Indeed neither city clocks nor personal timepieces function with due timeliness. But our people have now acquired the habit of checking and resetting their timepieces, and though we might not have brought timepieces to the villages, we have at least instilled in their inhabitants a taste for them. There are today a million village children wearing toy watches that we ourselves sold them! What this means is that when they grow up they'll all buy watches, with the help of the easy watch-exchange plans made possible by our Timely Banks. And if such toys are fundamentally useless, well, at the very least they are property their owners can pawn, or sell for a nominal amount, if they fall on hard times. We've produced women's watches in the form of delightful bracelets. And we have applied the same concept to the entire range of costume jewelry. May I draw your attention again to our garter belts adorned with miniature clocks, which are enjoying worldwide success? You may recall that you were very much opposed to these, saying they'd only be of use in music halls, whereas thousands of ladies in Istanbul wear these garter-belt watches today. A belle dame can lift her skirt in the most elegant way possible, to check the time as she strolls down a busy boulevard. But that is not all: remember that the International Clock Lover's Society has now approved my proposal to have a number of state awards marked with timepieces. This has sparked a tremendous promotional surge. Following on from this—and thanks also to your lecture at the last congress— there is renewed international interest in Mahmud II, he who presented golden watches to all those he dearly loved and appreciated. Books upon books are being written about this man. Why should I back down in the face of all this success? We may not have established a watch and clock industry yet, but we have expedited the adoption of new regulations that should make it easier to import timepieces. The country's finest timepiece emporia operate under our corporate umbrella! How can a functioning, and indeed thriving, institute go back on its word? What right does it have to do so? Why should I accept the doom and gloom of naysayers? And all this aside, why would I ever portray myself as vanquished or in the wrong? I am not in the wrong! I set but one condition, and those who can abide by it will do so."

"That's wonderful, sir, just wonderful, but as you see, they simply can't do it. It's just too difficult to realize."

"But it must be done!"

Deaf to his words, I pressed on:

"And anyway this isn't your fault! I was the one who added this 'inside and out' clause to the rules and regulations. I am only human, and I was angry with you because you were so insistent on the matter! Backing down here really doesn't count as a defeat!"

I felt my face flush crimson. I lowered my head and waited for his answer. Halit Ayarcı smiled softly, or, really, it was as if his voice were smiling as he spoke.

"I know," he said. "I'm aware of this. I'd like to thank you for saying it. But I'm going to thank you for something else as well. And that is for your flawed ideas in regard to such matters, or rather for your churlish disposition, which has forced these ideas upon you. Thanks to all this, we shall soon have a truly original building! I am a man made for results, not intentions. You did well in adding those words! Now we must remain steadfast. Don't forget that the International Congress will take place here, in April next year. I want to host this congress in our new building. But others have already taken the idea from us and surpassed us in our own field. If nothing else, let us create a building whose originality establishes us as leaders in our realm."

Ahmet Zamanı's April birthday had become the official International Time Day, as a matter of course. Our congresses were held every year on that date.

"All right," I said. "But how can we achieve such a thing? However will we integrate a clock into the body—I mean, the building's structure?"

He took his head in his hands.

"I don't know," he said. "Even I haven't the slightest idea. We'll leave it to the architects. They have to come up with a solution. Actually, the job falls to you. As it was you who added the condition, it should be you who comes up with the solution!"

He rose to his feet. He fixed his eyes on mine, and in his most serious tone of voice he slowly gave me his final word on the matter:

"You will have this building built, Hayri Bey. Is that understood? I will have no one else. You owe me this one—it's personal!"

And so that's how it happened. But only I know just how difficult it all was. The reason being that from the very beginning I was stuck on the idea of a pocket watch. Isn't it often the case that most of the difficulties we face in our lives come from our stubborn embrace of the first idea that comes into our minds?

Though I had spent my entire life in the company of timepieces, I have always been most fascinated by the pocket watch, and this must be why I had been searching for the secret of the building in such a form. First I imagined a round building very much like a pocket watch, with twelve pavilions, representing the twelve different hours of the day, circling this hall. But once

I'd tried to work out the idea on paper, I came to see it was impossible. Then I began thinking about how the watch might stand vertically. Stairs would provide access to a solid structure resembling a fat, swollen pocket watch mounted on four block pillars. Naturally the watch would have to have faces on both the front and the back, and windows would run down the sides of the building. So on each face of the building would be giant hands indicating the time, and in the middle of the facade would be a large door, accessed by stairs running up through one of the structural pillars.

But I had to give up on this idea as well, for Pakize was much too fond of it. I must admit that Pakize's taste had become a sort of gauge for me. I had begun to question everything for which she expressed interest or enthusiasm. And, truth be told, the final idea did in a way come from Pakize. When I told her about my first idea, she responded with her usual carefree smile:

"I already know about it. Last night I had a lamb sacrificed for the Blessed One. Its spiritual powers have come to our aid."

Initially I was taken off guard.

"Which Blessed One?" I asked. "What are you talking about?"

She calmly replied:

"Ah, my dear husband, you know—the Blessed One! Our prophet of a clock. You know it's in your aunt's house now! The one who comes to us in our hour of need!"

At first I thought I'd strangle her in a fit of rage, but then I suddenly embraced her. She had reminded me that the building didn't have to be constructed in the shape of a round timepiece, that the world had timepieces of all shapes and sizes—that the building could easily take on a rectangular shape, like any other building worthy of its name.

"My dear wife," I said. "I owe every success in my life to you. And now, thanks to your intercession, the Blessed One has come to our rescue. How can I express my gratitude?"

In fact it wasn't at all difficult to design a long rectangular space in the shape of a grandfather clock. There was nothing we had to do, save place structures representing the hours of the day along the sides of the courtyard. The central hall would no longer be harnessed to the startling and indeed impossible height of my initial idea of the pocket watch. At the top of the courtyard would be a round, clock-shaped construction representing twelve o'clock. Then four small pavilions on each side would lead down along the courtyard to the pavilion representing six o'clock, which would have three floors. It would really be quite easy to suspend walkways above the strips of lawn between the pavilions. The large central hall would be enclosed in glass. And on the face of each pavilion a Roman numeral would be displayed, from one to twelve, moving, from right to left, in a large ring, just as it would be on a clock. In the end I decided that instead of using the number twelve, I would make the front-gate pavilion, occupying that numeral's position, slightly larger than the others. To be sure to give the impression of a clock, I designed the front gate to resemble a dial. That said, my efforts to give a six-meter gate the appearance of a dial were truly exasperating. I would achieve nothing by putting yet more numerals along the sides of a normal rectangular shape. I needed a new idea. To this end I traveled as far afield as Bursa and Konya. And I visited all the mosques in Istanbul, looking closely at the many shapes of their doors, but they offered me nothing in return. Though all were beautifully crafted rectangles, they couldn't help me with my problem. Then one night the idea came to me when I spied a curtain hanging in the door to one of the smaller mosques in Istanbul: I would use curtains to represent the hour and minute hands! After this it was simply a question of deciding what time I wanted these curtains to indicate over the top of the entrance. It was easy to manage such details once I could envisage a door with two curtains pulled halfway open, like wings.

It was summer. As usual Ahmet wanted to spend his vacation at a summer school. But at my insistence he agreed to stay at home to help me. He knew that I was under pressure, but it was also the sort of project that appealed to him. After seeing me struggling for hours on end, he didn't have the heart to leave me stranded, even though he didn't quite understand what I was up to—or perhaps simply found it too absurd for words. For the first time since Emine's death, I felt truly happy. My son had not just forgiven me—he had undertaken to help me. I was overjoyed to have him working by my side, giving deep consideration to each and every possibility, and wrestling with matters that had no bearing on his life, just for the challenge. It was a true representation of the virtue we know as hard work.

Work makes us pure and beautiful; it is our bond with the outside world and makes us who we are. But work can also take possession of our souls. No matter how meaningless and absurd the job, we unwittingly become its prisoner: from the moment we accept responsibility for its proper execution we can never escape its grip. Herein lies the greatest secret of man's fate and indeed the history of mankind.

In our first father-son discussion, we decided that the minute and hour hands shouldn't be positioned at the same height, which would create an overly simplistic and classic symmetry.

So father and son sat together for hours on end, fiddling with watches, searching for the position that would best suit the curtains that would serve to represent the hour and minute hands by the angle at which they hung to either side. We wanted an angle that would seem natural at first glance but also out of the ordinary. A person rushing in would be sufficiently struck by the originality of the design to want to turn around and examine—if only for a moment or two—the large bronze numbers set into the white marble border around the door. If nothing else, he should think, "Oh yes, I really must have a look at that on my way out." We finally decided on forty-two minutes past four. In so doing we cleared the space for a six-meter gate. And then, a meter and a half above the lintel, we fixed two stone curtains at different heights, depending on the time we had selected. The empty space on the left would be slightly higher, but both sides, even the point closest to the stone curtain's edge, was just high enough for an average person to clear. To give a clearer indication of the hour and minute hands, we would place two thick, straight rods of engraved copper, or perhaps a copper-steel amalgam, in the folds of the stone curtains. A large pendulum would hang above the point where the curtains parted. This too would be forged of metal and sturdily affixed; as it swayed back and forth, it would represent the idea of regulation. And the awning

over the door would create enough shade to bring out the rich-
ness of the green lintel, the white marble, and the burnished
copper. Or so Ahmet thought.

By the time we had agreed on all these details it was mid-
night. It was not without trepidation that I asked my son:

"Do you realize what time it is?"

"No, I don't," he replied. "What's so important about it?"

"It's the hour of your birth . . ."

Suddenly he blushed and smiled. It was clear that he was
pleased. But then he furrowed his brow and looked down at his
feet. I understood from this that he was afraid I might be hurt
by what he had to say, but he couldn't keep quiet for very long.

"Father," he said. "There's no need to be overly sentimental.
We're not yet at the point where we'd give up on each other
over a difference in opinion. And I speak for all of us. But I do
feel much more comfortable with how we are now."

Perhaps it was the fear I felt hearing these words that led me
to ask what was missing in the design. What was I going to do
with this 720 square-meter central hall? All night I racked my
brains. Toward dawn I hit upon the idea of dividing the
space with a balustrade like the one from the cemetery of
the Kahvecibaşı Mosque that I still kept at home—then at least
the hall would not seem quite so vast on first seeing it. But this
wasn't enough. I needed something else to break up the space. I
was flipping through one of the architecture magazines that
Ahmet had borrowed from his classmates, when I chanced upon
a few pictures that suggested the perfect solution. Halfway
along the balustrade I would erect four large columns—as large
as those enormous funnels that one saw on oil tankers facing
north, east, south and west. But the hall's glass roof had no
need of such pillars. Then came my moment of sublime inspiration. If we had to have pillars, then we would also have to have
a second floor. A second floor would appear to reflect the Time
Regulation Institute's very essence. We had founded the institute to generate employment for ourselves, and now, having
created pillars to soften the look of the vast hall, we would give
those pillars a purpose. In the early hours of the morning I
was struck by the idea that allowed me to perfect the hall's

composition. The four pillars would stand in a row with a passageway running through them. To go from the right to the left side of the hall, you would pass first through the door in the Morning Pillar; then passing through the door in the Afternoon Pillar, you would climb the stairs inside the Evening Pillar; and when you at last descended through the Night Pillar, you found yourself on the other side of the hall. A visitor wishing to cross from the right side of the hall to the left would pass through Night, Evening, and Afternoon before finally exiting through the latticed door of the Morning Pillar.

After consulting Ahmet over breakfast, I was able to crystallize my idea. Ahmet reminded me of the minarets on the Üç Şerefeli Mosque. Everyone knows how the muezzins at Üç Şerefeli walk up three separated sets of stairs without ever seeing one another. Our pillars would achieve the precise opposite.

People moving up and down either wrought-copper staircase would be visible, as they would be encased in glass. I now saw I could arrange them diagonally across the center of the hall to disrupt the traditional four leaf clover formation. Of course all the pillars—each one a little higher than the next—would be connected by little bridges so as to allow those moving up and down them to cross.

So far so good. But I still felt uneasy about the upper-floor lounge. Far from solving our original problem, the pillars and the balustrade had resulted in our transferring it to the upper floor. Once again past experience, or really something I had picked up from all those newspapers I'd read out of boredom in the coffeehouse during the years I was unemployed, came to my rescue. Rather than create another hall, why not a roof garden of the type seen on skyscrapers? After settling on the garden, I realized I could illuminate the hall with natural light by putting a glass roof over the top of the columns and running two long, thick panes of glass along the full length of the courtyard. True, we would already have ample gardens around the building and most skyscraper gardens are on the thirtieth floor and higher, but at least our friends would be able to see a few flowers when they took a break from work, and if nothing else second-floor windows overlooking the courtyard would let in some natural light. I decided to landscape the garden in the shape of a clock, just as I had done with the garden at the front gate and the one located at the six o'clock pavilion. There would be just one difference—the roof garden would be adorned with a bust of Ahmet Zamanı. Thus our hall would be a fusion of both the traditional and the modern. Indeed this hall went on to become our crowning achievement.

I determined that only four of our pavilions would have more than one floor. The front pavilion with its large gate represented twelve o'clock, while its two neighboring pavilions, representing one and eleven o'clock, respectively, would have two floors each. Then I envisioned the twelve o'clock pavilion's counterpart, the six o'clock pavilion, with three floors. I left the first floor of this pavilion open and undivided, just one large room graced by two broad windows that let in light from both sides. Having designed the second floor as two overlapping circles, I thought it only natural to divide the top floor into separate rooms as in the other pavilions. But instead of designing internal stairs leading from one floor to the next, I arranged for the stairs leading up to the second floor to come from the five o'clock pavilion, with those leading up to the third floor originating from the seven o'clock pavilion. Thus two sets of stairs encased in glass—one relatively shorter than the other, which was less direct—connected the six o'clock pavilion to its neighboring pavilions. And its ground floor was linked directly to the main hall.

In time these rather architecturally redundant innovations—created as an homage to Dr. Mussak, though perhaps I had in mind the allegorical house that my dear friend Dr. Ramiz had used to explain the workings of the human mind and its subconscious when I was undergoing psychoanalysis—became as celebrated as the pillars I'd designed for the main hall; and as I mentioned earlier I was made an honorary member of the International Society of Architects and was even awarded some of its medals, and if my memory serves me, I was in fact awarded medals from two different foreign governments.

Needless to say, the first floor of the six o'clock pavilion was to be our conference room. And the smaller rooms of overlapping circles on the floor above would be used for smaller meetings. The top floor was reserved for Sabriye Hanım, as a tribute to her complex involvement with the public. Indeed there was no other way to free ourselves of our friend's relentless curiosity or her determination to subject all our affairs to needless scrutiny.

It should come as no surprise that I designed the overlapping circular rooms on the second floor to represent a clock's inner wheels and cogs. I also designed the large round room in the four o'clock pavilion to suggest the minute hand on the face of a clock. So in the end I paid the full price for my addendum of the words "inside and out" to the competition conditions—this despite the fact that I had added these words only to challenge Halit Ayarcı and force him into an awkward situation, only to be forced to invent a compendium of absurd architectural innovations to suggest the inside and outside of a clock.

The only good thing that came out of all this was the time I got to spend with my son, Ahmet. I had truly missed having my son in my life. And so I was sad as our collaboration came to a close. We were destined to live apart. Ahmet loved me dearly but detested the way I lived and the work I was doing. We spent our last night together in front of the strange models we'd constructed out of hundreds of matchboxes, thinking of Dr. Mussak. We were making the final changes.

As my son teased me about the building and its pillars and stairs, I looked at his eyes, which were dark like grapes, and his thin lips and his stubble of a mustache slowly altering his face. I thought of all the things that made him so different, this fragile little man who was a part of me, who helped me as a friend, yet never fully opened himself up to me as he glided over so many of his thoughts. It did not upset me in the least that he didn't take after me, that in his mind he rejected me. I harbored no resentment. I knew that his only salvation was in being unlike me, and that was fine by me. Indeed it even made me happy. But I wondered where he found his strength. Here was the last man in the line of Ahmet Efendi the Some Timer—what had driven him to this point? I was, nevertheless, truly surprised to find no anger or hatred between us. I took this to mean that my son had not just overcome close family ties and the comforts that came with our new wealth and prosperity but that he had also taken on a far more difficult challenge: he had overcome himself.

Suddenly my mind went back to the years after Emine's death, when Ahmet and Zehra would wait for me on the front stoop every night, fighting tears as they embraced each other in desperation. I felt the tears well up in my eyes. If I'd had the courage, I would have told him everything and asked for his forgiveness. But Ahmet had become that lycée student who, after completing his studies with due seriousness, erases all problems from his mind, and so he left me no opening. At one point, I asked:

"How are you getting on with your sister?"

A beautiful light shone in his eyes.

"I love her very much," he said.

Then his hand rose to his chest and gently tugged on his sweater.

"She knitted this for me."

We fell back into our usual silence. I thought that although my son was right there before me, we had again drifted far apart in our thoughts. With the end of our shared project, the chasm between us reopened. Once again I became a man he would only visit if I was ill or by appointment.

What a terrible thought, and what an impenetrable maze. "Perhaps to become his own person," I told myself, "he has no choice but to forget about me, yet only through him do I feel remotely like the person I should be." Perhaps this was something he'd never understand. He'd guessed that my run of good luck would soon be over, and he was right. But I could only tremble helplessly as I watched his life unfold.

There would always be a chasm between us. Every so often we would extend our hands to each other, only to return to our separate worlds; meanwhile my heart filled with bitterness and his with hope. Such were the poignant thoughts that weighed on me during the night we spent together. When morning came, I would be a different man, as I stuffed the matchboxes into a basket and marched off to work. And perhaps the very next day I'd meet with thundering applause. Halit Ayarcı would have to pay through the nose for the pleasure he'd taken in angling for the upper hand. And that wasn't all. Tomorrow night was my night with Selma. Once in her arms, I'd forget everything. And in two or three weeks' time, I would perhaps sleep with that young girl Sabriye Hanım had offered me as a gift; Sabriye had been holed up in the institute for three months and was keen to cause trouble for Pakize and Selma. This was yet another way to forget, and to change. And just the other day I had quite an interesting talk with Seher Hanım over afternoon prayers. I'd left knowing I'd not be able to neglect that woman any longer. I was doomed, therefore, to sink into the bog of forgetfulness I'd claimed as my own, and to forget. Never again would I experience such joy as I did over the three months I spent working on the clock building.

All this had come of a single event. None of this would have happened had Emine not died. As if hearing my thoughts, my son stood up slowly:

"There's no need to worry," he said. "I'll come visit you more often. I'm strong enough now."

And for the first time he gave me a genuine kiss. He had accepted me for who I was. I watched him as he left the room. And I thought of the girl he might have been in love with then, or perhaps the one he'd fall in love with in the future. I thought about his fate and fortune. Every child breaks with his father at that age. But my child had done so twice. That night, as I lay in bed, I thought of our old, humble home. I kept remembering the geranium that a tiny Ahmet had planted in a broken-rimmed pot that hung from our crumbling bay window. Every now and then I shivered in my bed, but I was pleased to know that I would see him one more time, at breakfast, in the morning.

II

Halit Ayarcı greeted my project with much enthusiasm, or rather he welcomed the strange architectural model made of empty matchboxes I had constructed in accordance with my son's entirely unprofessional designs. With each new detail I explained, his delight rose to new heights. When I finished, he leaped to his feet to offer me his heartfelt congratulations. On several occasions, I reminded him:

"But let's not be too rash! There's still so much to do, and so many flaws in the design. We have twelve large meeting rooms and forty smaller rooms—how shall we ever fill them?"

He wasn't even listening.

"My good friend," he said. "There is no need to disparage your wonderful work. You've done a sterling job. The hardest part is behind you. This central hall has been bothering me for the last two months now. And here you have hit upon a capital solution!"

"But that's not at all what I mean—."

"By now we should no longer need to share all our thoughts— we should understand one another implicitly! We each made the same mistake, basing the building's design on a pocket watch. But then we remembered the Blessed One instead and presto! Everything changed. But you have surpassed me. As for the meeting rooms and offices, there's no need to worry. We each have plenty of relatives and then, of course, there will be the others who come recommended, not to mention the people in the regulation stations who will wish to be promoted. What I'm trying to say is that an empty office or meeting room will find its own function, much in the way that a civil servant's function is guided by his title. And this spot you've set aside for Sabriye Hanım—it couldn't be better. How happy I shall be to see our dear friend perched at the top of the building, in her very own eagle's crag! But we'll think about these things later. Our next step is to arrange a press meeting, to alert the public to your achievement."

Of course a good many of my readers will remember those pictures of me posing before the outlandish and frankly gro-tesque model I had made out of detachable and expandable matchboxes—for why not admit now that the game was up. Even as I was applauded so vigorously for my building and its model, I was being subjected to criticism just as loud: it was perhaps fitting that I became known as something of charlatan, a cross between an amateur genius and a fraudster. But by then I'd become used to such things; those who looked kindly on innovation were enthralled with the novelty of the main hall's four ornamental pillars and the entirely original way in which different stairs ran in and out of the different floors of the six o'clock pavilion. One friend of mine praised me lavishly in the paper almost daily: "Innovation! From top to bottom, unfathomable innovation beyond our wildest dreams! Three cheers for innovation!" Another friend praised us for "our departure from dusty classical forms." And to quote a third commentator, who had earlier heaped me with praise for my unusual staircases and the two unnecessary bridges connecting them to the main building, the ample space left between three pavilions was only to allow for these: "As a new era of Turkish syntax dawns, a new architectural language has been given voice. Let's see what those opposed to inverted syntax will say in the face of Hayri İrdal's resounding success!" The fourth critic was even more ebullient. In his view I had not just designed a building worthy of inverted syntax: I had also created a work of abstract architecture. As for my matchbox model, it had a clear effect on the market. As the new architectural language took root, the state monopoly of matchmakers struggled to keep up with demand. We issued regular statements to the press that only served to add heat to the debate. And when I declared that I'd paint each pavilion a different color, the discussion lit up like a bonfire.

But still professional architects rejected my work out of hand. Such was their opposition that we had difficulty finding anyone willing to oversee construction or do so much as calculate the required amount of reinforced concrete.

As I mentioned earlier, I was very much indebted to Dr. Mussak, be it for his modeling techniques or the matter of my stairs. I'd now like to pay tribute once more to this dear friend of mine, a kindred spirit; indeed I never could understand why he'd not been born in our part of the world. Surely he would congratulate me when the building was finished. He would have been proud to see the way I avenged myself against those who refused to see daydreaming as a virtue. Indeed I felt I was atoning for him, with every round of applause I received. I was more than willing to share with him the bonuses I received from the Timely Banks and the institute for my work on the new building.

So how strange it was, when it came time to begin work on our Clock Houses, and Halit Ayarcı suggested I should draw up the plans for our residential neighborhoods; despite my brilliant success with the institute building, he could not find a single friend, even among those who had formerly admired my work, who thought I was the man for the job. Even our closest friends, who for months had claimed the institute to be the pinnacle of innovation, who had seemed so very pleased with it, who had come, if not every day then at least once or twice a week, to watch the new building go up, these dear friends of mine who had dropped by on the way home to push and shove outside my office door, just to offer me their congratulations—they all protested. The most levelheaded of them cried:

"These are private homes that we'll leave to our children! There's no need for any originality! Just let them be well built, affordable, and safe!"

Some of them went even further, shouting:

"We're not about to experiment with our hard-earned wages. We want a home, not a clever work of art!"

Even Dr. Ramiz, who knew me so very well, was of the same opinion.

"Impossible, my dear friend, impossible!" he ejaculated. "Who knows, you might just place the stairs on the wrong side of the house! It's simply out of the question."

As best I could, I explained to Dr. Ramiz that he himself had been more than a bit responsible for a floor inaccessible by stairs, and that my original inspiration for such a design had in fact been his description of the human mind. But my every attempt brought the answer:

"Don't confuse such things, my dear friend! A house is one thing—science and the subconscious quite another!"

Lazybones Asaf was the only one who kept his opinion to himself. With his fly swatter in hand—it was toward the end of summer and our friend had got in the habit of hunting flies—he sat through three meetings without understanding much at all, but during the fourth he came over to me and whispered:

"My dear friend Hayri, it's best you just drop it. There's a house I've inherited from my father, if you like I can have it fixed up and then give it to you! You can satisfy your curiosity there!"

My wife agreed. Though Pakize had posed for thirty-five photographs beside the matchbox model, she nearly lost her head when she heard that I might be designing our home. For the first time ever, my wife, my daughter, and my son-in-law were all of the same mind. My wife kept saying, "God forbid! Could anyone actually live in one of your houses?" while Zehra used all her womanly charms to convince me to give up the idea.

Truth be told, I really had no desire to design the Clock Houses. My interest—and frankly, my passion—was with the human soul. Were other people like me, or were they just a bit different? I was determined to find the answer. Surely they were like me, or even worse. Clearly they were self-centered. When public funds were involved, they were generous, enthusiastic, proud of my work, and enthralled by its innovation, but when it touched on their personal interests, they flipped sides. Indeed they even stopped listening to Halit Ayarcı.

"But please, you can only joke around with people up to a certain point." That was the common refrain. All in all, people showed their true colors. In this aspect at least they all seemed the same. Halit Ayarcı was really quite distraught and didn't have the slightest idea what to do; every now and then he came to me and complained.

"How is this possible?" he cried. "Here we have people who work in the world's most modern institute, steeped in innovations, and in conditions they acknowledge to be the best and most advanced in the world—how could they not understand this? If they do not understand, then for goodness sake, what are they doing at the institute? Why did they applaud the new building? Why did they congratulate us? Nothing but lies!"

I tried to explain the situation to Halit Ayarcı.

"No, they weren't lying," I said. "They were sincere on both occasions. They adore innovation providing it doesn't affect them personally. And they continue to adore it but with this one condition. In their personal lives they prefer to be safe and secure."

"How can that be? Can a human being think about something in two entirely different ways? Can two different sets of logic coexist in their heads?"

Halit Ayarcı was truly in despair.

"Of course. Or, better said, when personal interests shift, logic follows suit."

"Truth is, I just cannot comprehend such a thing! All my life's work has collapsed before me. This institute is no longer mine!"

Beads of sweat ran down his temples. I'd never seen him in such a state. He had held his own against much stronger and more powerful opposition. But now just a handful of people—people he himself had created—had taken him by surprise. He looked vacantly about the room.

"Have you ever been to a boxing match?" I asked. "At first we can't even bear to watch. Then soon enough we get excited and side with one of the boxers. Not long after that we're angry that he's not holding up well enough, and we scream at the top of our lungs: 'Come on! Hit him harder! That's the way!' And if he doesn't, we feel disappointed. But which one of us actually wants to be in that fighter's shoes? No one, right? These people are no different. They watched us fight and cheered us on and even applauded our efforts. And they meant it. But now that you've welcomed them into the ring, it's all changed. Now it's a matter of their personal interest and safety!"

"Then these people don't believe in me! We've banded together here for nothing! We have struggled in vain!"

"No, they still believe in you, providing their personal needs remain untouched. Besides, why do you need them to believe in you? This I don't understand . . ."

"But work is work!"

And so it was that the long and difficult discussions over the Clock Houses chewed up Halit Ayarcı from the inside out.

The fourth meeting was the most arduous. Halit Ayarcı went so far as to issue threats. Alas! The magic had worn off. The opposition was just too strong. They didn't even give him a chance to speak. The Clock Houses would be just like any other houses. That was the majority's final word.

He left the meeting early, ceding his seat to me. For the first time, I exercised my right to vote and, having succumbed to the majority, I left.

When I went into his office, I found myself with an entirely changed Halit Ayarcı. Sitting in the chair he had once pulled out for my aunt, he had his feet up on the table and was deep in thought. When he saw me come in, he said:

"Somewhere I went wrong . . . But where? Where did I go wrong? If I could just figure this out I'd feel so much better . . ."

"I don't know," I answered him. "Best to put it out of your mind. After all, they are private homes, and they can have them built whichever way they like. We'll wish them all the best and that will be that."

He looked at my face stubbornly, imploringly.

"Why don't you understand me?" he asked. "Somewhere I went wrong!"

Smiling, I tried to console him.

"Perhaps it's the fault of my architectural wizardry!" I said. "But you must admit, I know nothing about such work, and I could never . . ."

He shrugged his shoulders.

"What difference does that make?"

"We've played with everyone a bit too much. Wouldn't you agree?"

He looked at my face again and said:

"No, we didn't play with them. We did nothing of the sort. They were the ones who deceived us. We placed too much confidence in them."

He stood up and began pacing about the room.

"This institute is no longer mine! Now I'm just like everyone else here," he said.

And he left without taking his hat.

This was the first bout of depression that seized Halit Ayarcı. The whole matter flared up out of nothing really. Yet it didn't last for long. The old Halit Ayarcı was back when our building was inaugurated at the congress of the International Time Regulation

Institute. The congress was in awe of this radiant, kind, noble, and true gentleman. He spoke for two hours at the closing ceremony, receiving one furious wave of applause after another.

But still, as someone who knew him intimately, I could tell that this wasn't the same Halit Ayarcı.

There is no doubt that his decline contributed to the altogether unexpected and sudden liquidation of the institute. Had he been able to maintain the same force and enthusiasm, we never would have come to such a tragic and unexpected end.

If Halit Ayarcı had been at the institute on the day of the event that led to liquidation, things would have turned out very differently, for Halit always knew how to behave in just such situations. But he wasn't there. It had been months since he'd visited the institute. I was the only one present when the foreign delegation arrived. And, sadly, in spite of all my experience, I failed to grasp just how important this particular delegation was. What's more, by that point I no longer harbored doubts about the institute. I had slowly but surely come to believe what Halit Ayarcı had so long insisted: that the institute was a viable modern organization conducting truly indispensible work. Having been inundated with love and admiration for the new building and our many other achievements, I had lost all my former doubts. It was in this frame of mind that I gave the delegation a full tour of our adored institute, explaining in some detail precisely what we did.

Sadly this delegation was nothing like its predecessors. The symbolic clock over the front door, the strange floors and extraneous stairs, the synchronized typing of our seventy typists, exerting a startling degree of rhythmic control under the direction of our chief secretary as she waved her baton at the head of our grand typing salon—none of this impressed them. Though affable enough at the start of the visit, they showed nothing but indifference toward our work.

When we returned to my office, the head of the delegation refused my offer of an alcoholic beverage, heading straight to the phone to dial 0135 before asking me for the time. Glancing at the clock on the wall, he turned to me and asked:

"When it's that easy to ascertain the time, where is the need for such an institute?"

This was more or less the same question I had been asking Halit Ayarcı since the day the institute was established. And every time I did, he gave me the same grave and reasoned reply, which, if not entirely convincing, succeeded in silencing me. But sadly I wasn't Halit Ayarcı. I had neither his eloquence nor his incisive powers of reason, and the man who had asked me this question had no desire to be persuaded. Thus he didn't really listen to any of the answers I gave him. Every time I opened my mouth he interrupted me with the same question:

"Where is the need for such an institute?"

Finally I told him that such institutes existed all over the world, after which I outlined our system of fixed and relative remuneration. In the end the man got up and left without even saying good-bye.

I never doubted this strange visit would end the way it did. But to err on the safe side, I called Halit Ayarcı. He wasn't at home. I asked around as to his whereabouts, but I couldn't find him. Three days later we received the order to liquidate the institute. In a way this really wasn't such a terrible shock for me. For some time, I had been preparing myself for our enterprise to come to an end. It was after this American fellow's visit that I began to think our time had come. The Time Regulation Institute had played out its role.

All the same, it had become a part of my life. We had put so much into it. And I was quite fond of my office in the new building, which I had designed especially for myself, and the relaxation room just beside it in which I'd sometimes spend the night. My little American bar, my bathroom, my furniture, my pictures on the wall—I was so very fond of it all. I absolutely loved the garden I also had designed to suit my own particular taste. I would no longer be able to follow the growth of the trees I'd planted with my own hands.

I called Halit Ayarcı the moment I received the order. They were expecting him to be home in half an hour. I sat at my desk, with my hand still on the phone, thinking. Perhaps one day this institute would be of some use. Halit Bey always said,

"It will create its own function!" What a shame it never had the chance to do so. On the other hand, there were nearly three hundred staff members whose futures weren't as bright.

I was worried about those futures. What would happen to these people? How would they find work? What were we going to do now? No matter how absurd it is, a job is still a job. Well, yes, I could write my memoirs, but what were these other people going to do?

Half an hour later I had Halit Ayarcı on the telephone. When I explained the situation, he teased me, saying:

"I imagine you're quite upset."

"Well, aren't you?"

"No," he said. "As you know I no longer have the same relationship with the institute. It rejected me."

"If you'd been here, perhaps you could have stopped this."

"But I wasn't there," he said. "And doesn't the fact that I was absent show that the old ties have been severed?"

"But this doesn't concern just us! All our friends, the staff . . . We are nearly three hundred people."

For a moment it seemed he was thinking.

"Yes, all of them!" he said.

"Can I see you tonight?"

"I don't think so," he replied and hung up the phone.

This wasn't an answer. The old rage welled up inside me. I hoped he would come see me in the evening. But there was no sign of him. The following day I stopped by his place. They told me he had left on a trip early that morning. I spent nearly all that week dealing with the liquidation.

That weekend there was a social event that had been scheduled many months earlier. Given the bitter circumstances, I wanted to cancel it, but I just couldn't convince my wife.

This final gathering at the Clock Villa did not get off to a brilliant start. For the last six months, our employees (who were either already relatives or had by now married each other) had been living together, day and night, in the same neighborhood, and various hostilities had emerged. It had become so bad that they tolerated social gatherings and even everyday neighborly visits only because it offered them an opportunity to insult and criticize one another or wage war by innuendo. Though their suppressed anger and bad manners made such shows of decorum rare, our gatherings would, even if peaceful, provide the fodder for future gossip and backstabbing.

So I avoided these functions as best I could, and if I attended, I never invited extra guests. But over the last three years, we had made a tradition of celebrating my youngest daughter Halide's birthday with a party. And Pakize was not about to give up on this tradition, just because we had moved into a new home.

Here I should add that, in sharp contrast to myself, Pakize was a regular at our neighborhood functions. She paid no heed whatsoever to the hostile ring around her: in fact she even took it head on. What woman cannot help but retaliate with a giggle and a wan smile? I really don't understand it, but women are stronger and more courageous than men in this regard. We had purchased a new set of china, and Pakize had a new evening gown to display, and so canceling the soiree was out of the question. Those people who had criticized us for days on end— she would crush them with her beauty, youth, and affluence.

But Pakize had failed to consider how much the mood had soured since the dissolution of the institute. She was expecting nothing more than the odd innuendo slipped into an otherwise pleasant conversation. That was not how it happened. When the guests arrived, they were already in a rage. One look at their faces told me exactly the direction the evening would take. And indeed it did not take long for matters to come to a head. The strange thing was that we were not the sole targets of all their all-too-human ire. They targeted everyone else too. Husbands and wives and betrothed all seemed equally angry at one another. No flaw or imperfection was immune. And everyone knew the score. We were all to blame for the institute's liquidation. We were all guilty of a crime. But as Halit Bey and I bore the most responsibility, we were naturally the chief culprits. The more people drank, the more things got out of hand. These people who had been plucked out of nowhere by Halit Ayarcı—they joined forces to ask us to account for ourselves, and they were openly berating us.

Pakize was the first to be attacked. Oblivious to her new gown, they dropped all pretense of common courtesy. Even our younger employees, who knew it was only proper to pay her a compliment, went out of their way to avoid her. The wives of our closest friends discussed her age as they stood right beside her, and then they asked her what kind of hair dye she used.

It wasn't long before they were discussing the size of our home and our tasteless furniture and the money we had squandered for it. When approaching one group, I realized, when I heard the word "weasel," that these three people were talking about me.

Yet—as I've mentioned—this anger was not leveled against us alone. With the liquidation of the institute, the need for pretense had also disappeared, and without pretense, friendships foundered. So then everyone was in the same cold, sour, hostile mood.

By ten I had given up all hope of stemming the arguments, though I'd been waiting in front of the dining room, whose doors had been flung open for half an hour. Pakize, who just a little earlier had been challenging the crowd around her, had now taken refuge between her sisters. Only my aunt was holding her own, countering all attacks with apoplectic tirades.

And it was just then that Halit Ayarcı appeared, holding his valise, with his hat still on his head. Without paying anyone else any notice, he marched directly over to me. A growl rose from the crowd, which in the space of a moment flared up like a furnace that had just been fed new fuel. But Halit Ayarcı paid no heed. Shaking my hand, he apologized:

"Please forgive me. I could only make it back just now. I have had the decision amended. That's to say, the decision to abrogate had been suspended, but in order for the institute to remain in a permanent state of liquidation we need to form a committee for continuous liquidation. All our friends will have positions in this new entity."

After he uttered these words, my wife took his hand and kissed it. He strode into the dining room.

The crowd heaved around us. And suddenly everyone was just as they had been before; in fact they were even friendlier. A couple who had been on the brink of a divorce just two days before, and had been mingling about separately for the last two hours, made peace and kissed each other right in front of me. A couple whose engagement had turned sour suddenly sprang back to life right then and there. The groups of three reformed. No, these men were now as open and pure in their newfound joy as they had been hostile and embittered just a moment earlier.

At the dinner table, I asked Halit Ayarcı, "What about the others? The little people?"

Suddenly his face flushed.

"Well, that's why I've done what I've done," he said. "But as for those working at the regulation stations, there's nothing we can do. You will have to work with them."

"But you, why don't you work with them?" I asked.

He looked at me, astonished.

"I . . . I can see now how I was deceived."

And with that, he began devouring his food.

Later that evening, after the crowd had broken up, we met again in my office. But there was a strange tension between us. In fact he seemed even more remote than that first time I met him in the coffeehouse in Şehzadebaşı. We played a round of backgammon. And when the game finished, we parted with a "good-bye and Godspeed." The next time I saw Halit Ayarcı, he was laid out on his bed at home, following his terrible car accident.

Appendix

A GUIDE TO TURKISH PRONUNCIATION

a as in "father"
e as in "pet"
i as in "machine"
o as in "oh"
u like the *oo* in "boot"
ı like the *u* in "but"
ü like the *u* in "mute"
ö as in German: *schön*
c like the *j* in "jam"
ç sounds like *ch*
g as in "get" (never as in "gem")
ğ is almost silent, lengthening the preceding vowel
j as in French: *jamais*
ş sounds like *sh*

BRIEF DESCRIPTION OF TURKISH NAMES AND HONORIFICS

Ottoman Turks did not generally have surnames. But they had a great wealth of first names, most of which carried lyrical, even ethereal, meanings. The surnames that Atatürk obliged all Turks to adopt almost overnight in 1934 also carried clear meanings. By and large, they reflected the new range of secular virtues and attitudes. Tanpınar has great fun with this cultural disconnect, and never more so than with Halit Ayarcı: translated literally, he becomes the "Timeless Regulator." He and his sidekick, the "Blessed" Hayri, are similarly playful in their use of honorifics. This, too, is a time-honored tradition, and yet another double game: even as they and their associates defer to social hierarchies, they can savor the irony, and even the veiled insult, in the use of an overly elevated term.

It would be misleading to suggest that all Tanpınar's characters carry hidden jokes in their names. But it would be shame to lose them all in translation. Below we translate a few of the most significant names, along with a list of honorifics.

Names

Abdüsselam: the pacifist, a servant of God; also mandrake.
Aristidi: the best (interesting considering his struggles with Lutfullah).
Asaf: vizier, one of great insight.
Aselban: caretaker of one of the four waters in heaven.
Ayarcı: the regulator.
Cemal: one with the beautiful countenance (deliberately ironic: Hayri rearranges his face).
Çeşminigâr: an Ottoman winter soup made with egg and flour; the beloved's eye.
Halit: lasting, constant, eternal.
Hayri: blessed, auspicious, fortunate.
Lutfullah: blessed or loved by God (equivalent to Amadeus)
Naşit: the reciter of poetry (as he proves a smooth talker at the trial and in his newly elevated position after marrying the aunt).
Nuri: pertaining to light, the one lit by the spiritual light of saintliness (it is "nur" in our "honor").
Pakize: clean, pure, innocent.

Honorifics

Aziz: saint; dear, as in "my dear friend."
Ağa: lord, master, gentleman, village headman (sometimes spelled "agha").
Bey: gentleman, sir.
Beyefendi: gentleman, sir but of a higher status or degree than "bey."
Baldız: sister-in-law.
Efendi: master; also commonly added to a first name to lend a sense of higher standing or social rank.
Hanım: madam, lady.
Hanımefendi: madam or lady but of a higher status than "hanım."
Hoca: an imam, a teacher; used generally with first names to elevate the sense of status or importance.
Hoca efendi: same as "hoca" but with even higher status; that is, esteemed hoca.
Usta: master, specialist; also added to names to stress the individual's importance and/or capabilities.

Notes

3 *A Parrot's Tale*: the *Tuiname* or *Tutinama* (also translated as *Tales of a Parrot*), a fourteenth-century Persian series of fifty-two stories.

4 *Emsile* and *Avamil*: books of basic Arabic grammar and model language.

4 *muvakkit*: religious timekeeper and clock repairman, the official keeper of time in the Ottoman Empire, a learned man involved in the study of philosophy and astronomy.

4 Mehmed IV: sultan of the Ottoman Empire from 1648 to 1687.

6 *kalfa*: an apprentice, master builder, foreman.

10 Turgot: most likely Anne-Robert-Jacques Turgot, French economist and statesman born 1727.

10 Necker: a French statesman of Swiss birth and finance minister under Louis XVI.

10 Schacht: German banker born 1877.

11 Abdülhamīd II: Ottoman sultan.

14 Aziz: literally refers to a saint but is aslo used as a term of endearment meaning "beloved" or "my good friend."

20 Receb: the seventh month of the Arabic calendar; considered one of the three holy months.

21 karagöz: one of the lead characters in traditional Turkish shadow-puppet theater.

21 Efendi: literally "master" but commonly used for "sir."

21 *iftar*: the breaking of the fast at sunset during the holy month of Ramadan.

21 *sahur*: predawn meal before the day of fasting during Ramadan.

21 *bismillah*: a common oath meaning "dear God" or "in the name of God."

23 Egyptian Affair: either the first Egyptian-Ottoman War (1831–33) or the second (1839–41).

26 *makamsher*: a mode in Turkish classical music; each *makam* has its own particular mood.

26 *alaturca*: in the Turkish or Eastern style.

26 *alafranga*: in the French or Western style.

30 **in that era**: after the rebellion of the Young Turks brought about the reestablishment of the constitution in 1908.

35 *medrese*: a college for Islamic instruction; in English often spelled "madrassa" or "madrasah."

37 **Armistice years**: The Mudros Armistice, signed on October 31, 1918, called for total and unconditional surrender of Ottoman forces at the end of the First World War. A large allied fleet reached Istanbul on November 13, 1918. The allied occupation of Istanbul lasted until the departure of the final attachment of British troops on October 2, 1923.

37 **Declaration of Independence**: the birth of the Turkish Republic in 1923.

39 **Arab Mosque**: A former thirteenth-century Roman Catholic chapel dedicated to St. Paul. The only example of Gothic religious architecture in Istanbul. Renamed the Arab Mosque, after the Muslims expelled from Spain during the Inquisition. Located in Istanbul's historic Galata neighborhood.

40 **the emperor Andronikos**: Andronikos I Komnenos, Byzantine emperor born c. 1118.

42 *bağlama*: a stringed instrument also known as the *saz*.

46 **Mahmud I**: sultan of the Ottoman Empire from 1730 to 1754.

46 *kahvecıbaşı*: the imperial coffee maker.

47 *oya*: needlework flower chains often used to decorate the edge of a headscarf.

47 *saray*: palace.

53 **oud**: a pear-shaped stringed instrument commonly used in Arabic, Hebrew, and Greek music.

55 **Kahvecıbaşı Cemetery**: cemetery of the imperial coffee maker.

60 *han*: an Ottoman inn for commercial travelers, with a closed inner courtyard for animals.

61 **Ramadan**: the ninth month of the Islamic calendar, during which Muslims observe a fast.

61 **Kandil**: one of the five Islamic holy nights when minarets are illuminated.

61 **Şaban**: the eighth month of the Arabic calendar, which precedes the month of Ramadan.

69 *ahretlik*: from *ahret*, meaning the afterlife; a pious man; an adopted maid committed to a lifetime of service.

70 *mehdi*: prophet.

71 **Mahmud Şevket Paşa**: Ottoman soldier and statesman who played a role in the overthrow of Abdülhamīd II. Assassinated in 1913.

72 hoca efendi: an esteemed instructor.

75 *kuşdili*: a bird language that people use to communicate with one another.

83 **Tünel**: funicular going from the Galata Bridge to Beyoğlu.

85 **Şeker Bayram**: the festival of sweets following the feast of Ramadan.

86 **Kurban Bayram**: Eid ul-Adha, the sacrificial religious holiday celebrating Abraham's obedience to God.

86 **Burmalı Mescit**: Built in 1540 in the Vefa neighborhood of Istanbul. Literally, the Spiral Mosque, for the spirals on its single minaret.

90 **war in Anatolia**: the War of Independence (May 19, 1919–July 24, 1923) was waged by nationalists following the Allies' occupation of the land now known as Turkey in the aftermath of World War I.

94 *meyhane*: a tavern serving alcohol and meze.

98 **Saliha Sultan**: the mother of Ottoman sultan Mahmud I and the wife of the sultan Mustafa II.

126 **onomancy**: divinations based on a person's name.

126 **numerology**: the study of the purported divine or mystical relationship between numbers and perceived events.

126 **alchemy**: the medieval precursor of modern chemistry, the effort to turn other solids into gold.

135 **Bergson**: Henri-Louis Bergson, French philosopher active in the first half of the twentieth century.

135 **Kantian imperative**: or categorical imperative, the ethical system devised by Immanuel Kant, which describes a moral law that applies to all rational beings and is independent of any personal motives or desires.

135 *ortaoyunu*: a kind of improvisational theater common in coffeehouses in the Ottoman Empire.

136 *meddah*: a coffeehouse storyteller or stand-up comedian.

137 *bedesten*: a market where antiques, jewelry, and works of art are sold; a covered bazaar; can be used to refer to the Grand Bazaar.

138 *banu*: a common name, used to refer to a beautiful woman, a lady.

138 *cadu*: a derivation of the Turkish word *cadı* meaning "witch" or "sorceress."

145 **battle of Holy Ali**: either the Battle of Badr, in which Ali, successor of the prophet Muhammad according to Shia Muslims, defeated the Umayyad leader; or the Battle of Karbala', again with the Umayyad, at which Ali was killed and his succession put to an end.

180 **Taflan Deva Bey**: a name meaning "the cherry laurel cure."

215 **Balıkpazarı**: a lively street market in the historical Beyoğlu neighborhood of Istanbul.

223 **Bukağılı Dede**: an Istanbul saint; literally, the Hobbling Saint.

223 **Elekçi Baba**: An Istanbul saint; literally, the Garbler.

223 **Uryan Dede**: an Istanbul saint; literally, the Naked Ancestor.

223 **Tezveren Sultan**: a legendary saint some say was a woman.

223 **Yilanlı Dede**: an Istanbul saint; literally, the Ancestor of Snakes. People believed praying at his tomb gave them children.

223 **Karpuz Hoca**: literally, Master Watermelon.

223 **Sheikh Mustafa of Altıparmak**: literally, Sheikh Mustafa of Goldfinger.

223 **Deli Hafiz** an Istanbul saint; literally, the Crazy, who has memorized the Koran.

223 **Sheikh Virani**: literally, the Sheikh in Ruins.

223 **Gömleksiz Dede**: An Istanbul saint; literally, the Saint Shirtless.

226 *maşallah*: praise God, wonderful.

230 **baldız**: sister-in-law.

230 **Mahur**: a *makam* in Turkish classical music, known for its lively and soothing properties.

230 **Isfahan**: both a city in Iran and a *makam* in Turkish classical music.

230 **Rast**: a *makam* in Turkish classical music.

278 **Graham**: Benjamin Graham, an American economist and professional inventor.

278 *rabia*: split seconds, famous female mystic, the fourth.

281 **Çelebi**: honorific meaning "gentleman."

286 **Spengler**: Oswald Spengler, German historian of philosophy born 1880.

301 **Committee of Union and Progress**: A revolutionary political organization that aligned with the Young Turks in 1906 and oversaw the reinstatement of the constitution in 1908. After a brief flirtation with democracy, its leaders moved back to authoritarian rule and are thought by some to have orchestrated the mass slaughter and deportation of Anatolia's Armenians. Having taken the Ottomans into World War I on the side of the Germans, the committee was disbanded, and in some cases its members court-martialed, at the war's end.

342 **Osman Hamdi:** Ottoman archeologist, painter, and curator
    born in Istanbul in 1842.

346 **Bektaşi ceremony:** the Bektaşi Sufi order was founded in the
    thirteenth century, active throughout the Ottoman Empire, and
    linked with the janissaries until both were banned by Mahmud
    II in 1826.

350 *estağfurullah*: of Arabic origin, meaning "don't mention it" or
    "don't so think so badly of yourself."

353 *semaiye*: a style of poem in folk literature.

354 *maya*: a traditional folk song.

354 **Satan's Mountain:** a legendary mountain in southeast Turkey.

358 *zeybek*: a traditional dance from the Aegean region of Turkey,
    which calls for slow and high knee steps and arms swinging
    widely through the air.

378 **Üç Şerefli Mosque:** Built in Edirne in 1410 by Müslihiddin Ağa,
    master to the famous architect Mimar Sinan, the mosque has
    four minarets, one rising from each corner of a large courtyard.
    The highest minaret has three balconies, and each balcony
    (*şeref*) is accessible by a different set of stairs.